OF TIME
AND TIDE:
THE WINDHOVER SAGA

JAMES HAYDOCK

authorHOUSE®

AuthorHouse™
1663 Liberty Drive
Bloomington, IN 47403
www.authorhouse.com
Phone: 1 (800) 839-8640

Published by AuthorHouse 06/24/2017

ISBN: 978-1-5246-9747-1 (sc)
ISBN: 978-1-5246-9746-4 (e)

Print information available on the last page.

This book is printed on acid-free paper.

By James Haydock

Stormbirds
Victorian Sages
Beacon's River
Portraits in Charcoal: George Gissing's Women
On a Darkling Plain: Victorian Poetry and Thought
Searching in Shadow: Victorian Prose and Thought
The Woman Question and George Gissing
Against the Grain
Mose in Bondage
A Tinker in Blue Anchor
Of Time and Tide: The Windhover Saga

Until my ghastly tale is told,

This heart within me burns.

-- The Rime of the Ancient Mariner

CONTENTS

CHAPTER ONE

"We Gonna Be Movin' Out Soon"

O ur little ship lay in the roadstead off Hamilton in the Bermudas. Lovingly built by old-world craftsmen in one of the best shipyards of Nova Scotia, she was named the *Windhover* by her first owner. He had seen a small hawk riding the wind early one morning and never forgot the spectacle. After a few years he sold the *Windhover* to the present owners who kept the name. I stood on her deck that balmy day in June of 1871 and could see six other merchant ships lying to anchor and waiting for the wind. We would be hauling anchor and moving out as soon as the sou'westerly breeze grew strong enough to fill our sails. A larger ship silhouetted against the pink of the early morning sky was already piling on sail and gingerly moving out to sea. Gulls dipped and wheeled in her wake, scavenging for bits of food from the galley, slurry tossed overboard by the cook. Working a huge expanse of canvas, the crew chanted a salty song. It skimmed across the water to please my ear.

"We gonna be movin' out soon," said the man approaching me. "I would like to see more wind, but we gotta take what we can get. I do wish we could stay a bit longer 'cause I like the weather here. But the captain has to keep to a schedule, you know. So we gotta get underway with any breeze that'll have us."

"I've been expecting as much," I said in reply. "It's a long voyage ahead of us, and the captain wants a crossing without incident."

I was speaking to a short, squarely built man with a thatch of red hair accenting a rugged face. Intense blue eyes, as blue as any I've ever seen, shone like jewels in leathery skin tanned by years of sun and wind. He wore on a pointed chin a copper beard flecked with gray, and when he spoke his beard moved up and down in comic fashion. His name was Andrew Turpin, first mate of the *Windhover,* and a competent seaman. He was polite when speaking to me, the ship's second mate, but somewhat rough when giving orders to the crew, especially when they tried his patience. I knew from the moment I met him that he was proud of being first mate, second in command only to the captain.

When he walked away toward the forecastle (*fo'c's'le* in sailor parlance), his short legs carried him very well but with a slight limp he tried to conceal. A group of men stood near the galley chatting with the cook. Their banter ceased when Mr. Turpin approached but quickly resumed when he passed them by. I could tell even from a distance that Cookie was entertaining the hands with one of his bawdy stories. He was a fat man with a bulging belly and a florid face. Life for him was a short joke to enjoy and he laughed a lot. His mouth was seldom shut and behind the fat lips were two gaping spaces where teeth should have been. The missing teeth didn't seem to bother him at all. He wore a very dirty flannel shirt with the sleeves rolled above his elbows, and he was pointing to pigs in a pen near the longboat. Nearby were live chickens to be killed on demand, but only for the officers. My gaze went aloft to the sails. Most of them hung without luffing even though the royals answered to a soft sou'westerly breeze.

On the weather side of the poop, bracing himself against a quarterboat, stood the skipper conversing with our navigator. Captain Redstone was a tall, slim, angular man, strongly built and good looking. His coarse, iron-gray hair covered a well-shaped head and tended to complement a short beard. His eyes were small and dark, his nose aquiline, and his mouth compressed as though under tension. On this day he wore a shirt identifying his station, clean duck trousers, and square-toed boots. His appearance did not in the smallest degree suggest the conventional notion of the merchant-skipper. Lacking the bow legs, red and coppery nose and groggy eyes of the typical rough skipper, he demanded respect from any crew that served under him and got it. I had heard before I joined the *Windhover* that Oliver Redstone was a very able seaman though a bully to his men in times of stress and a strict upholder of rules. The rumor didn't bother me in the least. I prefer discipline aboard ship, and I thought I knew my duties well enough to steer clear of any temper tantrum the skipper might release. Knowing the seafaring life is often perilous, I would rather serve under a stickler for rules who knows his job than any mild-mannered man who doesn't.

The navigator, Peter Charnook, was a wiry little man suffering from a disability that left him cold even in mid summer, and yet he knew his craft and was respected by the crew. His features were more refined than those of the other men, and one noticed his long slender hands that always seemed too active and too white. I was watching the two men when Turpin came up to me again and said he was worried about how the ship's crewmen, all of them gathered in the fo'c's'le, were behaving. Something just didn't seem right.

"It's my belief we gonna have trouble with them fellas forward. When I ordered them to make ready to get underway, did you notice how they went to work all sullen like?"

"I did. And I'll tell you why they're acting that way. Last evening after dinner the cook told me the men were grumbling about nasty provisions. Some of the greasy pork he gave them had an awful stench and couldn't be tasted, much less eaten. The bread, a staple to fill a man's belly on any ship, was moldy and had weevils in it."

"I'm finding that hard to believe," said the first mate with a troubled look. "We put in good provisions on the mainland, and that was only three weeks ago. How in hell could the grub go bad so soon?"

"I can only tell you what I heard, didn't see it for myself. But you'll find out if it's true soon enough. The men won't stay quiet for long facing an ocean crossing with food they can't eat."

"At sea maybe they'll have something to cry over. Here at anchor even before the voyage begins they don't have no right."

Just the thought there could be such a problem was making him angry. He stalked away from me, went to the break of the poop, leaned squarely on the rail, and stared at the men near the galley. One or two stared back. Another had the gall to laugh, and it put Turpin in a passion. No common sailor would question his authority and get away with it. Of that he would be certain. He wanted to scream a few choice cuss words but remembered the captain frowned upon cussing and drinking hard liquor on a voyage. So loud enough to be heard he called out.

"Have you nothing to do, you lazy oafs? Get cracking! You, there! Clean the longboat's bottom. You and you! Go aloft and see that our halyards are clear for running. No more yakking with that worthless cook, you hear? He's got work to do too!"

He raised a clenched fist and shook it. The men got life into them at once and bustled about. I looked at the captain and navigator to see what they thought of Turpin's little outburst, but neither paid a smidgen of attention. Only when the first mate ceased to speak did Captain Redstone give the order to get underway. It was repeated without hesitation in a voice of thunder by the first mate.

"Move it, heathens! Haul anchor and watch out for the chain! To the ratlines! Unfurl the mainsail and hoist it! Get forward and get them headsails ready for the wind! Scoot you lazy hounds and look smart!"

The men moved sullenly and slowly and seemed inclined to disobey, but another order got them in the rigging where they did the job grumbling but making no attempt to confront Turpin.

"I'm just beginning with them," said the red-headed man with the temper. "They gonna do as I say or I'm gonna know the reason why. And I expect they won't be complaining about no food neither." Saying this he glanced at Redstone who gave him a nod and a smile. It seemed evident to me that these two had a silent understanding of each other.

The royals and top-gallant sails were clewed up and furled but released just as the ship began to move through calm water. Seabirds wheeled behind us, and from one of the anchored boats came a call on their horn to wish us well. The wide, wide ocean lay to the east of us and would be the only world we would know for several weeks.

At noon the navigator released his sextant from its water-tight compartment and began to shoot the sun to determine our position. With that instrument he could measure the angle of the sun to determine latitude. With the ship's carefully tended chronometer he was able to figure our longitude and thus fix our position in the open sea. We had a good breeze by then and our ship was moving smoothly at six knots toward our destination, a European port more than 4,000 miles beyond the horizon. I was walking aft when the cook came out of his galley to speak to me. I stopped to hear what he had to say.

"Beg pardon, sir. Would you mind tasting this?"

He was polite and serious, a big change from his usual jovial and joking behavior. He thrust into my hands a small gray biscuit and asked me to taste it. I looked at it, smelled it, found it moldy, gingerly bit into it, and quickly spat it out.

"There's nothing good about this," I said to him. "No person, not even your galley boy, should have to eat something this bad."

"It ain't fit for a dog," the cook asserted. "And what's more, as far as I know, all our provisions is the same. The sugar is like a block of concrete and the molasses is like mud and gritty and tastes like

James Haydock

the bottom of a copper pot. In twenty years of sea faring I never seen nothing like this. Not ever! Even the coffee has the taste of a rusty old nail."

"Tell the men to go as a group and complain to the captain. He can report the problem to the owners and get the ship's stores replaced. We'd have to turn back, a big decision for him, but we can't sail thousands of miles with rotten food no man can eat. Give me a biscuit, one not showing teeth marks, and I'll show it myself to Captain Redstone."

He thanked me and scurried back to his galley. Later I heard he sent his helper to the fo'c's'le to report the good news. The second mate would take their grievance to the captain, and if Captain Redstone had any milk of human kindness at all, he would solve the problem quickly.

6

CHAPTER TWO

Sour Provisions For Crew

Our merchant ship was a fully rigged vessel carrying three masts and a full complement of sails. Her hull was painted a gleaming white with a blue cove stripe below her bulwarks and a red boot top at her waterline. Her hardwood masts were carefully oiled to preserve them and tan in color. Her sails were no longer new but clean and white. Under full sail on a blue ocean under a blue sky she looked like a cloud skimming across the water. For that reason alone the second owners wanted to rename her and call her *Seacloud*. But when they heard it was bad luck to rename the ship, they yielded to nautical superstition and kept the original name of a bird riding the wind. Her lines were as perfect as any naval architect could make them. When I first saw her, I admired the perky way she sat in the water, her shining hull, and her lofty masts. Her decks were clean and uncluttered and she had a poop deck that served as the roof of the captain's cabin. Near the bow of the ship was another raised deck, the fo'c's'le. Below it was enough space for the living quarters of the crew. The ship on this voyage had a crew of fourteen.

Abaft the mizzen mast were the two cabins occupied by Oliver Redstone and Andrew Turpin. On the whole they were rather fancy, the captain's being the finest. My own cabin was under the break of the poop, and from its window I could look out on the main deck. Skylights let light to enter the cuddy, the common room of the ship, but not enough. That space, containing four cabins and the ship's pantry, was functional but plain. While each of the poop cabins had private heads, the cabins in the cuddy had but one sanitary facility. Forward in the fo'c's'le were two traditional heads, crude box-like stools above a hole close to the bow. The men often used them side by side when necessary and washed their hands in a basin filled with sea water. I wondered why the most trusted members of the crew were not allowed to use the cuddy cabins. "Reserved for passengers," Turpin told me. Yet we carried no passengers. I never knew exactly why we didn't because our voyage would take us to Europe and some of its best cities. Turpin, who seemed to have all the answers, was convinced the owners didn't bother to advertise the ship's departure and destination, or did it too late. So getting no passengers, they overloaded the ship with freight to gain revenue.

Our course would take us to Gibraltar and on to Italy, and Naples would be the southernmost port of call. The cargo consisted chiefly of American-made toys, bird cages, Remington rifles, grand pianos made in New England, door hinges, and other metal goods. It was a heavy cargo and made the ship sit deeper in the water than usual. On our passage from Baltimore to Bermuda we had seen already that in heavy weather with all that freight the *Windhover* was a wet ship. That meant she might not be easy to control in the kind of blow that screeches in as the hallmark of an extended storm. However, in spite of the overload the sleek little ship took us eight hundred miles to Bermuda in record time. She weathered a summer thunderstorm with ease and passed an old coal brig staggering under dirty canvas as if standing still. She was seaworthy in all respects, and not a soul on board had cause to worry about how she would kiss the seas. We knew she could take whatever lay in store for her a lot better than we could.

Leaving Cookie with the biscuit in my pocket, I went aft to the poop. The skipper, who spent most of his time there when the ship was under sail, had gone below with the navigator to drink mugs of coffee, look over charts, and check our plotted course. Mr. Turpin was leaning against the rail but began strutting back and forth on the poop when he saw me approaching. Coming closer, I could hear him mumbling under his breath about ordinary seamen not earning their pay. He was notorious for inventing work that wasn't really necessary, work such as turning the bitter end of a line into a Flemish coil to lie flat on deck. The neat circle of line pleases the eye of passengers but serves no real purpose at all when not underfoot. I greeted the first mate with a friendly hello and got a nod of the head in return. After looking aloft to check the trim of our sails I went below with Turpin to the cuddy, stepping aside in deference to his rank to let him descend the companionway ladder first. He cocked his head and smiled but said nothing.

The severe interior of the cuddy looked like an old Dutch painting, for the mahogany trim and dim light gave the place an antique air. We had daylight on deck, but here in this room with tiny ports that screwed shut in a storm we had lamplight and shadow. The skipper was drinking coffee while perusing a chart, and the navigator though not in the best of health was eating bread and butter voraciously.

"We got a good breeze from the sou'west, sir," Turpin said. "Paws on the water and seas building. Vessel moving fine."

"Let the breeze come," said the captain, "and hope it stays with us for a good long time. We can't afford to drift in a calm this voyage."

"Mr. Doyle," he asked me, "what's going on with the men? I heard them cursing freely aloft, and they know my orders are to go easy on the cussing. Seems strange they'd be acting up so soon. Not even time for boredom to set in and some of them cussing already."

"They're complaining about the ship's provisions, sir. The cook gave me a biscuit a while ago and wanted me to show it to you."

I pulled the biscuit out of my pocket and put it on the table. He looked at it with a decisive frown on his handsome face, touched it gingerly with one finger, pushed it aside, and stared at me.

"Now you listen to me, Mr. Doyle, and you listen good," he said in muted anger. "I allow no officer that sails with me to become buddy-buddy with my crew. It affects discipline shipboard. I won't have it. Do I make myself clear?"

"I'm no confidant of the crew, Captain Redstone," I stammered in reply. "I merely bring to you a message from the cook. The crew complains of rotten food served by the steward. You have the proof in front of you. I'm told other food items are as bad as that biscuit."

"It don't look all that bad to me," said the navigator, breaking open the biscuit and poking it with his finger.

"Eat it, then! Put some butter on it and eat it," I said to him.

"Are you forgetting your station, Mr. Doyle?" said Redstone with mounting anger. "You will not be getting out of line on my ship! Is that clear? Why don't *you* eat it? You must like it or you wouldn't be bringing it to the cuddy in your pocket!"

Reluctant to quarrel with the man who paid my wages, I held my tongue. Glancing at Turpin I could see that he too supported the captain. It would be three to one if I held my ground, and I didn't want to get off on the wrong foot as the voyage began. It would be a bad omen.

After a pause to catch his breath, Captain Redstone ordered me to return the biscuit to the galley and make it known to the cook that nothing at all would be done to correct the situation.

"Tell them," he said to me as I stood to leave, "if they don't like the bread they don't have to eat it. The bastards can starve for all I care."

"Mr. Doyle tells me they find the meat worse than the bread," said Turpin, chuckling. "I guess the ones doing most of the grumbling are from the slums of Baltimore. All their lives they've slurped watery soup and never tasted meat before now."

He laughed at his own wit, but I heard no laughter from the captain or the navigator. Already I was beginning to dislike the first mate, a bully and a martinet who walked in the shadow of the captain. Also, because he saw nothing wrong with the bread, I was beginning to have negative feelings for Peter Charnook, the navigator.

A trifle upset, I went to my cabin to get my pipe and then on deck to speak to the helmsman. Also I wanted to see that a man was near the bow with an eye out for anything in our path. A few men working on the main deck greeted me as I strolled the full length of the ship. Back on the poop, I sat down to smoke near the rail. Though it wasn't my intention to eavesdrop, I could hear the captain speaking to his first mate.

"I'd really like to know what sort of man they gave me for second mate. He seems a bit too soft for my kind of seaman, too much the gentleman. I like manly men on my ship, not gentle men. A bleeding heart he seems to me, so concerned with the crew and all."

"Well, sir, he's a soft-spoken young man all right. And he looks a bit soft, I grant you that. But he seems qualified to do his job, don't you think? In a civil sort of way? Maybe he could use some New Orleans training, as my old skipper Stoltz used to say. Treat the men rough and hard. Knock their guts out if they don't obey in an instant. That sort of thing. Old Stoltz often said it's the only way to maintain discipline."

The captain spoke in reply, but even though I strained my ears I couldn't make out what he was saying. If I could have heard his remarks, his reaction to Turpin's obsequious palaver, I might have gained some insight into his character. I might have learned how to shape my behavior under his command. It was important for me to know the man because I wanted to move up in my profession, and

I knew only too well that a negative report from him or any other captain could stifle that ambition. The welfare of a young officer in the seafaring life depends on reports and testimonials. A good report to a ship's owner can boost a man's career overnight. By the same token, especially when supply exceeds demand, a negative report can shatter hopes and dreams.

Neither the captain nor first mate appeared on deck. The navigator came up near suppertime and went directly to the binnacle. There he checked our compass course and spoke briefly with the helmsman. I thought he might stop to pass the time with me, if only for a minute or two, but he turned without saying a word and went below again. Half an hour later the steward informed me that I might take supper, along with my daily share of grog, at the captain's table.

"Did Captain Redstone send you?" I asked.

"No, sir, he did not. I saw you were missing and thought I might tell you to be there. The captain likes to have all his officers at the table when it's time to eat, and he likes promptness."

"Thank you, but I'll grab a bite when my duty is over. I want to be certain the breeze remains steady so we can make sail accordingly."

I lied. My real reason for not going to table was to steer clear of the captain until his temper subsided. I didn't want another outburst. I took some turns on deck, stopping to exchange a few words with a sailor or two, and soon afterwards went below to find no one at table.

Our day of slow sailing was over. A night breeze might increase our speed to take us farther eastward with sour provisions and possibly no return to Bermuda. It was Captain Redstone's problem, and with the help of Mr. Turpin he would handle it. In the fo'c's'le all crew members not on watch had turned in for the night. I heard no voices.

A profound silence had taken over the ship. I could hear only the gentle music of the bow wave. At last the moon arose, sprinting above the horizon, and growing silvery and smaller. The sea beneath the rising moon was lustrous with soft and twinkling light. Weather and winds were balmy and mild. I thought I might keep watch all night and have nothing whatever to report.

CHAPTER THREE

"Get Off My Ship! Get Off Now!"

In my cabin was a sturdy mahogany bunk I never used. When I first went to sea I was assigned a bunk snug against the hull and considered myself fortunate. Then one night we ran into heavy weather and high seas, and the call went out for all hands to shorten sail. I heard the command and tried to jump out of bed and get topside as fast as I could, but my body was glued against the leeward side of the severely heeling ship. I was forced to lie there until the ship righted herself. Had she run into more serious trouble and foundered, I would have gone to the bottom with the sinking vessel while still in my bed. After that I slept in a hammock that swings to any movement of the ship. However, on this voyage as slightly more privileged than an able-bodied sailor, I had a comfortable cot I was able to sling up as I would a hammock.

Even though the night was warm I slept soundly until 0200. In just my trousers I went on deck to find the first mate in yellow flannel drawers pacing up and down in the moonlight.

"No wind," he muttered. "The damn wind died on us! Maybe you can pray to your good lord to send us wind?"

Then saying nothing more he went below in a hurry, nearly tumbling down the ladder. I took a forward turn to check on our running lights and make sure the man on duty as lookout was awake. The decks were wet with dew and left my bare feet quite cold even though the month was June. Not a breath of air stirred, and so I went back to bed. Then of a sudden I found my cot swinging violently.

Mr. Turpin breathing hard had pushed it and was demanding a response. "Outta that sack, Mr. Doyle! We got a good breeze sou'easterly. Look sharp now and call the bo'sun to pipe all hands."

In minutes I made my way to the bo'sun's cabin, a deckhouse on the portside against the fo'c's'le. He and the carpenter were fast asleep in stacked bunks, having turned in "all standing" or fully clothed. I shook him awake and he quickly sat upright.

"All hands, sir?"

"Yes, bo'sun, all hands. Pipe all hands."

"Aye, aye, sir!" I heard him say as I was returning to my cabin to get boots and socks on my cold feet and finish dressing.

In minutes I heard his pipe sound, followed by the roar of his voice summoning all hands on deck. My duty station was close by the fo'c's'le, and there I went expecting to see sleepy sailors slowly emerging to sheet home all the canvas we had. I saw no one.

From the poop, that portion of deck above the captain's cabin and close astern, Captain Redstone cried out, "Mr. Doyle! Go below and find out why the men are not on deck."

Entering the fo'c's'le, I yelled. "Did you not hear the bo'sun?"

"Yeah, we heard!" a man yelled back. "But no use! We don't mean to sail this ship until we have something to eat! My name's Dan Cullen, able seaman first class. Tell the captain we can't work this here vessel with no food in our bellies. Nobody can eat his filthy provisions."

As I was leaving to deliver his message a lot of voices supported Cullen, all of them cursing the captain and their predicament fiercely. From the quarterdeck I repeated what the man had told me. Redstone flew into a rage even before I finished.

"Who gave you that message, Mr. Doyle?"

"A fellow calling himself Dan Cullen."

"Remember that name, Doyle. Cullen is due to be flogged. Do all the men refuse to leave the fo'c's'le?"

"They refuse to get the ship sailing."

"What about the bo'sun? Is he one of them?"

"I think not, sir. But I'm sure he knows what's going on."

When the captain saw the bo'sun standing near the longboat, he ordered the man to lead the crew aft two at a time. They were fourteen in all, including the carpenter, the cook, and the cook's helper. They assembled on the quarterdeck abaft the mainmast near the capstan. Three officers — captain, first mate, navigator — looked down on them from the poop deck. I, the second mate, stood on the quarterdeck close by.

Strong men capable of doing the hard work necessary to sail a fully canvassed ship thousands of miles across treacherous seas struck me as a sad and motley group of victims in the half light of early dawn. Some were men who had been to sea all their lives and had leathery skin to prove it. Some were pale and thin and dressed in patches, destitute when they signed on and no better at sea. Some were ugly in a bizarre way with silver earrings hanging from long ears. As a group they were almost comical in their appearance, and yet I felt sorry for them. I knew from experience and from extensive reading that these men stood little chance of redressing their grievance successfully. Inarticulate, most of them, they had few words with which to argue their plight.

Captain Redstone, stiff as a rail and clutching the rail with both hands, spoke loudly to be heard above the wind. "The bo'sun piped you out to get the ship moving. Why in hell do you refuse that order?"

Dan Cullen stepped forward to reply. "We don't mean to work this here ship until we get better food! The biscuits ain't fit for hogs and the pork stinks and the molasses you give us is like sand."

"And that's the truth!" several voices rang out.

"You sons of bitches!" the captain screamed. "How dare you! What do you know about food for dogs or hogs? Didn't you ship out of some flop house in a Baltimore slum where food like we have here is a luxury? Now into the rigging, damn it, and get this ship moving!"

"It ain't gonna happen," Cullen calmly replied, pulling a biscuit from his pocket and holding it up. "We don't do nothin' till you give us better bread than this. The sun's up now, sir. Put the bread in the sun and watch what happens. Worms gonna crawl out of it!"

Redstone glared at the seaman for a full minute. All on board could see that he was furious. I thought he might strike the man down and berate the men a second time. Instead he drew Turpin aside to say something to his first mate in private. I made no attempt to go near them, and within a few minutes they went below possibly to iron out kinks in more privacy. The navigator remained alone on the poop.

I was about to go to my cabin too when I saw Charnook calmly smoking his pipe as if taking the air on what promised to be a fine day. He nodded when I approached and said it was too bad to have the men refusing to work when the breeze was so good.

"True enough," I said, "but the captain and first mate are probably deciding at this moment to return to port for fresh stores. We couldn't be more than thirty miles from shore."

"According to my reckoning it's closer to forty-six," said the navigator. "While that ain't much I don't believe Redstone would return even it was only ten. He means to send word for another crew. He'll deploy a sea anchor, put them fellas in a quarterboat, and wait for a new crew."

"Oh, surely the man will order food the crew can eat."

"Don't think so, not in his character to give in to common-sailor demands. Tough old bird and loves a good fight. And he probably has something going with the owners about them stores. Probably got the bad stuff very cheap just to make a quick buck."

"You mean the rotten food will stay put and if a new crew comes on board they'll be up against the same problem?"

"Guess so. Sure looks that way."

"If that happens, you can look for a mutiny, Mr. Charnook, long before we reach Gibraltar."

"Well, I sure hope not. I think you know I don't like violence. And the men will identify us as belonging to the captain. And . . . I won't even think about it, could be the end of us."

That last observation made me shudder. And yet it was no exaggeration. I found it hard to believe that a seasoned and competent sailor such as Redstone could be so foolish. Couldn't he see he was fomenting disaster? But as the old saying goes, "The human heart is greedy; it will use any excuse to justify its greed." That in a nutshell was Redstone. He was willing to risk high dissatisfaction, even mutiny, to glean a few extra dollars during what should have been a pleasant voyage.

As the navigator was speaking, the steward called me down for breakfast. The air was charged with the sweet aroma of cooked ham, hot rolls, and black coffee. Helping myself to a full serving of ham and gulping it down with a ravenous appetite, I thought of what the crew was expected to eat and the contrast disturbed me. The cook was saying the men would rather starve than eat their moldy and rotting provisions. The steward confessed he didn't like walking the deck to bring our food from the galley for fear of being fiercely cursed or tossed overboard.

After breakfast I clambered on deck again and found the captain once more in a dark mood. He was standing near the fo'c's'le with his sidekick, Mr. Turpin, and nearby were several sailors quietly chatting.

"Get your belongings together and get off my ship!" I heard him shout. "You have exactly half an hour to be gone. If any man among you refuses to leave, I personally will flog him and toss him overboard!"

To my surprise the men obediently went below and without delay prepared to go. The mechanics of leaving the ship far from land had apparently been worked out beforehand, and so each man knew exactly what to do. They were to take the longboat with water and a crude compass and make their way back to land. None seemed to think it was an undertaking they couldn't perform. They came to the gangway carrying their bags and sea chests and expressing themselves freely.

"That dirty old bastard!" muttered one, flinging his bag into the boat. "He ain't human enough to feed us or even to take us back to shore. I wanna warm my fist on his ugly face!"

Turpin was wise to hold his tongue, nor did I say a word either. Every man departing in that boat was angry enough to murder any person confronting him. The older sailors only scowled at us and descended with a show of resignation into the longboat. Not so with the younger ones. They hurled curses upon the ship and those remaining behind. One that stung me was the fervent wish that in a few days the ship would founder, sink, and drown every one of the arrogant bastards commanding her. Years later I found it difficult to forget that beautiful morning filled with so much misery — the hungry, angry, abused men going over the side with bitter curses on their lips. I remembered with searing pain the first and second mate, Turpin and myself, standing like sentinels absorbing their curses and saying not a word.

CHAPTER FOUR

Peril And Suffering

A fresh crew came aboard the following morning. They came in a longboat almost identical to ours that was taken aboard as an equal exchange. I went to the gangway to receive them and stood there admiring how expertly they dropped the lugsail, came about, and eased up against the larger vessel to stop exactly in place. I caught the line that was flung from her and made her fast. In minutes the empty boat was ready to be lifted, and three skilled men did the job with dispatch.

Even though they came from Bermuda instead of Baltimore, the new crew had much the same appearance as the old. Only four of them had sea chests while the rest shouldered canvas bags. One mariner among them caught my eye, a big fellow who dwarfed the others. His arms were broad and muscular and he wore a bird-of-paradise tattoo on a very strong neck. I judged he must have done service in the southern ocean to want that tattoo. His name, I learned later, was Hector Sylvain. Another scrambling over the side of the ship was a wiry little man with probably the biggest head on narrow shoulders I've ever seen. He had a little boy's face with a pug nose, tiny black eyes, and coarse black hair that made his head look even larger. When he opened his mouth to eject a loud cackle, I saw he was missing three of his front teeth. Yet he strutted on deck with confidence and vigor and soon moved out of sight into the fo'c's'le. His name, I found out later, was Otis Bearclaw.

Still another was a swarthy man with broad shoulders they called the Dutchman. Even though his hair was light brown or blonde, his skin was quite dark. He wore a jacket with no sleeves, possibly to show off a wide array of tattoos on both arms. Or maybe he wanted to make it clear to anyone who looked him over that he had large and hard muscles, formidable biceps and a muscular torso. His neck was muscular and his jaw square. I didn't see much of his face.

Scarcely half an hour went by before Mr. Turpin was asking the bo'sun to pipe all hands on deck to get the ship moving eastward. Some of the crew brought in the sea anchor that had held us steady for hours while others climbed the ratlines to unfurl and trim sail. We had a good breeze from the southeast, quite enough to keep the lighter sails full, and the day was gloriously fine. The sea was green and sparkling. Our little ship picked up speed and lay over enough so that a man on the weather side could see her copper. She was heeling, as sailors say, and showing her bottom. The canvas, broad and white in the sun, towered nobly to the sky to make the vessel a thing of graceful beauty.

Near 1400, two o'clock in the afternoon by landlubber time, we had up all the sail the breeze and the ship could handle, and the sleek bow of the *Windhover* was cutting through the ocean's water like a hot knife through butter. The sound of the bow wave was music to my ears, and I wanted to stand near the bowsprit and listen but duty called. It was necessary to divide the crew into watches, and I had to oversee the port watch while the starboard watch went below for grog and a bit of food. Some in my watch had skipped breakfast, and as a favor to them I let them go with the others to the fo'c's'le for fuel on which to accomplish their jobs. That was when I discovered our new cook was an African with a sweaty copper face and a long scar on his left cheek. The men were joking with him as they went past the galley to a table carrying lumps of pork and steaming bowls of pea-soup. It seemed obvious to me they had not yet discovered the rank provisions that caused the first crew to complain, or maybe they were more easily satisfied.

It wasn't long before the cook was poking his head out of the galley and peering in my direction as I paced the deck. By the time I reached the poop and returned to the cook's station, he was walking toward me with a large piece of pork swinging on a string. My heart sank, for I knew the problem that had caused so much fuss had not gone away. I stopped and waited for him to approach and say his piece.

"You see this, sar? Let me tell you somethin'. I come from a country where we don't eat pork, but here on board ship I do. But I do only if it don't stink to high heaven, sar. And this pork stinks real bad!"

"You mean to tell me the pork is tainted?"

"Don't know if it's tainted, sar, but do know it stinks. And no self-respectin' man gonna eat pork that smells like this. Disgusting! Fork'sle smells like somethin' died in it, and men grumblin' like hell. I'm as good a cook as you gonna find anywhere, sar, but for sure I can't make stink sweet and easy to eat."

He pushed the stinking pork under my nose so that I could get a good whiff of it. Then with a show of disgust and anger he flung it over the side. Walking away from me, he was saying: "Them my rations, sar, my rations. Can't eat none o' that nasty stuff. Throw it into sea. Don't you go and eat the funny fish that swallow it."

As the cook entered his galley the man with the large head and small face came out of the fo'c's'le and confronted me.

"Beggin' yer pardon, sir, can I have a word wit' you? The meat on this vessel is just plain bad, real bad."

"I'm sorry to hear that, sailor," I replied with some impatience, "but I can't do a thing about it."

Captain Redstone in anger had accused me earlier of being a confidant of the crew. For my own welfare I couldn't let him believe it was true. "Talk to the captain," I said. "Make your complaint to him."

"The bo'sun done already told us talkin' to the skipper ain't gonna do no good. So we been hopin' you might do it for us."

I was about to repeat I could do nothing to solve the problem when Captain Redstone came on deck and asked what the man wanted.

"He's complaining of the pork, sir, and I referred him to you."

Redstone gave me a sharp look, his hard little eyes glinting under bushy eyebrows. Then taking a step forward he calmly remarked, "What's the matter there, sailor? Something bothering you?"

"Yessir, I been elected to come and tell you the pork is real bad, sir. It smells somethin' awful and what ain't a bad smell is brine."

"I'm sorry to hear that," Redstone kindly replied.

His tone of voice surprised me, and yet the man was full of surprises. At that moment Simpson, the steward, came on the quarterdeck and looked at his captain as a beaten dog would his master.

"What's with the pork, steward? I'm hearing complaints about it. This man claims it stinks."

"He must have a nose better than me, sir. I didn't detect no smell at all. I put my nose right to it and didn't smell nothing."

"The men say it has a strong and nasty smell. Am I right in saying that, sailor?" He was pointing to the man who had dared to complain. "What's your name, lad?"

"My name's Otis Bearclaw, sir. I'm part Indian. I do smell keener than your steward and taste better too, and I tell you the meat can't be eat. It'll tear the guts outta any man that tries it."

"I'm ordering Simpson to open a new cask and fling the old one overboard, you hear? I won't have the men poisoned. The cook will boil me a sample from the new cask and put it on my table. Go now and tell your mates what I've said. Your name is Bearclaw, you say? That's a name not easily forgotten."

At 0700 the next morning, according to the navigator's briefing, we were well at sea and on course. We had carried a strong sou'easterly breeze with us for most of the night, but as dawn came the wind diminished and remained light all through the middle watch. After 1600, however, it freshened from the same quarter and began to blow hard. Even so, we kept the fore and main royals hoisted and working all through the blow and found our decks running with water. We had seen when sailing to Bermuda that the *Windhover* was something of a wet ship with her heavy cargo, and now we were getting a repeat of her behavior. She lay steady enough but shipped water over her windward bow in heavy seas without rising to the waves. While that bothered me a bit, I put my faith in the captain's ability to handle his ship. I went to my cabin to get some rest just as sheets of foamy water swept over the bow and foredeck. The man at the wheel was dry, but those on lookout were already soaked to the skin. I would be on duty again at midnight.

I slept like a stone and resisted being awakened by Turpin when he came shaking me by the shoulder in the middle of the night. It isn't good to roll out of warm blankets after only a few hours' sleep and walk cold and watery decks for many hours. The rawness of the night air hurts even your strong man, and you think as a shower of spray patters your face of your comfortable cabin and warm cot. You wonder what in the name of common sense could have caused you to go into so painful a profession, and yet you know it's somehow right for you. In many ways in this respect the crew is better off than the officers. At night the watch can manage to find shelter on the lee side of the ship and even dose an hour or two. But the mate in charge must always be wide awake and walking throughout his watch in all kinds of weather. I had four hours to be on deck without rest in the black of night in high winds.

Captain Redstone stood near the wheel without saying a word, as far as I could tell, to the helmsman. The wind was east-southeast, our course easterly. Close-hauled, the vessel was beating valiantly against high winds and waves. If I had thought she was carrying too much sail when I went below, I knew she had too much now. We could have furled the main-royal and the two top-gallant sails and even reefed the topsails without losing half a knot of speed. The press of canvas was placing the ship's lee rail almost to the water, and that meant she was heeling thirty degrees when it should have been twenty-two at most. Redstone was calmly smoking his meerschaum pipe with one hand and holding the rail with the other. He was keeping an eye on the sails, calmly looking upward while puffing.

"She's performing well, sir, but maybe too much canvas?"

"No," he answered gruffly, "she has all the sail she can handle but not too much. We've lost time, as you know, and have to make up for it."

"She's a fast vessel, sir, fast and steady. We're doing better than nine knots, her hull speed, maybe more than ten."

He looked up at the sails again and squinted at the lee rail almost touching the water but made no answer. I was walking away when he ordered me to go forward and urge the men to keep a keen lookout. I did as told and went leaning against the wind to the fo'c's'le where I found two men in oilskins pressed against the wall. In the uproar of screeching wind and groaning timbers I made no attempt to talk with them, or to roust them from their position.

An hour later, chilled by the wind, I went to my cabin for a scarf to put around my neck. As I was leaving the cuddy I heard a loud cry from the two men huddled against the fo'c's'le, "A sail! You see it? A sail dead ahead!"

I shouted, "On which bow do you see a sail? Which bow?"

"Neither!" Came the reply. "Dead ahead. Bowsprit ahead!"

After a pause the men roared out, "Hard over! We're gonna hit her! Cutter rigged. Single mast. A fishing boat. Bring that helm hard over!"

I saw the spokes of the wheel flying round in a desperate attempt to avoid the collision, but it was too late.

"Oh my god!" cried the helmsman. "We've run her down!"

I looked over the weather side and saw a mast and dark-colored sail swallowed by the sea as our ship thundered past. Our rigging jerked with a crackling sound as though it were ready to snap, but Redstone grabbed the wheel and put us on course again.

"Shouldn't we make an effort to save them, sir?" I asked with feelings of surprise mingled with disgust.

"Save them and die in the attempt? Not on your life!" Those words came from his mouth like a pistol shot, brutal and direct.

I was taken aback by the inhumanity of his reply but could do nothing on my own. All I could do was look over the rail again where I thought we hit them. In the dark I could see only sea foam.

"Order the carpenter to go into the hold and check for damage," Captain Redstone was saying. I did as told and the carpenter, whose name was Harlowe Quine, later reported a normal four inches in the bilge. We had sustained no damage except perhaps at the bow. The wind now was reaching gale force and threatening to dismast the ship. Redstone was ready to shorten sail almost too late.

"Get some men up them ratlines now to furl the main-royal!" he bawled. "Have them furl the mizzen top-gallant sails!"

Conditions promised a long and fierce gale before morning. The slippery decks grew lively with shadowy figures running about, and above the noise of the storm I could hear good-natured cries of sailors at work. "Smartly now, lads! We gotta reef the main top-gallant sail! Watch out fer the scud! Don't let it smack yer face! Hey, Dawson! Get the lead outta yer pants! Move it, man!"

Then came the order I dreaded, "All hands! Reef topsails!" The watch below came tumbling out of the fo'c's'le and sprang into the rigging. The captain had carried too much canvas too long and now went to the opposite extreme to reduce sail. The fierce gusts that pounded the ship rattled him, and his order was to let go all three topsail halyards and double reef the sails. To put it mildly, the order caused a complicated confusion that went on and on. When dawn finally came it found the *Windhover* under all sails reefed, even the spanker, and wallowing in angry seas. The gale had raised a heavy beam sea and the ship, sluggish with too much cargo, took sheets of green water time and again over her weather side. The captain had gone below, leaving me in charge of the ship. It was a huge responsibility for a junior officer, and yet I was relieved to see him go. The time was already 0200, and at 0400 I would be warm and comfortable in my cot.

I was alone except for a skeleton watch forward and was troubled by unpleasant thoughts. Foremost was our running down and capsizing the smaller boat and Redstone's show of no willingness to turn back for even half an hour to help. How fast the whole thing had happened! A cry of another boat ahead, a bump in the night, a quick adjustment of sail, and then galloping out of sight. All within minutes! In the roar of the wind and the clatter of sail and rigging, not one person on the *Windhover* heard so much as a dying shriek. But the memory of that dark-colored sail, perhaps red in daylight, lying prone upon the water near the hull of the boat haunted me. Our voyage had begun pleasantly enough and without incident. Now a malicious fate seemed to hold us in its fist, and all we could do was hope for the best and wait.

As I looked toward the east where the morning light was building slowly over a rugged horizon, I felt strangely sorrowful and somewhat helpless. Above me in rank and commanding the ship were two men with scarcely one shred of human decency. Equal to that but not worse, they were unpredictable in a crisis. Thoughts of peril and suffering entered my mind and never again quite left it. Peril, suffering, and death — I was thinking as I went below — had come to those on that fishing vessel. Was the same in store for us? When I stood at the rail to absorb the beauty of Bermuda shortly before we got underway, perhaps without knowing it I was bidding farewell to a scene I would never see again. In fact, and I hated to admit it even though I knew it could certainly be true, I might never see land again.

CHAPTER FIVE

Kicking Up A Shindy

In my cot swinging wildly as the ship plunged and tossed in wind-swept seas, I slept fitfully. It didn't matter whether I had gotten enough sleep or not. I had to be on deck at 0800 for my usual four-hour watch. The gale had not let up. Although the topsails remained reefed, Turpin had seen fit to require the riggers to set the main top-gallant sail for balance, and the ship was galloping like a race horse. Her speed was a fast ten to eleven knots. Yet despite running fast she was rolling from gunwale to gunwale and pitching with a jerky motion that had the power to make even the most seasoned sailor seasick. I held on to the rail at the poop and made no attempt to walk the decks.

In the nasty weather not far from us was a small steamer crossing our bow. She was possibly hailing from France. I watched her pitch violently through my 'scope. At times she seemed to stand clear of the water, hang in midair for a minute or two, and crash into a wave or trough and disappear. Observing that spectacle, her decks completely under water, I was certain the sea with no remorse had taken her. Then some minutes later through the 'scope I saw her smoke on the horizon. It was clear the less seaworthy steamer was having a worse time of it than our sailing ship but somehow remained afloat.

First mate Turpin and Navigator Charnook were eating

breakfast in the cuddy. Captain Redstone had driven himself out of bed early and was ready to come on deck. I thought I might speak a few words with him before going down for breakfast. As I stood waiting for him to appear, the cook with the copper face came with two other men walking briskly toward me even as the ship rolled and pitched. Again Cookie complained to me about the provisions, speaking as if I had not heard the complaint earlier. And again I replied with some impatience that I had nothing to do with them. He would have to see the steward and the captain about his problem. I told him he could find Simpson in the cuddy and the captain in his cabin. They were about to look for the two when Turpin came on deck.

"Go get some breakfast," he shouted over the noise of the gale. "I'll stand you till you get back. Who are the men on the quarterdeck?"

"They came complaining again about the bread. Seem to think I can do something about it. Will you speak to them?"

"Well, I dunno. Why should I? They seem to be your buddies, fella. Anyway, I'll do it. Hey, there! You! What's going on?" he called.

"We came topside even in heavy weather to complain about the ship's bread, sir," one of the men said politely. "It just ain't no good."

"Damn bad bread, sar!" added the cook. "I seen bad bread before in my many year at sea but nothin' like this. It's the honest truth!"

"Get out of my sight, you scoundrels!" Turpin roared. "The bread's good enough for anybody! You wanna kick up a shindy? We got enough on our hands dealing with this storm. Now, go!"

The cook began to mutter something in broken English, but the two men with him took him by the arms and almost lifted him off his feet as they retreated to the galley. Believing himself more important than any ordinary seaman, he was ready to defy authority. But his mates with cooler heads took him below. It was good they did, for Turpin on the poop was ready to polish his knuckles on the man's face.

"The impudence of those sons o' bitches!" he exclaimed. "Now, Mr. Doyle, get on to your breakfast. I wanna turn in when you're done."

I entered the cuddy where the captain was seated. He took very little notice of me, occupying himself with some papers in front of him. The vessel was rolling so heavily that dishes on the table were sliding to the little bumper on the sides, and the coffee pot was swinging on its gimbal. I managed to pour a cup of coffee without spilling even a drop and was proud of the achievement. A rattle of crockery came from the pantry, and the timbers of our little world creaked incessantly.

"So what was that on the main deck just now?" the captain asked abruptly. "Sounded like a tussle of some sort."

"Almost came to that, but the cook's companions carried him bodily away. Turpin demanded they go, and they went. I got a feeling our new cook is gonna cause a bit of trouble. He seems to think he has more power than any ordinary seaman."

"Oh, does he, now? Well, we'll see about that. So the worthless second bunch is complaining! Damn them fellows!"

Then calling the steward from his pantry, he ordered the man to place the same pork served to the men on his table at dinner time.

"Aye, aye, sir! That I will!" said the obsequious steward going back to his pantry in some haste.

Captain Redstone fell silent again, and I made no effort to converse with him. I ate my breakfast quickly so as to relieve the first mate. As I was about to leave to go on deck again, the captain called me back.

"Mr. Doyle, a question for you. What would you have done after we ran that vessel down? You seemed upset that we went on."

"I would have backed the headsails and hove to," I replied.

"Are you aware that with all the sail we had up in a wind close to gale force you could have ripped the masts away trying to heave to?"

"I am indeed, sir. But plain human decency demanded we save the poor wretches we threw into the sea, or at least try."

His volatile temper was quickly reaching the boiling point. I could see he was searching for choice words to belittle me as too soft, too namby-pamby for my profession. I waited for a savage response when of a sudden his attention was no longer centered on me. The entire crew including the cook and even his helper stomped with heavy footsteps along the main deck, advancing aft. Redstone clambered up the companion ladder and I followed behind him.

In front of the men as their leader was the giant of a man who had caught my eye when he first came aboard. Beside him was the little man with thin shoulders, a big head, and a tiny face, the one who claimed he was part Indian. Earlier I had come to know the giant's name as Hector Sylvain, and the little man had told the captain when complaining that his name was Otis Bearclaw. The company gathered in little knots near the mainmast. They held in their hands a tin dish containing lumps of black meat, a dozen inedible biscuits, a pannikin filled with gritty molasses, and a glass jar half full of something that looked like liquid tar.

In a loud and throaty voice to be heard above the howling of the wind, Sylvain spoke first. "The able-bodied seamen of this here ship is come aft in stormy weather to make it known as best we can that this here food ain't eatable. Not even a starving dog would eat it!"

Captain Redstone retorted calmly, his famous temper under control. "Let all hands speak their piece. When done, I will do the talking."

The fellow with the biscuits came forward. "These here belong to the starboard watch. Not a man has sunk a tooth into even one. We brought 'em here coz you might not really know what god-awful slop your crew is expected to eat and work on."

"Bring one of them to me," said the skipper.

A man advanced with a biscuit. Redstone broke it in half, smelled it, tasted it, and handed it to Turpin who tasted it.

"What else do you have?" the captain inquired.

A crewman gave him the dish containing meat. Redstone jabbed at it with a penknife and even put a small piece in his mouth. I scrutinized his face for a grimace but saw only a wry smile. He gave the dish to Turpin who looked at the meat closely but didn't dare taste it.

"What else do you have? Make it fast now!"

"This, sir, is what we are gettin' for molasses. But it ain't molasses. It might as well be biled beetles or shellfish or sand. You need a toothpick to get it arter yer teeth!"

"Hand it to me!" cried the captain. Any moment I expected his temper to explode. He inspected the stuff but didn't taste it. He gave it to his first mate who quickly gave it back to the crewman.

"Is that all now? Or do you have more?"

The man with the glass jar stepped away from the others. "Maybe the steward calls this black stuff coffee, but it ain't nothin' like what we had on other vessels or what they sells on shore. It's more like coal oil."

The captain exchanged looks with Turpin and demanded to know of his hard-working and tractable crew if they had any more complaints. At length after some mumbling among themselves, Sylvain answered "No." Captain Redstone made a mental note that the big, muscular man with broad shoulders didn't attach a "sir" to his response.

"Very well, then," he said in summary. "I've heard your complaints about the food. You must know I can do nothing to rectify the situation here in this wilderness of water. You'll have to wait until we make landfall at some port beyond the horizon. Perhaps we can put in at Horta or Ponta Delgada in the Azores."

"I reckon that's two thousand miles from where we stand here," Sylvain complained. "And how do we hold out?"

"Our navigator can tell you the exact distance. And I will tell you my ship will go onward. I cannot and will not turn back. I may alter course just slightly for the Azores to satisfy you but no more than that. If the crew can manage on what we have or can wait, I'm willing to hail a passing ship for assistance if possible."

"It's our stomachs, sir, that can't wait," said Bearclaw. "It's our bodies that can't wait. You just can't expect us to work without food."

"Cookie tells us," cried Sylvain, "if we try to eat that stinking pork we gonna come down with cholera. You don't want vomiting and diarrhea on your ship, Cap'n. We wouldn't mind if the bread and molasses was right but they ain't. Nothin' is right!"

"Hold yer greasy tongue!" bawled Turpin. "The captain spoke fair, as fair as any skipper I ever sailed under. So quit yer belly achin' and get forward and finish yer breakfast. And you, Cookie, lead the way!"

The men moved away in a tight little group, grumbling among themselves, chastened by how little they had been able to accomplish, and lost themselves in the fo'c's'le. The captain had walked aft to the wheel, leaving Turpin alone with me on the quarterdeck. It was time in his mind to set things right with me.

"I'm gonna be blunt with you, Mr. Doyle. You gotta wake up and help me keep these rascals in their place. It's no used standin' and starin' and sayin' not a word. You gotta speak up and back me up and let 'em know we ain't gonna take no guff from 'em. Do you understand?"

"No, Mr. Turpin, I do not understand. I don't believe abusing a ship's crew ever works in the long run. I've seen it tried, oh tried more than once, and every time it failed."

"I take it you're one of them officers that coddles a crew," he said with a sarcastic snicker. "Captain Redstone ain't gonna like that much. He told me hisself he wants manly men for officers on any ship he commands, not gentle men."

"I believe I can get the men to do their work, assuming they're fed decent rations, without insults and threats of violence. The men come around when the officers work with them and not against them."

"Oh, that's a lotta crap!" he said with disgust. "I really believe you couldn't knock a man down even if you had a very good reason."

I looked him squarely in the eyes, smiled, and said nothing. He was looking me up and down as though measuring my strength. He was a strong man and knew it but perhaps I was stronger. I was taller and weighed more. My arms and chest were visibly muscular, my fists hard. My age was twenty-six, and while I didn't know his exact age I could tell he was pushing fifty. He backed off and said nothing. With the advantage on my side, I couldn't resist needling him a little.

"I think I could knock a man down if I tried, could knock him down, perhaps knock him out. But then I've never tried. You would have to insult me with cruel and vicious accusations for me to try."

His little blue eyes grew even more intense as he caught the shift from general to specific, from "a man" to "you." He heard me say "you" and moved back another step, his blue eyes squinting soberly at me and his copper beard moving up and down on his chin as he muttered something I couldn't hear. I think he was saying I was too fine a bird to be serving on Captain Redstone's ship. I chuckled as he walked away, found the captain, and the two of them went below.

As second mate on the *Windhover* I had fallen into conflict with the first mate, the protégé and bosom buddy of the captain. Also I knew the captain was convinced that my sympathy lay entirely with the crew. Moreover, he could easily see my contempt for Turpin, a coarse and ignorant toady. So for the entire voyage I was fated to be the stranger on board, the outsider distrusted by the captain and hated by the first mate. I had done as much as I could to be an affable officer well-liked by both, but now that the opposite was thrust upon me I resolved to meet it quietly head on. To put it simply, I would perform my duties with diligence. That would give Redstone no cause to find fault with me.

CHAPTER SIX

Screeching Came The Wind

The next day the wind that had rattled our timbers for two days subsided, and the sun rose bright and clear on a sparkling blue sea. In a fine breeze we unfurled and set our sails, and our navigator instructed the helmsman to steer south-southeast. That course would take us to nine volcanic islands, the Archipelago of the Azores. Located directly west of Portugal and more than 900 miles from that shore, Redstone could reach them without greatly changing his original course. On hearing that we were headed for the islands to replace the provisions, most of the sailors on board ceased to grumble and became more tractable. However, some were asking how could they survive a journey of some 1,800 miles, as calculated by our navigator, without sufficient food. It was certainly cause for concern.

Shortly after the noon hour the breeze we had working for us, with the hope it might increase to give us a speed of eight knots, quickly diminished and died. The captain was resting in his cabin when his ship began to stand still in calm water and roll in a surge. All along he had feared encountering a dead calm, for it meant losing precious time and perhaps not reaching our destination on schedule. Should that happen, it meant a considerable loss of money, a condition Redstone found intolerable. All afternoon he raged against the calm, raged against whatever gods may be, raged and made us miserable. Then when he went to eat his dinner at 1930 hours, seven bells shipboard, he grew silent and soon afterwards went to bed.

At eight o'clock I began my watch that would run four hours until midnight. A light breeze was rising aft of the ship. We ran up the fore topsail studding sails (stun'sails in sailor jargon), and the ship began to move again. The breeze held all night and freshened a bit the next day. But since it was directly behind us and we were running before it, our speed never reached more than six and half knots. Even so, that last day in June gave us weather as persistent as we could wish, and the crew was able to relax a little because of less work. The bo'sun told me they grumbled at meal time but managed to eat, and no murmurs of dissatisfaction came aft to the skipper. They had been told the ship would put into port at first landfall and take on new supplies, and they were willing to endure hardship until then. I too believed it was the skipper's intention to reach the Azores and later go on to Gibraltar. As time passed, however, and we gained snippets of information to the contrary, neither the crew nor myself believed the captain had ever intended to change the ship's course even slightly. I was forced to conclude his behavior was fraudulent and potentially dangerous.

Had I been on friendly terms with the man and his first mate, I would have mentioned how the crew was having misgivings about his intentions, and those misgivings at any time could erupt into turmoil and trouble for every person on the ship. Then as I thought about it I really believed he would try to turn my fear of trouble into a legal charge against me. He could toss me into the brig and swear later to a court of law that I had sympathized with the crew, had even urged them to mutiny, and had persuaded them to select me as ringleader. I knew only too well that the legal system in 1871 favored owners and captains far above any crew or junior officer. Also there was the distinct possibility that nothing even resembling a mutiny was afoot. A report suggesting the opposite would endanger every man of the crew and possibly end my career at sea. So with some reluctance I held my tongue.

When I left the deck at midnight, the favorable breeze was still blowing from astern and steady. The sky was clear though with a bank of clouds on the horizon to the southeast, and a swell was rolling up from that direction. The weather on the whole looked promising except for mist or fog that made the moon a pale round orb. Before entering my cabin I stopped to view the barometer and found it falling. That could mean a shift in the direction of the wind or a spell of rain or a drop in temperature with stronger wind or less wind. Yet beyond showing a change in the density of the atmosphere it might not signal a thing. Though I am certainly no Luddite, on occasion (or so it seems to me), the eye of a seasoned mariner is more accurate forecasting the weather than a barometer or similar machine. Through both of the dog watches (shorter than the standard watch of four hours) the weather held fair even though the glass continued to fall. The breeze that had been steady for many hours became erratic and diminished.

I went into the cuddy for a mug of grog before trying to get a few hours' sleep. Captain Redstone was there and bluntly asked what I thought of how the sea was looking.

"That swell increasing by the hour bothers me, sir." I said with as much courtesy as I could muster. "I think we're in for a real blow."

"Strong winds south of us are causing the swell," he said, appearing to agree with me but not saying as much. "A couple hours from now a gale's gonna batter this ship. If you're turning in keep your clothes on."

I was about to reply when Turpin sang out to the men on deck to get the fore-topmast stun'sail down. In the calm and darkness of night, the ship rolled from gunwale to gunwale in heaving seas. She rolled so violently it was impossible to walk safely on the best of sea legs. I stumbled to a nearby porthole and saw black and oily water with flashes of phosphorescent light beneath the surface. The swell by now was gigantic and shocking the rudder, making the wheel kick. I went to the binnacle and found the card swinging and the vessel in irons with no steerage whatever. In the rigging by degrees all the lighter sails were clewed up and furled, and the reefing of topsails began. Turpin stood on the poop delivering orders in a thunderous voice to the men in the rigging. Captain Redstone stood silently beside him observing the action. Not because of any wind but because the ship rolled violently, the topsails flapped like thunder until furled. In time she was made snug enough for any fluke of weather that might befall her. Under bare poles almost (except for topsails), in a dead calm and darkness we waited.

Then slowly as I stood by the binnacle, lights that looked like a fleet of steamers rose from the horizon to the southeast. One by one looking red before turning white they climbed into the sky, and I realized they were not ships' lights but stars. The sky was clearing. Then screeching across the water came the wind. In front of it was a white surf such as one sees when standing on a beach. It hit us with tremendous power. Our little ship rolled and pitched with such violence I thought her back would break. Then she righted herself and the helmsman with my help set her nose into building waves to ride out the storm, but with virtually no sail aloft and no forward sails aback we had to run under small canvas in confused seas. The wind was as strong as any I've seen, and its force soon leveled the monstrous swell. That allowed the ship to race faster than hull speed on a surface of froth, but for only a short time. Running before the gale that came from the south, we quickly lost all the ground we had gained during most of the day. Looking astern I saw a following sea with churning waves becoming larger by the minute.

The violence of the wind couldn't be fully appreciated as the ship ran before it, but as soon as the helmsman put the wheel to starboard with some attempt to get back on course, it seemed to me the ship would be blown like a leaf in autumn right out of the water. Two of the three mizzen topsails were ready to rip in half just as Turpin roared through a bullhorn for all hands to clew up and furl the topsails. No landlubber can possibly imagine what it's like to climb high in a ship's rigging in wind so strong it's difficult even to breathe.

When you're there at the top, the masts swing like an upside-down pendulum, and you hang on for dear life as you whoosh at high speed through air that batters your face. Somehow you get the job done and slither down to the deck exhausted. Then as you seek shelter from the elements the captain is there expecting you to do more work that could throw you into the sea. However, to my surprise, Captain Redstone allowed all but a few men to go below for grog and rest. He ordered the steward to serve their daily ration to them. The ship was now hove to under reefed topsail, staysail, two reefed bowsprit sails aback and riding well. As the captain had suggested or perhaps ordered, I fell into my bunk "all standing" as mariners say. I removed only my boots and I slept quite comfortably fully clothed.

CHAPTER SEVEN

We Encounter A Ship In Distress

All night the wind blew hard and raised as tall a sea as I've ever seen. It was wild and angry like a drunken man kicked out of a bar and tumbling head over heels on the dirty sidewalk. I've been told it's stupid to impart human characteristics to the great forms of nature, and yet that sea as far as anyone could tell was angry. I know people often laugh when they hear a sailor speaking of his ship as a person, and particularly as a female. But why not when the ship is beautiful and plainly alive? I will say with no exaggeration that my ship was alive that night. Just a few hard planks between me and the briny deep, she was groaning in agony. Angry seas were slapping hard against her, beating her without mercy, and not a one of us could do anything about it. I was sleeping from midnight until four and worn out when I went below. I fell into a sound, sound sleep as soon as my head hit the pillow and never moved until Turpin routed me with a loud cry a few hours later.

After an early breakfast I was back on deck again. Captain Redstone sent me forward to tell a couple of men to look smart and snug the inner jib tightly on its boom. The sail had been quickly stowed and the wind was blowing it loose. I managed to get around the water on the main deck by waiting until it rolled into the scuppers. But as I stood near the bow to give orders to the men, I was struck by a sheet of salty green water that knocked me off my feet and left me coughing and hacking for ten minutes.

Good oilskins kept me from getting entirely soaked and clinging to the portside rail kept me from being washed overboard. We were weathering one storm after another it seemed, and yet no man was seriously injured or lost. For that we could thank only dumb luck.

Before going aft I looked into the fo'c's'le where the crew was gathered. A sputtering oil-lamp fought to push the darkness away even though outside dawn was breaking with streaks of light. My eyes had to adjust before I could detect objects in the gloom, and then slowly the interior revealed itself. I saw more hammocks than expected and two rows of very narrow upper and lower bunks. Near them were a few sea chests securely lashed as a caution against heavy weather. Most of the men lay sleeping or resting in their bunks or hammocks. One or two were awake and chatting. A crewman propped up in his bunk saw me as I entered and cried out.

"Hey! Look who's here! It's Mr. Kevin Doyle, second mate! We gotta ask him when we gonna put in for fresh supplies and where. The cap'n said somethin' about the Azores but when? We gotta have proper food soon. I must tell ya we can't wait much longer."

"I wish I could help," I said hesitantly, "but I can't answer your question. I don't know any more than you do. I believe Captain Redstone will do the right thing by you. As to when I just don't know."

"We must have proper vittles to support us," came a voice from a hammock. "In this storm we been working like mules on a dirt farm, and I can tell you the mules eat better than we do. Every man you see here is terrible hungry. Stomachs are scraping backbones!"

I had not gone into the fo'c's'le to quarrel with the crew. My intention was to compliment them on the smart way they worked the ship during that raging storm in spite of poor rations. I wanted them to know their worth and feel good about themselves. I turned on my heel to leave when the cook cried out.

"Tell the skipper, Mr. Doyle, that if we don't get decent food soon we gonna have to kill a couple of them pigs under the longboat and have ourselves a barbecue. Then for dessert we gonna bake a few chickens!"

I was about to tell Cookie to go easy on the threats when as bad luck would have it, Captain Redstone emerged from his cabin and saw me exiting the fo'c's'le. He motioned for me to approach and asked me why I was keeping company with the crew. At a glance I could tell he was becoming angry for reasons I couldn't quite understand.

"I went among the men to let them know the officers of this ship saw and appreciated the good work they did during the storm."

"Did I order you to do that? Did I give you leave to represent the officers of this ship and speak for them?"

"No, sir, you did not. I acted alone because no captain I've ever sailed with has ever given me orders not to encourage the crew with a few kind words. In fact, it's been much the opposite."

"So you acted alone, did you? Consorted with the crew in their quarters without my knowledge or permission. Insubordination is what I call it. It's what every captain calls it, sir, or worse! I want you to know I'm on to your little game!" He was venting his anger without restraint.

"What game is that, sir? I don't understand."

"Oh, you understand, Mr. Doyle, you understand only too well. But hear this and hear it good. Any time you wanna start your little game, go right ahead. Then I will end it and you won't like my ending at all."

"But, sir, I don't understand. Will you speak plainly?"

"Your mutinous game, you damn rascal, mutiny! You think I don't know you're planning to take over my ship with them apes in the fo'c's'le to help you? I've had my eye on you, bully boy! I know!"

Half mad with rage he stumbled to the wheel and stood there glaring at me, his deep blue eyes almost black in a very white face. For an instant I felt sorry for the helmsman who sensed his rage and was embarrassed to be a witness to it. He was standing like a statue, gripping the wheel and staring at the bow of the ship, trying as best he could not to make eye contact with Redstone. I was vexed by the captain's outburst, but decided he was not in full control of his temper and would in time apologize. Yet to be charged with fomenting a mutiny was no small matter. Even for the captain to suggest such a thing was dangerous both for him, for me, and for the entire crew.

Were he to charge me of mutiny and none took place, a court of law could find him guilty of a severe offense and sentence him to prison. It goes without saying that no captain in his right mind would ever want to find himself in trouble with the law. By the same token, no sailor would ever want to be so charged. I was tired and needed sleep and with some effort managed to put these thoughts out of mind to reach a simple conclusion. I would endure whatever Captain Redstone had in store for me and leave the ship as soon as possible.

The storm lasted three days and drove the ship some eighty miles off course even though after running before the wind on the first day we hove to on the next two. Seas on the afternoon of the third day were as fierce as I've ever seen them. Had we attempted to run on that day, I'm fairly certain the *Windhover* would have been pooped, smothered, or pitched with all hands lost. But riding close to the wind hove to with fore topsail aback she held her own quite well. However, on the second day a rogue wave put out the galley fire, and until wind and waves diminished no cooking could be done. That meant all hands were thrown upon the ship's moldy bread for the better part of two days. The rotten pork and beef couldn't be eaten at all without some degree of cooking. During the height of the storm, subdued by its ferocity, the crew ate as best they could without complaint. Near the end of the third day they were grumbling again, and the cook was keeping a close eye on the live pigs. I felt it was only a matter of time before desperate men, motivated by anger and hunger, would make a concerted attempt to take one.

All along I had thought the captain would eventually come to his senses, relent, and feel a modicum of shame after berating me with insults and accusations. My supposition was a bit too optimistic perhaps, and yet when I went below for my daily ration of grog he invited me to sit in a rough attempt at politeness. I thought he might apologize, but instead he gave me a lecture on what it's like to be a captain year after year on a vessel hauling freight. Cargo sailors, he said, are the most ungrateful scoundrels in all the world. Every crew he had sailed with — he was careful not to say commanded — had gone out of their way to invent a grievance to growl about. Without exception, every crew had complained of the food, of too much work, of the ship being unseaworthy, of regulations they saw as too stringent, even of the time of year and the weather. And so he made up his mind to pay no attention to any complaint. If he attempted to redress one that perhaps seemed reasonable, the next day there would be three.

Even though I had never commanded an entire crew, I understood what he was saying and felt a shade of sympathy. Some men strive all their lives to become leaders only to find when they begin to realize their dream that what appears to be white and sweet sugar on their festive table is really powdered glass. Ah, vanity, declared the preacher. Which of us has his desire, or having it is satisfied? Although Captain Redstone had attained all he set out to do, he later felt no sense of triumph. I assured that good looking but very bitter man that I had never tried to ferret out complaints, had never willingly listened to any complaint. On the contrary, instead of wishing to stir up the crew I wanted only to placate those who might be thinking of rebellion. He looked into my face with a strangely sad expression on his own and said not a word. The next day in good weather he was sullen again and taciturn.

When I left my cabin at 0800, I found the weather bright and warm with a blue sky filled with fleecy white clouds. The decks were dry and comfortable and the ship in a fine breeze was barreling along at seven knots. Later in the morning I stood near the taffrail to view with fine enjoyment a shoal of porpoises frolicking astern in our wake. I marveled at the sight; they seemed to be celebrating the mere joy of being alive. I couldn't help but feel a stark contrast between them and the denizens on board the *Windhover*. As I turned to move away, Joshua Haythorne at the wheel caught my attention with a question. He asked me to look at the sea a couple of points off the starboard bow. Something black was on the horizon. He had seen it twice and wanted to know if I could see it. I gazed in that direction and saw nothing. I said it was probably a wave larger than the others playing tricks on his vision.

The breeze held good and the sun on the dry deck was warm and comfortable. Both Redstone and Turpin were below resting after the storm that kept them on duty longer than usual. The men on my watch were on the fo'c's'le sitting or lying in the sun. The hens in their enclosure were clucking, and the pigs were grunting. Every creature on deck was basking in the warmth. Then as the ship rose, breasting a wave, I distinctly saw a tiny black object on the horizon. Before I could blink my eyes and look again it had vanished. I went for the glass secured on brackets in the cuddy and pointed it where I had seen the black thing.

For several minutes, though sweeping the sea in a wide arc, I saw nothing but sea and sky. I was about to return the glass to its brackets when suddenly the hull of a ship deep in the water hove into view. Adjusting the glass for a sharper look, I saw that she was a sailing vessel all battered by a storm and dismasted.

"It's a ship in distress," I said to Haythorne. "No masts that I can see, no sails, and wallowing in high seas. It's our duty to render aid. Of course we must inform the captain, but keep the ship on her present heading and approach cautiously."

"Aye, aye, sir!" Haythorne replied. "I saw her first! I just knew in my gut that what I saw was bigger than a wave."

I kept the glass trained on the derelict as we moved in closer. Her cargo had to be timber and was keeping her afloat. A sinkable cargo would have taken her under, for she rolled deep in the swell as sheets of green water dashed over her. I gazed intently for any signs of life on board, and to my surprise I saw a figure huddled against the deckhouse frantically waving something white. We were close enough to see the ship with the naked eye but only a semblance of a person.

"There's a man on board!" I cried. "He's waving a white towel! Take the glass, Haythorne, and I'll find the captain."

I met him coming up the companionway ladder looking upward at the sails. "You're off course," he said.

"Just a little, sir, because ahead of us is a ship in trouble. There's a man on board trying to get our attention."

He took the glass from the helmsman and looked at the wreck for what seemed a long time. "Don't go near it," he said quietly but firmly. "Get back on course!"

"But sir!" I tried to explain. "There's a man on board. I saw him, and there may be others."

"We have to make up for lost time, Mr. Doyle. We can't lose more time with something like that. It will throw us completely off schedule."

"Captain Redstone," I said in as firm a voice as I could make it. "If you bear away and leave that wreck to sink, you will become a murderer. And believe me, you will reap the consequences of your crime."

"Are you threatening me, Bully Boy?" he shrieked in mounting rage. "Damn your insolence! I will not have it! I alone command this ship. You and all aboard her will do as I say!"

His blue eyes protruding, his jaw moving up and down but his mouth emitting no sound, clenching and unclenching his fists, he stalked off to Turpin's cabin. I pulled off my coat, seized a belaying pin, and stood ready. I really believed the two of them would assault me. The crew, seeing that something was happening, slowing advanced aft along the main deck to the quarterdeck. Bewildered by the commotion, Turpin came scrambling topside. Redstone seized him by the arm and cried, "That villain! He and those rascals behind him are hatching a mutiny!"

"No! No!" I answered. "He couldn't be more wrong! Do you see that wreck, Mr. Turpin? It's sinking and there's a man on board." Then turning to the men I asked, "Is there any person among you who would leave that poor wretch to drown without trying to rescue him?"

"No, sir!" several shouted in unison. "We gonna save that man. We're men of the sea and the rules of the sea is to give aid when needed. If the skipper don't like it, by god, he can lump it!"

Redstone came running toward me with something in his right hand. It wasn't a pistol but by now my fury was equal to his.

"Come within three feet of me, Captain, and this belaying pin will splatter your brains all over the deck!"

He stopped as if a lasso had been thrown around him and looked at Turpin. True to his nature the first mate screamed imprecations in foul language, threats I managed to ignore.

"Knock him down, Mr. Doyle! Give that bastard a taste of his own medicine!" a crewman cried. "We'll back you up all the way!"

Now the entire crew was on deck, roused by the roar of voices. Some were amused by the row and stood gawking and grinning. Others caught the gravity of the situation and immediately sided with me. I was making a stand against the captain and first mate, the two men they hated most for starving and abusing them. With one word I could have them do my bidding. In minutes they were ready to throw Redstone and Turpin in the brig to eat the bad bread they had been forced to eat, or toss them overboard as food for the fishes.

In the meantime the man at the wheel had brought the ship about so that she was barely moving. The captain slumped against the rail on the lee side of the poop, worn out by useless passion. Turpin eyed me furiously but kept his distance. Then he muttered something to the captain who got up and went below.

"I don't object," he said to me in a voice so thick I could barely understand him. "If you wanna save the man's life, it's up to you. Lower the quarterboat and see what you can do. I won't stand in your way."

In minutes with two men I was in the boat. Turpin came over to lower it. "Don't let him do it!" yelled a crewman. He'll drop you in the drink to be drowned!" Turpin fell back scowling and cursing.

We got away skillfully from the ship's hull and was soon rowing as fast as we could toward the wreck. One of the men, hoping to ease the tautness of the situation, said with a chuckle that Redstone was probably giving orders to sail on without us, leaving us alone on the sea with a wreck within minutes of sinking.

"Nope," Otto Jones, the man at the oars, replied. "That ain't gonna happen. I'll bet my britches on it. My mates would pitch the skipper overboard if he gave such an order. And that snivelin' first mate of his too. We don't have no love for either one of them."

Speaking with a nasal twang, he pulled at the oars savagely, glanced at the ship, and spat into the water. I looked at the *Windhover* too and found the ship as beautiful as any woman I've ever known. Though riding too deep because of her cargo, she was subtle and perky and rolled to the swell with marvelous grace. I sighed as I looked at her and felt the irony of it: a beautiful ship with a miserable crew abused by a tyrant. At that moment I sensed a radical change soon to occur, and I felt a profound sadness inexplicably mingled with alarm.

"Well, there she is!" shouted Eddie Calvert, our lookout. "Wallowing like a stricken porpoise. She's in her death throes for certain!"

We were close enough to the wreck to see a woman waving to us. All along we had thought the figure was a man. Now we were looking at a tall and slender young woman with golden hair streaming to her shoulders. Moving in closer I could see she was perhaps in her early twenties, and she was waving a white shirt or part of a sheet. I doffed my hat to acknowledge the girl, and we rowed around the wreck to find the safest place to board her. She had been a sturdy vessel and seaworthy before her masts came crashing down to crush her portside bulwarks level with the deck and damage also her starboard bulwarks. Her wheel was gone and heavy seas had carried away her binnacle and everything else except the deckhouse and galley.

She was rolled far over, and on the lee side we found a place to secure our footing and climb onto her. I went first with the help of the two men with me, and managed to throw to them a long line to let our boat drift freely astern. We couldn't run the risk of tying up to the side of the severely listing ship, and also the oarsman could rest while waiting for Calvert and me to return. While we were boarding the wreck the girl retreated fearfully to the interior of the damaged deckhouse. I called out to her to open the door so we might enter. Her face appeared behind the porthole, wild and frantic, and she stared at me blankly. I called out again, but she didn't move. It was obvious she didn't trust us.

"Do you understand English?" I yelled.

Imagine my relief when she answered "Yes!" For the third time I asked her to open the door, and slowly, slowly she moved out of my sight. I waited impatiently for the door to open, and while I waited my companion gained his feet after being swept hard a-starboard by a wave smashing the wreck. He approached soaking wet and cursing. The sliding door shook in its grooves, opened a couple of inches, and jammed. I inserted my fingers in the crevice and pulled as hard as I could. The door didn't budge. Then Calvert with big shoulders plunged against it, knocked it back in its groove, and opened it easily.

Inside I found only one compartment when I expected to find two. In the center was a table; on either side were two bunks. The girl lay shivering in a fetal position near the door. In one of the bunks lay an old man with gray hair and wide-open eyes that seemed to see nothing. In a chair slouched a sailor, a young man suddenly old and perhaps mad. He yelled in Portuguese, a language I understood only by its sound. He snapped his fingers as if listening to music and made grotesque grimaces that turned a handsome face ugly.

I seized the girl by the arm and drew her to her feet. "Come! There is no time to lose. Grab my jacket and hold on tight."

"My father first!" she cried. "Save him first!"

"I'll come back for him in a few minutes. You must go first. It's the rule of the sea! Ladies go first."

I lifted her off her feet, slung her tender body over my shoulder, and with Calvert's help clawed my way to the bow of the wreck. Hailing Otto Jones in the boat with the long painter, I ordered him to come alongside. Rowing with an energy I never suspected he had, he brought the boat skillfully to the right spot. Calvert joined him.

"Make ready to receive the lady," I called to them. "Otto, keep the boat steady while Eddie takes her."

The girl was stiff with fear but managed to let go of me and fall into Eddie Calvert's arms. He placed her gently on a seat and waited for more instructions. She was safe and I went back for the old man.

I was pleased to see he was no longer in bed. I had feared he was perhaps unconscious or out of his mind.

"My daughter!" he exclaimed. "Did you take her? Is she safe? You must take her even if it means leaving me behind."

"She's safe, sir. Come along now. We don't have a minute to lose."

I seized his thin old hand but shifted my grasp to his collar to exert more control over him as I half carried and half dragged him to the bow and dumped him into our boat as the seas lifted it. He tumbled in like a sack of potatoes, and his daughter quickly went to receive him. Then I scrambled back to the deckhouse when I heard Calvert screaming and another voice either cursing or loudly exclaiming.

"The bastard bit me, sir! He bit me and tried to kick me in the groin, and only because I tried to help him leave this god-forsaken wreck. He's cussing up a storm in gibberish and he's rip-roaring mad!"

"I'll see what I can do! We can't just leave him here."

Crouched in a shadowy corner of the deckhouse was a figure looking like a stricken animal at bay. When I opened the door he glared at me with eyes that seemed on fire and spat in my direction. Then before I could say a word he fled with incredible speed to the leeward side of the ship and jumped overboard. Otto in the life-saving boat saw and heard him splash into the sea and went after him. Eddie and I made our way to the wreck's bow to see the boat rowing away. A fit of terror seized me, but for only a moment. The boat was chasing the mad man in building seas and Otto was rowing like a mad man himself. He closed fast upon the wretch, dragged him from the water, tumbled him on his back, and wrapped the painter around his legs. Then he came alongside and I jumped awkwardly into the quarterboat with Calvert behind me.

Our sleek little ship the *Windhover* stood steady about a mile away with her foresails backed. I now had leisure to look over the people we had saved. The old man was sixty-five or older. He leaned against his daughter with his eyes closed and his chin on his chest. I feared he was very sick, even dying, and no help could be given him. The girl, perhaps only nineteen or twenty, was fair of skin and soaking wet. Her yellow hair was obviously darker when wet, and her face was deadly pale. Her lips were blue and her gray-blue eyes were filled with a mixture of horror and rapture. She cast them first at me, then at the wreck, and then at the *Windhover*. She shivered with cold even though the sun was warm upon us and the thwarts of the boat hot to the hand. The sailor lay sprawled in the bottom, chanting Psalm 118 in English: "Give thanks to the Lord for he is good. It is better to trust in the Lord than to put trust in man." Eyes wide open and grimacing as he lay chanting, he looked without blinking into the sun.

"Do you feel like speaking?" I asked the girl. "How long have you been on that derelict so close to sinking?"

"It happened maybe two or three days ago. I don't remember rightly," she answered in a dull monotone, gulping after each word. "In all that time we've had no water to drink, nothing to eat."

"My god, men, did you hear that? Move the boat faster!"

Eddie relieved Otto at the oars and rowed like a demon. The wind behind us made his job easier. Knowing that each word she spoke was like a shard of glass in her throat, I didn't say more to the girl. After twenty minutes, which seemed much longer, we reached the vessel and made fast to the gangway. The crew cheered when they saw us. Redstone and Turpin, standing like Napoleonic figures on the poop, grimly watched without a word.

"Up with the lady first," I called. "And get some water for her soon as she touches the deck. She's dying of thirst, all of them."

In record time the young woman and her father were on board sipping cool water and nibbling on canned peaches. Then we devised a way to haul the mad sailor topside as though he were cargo. The man was gulping water when suddenly he threw back his massive head with long and tangled hair, screamed in Portuguese, and sank to his knees. He held that position for a moment, and then with fierce bloodshot eyes half out of their sockets he fell dead. I was there to see it all and shuddered at the sight. Turpin looked surprised.

"Wrap the poor devil in a tarp and heave him overboard," he said to the men who had gathered around the body. "We have no place on ship for a dead man. Corpses stink."

He was really saying a dead man on a ship brings bad luck and must be disposed of soon as possible. It was a time-worn superstition among sailors, and Turpin wasn't free of superstition. Sylvain and the Dutchman did as they were told. Without ceremony of any kind a young Portuguese sailor was given to the sea to become food for the fishes.

CHAPTER EIGHT

"Clap Them Shackles On Him"

In my cabin I heard the men hoisting the quarterboat. Mr. Turpin, complaining of lost time, was ordering the watch to get the ship underway. I wanted to get Captain Redstone's reaction to what had taken place but lay on my cot in dry clothes for half an hour before moving. Then as I was pulling on a boot to go on deck I heard a loud knock on my door. Before I could open the door or even say enter, Turpin with a silly grin on his weathered face barged inside. Behind him holding iron shackles in his hands was Harlowe Quine the carpenter.

"Captain Oliver Redstone orders me to put you, Kevin Doyle, in irons," Turpin announced as the officer in charge. "Carpenter, clap them shackles on his shins good and tight."

I jumped up, one boot on my foot, another in my hand, to remonstrate. Though it was not my intention to resist, Turpin immediately decided I was bellicose and dangerous. Quickly he drew a knife, and putting it close to my throat, hissed a message I couldn't ignore: "By God, if you don't let the carpenter do his thing, your blood is gonna spurt all over! Believe me, Mr. goody-goody Doyle, I'll cut your throat!"

I did believe him. I think he was aching for a good excuse to carry out his promise, but I sat down again to deny him the pleasure. Quine locked the irons on my ankles and turned screws to make them tight. He didn't look at me and didn't speak. I got a fleeting impression he didn't like what he was doing, maybe acting under duress.

"Now, you mutinous son o' bitch, I reckon you ain't gonna give us much trouble for the rest of the voyage," Turpin hissed.

A low-life calling my mother a bitch was more than I could stomach. In an instant I threw myself against him, caught him by the throat, and dashed him to the floor. The carpenter made himself scarce, leaving the door open. Turpin already was trying to get to his feet. I grabbed him by the neck and hurled him through the doorway to crash against the cuddy table. Blood oozed over his face and nose, and he howled like an animal. He rolled under the table and lay there in a heap. I slammed my door and sat down, breathing hard. Then to my surprise a hand opened it just wide enough to push a pannikin inside. The bo'sun, as I later learned, had brought me rum and water as refreshment. I was sorely in need of it and drank it all in one gulp.

Trying to evaluate my situation, I wasn't able even to guess what was in store for me. All I could do was hold my aching head in my hands and look down at the shackles on my ankles. They were so ugly as to be obscene and I shuddered at the sight of them. I waited for the first mate to hurtle himself upon me, knowing there would be little I could do to defend myself. Leg irons have been around for centuries because they do their job well. Any man who was ever a slave will tell you a man can't defend himself very well at all in leg irons. I waited but nothing happened. Then half an hour later I saw him pass along the main deck with a big lump above his left eye. He appeared to be heading toward a group of sailors quietly talking near the fo'c's'le. I questioned his authority at this juncture to command any of them.

I knew that in some measure the crew sympathized with me, and that nurtured the belief they would not for any reason see me abused without cause. But the thought that a mutiny was brewing among them gave me no pleasure. The captain would swear once it ended that I had been the leader, and his first mate would surely support him. I had defied his authority in the matter of the wreck, and that would tell against me should there be a Court of Inquiry. I could lose my livelihood as a seaman, my status as an officer, even years of my life in prison. These thoughts bit into my conscience as painfully as the leg irons on my shins and ankles. Then suddenly I realized I was faint with hunger. The day had been one of peak exertion with not a morsel of food.

In a way I was fortunate to have a cabin so close to the pantry, for without too much difficulty I could shuffle there for something to eat. I knew the captain was eating his dinner in the nearby cuddy. I could smell the food and hear him talking to the steward. Perhaps old Mr. Waterhouse and daughter were with him, but I could hear no other voice. The steward's reply to a few questions had no volume whatever. Then when a period of quiet came I knew Redstone had left the cuddy to go back on deck. That would be my chance to enter, but as I was about to do so I heard Turpin speaking in a loud coarse voice to the steward.

"What are you gonna feed that mutinous son o' bitch tucked in his cabin there? He don't deserve nothing better than what the crew gets."

The steward made reply in so low a voice I couldn't hear a word from him, but Turpin heard.

"That bastard deserves every bit of it," snickered the chief mate. "I just wish we had a pair of handcuffs on board. I'd put 'em on him and spoon feed him like a dear ol' mama feeding her babe."

He deliberately spoke in a harsh and loud voice for my benefit. It didn't bother me in the least. All my life I had heard talk like that from bullies and had dismissed it as bluster. I was worried more about the old man and the girl than about myself. If they were listening to Turpin's blather, they might conclude they had been rescued by a band of brigands. At length the first mate left to harass a poor sailor on deck. I could hear him ordering the man aloft and cursing a blue streak when he didn't move fast enough. Then I heard a self-satisfied snicker. He had found a way to take the humiliation I had delivered him and thrust it upon an innocent victim. Through the window that overlooked the quarterdeck I saw him sauntering aft to the poop, and I could tell he felt good about what he had done.

I was hungry and decided to shuffle to the pantry and find something to eat despite the leg irons restricting movement and cutting into my flesh. When I reached the door I found it locked from the outside. I had no way of knowing who did it but quickly concluded Turpin had locked me in my cabin and sneaked away with the key. Rattling the doorknob and shaking the door, I had half a mind to call out to the steward who might hear me in his pantry. Then thinking I might get nothing but silence in reply, I squelched the hunger pangs and slept through the afternoon. I awoke as evening was coming. A strong breeze was blowing and the nimble ship with plenty of canvas was heeling right well to it.

On the floor near the locked door was a tin dish containing biscuits and a pewter mug of water. I fell off the bunk and crawled a few feet in the painful shackles to reach the food. It was easier than trying to walk. Eagerly I bit into a biscuit to find it was the ship's bread so despised by the crew. Famished, I ate it in one or two gulps and went for another. Then the metallic taste of mold lay heavily on my tongue, and the stench of rotten biscuit pervaded my nostrils. Even in half light I could see white weevils infesting the brown-black bread. Hunger drove me to devour two odious biscuits washed down with unclean water. To get rid of the awful aftertaste, I lit my pipe and smoked until the tiny room with little ventilation began to assume a bluish mist. Then I lay the pipe aside and went back to sleep, for there was nothing more I could do. I gave considerable thought to my situation before sleeping but reached no conclusion. How long my bondage would last I couldn't guess.

I remember waking up when the wind freshened and the sea began to beat against the hull. Above me on deck I could hear the captain ordering the crew to shorten sail. When their work was done the vessel moved smoothly along on a more even keel, and I went back to sleep. Later in the darkness of night I was awakened by a metal object striking the thick glass of my porthole. Someone had lowered himself on the chainplates of the windward side of the vessel and was trying to get my attention. With difficulty I managed to hoist my shackled legs out of the bunk, get over to the porthole, and open it. The wind blowing through the aperture deposited a damp spray on my face. Muffling my voice, I asked who in hell was out there. A face appeared, shutting out the wind, and Harlowe Quine the carpenter spoke in a whisper.

"I come from the crew with a message. You gotta tell me you gonna be wit' us or agin us in what we plan to do."

"I can't promise anything until I know your intentions. I can only suppose what you have in mind. I must warn you that going against our unreasonable captain would be a serious offense. It could land you in jail for the rest of your life. The courts don't look kindly on mutiny."

Quine was silent for a long time. I thought he might climb back to the deck and tell the crew his mission was a failure. Then he brought his face close to mine again, so close I could smell his dirty breath, and gave me details in a hoarse whisper.

"I understand, Mr. Doyle, but you need to understand. I speak for the crew, not me alone. We'd rather go to jail in the worst prison in Europe than work this here ship another week on rotten provisions. Cookie wants to kill the pigs and chickens for us to eat. Captain Redstone said it would be mutiny if we touched even one. He said he would shoot in the head or face the first man to touch one of them animals. His chief mate Turpin backed him up without batting an eye."

"And he would do it too and get away with it. He's an angry man prone to violence, and he knows the authorities would side with him."

"What we wanna know is this in few words. Will you take charge o' the ship and take her to whatever port we choose?"

"You speak of mutiny, man. I wish I could say yes, but cold reason tells me I can't. Conditions are bad on this ship, Mr. Quine, but my advice is to hold out as best you can till we reach the Azores."

"Redstone said he would take us there, but we got wind he won't. He lost too much time. So he's goin' straight to Gibraltar. Won't detour."

"I'm a prisoner and must live on the same food you eat, but I can't go along with mutiny. It's too drastic, don't do it."

"I never cussed an officer, sir, but now I gotta cuss you. I swore to the men you had courage. Now I see you got a yellow streak down yer back. So damn you, Doyle, and be prepared for what's coming."

He had hardly spoken his last word when he was up the side and on the deck, leaving me to ponder my fate in darkness. I screwed shut the port and shuffled back to my bunk. I couldn't disclose what I had heard. If I did, the crew would kill me. And what good would it do anyway? Redstone couldn't count on more than two or three men to support him — his chief mate, his navigator maybe, and the steward. The crew greatly outnumbered them, and they would be overpowered and killed, within minutes. Though I dreaded the thought of violence and bloodshed, I dreaded even more being imprisoned in a dark and tiny room subsisting on rotten, insect-ridden food. I also knew the leg irons if not soon removed would leave festering sores on my ankles to become infected. Already the skin was raw and broken and unclean.

Thinking it over, I half believed I might fare better if the crew did as Quine insisted they would do, namely wrest all power from

Redstone and Turpin. The two could be locked unharmed in a vacant passenger cabin, and Peter Charnook could be persuaded to continue as the ship's navigator. Upon reaching a port the ship's officers could be released and the mutinous crew could fade into the population and escape reprisal. These thoughts floated like confetti in my head as the night wore slowly away. I tried to sleep but the shackles caused steady streaks of pain to run up both legs, and I could find no comfort. Also I could reach no conclusion as to whether I would or would not join the crew in mutiny. Then in the middle of the night the ruckus began.

I heard men running the length of the ship to the poop, heavy boots pounding wood and a rabble of voices where Redstone and Turpin were asleep. I lay in my bunk holding my breath and heard shouts and groans and men fighting. In the chief mate's cabin they found a foe who was not ready to go down easily. Believing he was fighting to save his life, Turpin was a match for three strong men. The struggle was brief enough in reality but seemed to go on forever. Then came a pause and I heard someone howl, "Don't kill him now! Wait till we have light! We'll make it a special event and then feed the scum to the fishes!"

The ominous little speech was painful to hear. Turpin had abused me and made me suffer, but I had no wish to see him dead and tossed into the sea by a violent, unruly crew on a rampage. And yet I was helpless, locked in my cabin and hindered by leg irons. I couldn't even call out and be heard above all that was going on. Then someone turned the handle of my door, pushed hard against the door, and tried to open it but the lock held. After a pause a quivering voice as if from a ghost came through the keyhole to reach my ears.

"Mr. Doyle! Mr. Doyle! They killed the captain and first mate! And I think they're coming to get you the second mate. And me too! Oh my God, sir, please tell them to spare my life, please! They might listen to you, sir. Oh, please do something to save me! I got a wife and children."

"Who are you, man? Navigator or steward?"

"I'm Simpson, sir, the steward. They got Mr. Charnook but won't harm him, I s'pose. He's the only one except maybe you that knows how to guide this ship and take her to a port."

Then even as he was speaking I heard a man on the quarterdeck shouting, "Where's that no-good steward? He's the one that tried to make us believe the pork was good."

Simpson also heard the shouting and ran like a rabbit to find a place to hide. Then for a few minutes all was quiet until a group of men entered the cuddy, pounded on the table, and ransacked the pantry. While they were filling their hungry bellies with anything they could grab, someone saw my cabin door nearby.

"The second mate's in there! Let's get him too!" I heard one of them say. His remark came only seconds before a booted foot slammed against the door. The kick broke the lock and the door swung open.

I was seated on my bunk when they entered, and I said to them calmly and even playfully, "What took you so long?"

The gang of sailors laughed and said until that moment they had important business to finish. Now it was time to take care of me, and that business wasn't important at all. They were laughing when they said that, but I wasn't laughing. I decided to play it straight with as brave a face as I could muster.

"I'm glad you've come to care for me," I said, choosing to take the positive meaning of the phrase, "glad you thought of me, fellows. Now will someone get these rusty irons off me?"

Though they seemed indecisive, I detected not a shred of hostility among them. I think my condition convinced them I was one of them. I had been locked in my cabin on bad bread and water in shackles and was obviously a victim. And I had spoken as one of them.

"I'll get a mallet and chisel and have them irons off yer in minutes," the man called the Dutchman said, backing through the doorway.

He returned in minutes and with only two blows cut the irons away. I rubbed my ankles to find them not only bruised but bleeding. Otto Jones, with me when we went to the wreck, said he would go to the ship's dispensary and find a soothing ointment for me, and that he did.

"Now, my lads," I asked with some concern while applying the ointment to sores on both ankles, "what in hell have you done?"

CHAPTER NINE

"Are You Wit' Us Or Agin Us?"

The Dutchman, an easy-going fellow well liked by the crew, began to answer my question. He fell silent when the leader came into my cabin. He was Hector Sylvain, the big man I've spoken of earlier.

"So you wanna know what we done, Mr. Doyle? We took over the ship, that's what. This here ship the *Windhover* and all aboard her, including them fancy pianners in the hold, belongs to me and my men. She's our'n now, that's what."

"I reckon the skipper's dead up there," said Cookie who had come in with Sylvain and seemed to be his lieutenant. "And if you wanna come to the main deck, you gonna see what's happenin' to Mr. Turpin!"

"Not so fast, Cookie," said Hector Sylvain, touching the smaller man's shoulder with a hand as big as a pewter plate. "We don't wanna get ahead of ourselves in this thing. We gotta move with caution, and the big question is this — are you with us, Mr. Doyle, or against us?"

Before I could answer, the carpenter followed by several rough-looking men barged into the cuddy and stood in my doorway, almost blocking the light from the cuddy lanterns.

"Ah, there's the one that can't make up his mind!" he cried. "Well, we gonna help him make it up for him, right men?"

His companions shouted in the affirmative, but Sylvain remaining silent scowled at the audacity of the carpenter and looked patiently at me. I had not replied to his question, and he wanted an answer. He took me by the arm, pushed the carpenter aside, led me into the cuddy, and ordered me to stand at the end of the table. Then with powerful lungs he bawled to those on deck, "All hands into the cuddy!"

The men came shuffling in and stood in a crowd on either side of the table, a scene I am not likely to forget. Some were dressed in yellow storm gear, some in heavy sweaters with skull caps, and some in coarse shirts with short sleeves. With their black beards and sunburned complexions, they looked sinister in the crude light of the cuddy. Not one face seemed to have a friendly or compassionate look while the squinting eyes of several hinted cruelty and hatred. Some were pale with demonic excitement, and all of them, even the youngest and particularly the youngest, wore a reckless and malignant look. It was clear to me they had taken it upon themselves to commit mayhem and were ready to fly into havoc and chaos again. They had killed a man, perhaps two men, and were ready if need be to kill another.

In the moments before the proceeding began, they ran greedy and curious eyes around the room. During all their weeks on the ship not a person had visited the cuddy even once. Several exclaimed how posh it was compared to the fo'c's'le where they took their meals.

"Oh don't it look rich," Otis Bearclaw said, "with all that mahogany trim and stuff, and the fine furniture."

Then taking a glass from an overhead bracket where it would be safe in a storm, he held it high as if giving a toast. Grimly but with a cheerful note of hope and comfort, he intoned — "By God, mates, we gonna have somethin' fit to eat now! No more starvin' on rotten pork and stinkin' bread! No more dirty water to drink! Gonna be rum now!"

I could see every face clearly as they glared at me. I noticed in particular the bo'sun, whose peculiar name was Rinehart Burdick. Half hidden from the others and pale as a sheet was Peter Charnook, the navigator. Those two were the only quiet faces in the crowd. They met my glance and instantly looked downward. The chatter ceased as Sylvain at the opposite end of the table began to speak.

"Yo, all hands! Let this proceeding begin. We're all equals here as every man in this room knows by now. But I'm the biggest and strongest, though maybe not the brightest. Anyway, I'm the leader of this rebellion. So I'm gonna act as judge here and jury too. Let no man interrupt me as I speak. We are gathered in this room to discover one thing regarding this mariner, Mr. Doyle. So I ask you again, sir, are you with us or against us? Your answer was delayed a while ago when Harlowe Quine interrupted. Now with no interruption let's have it."

"Are you wit' us or agin us?!" several men cried at once.

"I am with you," I said as firmly as I could. "I am with you in everything that has to be done, but I wish to make one thing very clear. I am not with you in murder."

"We don't know what you call murder," growled the carpenter. "And what's done is done and I've heard of accidents shipboard, and that's the proper word for what we done."

"You will not speak again, Harlowe, unless I call upon you to speak," Hector Sylvain admonished. "Let Mr. Doyle explain himself."

"I wish to speak plainly before I'm asked any more questions. All of you know I sympathized with you when I learned what god-awful food you were obliged to eat, and I spoke to the captain about it. That brought me into conflict with Captain Redstone and his chief mate, Andrew Turpin. Later I incurred the captain's wrath when I defied his authority to save survivors on a miserable wreck. As you well know, he clapped me in irons as soon as I returned from the rescue, charging me with unscrupulous insubordination and even mutiny."

"That's right!" said Eddie Calvert who went with me to the wreck. "We risked our lives to save three people, but that bastard Redstone didn't wanna stop even to take a look. Then he had the gall to punish Mr. Doyle for doing a good thing."

"Eddie speaks true," said Otto Jones. "I was there and I know."

"All right," said Sylvain. "We're gaining some facts now and that's good, but let Mr. Doyle speak his piece."

"I suppose I'm on trial here, on trial for my life, and I won't say I don't care. I value my life, any life. But if you decide to kill me I will die with dignity. I will not cringe or cower or beg for mercy. But in the hope that you will spare me I will tell you this. If you take my life you will be killing the one officer on this ship who sympathized with your condition and was at heart a friend. I became the enemy of the captain and first mate when they believed I consorted with you to make secret plans. They feared that sooner or later I might lead you into mutiny, to do what it appears you have done sooner on your own."

That said, I folded my arms across my chest and gazed with fixed calm upon the face of my judge. The entire crew listened to me in profound silence, and now several began to talk all at once.

"What you say is truth," went the general response. "Redstone and Turpin, high and mighty, had it in for you coz you dared talk to us."

"We never had a grudge against you. It's them other two that got our goat and maybe the steward. Not sure about Charnook."

"Sylvain brought us here to sift through the facts. We don't have a hankerin' to take yer life. You're more valuable to us alive."

I heard every remark and breathed a sigh of relief, but keeping my eyes resolutely upon Sylvain I pretended to hear nothing. He was their leader, their mouthpiece, and my judge. I would deal only with him. He was a fair-minded man, this Hector Sylvain. After examining the evidence in a rare, democratic meeting he absolved me of all blame.

"All what you say is correct. All what the others said in support of you is correct. Not a man here finds fault with you. Now I ask you another question. Will you take this ship working with the navigator we gotta keep an eye on to a port of our choosing? Answer yes or no."

"Yes, but with one condition."

"And what is that?"

"That there be no more killing. I'm given to understand you've killed the captain. You must promise me, and swear to it on the good book, that you will take no more lives."

"By god, no!" shouted the cook, looking to Sylvain for support. "That man has no power to tell us what to do! I won't agree to it."

"You don't have to agree," Sylvain replied. "We'll put it to a vote, Yay or Nay." The vote was taken; no more killing was the verdict.

"And now I must warn you, Mr. Doyle. If you get with Charnook to take us where we don't wanna go, you will die. If you put us in the way of some ship of state with people to arrest us, you will die. If you try to flag a passing ship to report this dizzy business, you will die. If you behave as we expect you to behave, you will live and prosper."

"We have an old man and a young woman aboard. Are they safe? I haven't seen them even once since bringing them aboard."

"They are safe," several men said at once. "No man on this vessel has the guts to touch either of them, particularly the girl. They are safe."

"And what about the navigator, steward, and first mate? Are they your enemies too, or will you tell me they're safe?"

"The navigator is trying to make himself invisible over there in the corner. We need him and won't harm him, at least for now. The first mate and the steward are bad men and oughta be flogged. Turpin got knocked around a bit but no flogging. That's somethin' we gotta think about when the breeze goes down."

"If I am to command this ship, there will be no flogging of anyone for any reason. I wish to make that very clear. You will not flog any person on this ship for any reason whatever. Flogging must go!"

"That Turpin nearly broke my jaw!" screamed the cook. "And he kicked me like a dog! No mercy due him! I say no mercy due him!"

"Now listen to me!" I said, raising my voice to be heard. "I am one man against many, but if you choose me to take this ship to safe haven I will demand discipline and obedience. I will not abuse any one of you, but all of you will be obliged to do as I say."

"We're listening," several men replied. "And what you say sounds good enough. You keep your promise, we keep our'n."

"Then you will spare the lives of Turpin and Simpson, and you will not harm either one of them further. Civilized men don't kill in cold blood, and civilized men do not torture prisoners. You are not savages."

The strange little man calling himself Otis Bearclaw and claiming to be part Indian raised his hand for permission to speak. "Beggin' yer pardon, sir, but the crew ain't gonna let that son o' bitch Turpin off that easy. I guess we can let the steward go, but we gonna have our just revenge on Turpin. And I'm a real savage, been told that all my life."

"He's right!" shouted several men speaking as one. "We gonna make that bastard Turpin pay. He desarves everything we gonna give him, and to hell with your sermons!"

"Then you'll have to make me pay too! I cannot be your commander if you will not follow my orders! You can't have it both ways."

Again ominous growling came from angry men, all of them gesticulating and talking at once. Their confab was interrupted by the helmsman calling through the skylight.

"It's blacker than all hell to leeward, fellas! Looks like a doozy of a storm is heading our way. Better get a watch on deck and some men in the rigging, or we gonna be in big trouble."

"A moment more before you go!" I yelled as several men began to move. "I must have an answer! Do I command this ship or not?"

"We give you command, Mr. Doyle. Spit out yer orders and we'll obey 'em! The welfare of this ship comes first! Nothing else matters."

The meeting broke and within minutes the cuddy was empty. The men returned to the fo'c's'le and to their stations on deck. On the poop I threw my glance upward to survey the rigging and sails. The wind was coming from the south and increasing, but our canvas was small. The mainsail, crossjack, three royals, two top-gallant sails, spanker, and flying jibs were furled. In the fore and mizzen topsails we had a single reef, and so the yards swung easily. Because sky and sea were threatening, I ordered the remaining top-gallant sail to be furled. The men sprang into the rigging with alacrity, working skillfully and singing out lustily. Standing on the poop and giving orders, I felt as though I had been doing it a long time. Then all that had happened during the last hour drew me back to reality. I recalled I had eaten only two moldy biscuits all day. Feeling faint with hunger, I put Sylvain in charge to go below.

On the quarterdeck I saw the bodies of two men sprawled close to each other just outside the cuddy door. The lamps inside threw light on them, and at once I knew they were Redstone and Turpin. The captain lay on his back and the first mate on his stomach face downward. Redstone with eyes wide open stared grotesquely at me. I saw no blood on his handsome face and no grimace or sign of pain. Apparently he had been struck hard from behind and killed instantly. I grasped Turpin by one arm and turned him over. Lying on his back I saw his eye lids flutter, and a barely audible groan escaped his lips. With a new and obvious swagger the carpenter came up and stood beside me.

"Looks like he's dead. You think he's dead?"

"Either dead or very close to it. No doubt at all about the captain. Have a couple of men take his body forward and cover it with a tarp."

"Why do you want it covered? Why not heave the old bastard into the sea just as he did with that crazy Portugee from the wreck?"

"Because I believe you are better than him. Captain Redstone was bitter and full of hate and proved himself a brute. But you and I can take a higher road. As civilized folk, whether Christian or not, we should conduct a brief ceremony before we commit the body to the sea."

"Every man on this ship hated that son o' bitch," the carpenter muttered. "Who is gonna say words ovah a man so hated? Hey, fellas! We got a squabble going on here. Mr. Doyle wants to read the good book over Redstone's carcass. I say chuck it into the sea. What do you say?"

Three men without speaking a word came up to the body, picked it up, and flung it into the sea. For them the captain's corpse was nothing more than a bag of garbage to be disposed of hastily. I stood appalled as I watched them hurl the object that had been the formidable Captain Redstone over the bulwarks. I heard it splash into the sea even above the wind. Perhaps he brought it all upon himself. Had he chosen to act in a different way, he most surely would be living even today. Quite simply, he chose a negative approach and it led to an untimely death.

Though I despised the man, I will not say he deserved what he got. He didn't. No man deserves to die by violence and be treated like an unclean animal, or a festering disease, after death. I really misjudged how intensely the crew hated the man. Their hatred also reached out to maim and destroy the first mate, Andrew Turpin. Whether he deserved it I will not say.

One simple act of brutality may have caused Turpin's death. When the cook wouldn't cease complaining about the putrid meat, Turpin in high anger had assaulted him. When Cookie least expected it, the first mate had punched him hard in the face and had kicked him in the groin as he lay sprawled on the deck. The man had limped away cursing and vowing revenge, and now apparently he would have it. He approached half drunk supported by two men on either side of him.

"Here's your friend, Cookie," said Quine. "What you gonna do with him? He's been waitin' and wonderin' what's to become of him. Been just layin' there takin' his ease waitin' fer ya."

"Oh, he's a gentleman, mind you!" said the cook, kneeling to get a better look at the prostrate first mate. "But he got a bad temper! He give me a hard knock right here on my jaw. And he give me kick right here in my balls, and it hurt like hell. You hear what I say? It hurt like hell."

Then standing up to look downward at the huddled figure, he kicked the dead or dying man viciously in the head and face, stepped back to take a deep breath, and kicked again even harder.

"I'll skin him fer ya! I'll gouge his eyes out and make him eat 'em. I'll tear his guts out! Would be better than the biscuits he tried to make us eat. Would be better than the rotten pork he tried to force on us. Oh, goddamn him! I'll cut his stinking balls off! Give me a knife, somebody!"

"That's enough, Cookie!" Hector Sylvain cautioned. "You've had your revenge. Now overboard with this thing! If Cookie wants more vengeance, fling him overboard too. Let him kick and cut Turpin all he wants there in the water with the sharks!"

Two men seized the first mate as they had seized the skipper and unceremoniously flung him overboard. I thought I heard a hoarse moan or groan from the supposed corpse as it went flying over the bulwarks, and I turned away in disgust to see several men surrounding the cook and shouting, "Overboard with him too! Overboard, Cookie! Go after Turpin and finish what you started!"

The carpenter was laughing and joking and egging the men on, but the cook didn't see any of it as a joke. With tremendous energy he wiggled free of his oppressors and screaming in terror ran as fast as he could forward to the fo'c's'le. When no one bothered to pursue him, and while the men continued to laugh at their joke, I asked Sylvain to mind the store while I went below to the cuddy.

"What you gonna do there?" he asked suspiciously.

"Well, I'm hoping to eat. I just realized I've had nothing all day long except two moldy biscuits reeking with weevils."

"My god, man, you're right! You must be starving. But before you go I wanna tell you what's agreed on. You gonna take charge as skipper. I'm gonna be first mate, and the carpenter wants to be second mate. We keep a firm eye on the navigator. You work with him and check all his sightings, readings, headings, and we check later. Agreeable?"

"Yes, agreeable."

"You gonna do the piloting. You'll take us where we wanna go with help from the navigator. Maybe we can trust him, maybe we can't."

"There shouldn't be a problem with Charnook. As you know, he's not entirely well and won't pose a threat to anybody."

"Good! Three new officers will occupy the poop cabins aft, and the ship's crew is gonna be forward as usual. You can have the skipper's berth, I'll take Turpin's, and the carpenter can have your cabin."

"That sounds all right, Mr. Sylvain. With provisions served equally to all persons on board, I'll take the ship to any port you name. It seems we have no need to make the Azores. We have stores and water to take us into the Mediterranean to any port you choose. I won't try to trick you, and I expect the same fair play from you."

"Fair play, Mr. Doyle. You got it right."

"What about the two people we saved from the wreck? And the steward. You have promised not to harm him."

"They'll have a comfortable cabin and be cared fer, and the girl won't have no worry about any of the men taking liberties with her. But I didn't promise to spare the steward. The men say he's gotta pay."

"If you murder the steward, you will have to murder me. I don't wish to sacrifice myself for that man, but I will not have more violence and more bloodshed on this ship if I'm to be your captain."

"I understand, Mr. Doyle, but I'll hafta talk to the crew."

"See that you do, Mr. Sylvain. Call all hands aft and decide. When your meeting's over, you'll find me in the steward's pantry looking for something to eat, or maybe eating at the cuddy table."

CHAPTER TEN

"Three Hits O' Grog A Day"

I n the pantry I found some cold meat and bread, a plug of cheese, and a bottle of wine. The steward couldn't serve me because he was hiding, or the crew had locked him up. I helped myself and went to the cuddy table to eat the ham and cheese and good bread. I was glad to be able to wash it down with a small bottle of passable wine. Although a heated debate was going on above my head, I felt but little concern. With the help of Charnook they could take the ship to a port without me, but it was obvious the navigator wasn't well and could die in a vast desert of water at any time. Also in a pinch, in a violent storm, the crew would not be able to work the ship without direction from me.

I was bolting down the food like a hungry wolf when a hand touched my shoulder. Had they reached a decision in so little time? I turned expecting to see the face of a sailor and saw a pretty girl. She was the young woman we had rescued, and this was my first time to hear her speak after depositing her on board. In dry clothing and rested, her appearance was much improved. The stringy wet hair was now dry and shining in the lamplight. It hung attractively over pretty shoulders half concealing a firm jaw and slender neck. She was as pale as a new moon but with a touch of color in her cheeks. I could tell she wanted to speak to me but was having trouble getting the words out.

"I'm here to thank you, Mr. Doyle," she said with some effort, "for saving my life and my father's life. I didn't have a chance to thank you when we came aboard. Later when I asked that I might see you, the captain told me you had been charged with mutiny and put in irons. I was so amazed to hear that."

"I disobeyed his order to sail onward. He had to make up for lost time and was unwilling to stop. I saw your signal and went against the captain's orders to help you. He was forced to wait for my return, to lose precious time on a tight schedule, and it made him furious. I was quickly arrested, shackled, and charged with insubordination. Then he changed his mind and called it mutiny."

"As I lay awake wondering what was happening on this ship," the girl said, "I heard scuffling on the deck and shouting and finally learned a mutiny really had taken place. The ship's carpenter told me. I think he called himself Quine. He told me the captain and first mate were dead, and the ship was in the hands of the crew."

"Terrible things have happened since I brought you and your father and that Portuguese sailor aboard. But I believe the worst is over. In a few minutes a spokesman for the crew will tell me whether they have chosen me to be their skipper or someone else."

"I know that you are caring and competent, Mr. Doyle. I do hope they'll place you in command and cease all violence."

"I'll find out shortly. In the meantime I want you to go back to your cabin. Comfort your father and sleep if you can. Lock your door, if you wish, but understand no harm will come to you."

I was now more willing than ever to work with the crew as the only way to protect the girl. If after debating they chose sickly Charnook to navigate, intending to kill him when his job was done, they would kill me too. With freedom to let their appetites run wild and with no resistance from anyone on a lawless sea, the girl and her father would also become their victims. She would die an unspeakable death but only after becoming the darling of the ship for a day or two. As I was trying to erase that odious thought, ban it from my mind entirely, excited voices overhead underscored my predicament. In a few minutes I would get the results of their meeting.

I finished my meal and feeling stronger decided to inspect the ship's log in the captain's cabin. My intention was to find out the *Windhover's* position at noon on the preceding day. I was about to light the lamp to read what appeared to be an entry when I was startled by a shadowy figure crawling on its hands and knees from a corner.

"Oh my God, please help me, sir! Am I to be killed? You can save me, sir. They'll listen to you, obey you. Please, sir, talk to them!"

I had thought the crew had placed the steward under lock and key as their prisoner until they could decide whether to kill him or let him live. He had run when he had the chance and was now hiding in a place no crew member ever visited. Terror had made him clever.

"Go back to your hiding place," I said with some impatience, "and don't let anyone see you. I'll try to help you but can make no promises. Be resolute, Simpson. If you must face them, meet them bravely. Cringing and whining will only amuse them. They will play with you like a kitten plays with a mouse. Show a little backbone."

He crawled back into his tight little corner, and I lit the lamp to read the noon sighting of the day before. The entry was done with a shaky hand, meaning our navigator was under stress but doing his job. How long he would be able to calculate our bearing was anyone's guess. Even though I knew most aspects of celestial navigation, my knowledge was certainly not up to Charnook's. I hoped he would live and carry on as I hoped Simpson would be spared to serve wholesome food. The thread of life for three men had become very thin: those two and me. I put the thought out of mind and mounted the poop.

Dawn was breaking in the east with a bank of heavy gray clouds that obscured the rising sun. The wind had freshened to keep the ship well over, and the sea was running with waves of two or three feet. Glancing aloft I could see in an instant that we needed more sail, more canvas to set for the good breeze. Yet not a person among the crew seemed to care whether the ship moved or not. A skilled crew wasn't sailing the *Windhover*; she was sailing herself. The fellow at the wheel was making a show of steering but also posing grotesquely to let all the other hands know he wasn't ordered to be there by anyone. We were all equal now. Demon democracy, a bumbling bugbear on a ship, ruled entirely.

Looking forward along the deck I saw a group of men lounging on the roof of the fo'c's'le. Squatted in the middle of them were the bo'sun and the carpenter. Hector Sylvain was not among them, and I saw no sign of the cook. Several were smoking and all seemed to be chatting or discussing something in pleasant camaraderie. For a moment I thought I might stroll over and join them but decided they would have to summon me first. So I turned in the opposite direction and went to the ship's compass to check our heading. It was roughly the same as before the mutiny. Ben Webster, a young man of nineteen and notably the youngest of the crew (excluding the cook's helper), was at the wheel.

"Ah, Ben, have they left you alone to do all the work?" I asked, hoping to make a joke of our situation.

"No, Mr. Doyle. Nobody is demanding work from anybody. I thought Hector would be our leader when we got rid of the officers, but he don't seem to be leading much any more. I'm steering 'cause I like it."

"Well, it looks like our heading hasn't changed. Remains the way I set it days ago, east by southeast toward Gibraltar."

"Guess so, sir. Nobody I know of set a different course. I think maybe they're waiting on you to do that."

I took my eyes from the card to see the bo'sun and carpenter with a few others behind them approaching. I felt a little tremor of agitation, as I prefer to call it, when they came up to me. But having made up my mind to show no emotion when confronting them, I remained calm and said nothing. Later I learned the pretense of tranquility told in my favor.

"We been talkin'," said the carpenter, "and most of us say leave the steward alone to do his job. But two or three say the man is a snivelin' little coward that licked the ass of a bad skipper and lied about the rations. He said the pork was sweet when he damn well knew it was rotten. And so the men want some kind of revenge."

"Perhaps the best revenge," said I "is to require the poor wretch to serve you cuddy provisions and let him have only the ship's stores to eat, the same spoiled food he insisted was good. Will that do?"

"Oh my God, yes! That'll do for sure!" several voices cried out as one. "Damn good idea and sarves him right!"

"All right then. No more blather about the steward," the bo'sun demanded. "And no more about wantin' to punish Charnook. You do your job and let them do theirs. It's over. The big thing is where we goin'? I don't wanna be strung up and hung soon as we gets ashore."

"I'm hoping you'll get an answer to that question soon," I replied, breathing a sigh of relief. The steward's life was no longer in jeopardy and there would be no violence against me or the navigator, at least for the time being. Also I had to assume I would be in charge of the ship as they hinted earlier, but couldn't be certain until I heard it directly. Then the carpenter made it clear to me, and I heaved another sigh of relief.

"You're a seafarer, Mr. Doyle, and we gonna place our trust in you 'cause we know you can sail this here ship. And we hope you'll get us out o' this mess 'cause we made you skipper."

"So it's official now. I'm your skipper and you will obey my orders. We can't work the ship with every man doing as he pleases. Someone must give orders and others must obey. Do you agree to that?"

"Of course I do!" Quine replied. "We all do! This mutiny began when the late skipper, the devil take him, wouldn't feed us decent food and treated us like dogs. If he had acted fair and proper, he would've got the same from us. But no, he didn't. So we had to do what we did. We didn't mean to kill the old fool. The biggest among us hit him too hard accidental like. And the other fought like a tiger and just wouldn't give up."

"Aye, that's so right!" said a man I didn't recognize. "He wanted to gouge my eyes out and would have. I had to bite his damn fingers and strangle the bastard to keep him quiet." To punctuate his remark, he spat a stream of tobacco juice to leeward over the rail.

"As I was sayin'," resumed the carpenter. "When we made up our minds to get rid of the skipper and his bully sidekick for the nasty way they was treatin' us, we couldn't decide where to take the ship. Some said come about and head back to America. Others said sail on to Europe and the Medi'ranean. Still others wanted to go south to Afriker. Nobody could agree on the safest place. And we can't set a course until we do agree. I'm for drawin' lots to choose the coast you'll run us to."

"So what is your plan if and when I do find a suitable coast?"

"Oh, some of us gets in the longboat and some in the quarterboat, and we pull off for shore. And when we get ashore and run into anyone that seems curious, we jest tell 'em we're destitoot mariners, sorrowful children of a cruel fate. It's a good plan, right?"

Quine paused to hear what I had to say. "If you could land in a fairly remote place without police or politicians asking questions, your plan could work. Trouble is, in a primitive village strangers would stand out, and you might not be able to melt into the population. In a large city you might be able to do that."

"Can you advise us, Mr. Doyle?" asked one of the men. "Give us a well-populated shore somewhere in Europe maybe? But one that's not too orderly? What I'm saying is a place with no sojers patrolling."

"Captain Redstone had said he would take the ship to Horta or Ponta Delgada in the Azores for new food supplies because the islands wouldn't be greatly off course. But you wouldn't want to land on an island and later have to get to the mainland. You want as little exposure as possible, and so I'm thinking of some place north of Gibraltar."

"That's good!" cried the bo'sun. "Maybe Portugal or Spain! Wide open stretches of beach on them coasts and not many people."

"It does sound good. Then it's all settled, Mr. Doyle, all settled!" the carpenter exclaimed. "The crew is gonna do as you tell us as skipper, and I'm gonna be yer first mate. You won't get no more trouble from us now. Just keep this li'l ol' ship on course till we make landfall."

The sudden leadership of the carpenter puzzled me. Yet I began to feel better now that the men had shown they were willing to follow orders. Speaking with them I could tell they were somewhat alarmed in afterthought by what they had done. That assured me they were no longer disposed to wreak the kind of havoc that took the lives of two men. Suspicion would be the order of the day for a long while, and yet I was fairly certain there would be no more violence. Their plan to quit the ship when near land and go ashore in lifeboats seemed practicable and workable if all went well. In time they might ship as single individuals on vessels sailing to all parts of the world.

How the plan would affect me I didn't know. I would have to keep my guard up and be on the lookout for any behavior among the crew that might be interpreted as hostile. We had worked out an agreement and they had made promises, but I was not so naive as to believe I could trust a band of cutthroats to keep any promise if necessity dictated otherwise. They were a bunch of rough men who could turn on me or even on each other without discernible reason, for circumstance had made them desperate. That I had to keep foremost in mind, not merely for my own safety but also for that of the girl and her father. In a way I was also the guardian of Simpson and Charnook, but in a pinch they would have to shift for themselves as men.

The dawn was now bright and pink and purple in the east, and a good breeze was coming from the south. The ship was skipping along on a friendly sea heeled way over and moving fast. In the air was the promise of good weather for several days. Watches of men, customary before the mutiny, were now on hand to sail the ship four hours before being relieved by another watch. Morale seemed to be good. Well-fed men did as they were told and did the work of sailing the *Windhover* with no complaints. I was observing the sails when Quine the carpenter called to me. I deliberately took my time going over to speak with him. Since becoming skipper I had kept my distance from the crew, as Captain Redstone had done, and as tradition and practicality dictated. The old saying, "familiarity breeds contempt," is so applicable to sea captains it must have originated with them. My aim was to earn the respect of the crew but as their commander living apart from them.

"We been talkin' it over day and night, Mr. Doyle," said Quine, "and we finally agreed the best we can do is sail on toward Gibraltar and turn northward before entering the straits. Then some distance off the coast of Spain, or maybe Portugal, we leave the ship for the shore."

"I do believe it's the best you can do. And I believe you can carry the thing off if you work together peacefully. You can't allow dissension within the ranks. One man dissenting could throw it all off."

"What's dissension?" Quine asked sheepishly. "Sorry, but us common sailors don't have the book learnin' you have."

"Disagreement, difference of opinion, argument, tension. Or to put it simply, no quarreling as you go."

"Oh, there won't be no quarrelin', Mr. Doyle. Hector Sylvain and the Dutchman are gonna see to that. Any man that gets outta line goes overboard. Now can you tell me what our course is right now?"

"Wait here. I'll go check the chart and tell you exactly."

"Steward!" I called when I entered the captain's cabin.

"Here, sir!" came a voice hoarse with fear.

"Good news, man. I spoke with the crew. They won't hurt you."

He rushed toward me crying, "Bless you! Bless you! Thankee, sir, thankee, and my family says thankee too."

"Remain here for the present," I said. "I'll call you out later."

He went back to his corner and I left the cabin with the chart. I spread it on the skylight the better to show our position. Several men bent over the chart to study it curiously. They could see that our course by dead reckoning was south by southeast with many miles to go. They agreed it was the proper course but wanted to see evidence of it after the noon sight every day. I assured them it would be their right to see and know all I did, and they went back to the fo'c's'le satisfied.

The carpenter and the bo'sun remained on the poop to talk about the daily routine to be followed until landfall could be made. Of importance was whether our supplies of food and water would hold.

"If you're willing to take my advice, you'll let the steward serve the food as he is trained to do in the regular way. If every man has the liberty to eat whatever he likes any time he feels like it, we could run out of edible food before journey's end and have to fall back on the bad stuff."

"That's good thinkin', sir." said the bo'sun. "And if we treat Simpson with a little bit o' kindness he may open stores hidden away somewheres deep in the ship's hold. We got a rumor goin' round he has backup supplies just in case daily supplies run out."

"I can't vouch for that. I've never heard a word about backup supplies from either Redstone or Turpin, and certainly not from Simpson. Yet I don't deny they could exist. About the alcohol on board, I must have control of it. We can't have a drunken crew trying to run the ship."

"And how much per day do you plan to give us?" demanded the carpenter. "The men won't work without their rum."

I hesitated as if thinking it over and then asked, "How much do you think they should have each day?"

An appeal to his sense of self worth, my question was exactly what Quine wanted to hear. He pulled off his cap, scratched his head with its thinning hair, and frowned in thought.

"Say, three mugs a day? A pint morning, noon, and night?"

"Are you not sure Mr. Quine? You phrase that as a question. Declare a positive decision, man."

"All right! Three hits o' grog a day. That's what it's gonna be, but let me check with some of them men in the riggin' 'fore I say fer sure."

"Now you're talking, Mr. Quine. As a leader you want to get approval from the majority before setting a rule. Then you don't run the risk of that dissension I spoke of earlier."

"Yeah, that disenshun. Gonna keep it in mind." Looking aloft to the men ready to sheet home the top-gallant sails, he called loudly. "Hey, fellas! Will three pints o' grog a day keep you on yer feet?"

"We can go with that!" someone shouted back. "But no stinting! It's gotta be a full pint morning, noon, and night!"

"Fair play for everybody, boys!" yelled the carpenter. "Good food and drink aplenty all the way to the promised land!"

CHAPTER ELEVEN

A Pistol And Silver Dollars

On ratlines in the rigging the men broke into song, chanting and singing with gusto a salty sea ditty. With the precious chart in hand I returned to the captain's cabin to put it in a secure place. As I entered the best cabin on the ship, I suddenly realized it was mine. But quickly I understood I was not alone there. Simpson had been hiding in a corner without food or water for many hours. I lit the lamp, for even in the day time the cabin had little natural light, and called out. Haggard, thin, and almost fainting for lack of nourishment, he shuffled out of his corner and stood before me. He couldn't be sure his long ordeal was over, and when I told him it was he fell on his knees and thanked me profusely.

"Stand up, man!" I ordered. "Stand on your own two feet and behave as though nothing at all has happened. Return to your pantry for food and drink and have no fear of the crew. You'll serve them stores intended for the officers aboard and do it without confronting any one of them, especially the cook. If any man gives you trouble, come to me. Now go and take care of yourself. Then go on duty."

Again he thanked me for saving his life, and yet I doubt his life was ever in genuine danger. The cook and the carpenter believed the steward knew of secret stores to be used when absolutely necessary, and that alone would have kept the man alive. After he left I found a bottle of sherry in the captain's private stash to bolster my flagging energy. Seated at the desk bolted to the cabin sole, I looked over the ship's log and made my first entry. I found not a word in the log relating to the mutiny and was careful to record only weather observations and how the ship was behaving. We were approaching the noon hour when Charnook would use his sextant and chronometer to fix our position. That would mean another log entry.

Since returning from the wreck and becoming a prisoner in irons, I had not seen the navigator. Vaguely I remember he was there when Turpin and Quine clamped me in shackles but said nothing to me and quickly left the scene. All the time the mutiny was taking place he was holed up in his cabin with the door securely locked. In the excitement of combat against Redstone and Turpin, he was perhaps forgotten. His name came up again when I agreed to take command of the ship and sail her to whatever destination the crew would choose. I didn't like the man all that much — he had said the bad biscuit was good — but was careful to speak in his favor. Though sickly and reclusive, he was a good navigator fully capable of doing a job I found difficult. "Speak of the devil," the old saying goes, and sure enough Charnook stood in my doorway.

"I'm here for the sextant," he said in a very low voice implying he was very tired or very unhappy. "The captain always kept it tucked away in a water-proof box in his cabin."

The man didn't look well. "Have you been ill, Peter?" I asked. "You look as though you should be in bed recovering from severe sickness."

"I'm not in the best of health, Mr. Doyle, but if you will allow me, I will help you navigate this ship to wherever you want to go."

"Then you will take your sextant, Mr. Charnook, for a noon sight. Your chronometer is there in its box. The *Nautical Almanac* is in the same box with the sextant, and the chart is there before you.

When you have a good fix on our position, I'll enter our longitude and latitude and the ship's heading with weather information in the logbook."

He fumbled in the place where Redstone insisted on keeping the sextant, released it from its box, looked at it carefully, and made a few adjustments before going on deck with it. Later he consulted his *Almanac* and chronometer for a complete reading. I knew him as a taciturn man and so made no attempt to speak with him further. As the days passed we would be working closely together, and so I expected he might reveal at that time whatever was troubling him. As it turned out, I never really got to know Charnook, for he never took me into confidence.

I left the cabin and went back on the poop to make sure the watch was changing. The men who had come on at 0800 now went below for their lunch. Those coming on watch at noon had already eaten and had taken their midday ration of grog. The rum, as decided by the carpenter, would be served at breakfast, noon, and dinner time. Some hands were claiming it was not enough, but Quine made it clear to them that if they continued to complain he would bore a hole in each of the rum casks and let it all drain out. That chastened even the diehard members of the crew, and we heard no more about the rum ration.

All this was reported by the bo'sun, Rinehart Burdick, who had returned to the poop. Now that I was alone with the man I wanted to ask him what he knew about the mutiny, for I knew very little about it. He told me that Hector Sylvain had been the leader in the planning and carrying out the thing, but had later yielded his position to Harlowe Quine, the carpenter, because he and Quine had begun to squabble on what had to be done. That cleared up a bit of confusion on my part, for I had wondered why Quine seemed to be doing all the talking. Burdick said all the able-bodied sailors were bent on rebellion because if they didn't oppose Captain Redstone and do it soon they would die of food poisoning from the bad rations or from starvation or both. He went along with the action to save his life. Sylvain had made it clear that any man not willing to act would be tossed overboard to feed the sharks.

I asked for details as to how and when the first blow was struck, and he gave them to me as closely as he remembered. He said Sylvain and three other men — the cook, carpenter, and Dutchman — confronted the captain on the poop and demanded satisfaction. Redstone cursed them, drew a knife from his waistband, brandished it, and yelled for the first mate to back him up. Turpin came running to help his master but was overcome just as someone delivered a mighty blow to the captain's head. The men didn't intend to kill the captain, nor did they intend to murder Turpin. And yet it was done and their bodies tossed overboard. The navigator, the steward, and the second mate they spared as I already knew. After a quarrel that almost became another murder, Sylvain relinquished leadership to become one of the crew. The bo'sun reluctantly became second to the carpenter in command.

Before Quine came from the hold (where he said he had strengthened some cargo brackets as the ship's carpenter), we exchanged remarks on the mutineers' plan to leave the ship. They would go in open boats to reach the shore. Burdick said the plan was feasible and might work but only at high risk. They could lose their lives should the seas turn angry, or in mild weather they could be taken into custody. If they were spotted by a ship while in the boats, they couldn't refuse to be taken aboard. Once in the company of mariners on a powerful ship and required to answer many questions, the truth might certainly leak out. Events would probably unfold much the same were they to reach land. People would ask questions, get different answers from individual sailors, become suspicious, and have the authorities investigate. One sailor would break under relentless interrogation and so betray all the others. The bo'sun believed they would not be able to escape justice.

When the carpenter and bo'sun went below to get some

much-needed rest, I was left alone on the poop. To the south of us and headed westward was a small topsail schooner. Since we were moving in opposite directions, even with the glass I lost sight of her in minutes. Viewing her with a heavy heart burdened by uncertainty, I began to imagine what life was like on that vessel. They were surely looking at the sleek hull, tall masts, and many sails of the *Windhover* and perhaps believing life on our ship was much better than on theirs. The irony of the situation was painful: a beautiful sailing ship from a distance but on board and up close a pungent atmosphere of ugliness. These were negative thoughts, and I quickly put them out of mind to ask what would happen in a week or two when we arrived at our destination.

The answer flooded my mind with anxiety. How would the crew behave when that fateful day arrived? Would they really leave the ship in orderly fashion with a hearty goodbye to a person who could send them all to the gallows? Would I really have a chance to save my life and that of several others by somehow sailing the ship to a nearby harbor? I couldn't place any confidence whatever in their assurances. They were desperate men, and they would murder me in an instant if they thought it would improve their chance to escape justice. But it was not just my life I had to think about saving. The girl and her father were also important. Then I remembered the steward and the navigator, only two men to help me sail the abandoned ship, and both weak and sickly.

My agitation was more intense than I care to admit. I had to accept the fact that I would not be able to sail a ship the size of the *Windhover* safely to a port even in good weather. And that was assuming the crew would leave me on board in good health. So I began to consider any number of ways I might leave the ship with the four persons in league with me. I thought of persuading the bo'sun to come with us in a quarterboat with provisions for a day or two. He was a capable man and could help me launch the boat and sneak off under cover of darkness with four passengers. Then

I realized how impractical was that plan. The night watch would surely see us and sound the alarm. The strategy was no better than trying to sail into a port under false pretenses.

To let the men know that I was willing to be on duty as under normal circumstances, I gave my full time to every watch I supervised and was careful to have the men sail the ship expertly in all conditions. The carpenter, who now saw himself as my first mate, relieved me after each watch when rousted from sleep or rest. He had chosen my old cabin instead of Turpin's, and there I went to tell him to be on deck. I found him half asleep in my bunk fully clothed with his boots on and puffing on one of my pipes. The wind had diminished during my watch, and I told him the ship could carry more sail. He seemed to be in good temper and was about to climb the companionway ladder to his post when I asked if he would see the steward.

"Of course," he replied, "bring him on."

"I thought it best for you to speak to him about serving the cuddy stores. Your instructions best represent the wishes of the crew."

"Of course, of course! Where is the man?"

"Simpson!" I called. "Mr. Simpson, come here please."

After a pause the door of a cuddy cabin opened, and the man came forward in mincing steps as if terrified. Pale and haggard with watery red eyes from lack of sleep, crestfallen and miserable, his lips quivered in a sorrowful, desolate face. I disliked the man but felt sorry for him, particularly when Quine began to grill him.

"Ah, the steward, our beloved steward! Here you are! I been wonderin' where you been keepin' yerself. Now what do ya think this here crew must do to make things right with you? Hangin' from a yardarm maybe? Or is drownin' more to yer likin'? Maybe you wanna be gutted by the cook. I hear he's pretty good at carvin' meat."

"Mr. Quine is only joking," I said. "He wants to talk to you about the cuddy provisions reserved for the officers of the ship and how you will serve them from now on to the crew."

The carpenter with a half grin on his wrinkled face stared at the frightened man fiercely, waiting for some response. I could see he was taking pleasure in the terror he had drawn from the steward.

"Yes, sir?" the miserable man inquired, folding his hands in an attitude of involuntary supplication and looking humbly and woefully at the carpenter. "Is there anything you wanna tell me, sir?"

"Well, I'll tell ya this! We're all equals aboard this here vessel now, barrin' you, Mr. Simpson. We can't make you equal coz you was the skipper's toady when he was a-poisonin' us with bad food. You sarved out the rotten stores with pleasure. Now you will sarve out the cuddy stores to all the men at the proper time, and you will sarve them three mugs o' grog mornin', noon, and night. Also each watch is gonna get a share o' the pigs and poultry. But you gonna eat only what the crew's been eatin' till now, and you won't touch even half a cuddy biscuit. If we find out you broke even one of them rules, you gonna die."

That was all to be said. Simpson wore a hangdog look as he turned and crept away to his pantry, Quine mounted the ladder to the deck, and I returned to my cabin known to all the crew as the captain's cabin. I sat down in a comfortable chair and attempted to draw it closer to the wide table when I discovered it was, like all the furniture on the ship, bolted to the cabin sole. Though at times a nuisance, it was a necessary precaution against sudden and violent stormy weather. The book shelves, for instance, were not bolted to the wall but hanging from the ceiling gimbal fashion. A detailed map of the world lay on the table along with several nautical charts. A large colored print of the *Windhover* under full sail in a very blue sea adorned the wall. In a corner was a well-made cot near mahogany lockers offering plenty of storage. I decided to go through the lockers to see what they might hold.

In one of them I found a loaded revolver. I placed it in my waistband under my coat. Later I found a box of bullets and that too I pocketed. I reasoned it was better for me to have the pistol than for one of the crew to seize it. Even though I hoped I would never use the weapon, I felt better having it. Our present situation, on the surface stable and peaceful, could suddenly unravel. Now should that happen, I could defend myself with something far more powerful than fists. I went through the lockers searching for more firearms but found none. All that I found were clothes belonging to Redstone, some old charts and logbooks, some illustrated magazines, a box of cigars, and a small bag of silver dollars. I counted eighty-five in all.

As I was replacing the bag of coins under clothing in the locker, a soft knock sounded on the door. I called out and Miss Waterhouse stood in the doorway. She looked much better than earlier but was pale and thin and seemed rather unsure of herself and nervous. I asked her how she and her father were getting along.

"My papa continues very weak," she said with a heavy sigh, "but is perhaps on the mend. He seems a little better today. Wants to stay in bed, but I'm encouraging him to get up and sit and move about a little."

"I wish I could invite him on deck to explore the ship and take the fresh air and get the exercise he needs, but at present I'm not able to do that. I'm not at all sure what an unruly crew might say or do."

"I understand. I would like to see him do that too even though he's probably too weak to do more than just sit. He's in his bunk resting. I saw you enter this cabin and would like to talk with you."

"Of course we can talk," I replied. "I've been waiting for a suitable time to hear your story and become acquainted. Right now is a good time for me if it is with you. A shipwreck at sea is the one thing in all the world that captures a sailor's attention. Nations can rise and fall with not even a groan from him, but the prospect of another ship wrecked and sinking is another matter altogether. Captain Redstone, however, was a bird of different feather. Obsessed with making money, he abandoned the rules of the sea. He ran down a small boat and wouldn't stop to render aid, and he didn't want to stop when seeing your wreck."

"You got yourself in trouble when you went to rescue us," she responded simply. "I'm so sorry for that."

"Oh, dear lady, you need not apologize for anything whatever. We went to your rescue because any sailor worth his salt will risk his life to help unfortunates at sea. And yes, I was in trouble for a time. But worse trouble came later. Oh, please excuse me! I'm forgetting my manners. Come in, Miss, and please have a seat."

CHAPTER TWELVE

Emma And Gilbert Waterhouse

The young woman stood in the doorway until I asked her to have a seat. She was tall and slender with an expressive, sensitive, lovely face that wore a tired and worried look. When she walked over to the sturdy captain's chair with its soft cushion, I couldn't help but notice how gracefully she carried herself. She sat down with a similar fluid motion and crossed her long legs. She seemed timid at first but soon gathered confidence. Her blue eyes, well set beneath a smooth and broad forehead, were deeply sad but flashed as she spoke.

"My name is Emma Waterhouse," she began. "My father has always called me Emmie. He owns a maritime shipping business located in Baltimore and Philadelphia. He was planning with his partner Mr. Dukenfield to open offices in New Orleans and Charleston. They own ocean-going vessels — I really don't know how many — and the wreck you found us on was one of them."

"I gather your father's business is thriving in spite of the uncertain economy at present. I've been reading that 1871 has been a good year for shipping goods to all corners of the world. I'm sure you know the age of sail is fast giving way to steamers. They are more reliable and move faster even in bad weather. But tell me more about you and how you came to be stranded on a ship ready to sink."

"It was a terrible ordeal, Mr. Doyle. No living soul should have to endure the kind of suffering thrust upon us. We were so helpless, and for many hours we expected to die at any moment. I can't believe strong men suddenly appeared to save us. I thought your ship was a phantom, a figment of fever, that would suddenly vanish. But she was real!"

"She was indeed, but if we had listened to the captain of the *Windhover* we would have gone on without rendering assistance, would have vanished quickly in the mist. He didn't want to stop. He observed your wreck through the glass for a long time but said we must go on. At that moment I really had to go against him."

"If not for your decision, called mutiny by the captain, I would not be talking with you at this moment. My father and I do thank you so very much for all you did. And we must thank your comrades too."

"You are most welcome, Miss Waterhouse. I will certainly convey your gratitude to Eddie and Otto. It will please them to hear you are doing well and grateful for their help."

"It was horrible being shut up in the deckhouse with that mad sailor. I couldn't be sure what he would do to us or to himself. And we couldn't leave the shelter we had for fear of being swept overboard. We waited and waited in terror, and then you and your men came. As you know, at first I was afraid of you."

"How were you treated after we brought you on board our vessel? As it so happened, I was never able to find out. Well, I hope."

"We were made to understand the captain didn't want us. He said a woman on board would bring bad luck, and yet he treated us civilly. He ordered the steward to give us food and drink. I think the wine he sent us made Papa stronger. He rallied after drinking just a little of it. And of course the food made us stronger too."

"A woman on a ship bringing bad luck is an ancient superstition the nautical world can't seem to shake even in our time. But it's good he treated you well. Is there anything I might have you could use? You two left the wreck with just the clothes on your backs. I'm afraid we don't have any women's clothing aboard, but you might be able to find other items. And just yesterday I came across this roll of serge. If you think you can use it, I'll find a needle and some thread for you."

"Oh, I can use the serge! Do you have scissors too?"

"I'll find scissors, needles, and thread and bring it all to your cabin. And in a few minutes the steward will come to you with a clean comb and hairbrush that have seen little use."

"Thank you! They will get plenty of use from me. Recently my long hair has become a nuisance. I've been reading that some women in England and America are cutting their hair short, even thinking of less cumbersome clothing. Father would scream if I cut even one inch of my hair. As for clothing, it seems a good idea. Oh, I'm talking of things that couldn't possibly interest you. Our situation on board this ship demands discussion. Will you tell me what the mutineers plan to do after seizing the ship and gaining control?"

I told the affable young woman all that I knew, seeing no need to hold back on anything. I was careful to assure her that she and her father were safe, that the leader of the mutineers had said nothing at all would happen to them. I tried to put a cheerful face on all I said, assuring her there would be no more violence on the ship. And the mutineers would possibly leave soon.

"What happens then?" she asked. "Do we remain on board?"

"Three men plus you and your father will probably remain. And I may be able to persuade the bo'sun to stay with us. With his help there will be nothing to prevent us from sailing this ship to a destination."

Judging by the look on her face it seemed she was ready to

express doubts that such a plan would work, or that the bo'sun could be persuaded to come over to my side without consequences. Instead she exclaimed, "No matter what happens, Mr. Doyle, Papa and I will feel safe with you." Then rising, she asked me to look in on her father.

Mr. Waterhouse had been sitting in a chair when his daughter left him to come to me, but now as we entered I saw that he lay in the upper bunk under a thick blanket even though the weather was warm. He lay perfectly still with his eyes closed and his thin hands outside the blanket. He was so pale I thought for a moment he was dead or in a very sound sleep. But when she whispered something to him, he opened his watery eyes and looked at me. Then with some effort he extended his right hand, and I shook it. The hand was fragile and cold.

"May God bless you, Mr. Doyle," he said weakly. "If you are able to place us on the good earth again, you will be well rewarded. I'm a wealthy man you must know, and for the rest of your life you too will be wealthy without a worry in the world."

"I assure you, Mr. Waterhouse, I don't ask for any favor whatever. I just hope that you and your lovely daughter will see your home again soon. How soon I don't know, but I do know that no harm will come to either of you all the time you are on this ship. You will be under my care, and I wouldn't think of accepting a reward for any help I might give."

"I'm been wondering," said Miss Waterhouse, "whether you have some headache powders on board. Papa is suffering from severe headaches that seem to come and go."

"I may have just what he needs and also something that will do you both good. We have some laudanum in the dispensary. It will quell the pain and also help him sleep. The other item is in the steward's pantry. I'll be with you again in a few minutes."

In the pantry the steward was sitting on a chest head in hands, disconsolate and almost weeping. I spoke to him in a joking sort of way, telling him he wasn't dead yet and so had no reason to be so sad. And then I asked for brandy. He pointed to several bottles secure on a shelf. I poured out half a tumbler for him to give him some pluck. Then I asked for eggs. He opened a drawer to show four or five fresh eggs from the clucking hens under the longboat on deck. I mixed two tumblers of eggs and brandy and gave them to my passengers. They drank the contents and almost immediately felt stronger. Mr. Waterhouse in particular spoke with a stronger voice and sat up in his bunk to thank me.

"Now," I said, "let me leave you again. I hope to return quickly with medicine that will ease your headache."

"Oh, please don't leave us just now," pleaded the old man. "Your being here with us does us good, puts life in both of us. Forget the headache, let me tell you more about us."

"By all means, sir. I would like to know more about you. I'm off duty at present and will listen without interrupting."

"My name, sir, is Gilbert Waterhouse. The *Diana Huntress* — her name was probably underwater when you came to save us — was my own vessel. I'm a shipping merchant doing business in America and Europe and soon in South America as Waterhouse and Dukenfield. A few months ago I sailed with my daughter to Spain, to Cádiz. I'm sure you know that port. I went on to do business in the Mediterranean, and Emmie made her way to Seville where she and some friends rented a villa for several weeks. When it came time to return home (we live in Baltimore), I went back to Cádiz on the *Diana Huntress* with a good crew and a very capable captain. She was a snug ship and her hold was filled with cargo, wooden barrels of good wine mainly. We set out to cross the Atlantic en route to Baltimore and ran into a vicious storm. It came up so fast! All hands were ordered on deck to shorten sail but too late. It was truly a vicious storm, the wind so hard our sailors couldn't breathe. Not a soul was prepared for such a storm . . . ah . . . I must rest now. With your permission I shall tell you more later."

"Father, are you all right?"

"I am, dear Emmie, but suddenly feel very tired. I'm sure Mr. Doyle will let me tell him the rest of my story later."

"Of course, sir. Tell me more when you feel stronger. I'm on call any time you need me. I must go now and talk with our navigator. His name is Peter Charnook. You'll meet him in time. Please rest, both of you. I must get some rest too before going on duty again."

"Well, sir," Waterhouse continued the next day while eating lunch in the cabin he shared with his daughter, "a vicious storm it was, vicious. No other word for it. The storm came on suddenly without notice, gale force winds. They caught the ship unprepared, and before the crew could shorten sail and point her nose into the wind and waves all three masts were down, broken in half as easy as you would snap a match stick. Several men were in the rigging when the masts came crashing down. They uttered no scream, no cry of fright. They were brave men, those. They had courage. They died courageously. Night came on. Pitch black darkness and the gale growing fiercer. It was a night of total confusion and sheer horror. The men crowded into two lifeboats. One went whirling away in the darkness and the other capsized.

"The captain — his name was Jonathan Field — said the ship was sinking. Emmie and I scurried from our cabin to the deck. The ship's starboard side was pierced by one of the yards when the masts fell, and the seas were pouring inside and over the decks. We got in the deckhouse where you found us. The captain was coming from the poop to join us, but just as he reached us a rogue wave washed him overboard. That left us alone with the mad sailor. His name was Enrique Santos. How and why he went mad I never knew, but we were afraid of him. You tell Mr. Doyle the rest Emmie. I can't bear to go on with it!"

"Let's make it some other time, Papa. You are not feeling well and neither am I. Telling the story means reliving the ordeal. I can understand, and so can Mr. Doyle, why you can't bear to go on with it."

"Yes. Another time, Miss Waterhouse," I exclaimed, seeing the look of reluctance on her expressive face. "If you wish, why don't you tell me what you plan to do when you get home again in Baltimore. We sailed from there at the beginning of this voyage, a fine port."

"Baltimore has its good parts and bad," she answered. "Fortunately we live in one of the best neighborhoods of the city, and Papa has a modern office near the waterfront. We have a house in upstate New York where we spend our summers, and sometimes we travel west as far as Chicago. We may own another house in Charleston or New Orleans if plans for offices there are realized. I've been to Charleston and like the city very much. Haven't seen New Orleans yet."

"And your mother? I hope she's in good health."

"Mama did very well until a year ago," the girl replied. "She went to our place in New York state every summer and liked being there but didn't like to travel. She wouldn't take an ocean voyage with Papa and me, and in the last year kept much to herself. She died of pneumonia."

"Tell me, sir," Mr. Waterhouse interjected. "Are you not the captain of this ship? I think Emmie said something about you being the mate. If you are the chief mate, then who is the captain? I am yet to meet that gentleman, and I'm wondering what keeps him from visiting us."

I was about to answer when the young woman put a finger to her lips. For a moment the gesture puzzled me, and then I realized she didn't want me to speak of the murdered captain and the violence that led to Turpin's death. For fear of making him sick with dread, she had not told him about the mutiny. He didn't wait for me to answer his question but asked where the ship was heading. Mr. Waterhouse thought we were sailing westward and was surprised to learn that our next port would be somewhere in Europe.

"Oh, dear!" he mumbled. "That means another ocean voyage to get home. And I'm not at all certain I'm up to it. Are you up to it, Emmie?"

"I am, Father. When it has to be done, we do it."

"Of course, dear, of course! We can return home on one of those fine mail packets. I hear they are comfortable in all seas and go very fast. Interesting how things shape up, interesting."

He lay back on his pillow, uttered a mirthless laugh, and became silent with eyelids drooping. The horror he had witnessed had shaken him to the core, and the suffering perhaps had affected his intellect. But then he was old, well into his sixties. His daughter in full recovery didn't appear to be older than twenty. In time I learned that he had married the girl's mother as his second wife late in life. I liked the old gentleman and liked his lovely daughter even more. They needed items to make their stay on the ship more comfortable, and I decided to get them if I could. I gave the captain's hairbrush to the steward, told him to sanitize it in soap and hot water, and deliver it to the couple. When he returned, I asked him to prepare a hearty breakfast for them and deliver that too. On a large tray he placed deep-fried pieces of chicken, white biscuit with butter, two small glasses of orange juice, thick slices of warm ham, and some fruit from a tin can. They could have coffee later.

It pleased me to make the couple more comfortable. On another occasion I sent to their cabin a good suit of clothes from the captain's cabin, a warm overcoat, and some clean underwear I found in a locker. Simpson humbly delivered those items and later informed me that he had in steerage a box of women's under garments he had intended to sell in Italy. Because I had been kind to him, had perhaps saved his life, he wanted to give it to me for the young woman. We went to the hold to fetch the box and found it after half an hour of searching. He took it to her cabin. She blushed on receiving it but keenly thanked him.

It's been said, and I will say it again, that shipwreck is a very effective leveler. Powerful people suffer as much in disaster as the lowest of their servants. It matters not when catastrophe strikes how rich or poor a man or woman may be, for they are human and suffer the same distress. So it was with Gilbert and Emma Waterhouse. Shocked victims of shipwreck, they had been reduced in spite of wealth and power to owning nothing but the wet clothing they wore. They were beggars, in effect, when they came to my ship. At home the girl had all that money can buy. Her doting father owned ships and a thriving business. The indifferent sea, however, cares little for things or for us. It will strip a monarch as soon as it would a poor sailor and set him afloat naked to struggle and die. The sea has no human emotion, no love of humanity, and no mercy. It has no love of anything because it has no power to love. It is simply there without feeling of any kind and therefore steeped in total indifference. To know this is to know and respect the sea.

CHAPTER THIRTEEN

The Carpenter's Diabolic Plan

A t seven bells, half an hour before eight in the morning in landlubber language, the carpenter was shrilly shouting for the steward. I opened my cabin door to tell the man to go at once. To shilly-shally would make Quine angry, and possibly all he wanted was to give Simpson orders concerning the crew's breakfast. When I went on deck to keep an eye on what the carpenter was up to, I found him leaning against a capstan and nonchalantly smoking his pipe. Several crewmen sat nearby smoking also. All sail was in balance and working well, and the ship was responding with verve and grace. Both sky and sea were a brilliant blue and the weather warm and clear. Off our portside quarter was a large steamer heading southward. As I watched the vessel Quine stood up from his lounging position and called out.

"Wouldn't take long for her to catch us, would it? I'm hoping no sea dog on this here vessel wants to see her alongside. I wouldn't want to be the man that'd bring her near, would you Josh?"

"Not unless I had time to make out my will," Joshua Haythorne replied with a chuckle, looking up from the binnacle as he steered.

Quine sat down again and struck a lackadaisical pose before addressing me. "I'm glad you come up, Mr. Doyle. Curious to know what's going on, I guess, even when you need rest. Got a question for ya. Whut would you do if a ship like that started asking questions?"

"She would have to signal us first," I said, "and then we could reply as we thought necessary."

"Luff a few sails, let her cross, and go on her way," the Dutchman said. "Let her go on about her business and us about our'n."

"Anyone on the bridge seeing that might become suspicious," I replied. "Then what would happen? Maybe trouble. However, the crew controls this ship and you can do whatever you decide."

"Mr. Doyle is right as rain," Otto Jones interjected. "Why you asking him that? He knows more about them things than all us put together."

"I estimate the steamer is moving at thirteen knots and will cross our bow in no time at all. Let her signal. There's nothing in the books that says we have to answer. Stay on course with no answer."

"Again Doyle is right," Otto insisted.

Sighting another vessel in the wide-open sea is always cause for conversation and speculation, and I could see any number of men looking at the steamer with some degree of anxiety on their faces. As for me, I gazed with indifference. The help I needed wasn't likely to come from another merchant vessel or a passenger ship. Only a government vessel from England or America might become inquisitive and hail us, and that was only wishful thinking. Rarely did one see them in mid-ocean.

"Let her slip off a point," I said to Haythorne. "They won't notice any change in course and will cross quicker."

He did as I ordered, and within minutes a luxurious ocean liner with hundreds of passengers was near enough for us to see people staring at us on the afterdeck. Magnificently she clipped through benign water, leaving a long wake astern and becoming small in the distance. Her wake tossed us gently as we crossed it and got back on course. The carpenter now got up from his lazy position, shook himself to settle his clothes, grinned a wry smile, and spoke to me.

"Got somethin' funny to tell yer Mr. Doyle. I went and told the steward to get the men's breakfast and sarve 'em as if they was officers, and I swear he thinks I'm the skipper. Never saw a man so meek. Anyway, it seems to me things are goin' good."

"Yes, I think so," I answered, "and I hope they continue that way. Even so, I'll be glad to be on dry land again. We've had some good weather, and so we're getting closer. You know, of course, the courts always hang the skipper of a mutiny. I'm your skipper as taken by a democratic vote, and the sooner we get out of this mess the better."

"You hit the nail on the head there, Mr. Doyle! The sooner the better! And we're dependin' on you to get us out of it sooner."

"I will do what I can, you understand. I can't do more."

"Oh, we don't want more. Just enough is all we want. And enough is to know every day exactly what our course is. We don't want to discover overnight that we're back in the Bermudas. So let us see yer reckonin's, yours and Mr. Charnook's, every day."

"Bermuda is 2,000 miles behind us," I said without hesitation.

"Just remember, Mr. Doyle, we're dependin' on you," he said in a tone of voice conveying more meaning than his words. "We're dependin' on you, and I'm hopin' you don't ferget it."

"It's nearly eight bells," I said, changing the subject, "the men can take their breakfast now, or if you prefer I can go first."

"I'm agreeable any way you want it. Me and the bo'sun can have our breakfast arterwards with you. Just say the word."

"I think it better if I remain on deck till you finish. Take your time and have a good breakfast. No hurry at all in fine weather."

He made his way to the cuddy and I went to the poop rail and leaned over it to watch the men come to a part of the ship they seldom visited and receive food much better than they ever expected when signing on for the voyage. They were decent in behavior, even courteous at times, as they gathered on the quarterdeck and entered the cuddy one by one to receive stores the steward was serving.

The food, judging from what I saw, was a fine collection of biscuits with butter, thick slices of ham, fried potatoes, corn mush, coffee or hot chocolate, and a small glass of rum. It was excellent fare for men who had been starved or sickened for too long on rotten food. Each man slowly gained weight and strength again, and I could tell the crew as a whole had thrown off the despair it felt when Redstone was alive. They took their breakfast to familiar ground, the fo'c's'le, to eat and enjoy it, leaving the carpenter and the bo'sun at the cuddy table.

They didn't seem to care whether those two assumed the privilege of occupying the cuddy and eating at the off-limits officers' table. They were happy enough to have good provisions to eat, food they later called delicious. How they treated the steward I didn't know. Later I learned that even the cook appeared to harbor no ill feeling toward him. Even though they had warned him not to taste a morsel of the cuddy stores, Simpson himself reported he was back in favor with the crew. So long as he served them good fare, they wouldn't abuse him. They would never treat him as one of their own but wouldn't bother to hurt him.

After forty minutes or so the carpenter appeared on deck. He had taken longer to eat than expected, but I didn't begrudge him that. In the fo'c's'le he had fasted for a long time and now deserved to take his time, to savor food perhaps he never had tasted in all his life. He approached me smiling and rubbing his belly. With a dirty finger he was picking his yellow teeth. We exchanged a few words and I went below to find the bo'sun still at table. He stood up when I entered as though ready to leave the table. I enjoined him to keep his seat. Then calling Simpson, I asked how the men had treated him.

"Fair to middling, sir," he replied with more spirit of manner than usual. "They're not a bad lot, sir. The cook didn't say a word. Mr. Quine has a bitter tongue, but I guess that's just his way."

Burdick the bo'sun laughed and asked him if he had eaten his breakfast yet. Then looking him over he said, "Why, man, you're so thin a breeze on deck could blow you away. Go and get somethin' in your belly. We can't afford to lose a good steward."

"Oh, thank you, sir, but I can wait. I'm not really hungry."

"No need to call me sir, Simpson. I'm just a common sailor. Call Mr. Doyle sir, if you please, 'cause he's the skipper of this ship but not me. There on the table is plenty to eat and drink. Help yerself."

"Plenty to eat and drink," the steward repeated in a monotone. He viewed the bo'sun as a ringleader of the mutiny and feared him as much as he did the carpenter. "Plenty to eat and drink," he murmured.

"Well, then," cried the bo'sun. "Dig in! Mr. Doyle don't mind and neither do I. Sit here at table or take what you want to the pantry."

I was observing the steward's face carefully, and I could see he thought the bo'sun's invitation was a trick to get him hanged. The carpenter and crew had made it clear to him he was not to touch or taste any of the cuddy food, and so it had to be a trick.

"I do thank you, sir, but I'm not hungry at present. I can wait. I'll have a biscuit in a little while, sir, by your leave." A polite little bow and he shambled into the pantry, his frame extremely thin and his shoulder blades sharply pushing upward under his shirt.

"Strange customer, that one," said the bo'sun. "Scared to death, a walkin' corpse. Well, there ain't nothin' quite normal about a steward, you know. He ain't a sailor and he ain't a landlubber, somethin' in between, and I guess that accounts for the odd behavior."

"You can't expect him to eat the cuddy food under threat of

Of Time and Tide: The Windhover Saga

hanging or being eaten by the sea," I replied. "The man's overreacting but he'll come around if and when the threat is lifted. Has Quine said anything more about where he wants to go and what he'll do when he gets there? I'm supposing the crew sees him now as their leader. That man Sylvain is certainly no saint but a better man than Quine."

"I gotta agree. That carpenter is a bad 'un, as bad as any you gonna find anywhere. No man can trust a sleazy fella like him."

"Did Quine beat in the captain's head? I heard the man was hit hard from behind, so hard the blow split his skull. Maybe Sylvain did it? He seems to be the only one among the crew strong enough. Also Quine made it pretty clear to me it was him. Said 'the biggest among us hit him hard.' Didn't name names but Sylvain is certainly the biggest."

"Nah, that Quine is lyin' through his teeth. You gotta know he's a liar and a thug and now a murderer. The carpenter snuck up behind the captain with an iron-tipped mallet and slammed him. He and the cook took over when Sylvain said he wanted no more of it. Guess he was glad to see the big man step down. Didn't try to punish him for givin' up his post, too big I guess, but put the fear o' God in Cookie when the brute wanted to carve up Turpin. So Quine is now goin' it alone."

"I'll tell you what bothers me, Burdick. I have reason to believe the carpenter has some other plan behind the visible one and has taken pains to conceal it. Does he really want me to take the ship within fifty miles of the Spanish shore?"

"Yes, sir. He does," replied the bo'sun leveling his eyes and looking me squarely in the face. "And he plans to lower the boats and make for the Spanish coast. They'll drag the boats onto the beach and tell any curious people they are survivors of a ghastly shipwreck. They'll have enough food in them boats to last for several days right on the beach. Then they expect to go their separate ways and sort of melt into the population and live happily ever after. At least that's the plan."

"And he figures on leaving me with Charnook and our passengers and also the steward to shift as best we can? I can't believe he would take us along with the others even if we begged him."

"He plans to leave you on board all right," the bo'sun said, lowering his voice as if someone might be listening. "But he's gonna scuttle the ship after the boats are dropped in the drink."

"Did he tell you this himself? Or is it just hearsay? How does he plan to do it? Not easy to scuttle a ship this size."

"Told it to me hisself, bragged about how he'll do it. Said he would splash lamp oil on them pianners in their wooden crates in the hold, toss a match, and run like hell."

"So it's not water he'll use but fire. That sounds odd. A ship miles and miles away could see the fire at night and the smoke in the day time. Sounds like he's just inviting trouble."

"He said he's willing to take the risk 'cause fire will sink the ship faster for all five left on her to fry."

I felt dazed and disoriented, like someone had mauled me with a the same iron-tipped mallet that put Redstone away. But somehow I managed to pull myself together.

"There must be others like you, Burdick, others who believe his scheme can't possibly work. Give me just two men and yourself and we can turn the tables on Quine."

"Take it easy," the bo'sun said, hesitating. "Don't rush it. Gotta go on duty now but I'll think it over. Time's on your side, so no hurry."

I sat alone at the cuddy table, stupefied by what I had heard, confused thoughts racing through my mind and my emotions on edge. For a few minutes I felt totally defeated, overwhelmed. Then slowly despair gave way to fury. I wanted to rush on deck and shoot the bastard where he stood, blast him right between the eyes, or beat him to a pulp with my bare fists. From the beginning I had shown the man sympathy and understanding, and this was the way he was planning in that warped little brain of his to pay me back. Not only did he intend to murder me, but he was scheming to take the lives of innocents who had done him no wrong whatever. I felt utterly betrayed by a creature with no moral sense whatever. I wanted to snuff out his miserable life like a sputtering candle flame but stumbled instead to my cabin and locked the door.

I plunged into deep reflection centering on my condition and that of our passengers. There was no way I could put together effective resistance. Who could I count on? The bo'sun? He seemed to be leaning in my direction but was still with Simpson and his gang. Also I couldn't hope for him to try saving my life at the expense of his own. The steward? I wouldn't be able to depend on him even to steer the ship. He would be a hindrance, I was thinking, more so than old and feeble Gilbert Waterhouse. The young woman? A fast learner, I really believed that in a pinch she could steer the ship. And finally there was Charnook, our navigator. Sickly Charnook had more courage than the steward but wouldn't be able to help me in a brawl. If I could win over just one or two able-bodied seamen plus the bo'sun, I might have a slim chance at putting down the mutineers and reaching a port. But would I be able to depend on them when things got rough and turned violent?

In that state of mind I felt helpless, and there in the half light of my cabin I could vividly imagine how it all would go down. The ship would be hove to in moderate or mild seas; the boats would fill fast and move away; one or both would linger to watch the *Windhover* burn and sink; then before moving on they would circle the area to look for heads bobbing in the water. They would have to be sure that all aboard had perished. All this would take place early in the morning as dawn was breaking or in twilight before darkness. No other vessel could be within sight. An assigned man would be scanning the sea with the best glass we had. If the ship were to burn before sinking, it had to be done when no other ship could see the smoldering fire and smoke.

The bo'sun had said he doubted the men could carry the thing off without failure. It was all very complicated and someone would slip up, but that would probably happen long after the ship lay on the bottom of the sea and after the mutineers reached shore and civilization. In that presentiment of their fate I found no solace at all. To destroy a beautiful ship was unthinkable. To sink the ship with innocent people on board was even more unthinkable. To render neutral the man in back of it all was not unthinkable. It occurred to me that somehow I might be able to take the carpenter by surprise and pitch him overboard. But the odds of doing that without a witness were astronomical. Also, if by some fluke of chance I could do it without a witness, without noise or struggle, as soon as he was missed his followers would suspect me.

What then was I to do? Anyone's guess was as good as mine. The crew knew already the course the ship was taking, and I couldn't change it more than one or two points at best without their seeing the change. And because they now had control of the ship, they could set her course to any destination they found desirable. No longer starving and with plenty of food to sustain them, they could sail the *Windhover* even to the coast of Africa. If we managed to get into a shipping lane, I might be able to signal a passing vessel. But what would be the consequences of that? Before the ship could reach me I would be dead and bleeding and turning a little patch of water red to attract the sharks. Neither my reason nor my imagination could invent anything that seemed workable.

I knew I was in a formidable situation and was fully aware of its danger. But I could think of no solution. Though I racked every molecule of my brain, I could think of no feasible way to improve my condition, or short of death to escape the misery thrust upon me. I now remembered that just about everything I owned was in the cabin occupied by Quine. I called for the steward, thinking he might retrieve a pair of boots better than the ones I had on. Emma Waterhouse heard my voice and came to where I stood. She wanted to thank me for all the things I gave her and said she made good use everything. At once I saw her complexion was clear and her hair clean and combed. She had arranged it on her head in a becoming coiffure. The sickly pallor she manifested when I first met her was now replaced by subtle color on well-formed cheeks.

"Papa speaks of you all the time," she remarked. "He speaks of a time when he may offer you a job you can't refuse. He tells me one of his best ships is waiting for you to take command as skipper. I tried to tell him his daydreams are premature, and yet they bring him comfort."

"If his daydreams make him feel better, then by all means let him dream," I chuckled. "There's no harm in speculating what the future might hold, but it's the present that concerns me now. And of course I wouldn't ask your father to reward me in any way whatever."

"But you saved his life and mine, and he owes you an inestimable debt. He really does want to pay you back somehow, and yet I know this isn't the right time. I know, too, Mr. Doyle, that you seem more worried than usual. Do you wish to tell me why?"

"I am a bit worried, Miss Waterhouse. Troubled might be a better way to put it. The men have mutinied, as you well know, and I'm in the middle of it. I'm walking a tight wire and trying not to fall off. Have to be careful the way I speak and act both for my sake and yours."

"I know," she replied, "but please call me Emma. The little formalities of polite society seem out of place here. We face a problem that spells life or death. Social graces merely get in the way."

"If I may call you Emma," I said to her in a jocular mood, "then surely I must ask you to call me Kevin. It's the name my grandmother gave me. Good enough I guess for an Irish lad."

That brought a laugh from her, a melodious laugh that sounded almost like music. She assured me Kevin was a fine name for an Irish gentleman and a good traditional name.

"I like your name, it fits you! Of course I'll call you Kevin."

I studied her face as she spoke, debating with my gut whether I should tell her what the carpenter really had in mind. Certainly I would have kept it all to myself had I not seen proof of strength and courage in the pretty face. Her confidence in herself convinced me she could handle the truth as well as I or even better. So I held nothing back.

"Come into my cabin and you will hear the thing that makes me wear this troubled look. I'll tell you what I've heard just now in as few words as possible. Quine intends to scuttle the ship when they quit her. And he is planning to leave us on board."

"To perish? To go down with the ship?"

"He plans to burn the *Windhover* to her waterline. If we don't jump into the sea, we burn with her. And if we jump we drown. If we don't drown, he will split our skulls with a heavy oar. It's a diabolical plan that savage has in mind, but burning is easier and faster than opening the seacocks or trying to pierce the hull. Maybe not better because there's always the possibility someone may spot the fire."

"How does the old saying go?" the girl replied thoughtfully. "Something like 'Caught between the devil and the deep blue sea?' Seems to apply specifically to us. We have the sea for certain, and that carpenter intent on making our lives miserable is truly a devil. A dilemma but we can't afford to panic."

"You keep a cool head in a crisis, Emma. I admire that so very much. Working together we may be able to come up with something.

I believe Quine will do what he says he will do, if he can. I've been trying to think how to foil his plans, but so far I've come up with nothing. Even so, we have a couple of weeks or more before landfall. Time is on our side."

"So during that time we may be able to think of something," she added, finishing what I would have said. "We don't want to say anything to Papa about what's going on. It would only worry him."

"Not a word to your father. And not a word to make any crew member suspicious. We must appear ignorant of their intentions."

"Do they have weapons?"

"Only their fists and whatever their big hands might hold. No firearms I'm aware of, but I have a pistol with ammunition."

"Only one?"

"Only one. But if we had twenty we'd have nobody to use them. Well, maybe somebody. You, me, perhaps the navigator. I'm hoping the bo'sun will join us, but he won't if he believes we can't win."

Just then I heard a step outside my door. Before I could open it to investigate, the door was roughly pushed open and Quine appeared. He stared at the young woman and stammered —

"Oh, sorry to barge in like this. Hope I didn't interrupt somethin'. Didn't know you was here behind that door, Ma'am. Thought you and yer daddy was already turned in." Then addressing me, "I'm here to look at the chart, Mr. Doyle. Need to know how far we still gotta go and how long it's gonna take us to get there."

"Our most accurate calculations, Charnook's and mine, show perhaps three weeks for Spain, a bit more for Portugal."

"Well, we got food enough. I just told the cook to prepare one of them porkers for a good barbecue. All hands achin' fer some good roast pork. You and yer daddy, Ma'am, will get some. Cookie knows how to do up a juicy pig just right. And you too, Doyle. It' good eatin'."

He bent over the chart and I showed him the course and position of the ship according to dead reckoning. He traced a dirty forefinger along the ship's plotted course, and asked, "What's this here? The numbers?"

"Those," I replied, "are the coordinates determined by Mr. Charnook when he took his noon sight yesterday. They show latitude and longitude. Latitude specifies our north-south position, and it ranges from zero degrees at the equator to ninety degrees at the poles. Longitude is a coordinate that specifies our east-west position. Lines of latitude on the earth's surface are horizontal. Lines of longitude are vertical. When two lines cross, the navigator gets our exact position in this huge ocean covering much of the earth. You've seen him using his sextant. It's celestial navigation and far more accurate than dead reckoning."

"Yeah, I know about the sextant but don't know nothin' about that celestial navigation. Know about latitude and longitude though, now that you explained it. Guess Charnook is valuable for what he knows."

"He is indeed. You and the crew must respect that and respect him. The man isn't well but does his job in spite of poor health. I will help him all I can, but you should know he is by far a better navigator than I."

Nodding but not speaking a word, Quine took from his pocket a little pad and with the stub of a pencil jotted down the coordinates. It was his way of making sure the course would remain the same until landfall. With clumsy politeness he tipped his cap to Emma, clicked his tongue, and made a quick exit. She returned to her cabin, and I was left alone to ponder my predicament.

CHAPTER FOURTEEN

The Bo'sun's Bold Stratagem

We had a role to play and I knew Emma would play it well. Without sacrificing any dignity whatever on her part she would speak kindly to the men and hope to win their approval. The carpenter was a cunning and suspicious man, and so she would have to choose her words carefully with him and sound totally sincere. She had that opportunity sooner than expected. The next day when Cookie had roasted a pig and the steward was serving big chunks of succulent meat to every man in the crew, Quine directed him to take a platter of pork to Emma Waterhouse and her father Gilbert.

Then on second thought he decided he would make delivery of the meat himself. That's when he had a chance to chat with the young woman, who thanked him politely for his gift. In the comfort of the cuddy where I sat drinking my daily ration of grog and consulting the *Nautical Almanac* to assist Charnook, they chatted for half an hour. I made no attempt to join their conversation but heard every word.

"I thought you and your papa would like the pork," he said with a crooked grin, "and so I took it on myself to bring it to you. I know you been through a terrible experience, Ma'am, even heard you was nearly drowned, but good food and rest is gonna make you strong agin."

"My father and I owe our lives to the strong and generous men on this ship," she replied, slipping into the role she would play. "They just had to be very brave and good men to risk their lives to save us, and I thank them from the bottom of my heart. They were so kind, so good!"

"Well, bless yer, Ma'am, for sayin' that but it warn't no risk. It was a job we had to do and we done it. It's not every day we do it, but I'm glad you and yer papa are safe and sound now."

"You speak with a high degree of modesty, Mr. Quine," she said with a smile he found difficult to ignore. "It's well known that sailors always make light of their good deeds, but happily my father is wealthy. When we make land, he will take care to see that every man on this ship will be amply rewarded. Not a one of you will ever have to work again."

"Oh, yer papa is rich!" the carpenter blurted.

"Yes, Mr. Quine, quite wealthy."

"How rich, Ma'am? If you don't mind me askin'."

"He owned the ship that was dismasted in a storm and sank, the one on which you and your brave companions found us. Owned the cargo as well, a shipment of fine wine from Bordeaux in France. His firm owns several ships. I don't know the exact number."

"Well, bless my soul! The ship and all that good wine lost! And more ships to bring in money from all over." His eyes glinted with greed.

The young woman's astute and intuitive mind was serving her well. Not only was she a good actress but a clear, insightful thinker. She couldn't have offered a better illustration of her father's wealth. Quine was a carpenter but also a seasoned mariner and knew ships. He could fully appreciate the worth of a vessel the size of the *Diana Huntress*. And in a wink of an eye he could estimate the value of her cargo, fine French wine to be sold in America.

"How much do you think yer papa will give to the men, them as saved him and you, I s'pose?"

"Oh, he won't single out just the ones who went to his ship. He owes a debt to all of you and will reward all of you accordingly. He knows the captain wouldn't have stopped for us if the crew had not insisted on it and even disobeyed his orders to go on."

"That's true enough, Ma'am, true enough," Quine replied. "Old Redstone was hell-bent to go on and make up time he lost. Well, it turned out he lost more than time, but I ain't gonna go into that. So how much do you think yer papa has in mind? Cold hard cash, I s'pose."

"My papa wouldn't offer less than $700 to each man, maybe more. He would probably ask what is the man's income for an entire year and then double or triple it. Whatever the sum, it'd be generous."

"Yup, that is generous. Most of us common sailors make only a dollar a day if we get paid, and sometimes we don't get paid at all, and some of us make less than a dollar a day. I guess you know, bein' a ship-owner's daughter, a sailor's life ain't easy. Well, thankee, Ma'am, I gotta go."

Quine rose abruptly from the cuddy table as if someone had called him. Twirling his seaman's cap in his big hands and casting a sideways glance at the young woman, he blinked his little black eyes rapidly, pulled his cap down over his ears, and quickly departed. He was mumbling something as he left that Emma couldn't decipher.

I was impressed by the skillful way she played upon the carpenter's greed, leading him to believe that her father would reward him handsomely at a later date if all turned out well. Yet I could tell even as she spoke that he was evaluating that possibility in the light of what he had already planned to do. He was seeing riches on the one hand and poverty on the other. But the riches could come at a terrible price were he and his men hauled into a court of law. They could lose their freedom, even their lives. Landing on a barren shore to forage for food and shelter would also be risky but might take them farther than the money. So when Quine rose from the table and left abruptly, thoughts of this sort must have been going through his mind.

Thoughts of Emma Waterhouse were in every corner of my mind. I had revealed to her the heinous news that if we did not somehow overcome our oppressors we had but one thing to look forward to, an untimely death. In no way did she react with a show of weakness. She remained calm, firm, and thoughtful as I spoke, and I knew at once that when things got really dangerous I could rely on her. She had been rescued from an ordeal so ugly it had driven a strong man mad only to be plunged into a situation that could prove even worse. Yet calmly she confronted its terrors and began to think of ways we might extricate ourselves. Fruitful and keen of mind, like the wind blasting a ripe dandelion, she scattered hope in all directions. So quickly and adeptly she had conceived and expressed the reward idea, believing it could move the men away from Quine. It's a known fact the promise of money is a powerful motivator for those without it.

It seemed to me a good idea that might work, and so I decided to go on deck and get the bo'sun's opinion. However, before leaving the cuddy I knocked on Emma's door and asked if she would like to get some exercise in the fresh air of a good day.

"Bring your father along," I said, "the air and exercise will do him good after endless hours in that stuffy little cabin."

"He's sleeping now," she replied, "and I shouldn't awaken him. But I will come on deck with pleasure if it's all right to be there. That little cabin of ours while comfortable is slowly becoming a prison."

"Of course it's all right. You have nothing to fear from any of the crew. Order has been restored and they answer to the authority of the officers over them — the bo'sun, the carpenter, and Kevin Doyle."

"I'm confident Mr. Kevin Doyle will protect me handsomely," she laughed. "But oh dear, I have no hat! How strange to find oneself without even the most basic necessities of life."

"I'm not certain a hat, dear lady, is a basic necessity. The times in which we live require us to wear hats. There'll come a time when nobody will bother to wear hats, not even seamen in the tropics. Well, the sun is shining hot, and so why don't you wear one of mine?"

I had a straw hat I had picked up on a whim in Bermuda, and that I gave her. She put it on her head and was surprised to find it wasn't too big. Her abundant hair made it look right for her. Together we went on deck to find the day bright and sunny. The breeze had freshened but the azure sea was almost calm with sparkling cat's paws racing across the surface. The *Windhover* beat against the wind with all sails set and every sail exerting a special power. Her motion was strong and steady and outboard, say from another vessel close by, she must have been a glorious picture of white and hard-working canvas on tall and slender masts, taut rigging interlaced, a piercing bowsprit, and a shiny white hull flashing its blue cove stripe and red boot top. Deeply I breathed the salt air and Emma beside me did the same.

I ran my eye along the decks of the ship forward. Most of the crew were lounging near the fo'c's'le, smoking and chatting and doing no work whatever. Had Captain Redstone been in command, either he or his man Turpin would have found plenty of work for them. But in near-perfect sailing conditions with their work aloft already done, there was no reason at all why the crew shouldn't relax and enjoy the day. It didn't bother me to see them idle, and it didn't bother me to see them in their assigned place rather than running all over the ship. They owned her now, and they might have come aft to swarm through all the cabins and ransack the pantry, steal drugs from the dispensary, occupy the cuddy, and do as they pleased any time they felt like it. Yet they didn't and that was good to see even though I wondered why.

I recalled that I alone with small help from Charnook, who by now had taken to his bed with a severe cold, could take them to where they wanted to go. They knew I deplored violence and had warned them against it, and so it was necessary to appear tame in their behavior to please me. They felt they had to assure me that I exerted some control over my destiny and that of others who depended on me for their safety. And then the irony of it all struck like a runaway train. The mutineers, criminals obsessed with eluding the law, depended on me to do the right thing by them. If I failed them, undeniable doom was in store for them. Capture, shipwreck, starvation on a ghost ship were more than probable. If I failed them, and it was this that haunted me, I would also fail myself and those I had sworn to protect.

Emma stood at the rail looking at the changing face of the ocean and then sat down near the break of the poop. The men forward, warming themselves in the sun and languid as a lizard on a rock, suddenly woke to the girl's beauty and stared at her. I was glad I couldn't hear the remarks they exchanged, for their stares alone seemed insolent and dirty. Yet even as I felt a cold disgust in the pit of my stomach, I knew I could do nothing if things got out of hand. I turned my back on them and walked over to the binnacle. Haythorne was again at the wheel.

"Yes, that's our course," I said as I looked at the card. "Let's hope the wind holds. The slightest shift in direction could throw us off course and cause us to lose time."

"Mr. Charnook said three weeks or thereabouts, and it's gonna be a long three weeks, I warrant, at least for me."

"Long enough certainly even in good weather," I said.

"Will you take the wheel for a minute, sir? I wanna get rid o' my quid. Don't wanna mess up the deck. Gonna spit my tobacco juice overboard on the leeward side. Not good spitting to windward."

I took the wheel and wanted to stay with it longer than a minute. As helmsman I was sailing a beautiful ship, alive and alert and responsive to my touch. Reluctantly I gave the wheel back to Haythorne and went back to the poop where Emma was talking with the bo'sun. I could see she was using her special talents to charm the man, and for a few minutes I remained silent. When she began to speak of Quine in a general sort of way, I thought it time for me to enter the conversation.

"I can see that you two seem to be coming to some sort of understanding," I said to Burdick. "So maybe it's time to tell you I've revealed to Miss Waterhouse what you were telling me this morning at breakfast. She has courage and is very capable. She tells me she can steer the ship if it comes to that, having learned on one of her father's ships."

To the bo'sun the news didn't seem to come as a big surprise. He merely looked at her and nodded and then looked at me. He spoke looking out to sea so that anyone seeing us would not detect any talking.

"If she's as brave as she's pretty," he said to the wind, "then you have a companion far more worthy than Charnook or the steward."

"She's not only a brave young woman but smart too," I replied with my gaze on the brass trim of the poop.

Emma stood at the rail smiling and happy to accept our compliments but seemingly concerned more with the horizon than with us. Every day we were coming closer to the Spanish coast, and we had to hit upon a scheme to save our lives when we got there.

"I want you to understand," said the bo'sun, "I ain't agreed to leave the crew and come over to yer side just yet. Quine don't trust me much but most of the crew do. If I value my life I gotta keep it that way."

"I'm here to explain an idea given me by Miss Waterhouse and get your opinion on it. Her father is wealthy, owner of the wrecked ship and several other ocean-going vessels. The cargo on the lost ship alone was worth many thousands of dollars. The ship and cargo were well insured, I'm told, and so in time Waterhouse won't suffer any great loss."

"Is that Waterhouse and Dukenfield, ship brokers outta Baltimore?" the bo'sun interrupted, addressing the girl.

"Yes! Yes, indeed," she replied without turning her head. "My father and his partner. In business for a long time."

"Three years ago I was sailin' in one o' yer papa's ships as bo'sun's mate. She was called the *Robert Jones* to honor a seaman that fell from the topmost part o' the riggin' to the main deck. He was a good man, they said, and I was glad to know they named the ship after him. Ordinary sailors don't usually get no kind of honor. They work hard and risk their lives but don't get no recognition and very little respect. He got some and it was good but rare. A good ship she was too, well equipped and commanded. A comfortable ship she was."

"Oh, really?" Emma exclaimed, not able to resist looking at the mariner. "Small world indeed! You were on the *Robert Jones.* That ship, I remember, was then commanded by Captain Harcourt."

"Exactly, Miss, exactly! Evan Harcourt was the name. And the first mate's name was Thompson. And the second mate was Green or was it Black? And Captain Harcourt's son Gregory was on board too."

They stood looking each other full in the face and smiling, forgetting all about any curiosity the crew might be having. The bo'sun was calling the matter a happy coincidence, and I could see he was pleased to meet the winsome daughter of the ship's owner.

"Mr. Doyle," she said, "raising her deep blue eyes to mine, "there must be others on this ship cut from the same cloth as Mr. Burdick."

"I'm not at all sure about that, Miss Waterhouse, but maybe the bo'sun can throw some light on it if anyone can."

"Well," he said, glancing at the men forward and then at Haythorne at the wheel, "I can't really say there's another man we can trust. You see every single man was in on this thing 'cept me. They were badly treated and they acted without thinkin', and it got out of hand. I don't think they meant to kill the captain and first mate, and no single man did it. Oh, it was Quine that clobbered the cap'n all right, but when he was down all the crew kicked him in the head and groin and ribs. So if Quine didn't kill him with that one blow, they did with several. Then three men or more went after Turpin, and so you see it's a crime they all did. No man is gonna leave the group thinkin' he's less guilty than the others."

Before either one of us could answer he deliberately walked over and looked at the compass and cast an eye on the sails and the leeward side of the ship. Then he walked back and forth on the poop for several minutes with his hands clasped behind him. It was obvious he didn't want the men to notice the three of us in close conversation for more than a few minutes. He went and stood away from us, leaned against the rail, and stared at the sea and horizon.

"Bo'sun," said I with my eyes on the deck to show any curious crew I was not speaking to anyone, "Miss Waterhouse told Quine her father would reward every man of the crew with $700 or more upon safe arrival in any port. That's twice as much as most of them make in a year. If they got wind of this, how do you think they'd react?"

"Oh, it's certain they wouldn't believe it. Even if he gave them somethin' in writin' they wouldn't trust him. They'd think he was tryin' to put somethin' over on them, tryin' to trick them into custody."

"But my father would give them documents from his bankers," Emma eagerly exclaimed, "certifying the existence of the money marked for them. How could they possibly see that as a ruse?"

"Sailors don't know nothin' about banks, Miss. We have fourteen men in the ship's crew, countin' the cook and the cook's helper and the steward. Call it thirteen 'cause the helper is only a boy. If yer daddy had several bags o' silver dollars on this vessel and counted out 700 for each and every man as a special reward, all of 'em would gladly take it but scuttle the ship in the next hour."

"Oh, I find that hard, hard to believe," Emma cried. "Really?"

"Make no mistake about it, Miss. Them fellas are proud of their vagabone lives and don't wanna live like decent people. And the carpenter's got them all fired up and believin' the only way is to get ashore near a big city leavin' no evidence behind."

Burdick walked away again and pretended to study the compass while chatting with the helmsman. I was thinking what he had said made sense. He knew the men, having lived among them, too well to think an offer of money could turn them against their leader. Moreover, growing up in poverty, all their lives they had distrusted people of a higher class and particularly people with money.

"Papa would insure they would run no risk, Kevin. They wouldn't have to appear in person for the money. It could be sent to them."

"We know they would run no risk, but how can we get them to believe that? Not easy for sure, but at least we can try."

"No," said Emma firmly. "Let us not try. I gave Mr. Quine details concerning the offer. Now let *him* talk among his men and bring it before them. Perhaps they will conceive a plan to accept the money and still betray us. Who knows? I do know Quine is a villain and greedy."

"The bo'sun knows Quine don't fully trust him, knows his life's in danger. He'll think of something to get us out of this. He'll join us."

"I just hope my poor father regains enough strength to help us. Until now he was always strong and vigorous. His business demanded activity and judicious thinking. Sadly he seems to have lost all that, grown old too soon, spends each day in his bunk."

"Peter Charnook is also confined to his bunk. He's down with a terrible cold, but I think it's more than that. The man is sick. Neither he nor your father could help us. So if we came up against the crew it'd be thirteen to two, or twelve to three if the bo'sun joined us."

"And what about me? I may be a woman but I'm also an able-bodied adult. I can fight if my life and that of my father depend on it."

"Oh, sorry. I wasn't thinking. I really must apologize. Let it be twelve to four. If we could somehow find some guns we might even the odds. The steward might do his part with a rifle, and you too. We carry tons of Remington rifles as cargo but not one shell of ammunition."

"Don't you find that intensely ironical? Hundreds of rifles and all of them useless? But I can understand why. Boxes of ammunition on board a ship can be dangerous. Could explode, cause a fire."

"Yes, true enough. Any firearms on board would likely be hidden in the captain's cabin, and I've already searched there. We have to devise a plan, a strategy you might call it, that doesn't involve firearms."

Just then the bo'sun came ambling toward us on sea legs well adapted to the heeling ship. He flung a coil of hempen line over a belaying pin, adjusted it for hasty use when necessary, pulled out his pipe and asked me for a light. I found a match in my pockets and lit the old clay pipe stuffed with coarse tobacco. He puffed on it and began to speak.

"Not suspicious standin' here in daylight fer all to see as it would be in the cuddy. I'll tell you what I been thinkin' but can't stand here long enough to set the men jawin'. So listen close. When we come to fifty miles off shore and heave to as night comes, I'll fall overboard.

Won't be me for real but a packin' case from steerage. With them rifles inside it'll sink right away and you'll sing out man overboard, bo'sun! I'll be in the hold and the man that comes there to set fires I'll choke. Then I set old oily rags on fire to cause a lot of smoke, and Quine is fooled."

"It might work," I said looking aloft at the sails and rigging as if ready to order some work there. "It really might work."

"Now I'll tell ya this. I'll lay ya ten to one that Quine won't wait fer the man he's sent to the hold. Too risky. He'll go as fast as he can."

"I see your point. It takes time for a man to come topside from the hold. It'd take even more time for him to claw his way out of there with fire and smoke all around him and get into one of the boats."

"As soon as they shove off we bring them mainyards around and get underway soon as possible. If they get in our way we run 'em down. If they try to board us . . . well, we have the advantage."

Without another word Rinehart Burdick knocked the ashes out of his pipe, trundled away from the poop, and went forward to be with the men. Emma looked at me and I at her in silence. We were both thinking the bo'sun's bold plan might work. And if it didn't? The answer to that we quickly put out of mind.

"I will think about Burdick's stratagem and try to smooth away the rough edges," she said as she entered her cabin. "I hope you will do the same. Look for flaws that might compromise it. I must look after Papa now. Please keep me informed."

CHAPTER FIFTEEN

"This Man Will Fear No Evil"

In my bunk at night and even on duty I thought of Burdick's plan, carefully examining every little detail that might go wrong. If any part of it proved defective, as with a weak link in a chain, we would have to discard the entire plan and begin to think of another. But the more I considered the proposal, turning it over and over in my mind, the more I liked it. The one thing I didn't like was having Burdick fall overboard during my watch and I alone having to sound the alarm. Quine was rough and uneducated but not stupid. Instantly he would become suspicious. Not a one of us had been lost at sea. So why now in the dark of night only a day or two before the crew would leave the ship? And why the one man he didn't fully trust suddenly going overboard? I had to admit the stratagem was weak in places.

During the bo'sun's watch from eight in the evening until midnight, I sat for an hour with Gilbert Waterhouse and his daughter in their stuffy little cabin off the cuddy. The steward in his pantry was nearby, and I asked him to bring us some bread and cheese and a flask of wine. When he quickly obeyed my request, I said he could eat as much as he liked of the roast pork he had served the crew at dinner.

"But sir," he remonstrated, "I'm not allowed even to smell the good provisions. If I so much as nibble on a crumb they'll kill me."

"Listen to me, Simpson. You are killing yourself by not eating. You're growing thinner and weaker every day, and I have to rely on you. I know what the carpenter has told you, but I'm the skipper of this ship and stand above him. Eat the roast pork, man, and the good biscuits, and take a spot of rum when you feel like it. But tell nobody."

He created a scene as he fell to his knees and kissed my hand and thanked me profusely and profoundly, asserting that for a second time I had saved his life, and his wife would be so very grateful, and his children would be grateful, and his old mother, and so on. I insisted he stand on his own two feet and go. He stood and shambled off to where food was stored, and slowly and in secret he got stronger and less wimpy. I got to thinking I might be able to use him in a fight after all.

The health of Gilbert Waterhouse had improved over several days, and the old gentleman was curious about the workings of the ship and the progress she was making, and asked many questions. I said not a word about the potential conflict or peril threatening us, and he seemed quite ignorant of it. His daughter was keeping the facts from him because she feared stress or anxiety would weaken his mental condition already strained by the wreck. He didn't know about the mutiny and thought I had always been the skipper of the ship, even calling me Captain. He said very little about the loss of his ship, not remembering the details. In fact, as his health grew better his memory seemed to get worse. When I rose to leave he was asking Emma to tell him my name.

I left them at nine-thirty and went on deck. The days in July were long, and the sky bright and sunny all day retained streaks of light. The ship and her decks, however, were already in dark shadow. I tried to identify the man at the wheel but couldn't make him out. I could tell by his size and the way he held himself that he wasn't Haythorne or Webster, was perhaps the Dutchman, and so I decided not to approach him. At my station I could see the ship was under topsails and main top-gallant sail, the wind from the east-southeast and rising. The glass was steady and foul weather appeared to be a long way off.

I could hear the bo'sun calling to the man forward of the fo'c's'le to keep a sharp lookout. I had not spoken to him since the morning, and so walked forward and touched him on the shoulder. He swung around quickly and stared at me, almost combative in semi-darkness. Then recognizing me, he muttered softly, "Ah, Mr. Doyle, how goes it?"

"Let's get in the lee of the deckhouse and talk," I said. "We'll be away from the wind there and can hear each other speaking low."

"Come to the binnacle first. We'll talk about the ship's course, and the Dutchman at the wheel will think you're giving me sailing directions as we walk away from him. Can't be too careful, you know."

Relaxing against the lee side of the deckhouse, I told the bo'sun I had thought over his plan and liked it.

"The one part I particularly like is knowing you'll be in the hold when they send a man there to scuttle the ship. You'll have to hide among the piano crates. That's likely where the fire would start."

"Them dry pianner crates will burn like tinder. They plan to splash kerosene on 'em to get the wood burnin' faster. I'll have to be on the spot to stop even one drop and hit the man hard. Can't be a glancin' blow neither, can't afford to have the booger cry out and be heard."

"The human eye can't see a shore at fifty miles even on a very clear day, and the mutineers know it. So what's the difference to the naked eye between fifty miles from shore and a hundred?"

"That's a good idea, sir. Less likely for them to reach any shore a hundred miles out. Them boats were never designed for that. And we might as well get it over with, the sooner the better."

"It means double reckonings, one for us and one for them. You, of course, will have access to my reckoning. The helmsman and the carpenter will have the false one. It won't be difficult to do a little fudging with Charnook too sick to do his job. When Quine sees the ship at what he thinks is fifty miles off shore, he'll gather the men and put his scheme into action. If all goes well we too will spring into action."

We shook hands on the decision and parted. I felt better on leaving Burdick to go below than I had felt in a long time. I had a good man and a very capable woman on my side now. Also the steward was getting stronger on good food and might be of some assistance. Although the odds were surely not in our favor, we were no longer helpless.

The next morning we threw the logline overboard to measure our speed. During the night I had tampered with it a little to space the knots closer to one another. So when the line was thrown over the stern with the sand in the glass running, we immediately saw a greater number of knots and I called out thirteen.

"I reckon even more than that," said the bo'sun loud enough for the Dutchman to hear. "Can tell by the way she's movin'."

"Nah," said the man at the wheel. "I allow we're doing ten."

"Nope," asserted the bo'sun, "at least thirteen and maybe more."

The Dutchman looked at the water and the logline before venturing to utter another opinion. "Well, this sweet little ship sure can sail! If she can't do nothin' else, she can eat the wind and scream all the while like a constipated banshee. I don't mind gettin' early up to sail her."

The true speed of the vessel wasn't more than nine knots, but convincing Quine she was going faster meant arrival at our offshore destination in a couple of weeks. He would think the ship was fifty miles from shore at that time when actually the distance would be one hundred or more. I instructed the bo'sun to log our speed every hour and maintain a careful record. Then feeling hungry I went below for breakfast. There at the table, feeding his face as if food were going out of style, sat Quine. Beside his platter of food was a flagon of beer, and I wondered where he got it but didn't inquire. He raised it in salute as soon as I entered. The steward came immediately to serve me, knowing what I usually ate for breakfast. I looked into his face, saying nothing, and was pleased to see some color suggesting better health.

"Tell the ol' gent and his darter their breakfast is a-waitin'," Quine said to Simpson. When Simpson hesitated to reply, I explained that the old gentleman was too ill to leave his bunk.

"Then let the gal come by herself," he said as he sipped his beer.

"She can't leave the invalid all to himself," I replied.

"P'raps I'm not genteel enough for her. P'raps she can't stand the scent o' me armpits. Or maybe my tobacky breath ain't sweet enough?"

"No, Mr. Quine. The girl is not a snob. The old man is sick and she must look after him. It's her solemn duty. As for how you come off in her eyes, I would say rather well. Not many carpenters become captains of ships, you know. You call me skipper but you are the one in charge, and she knows that very well."

"Well, thankee Mr. Doyle. Glad you know where I stand. And of course I know to the very inch where you stand. Now bring me some more o' that roast pork, steward. A fella can't eat too much pork!"

I didn't feel like eating breakfast with Quine. I had said his table manners were not all that bad, but I lied. Gnawing at the meat, slurping the beer, feeding his gaping mouth with both hands and trying to talk at the same time, it was all rather disgusting. Yet the time was good to let him know we might arrive off Spain in a couple of weeks.

"How do you figure that? You said three weeks yesterday."

"And depending on our speed it could be a month," I answered. "But if we keep sailing at this speed I'm thinking a couple of weeks."

"I understand," the carpenter said. "I ain't no idiot, you know. Just hope it won't be too long 'fore we get there. I'm itchin' to get off this tub and feel some steady ground under my boots."

"So am I, Mr. Quine. You can count on me to put the crew on shore safely, and that includes every person on the *Windhover*. We can land on some uninhabited part of the coast, walk along the seashore until we find a town, and tell the citizens we're shipwrecked sailors."

Receiving my remarks as though they were coming to him for the first time, he looked at me with a half scowl on his weathered face. For an instant his eyes met mine, and then he turned to his beer, drank the last of it hastily, rose from the table and left. I didn't see the man even once for the rest of the day, but that evening he told me the men would move as I described as soon as we got within range.

"Bring the vessel to fifty miles," he cautioned. "Don't make it no closer and don't let it be no farther. We can't risk gettin' in too close or leavin' the ship too far out. And we all gotta tell the same story ashore."

"Yes, that goes without saying. Tell the men to rehearse what they will say. Tell them to dress warmly but go only with the clothes on their back. The plan is to leave the supposed wreck fast as possible. All of us will have to endure the high seas for a day or two and look tired and bedraggled when we make it to shore."

"I'm sure we gonna look plenty tired when we finally make it to shore. Won't be no pretendin'," the carpenter was saying as he left me.

I remained on deck until my watch was over at midnight. We had a good breeze in good weather and a lop-sided moon. Haythorne was lounging lazily at the helm because the ship was sailing herself. I walked the decks from stern to stem and back again several times to keep an eye on the men of my watch. I found no one sleeping on the job, and that pleased me. However, under the circumstances I'm not at all certain I had enough power of command to keep any sailor awake. I was merely the de facto skipper. Every man on board knew Quine was the one who truly gave the orders, and he was growing more offensive as his sense of importance went to his head.

Charnook, as I have already mentioned, was confined to his bed unable to come to the cuddy table to eat. The carpenter ordered the cook to take a plate of food to his door and leave it outside if he didn't answer the knock. When the cook refused, saying he was not an errand boy but one of the best cooks on the high seas in charge of the ship's galley, Quine beat him as Turpin had done. Cookie complained bitterly to the crew, got no sympathy from any man, and was beaten again for complaining. Beating the cook confirmed Quine's influence over the crew, and it made him even more arrogant and assertive. However, the beatings alienated the cook even more and left him seething.

A few days later I went to Charnook's tiny cabin to check on him and found him lying on a narrow, rumpled, stinking cot pushed up against the hull of the ship. Overnight he had become an exhausted old man. Though his eyelids flickered as I entered the room, he said nothing to acknowledge my presence. I had never smelled the odor of death before, and yet I had to believe the man was dying. Never rotund but certainly robust when he signed on for the voyage, he was losing weight rapidly and was almost skeletal. His long gray hair was thin, dirty, greasy, and reeking with lice. His once-ruddy face was deathly pale and drawn into a frozen grimace. Haggard, disheveled, and suffering from diarrhea, the man was obviously in pain. I tried to speak to him but got no response. He died the next day.

The bo'sun found his body when he took it upon himself to take food to the man. Without notifying Quine or the crew, he came to me with the news, asking if we could possibly give Charnook a dignified burial at sea. He was not an ordinary seaman, Burdick insisted, but for years had been a competent officer navigating good ships. He deserved more than the treatment given to Redstone, Turpin, and the mad Portuguese sailor. Inclined to agree with the bo'sun, I decided to conduct a simple ceremony with words from the good book before committing the body to the elements. I would do it whether Quine liked it or not. If he objected, and chances were good he would, I felt the crew would back me up, for even a coarse, put-upon, common sailor wants to die with dignity.

Except for Mr. Waterhouse whose mind seemed to be wandering, it wasn't long before everyone knew we had a dead man on board. Sailors for centuries have been the most superstitious of people, and the *Windhover's* crew was no exception. When they heard a man on their ship had died of natural causes, to a person they became fearful and antsy. Most of the men believed an evil spirit had quickly occupied the body to bring unspeakable bad luck. If the body were not disposed of posthaste, accidents would happen and men would die. The sea is consistently a dangerous place, for man was never meant to live on water. Between him and death is a mere inch of wood bolted and braced and sealed with oakum. Even with good luck the life of a man at sea is can be taken at any time. When bad luck comes, hell breaks loose and the sailor's dilemma becomes catastrophic. So Quine and his crew wanted Charnook's body off the ship as soon as possible.

When they came in late afternoon to wrap his remains in a sheet, I was there and didn't object. But when Quine ordered Hector Sylvain to carry the emaciated corpse to the main deck "for burial," I asked the big man if he were willing to see Mr. Charnook go without ceremony.

"I can't say, Mr. Doyle," he replied. "All I know is we gotta get rid o' this here corpse 'fore what's inside burns the ship or sinks her or sets a plague on board to kill us all."

"Perhaps a few words from the good book will paralyze that spirit you fear just long enough for the man to be sent into the unknown. It's a conflict between good and evil, you know, and I really believe good can win if we just give it a chance."

"Take it, Hector," the carpenter howled gruffly. "Throw it over them big shoulders and get it topside. We'll let Mr. hoity-toity Doyle have his say maybe, but only if he makes it fast. Guess it can't do no harm. In fact, it just might keep some of us from being bored outta our skulls when there ain't much work to do."

To my surprise I did have my say, and I attribute my good fortune not to Quine, but to the fatigue and resignation all of us felt. A mutiny had taken place, and we had lived with it for weeks. It was apparent no one wanted more conflict, even Quine who looked as tired as the rest of us. So just as the sun was setting we placed the sheeted body on a platform made of crates, and the crew gathered around it. Their faces pale and serious, they looked to me to begin the ceremony.

I stood on a crate so they might hear me. Earlier in my cabin I had gone through the good book in search of suitable text to illustrate what I would say about the departed. I read a few passages, and the words of Psalm 23 appeared like graffiti on a wall in my mind. I knew I couldn't read the graffiti verbatim but would try to make sense of it in paraphrase. I began slowly, almost faltering, and then gathered steam —

"The earth, this world around us, belongs to the Lord," I intoned. *"He hath founded it upon the seas, hath established it upon the floods. He sees the mariner's life, and this mariner in particular, as worthy. Therefore, the Lord is this man's shepherd, and he shall not want. He maketh this man to lie down in green pastures. He leadeth this man beside the still waters. He restoreth this man's soul. Yea, though he*

walks through a valley of shadow and death, this man Charnook will fear no evil. His Lord is with him and he will dwell in the house of the Lord forever. Now with heads bowed we commit this man's eternal soul to the Lord and his poor body to the sea."

Someone in the group mumbled *Amen*, and the service was over. I stepped off the crate and mingled with men who murmured I had done a good thing. Even the carpenter made a gesture to show approval. Two men lifted the body gently, walked to the bulwarks with it, held it over the side of the ship for a moment, and let it drop. When all of us heard the splash, the water receiving the body, someone said "Bless the Lord, for he is Good!" and the group silently dispersed. I was moved by the essential humanity of hoodlums who had killed. They were not monsters in any sense of the word; they were men, ill-fated men caught in a web of circumstance that would most likely doom them all.

CHAPTER SIXTEEN

A Plot Set In Motion

I went to my cabin to rest for an hour before going on watch but fell sound asleep. When Quine came to wake me, shaking me gently by the shoulder, he was almost kind when he spoke of "the burial on deck." I found it hard to believe that a man of his ilk could show emotion other than anger, and yet he was saying I did a good thing for all concerned. I began to have a better opinion of Quine but knew it was dangerous to forget what he had done and what he was planning to do. I had to remind myself that the man was a villain and couldn't be trusted.

As for the crew, they conducted themselves much better than expected. I thought within a week, as masters of the ship and answering to no one but themselves, they would be running amok. Instead they behaved with moderation and did the work assigned them as though nothing had happened. There were times when the cook asserted himself as more important than his comrades and behaved offensively, or times when Hector Sylvain complained of losing his leadership, but others in the crew quickly put them in their place. The power that Captain Redstone was unable to sustain had become that of the crew.

All the same, I couldn't allow myself to be deceived by appearances. They had murdered two men and would murder again to escape having to pay for their crimes. That I had to remember at all times when dealing with the crew and particularly when talking with Quine. I felt I could trust the bo'sun to side with me when the chips were down, and in time, as I observed his behavior, I began to think the two of us might be able to win over Sylvain. After initiating the mutiny and performing as its leader, he was shunted aside by the carpenter who acted with more nerve. The bo'sun told me the man wasn't pleased with Quine's barbaric plan to leave a burning ship with innocent people on board. Yet it was dangerous to ask him directly to join us. We could die if he refused.

Sunday came but no one on the ship observed the day as Sunday. Although I was unaware of their religious affiliation, Emma and her father may have said a few prayers in the privacy of their cabin. And certainly I would have prayed too had I thought it would have helped even a little to alleviate the stress I felt as the *Windhover* bounded along in good weather to come closer and closer to the **X** I had marked on the chart after taking over Charnook's duties as navigator. Because the weather was fine and the ship was moving upright at six knots or less, I invited Gilbert Waterhouse on deck during my watch. It was his first time to be there, and he came with his daughter. He shuffled slowly along, aided by her at his side, and was smiling as though for the first time in all his life he was breathing fresh air.

I had feared he was losing his memory, and I soon found his short-term memory was just about gone. Emma had said even before they embarked for America he was having trouble recalling business transactions completed only days before. His long-term memory seemed to be intact, and so she thought the inability to recall more recent events was only temporary. Disaster at sea, however, was the catalyst to dissolve memory. He knew nothing about the shipwreck that put him on the *Windhover* and nothing about the mutiny that had taken place. He thought every person on board was happily doing his job to make the ship run smoothly under my command. While his condition worried his daughter, she believed it wasn't altogether a terrible thing.

"I think it's perhaps better," she said, "that he not remember the horror we endured when our ship was wrecked. And certainly his mind is more at ease not knowing things are not as they seem on this boat. If he knew the truth, he would worry dreadfully about my safety but not his own. In some misguided attempt to protect me, he might get himself into real trouble with that mutinous crew. So while I find it very painful to see my father this way, I'm relieved too."

She was a devoted daughter, tender in her care of him and unremitting in her efforts to see him whole and healthy. At times when he didn't feel like eating, she persuaded him with exhaustive patience to take food and drink directly from her hand. When she knew he needed a bath, she bathed the old man with a large sponge dipped in warm and soapy water from the galley. So on this Sunday after lunch Gilbert Waterhouse was able to take the fresh air on deck. We were on the poop most of the time, that being my station, but at length he wanted to stroll the expanse of the entire ship. I couldn't resist his desire to do that and walked along with him. Deckhands at work looked at him curiously and tipped their caps to him to show respect. I was surprised and pleased to see that, and so was Emma. Both of us had thought a rough and unruly crew might make fun of her father and reduce him to utter confusion.

The exercise in salty air did the old man good, strengthened him and made him lively again. Near the capstan he stopped to exchange a few words with Ben Webster. They looked at each other, one very young and the other old, and seeing the contrast they laughed. Emma told me later that it did her a world of good to hear her father laugh again after so long a time. From the stemhead we returned to the poop, and there I found a chair for Mr. Waterhouse to enjoy the warmth of the sun. In minutes he dozed off and that allowed me to speak secrets to his daughter with no worry that either he or anyone else would hear my words.

"The moon tonight will be a waning crescent hopefully obscured by clouds. So if tonight is dark enough, our friend the bo'sun will fall overboard and be drowned."

"Are we truly within a hundred miles of the Spanish coast?"

"Probably not but it won't be too soon to make our move. The first step is to have the crew believe the bo'sun is gone. The second is to get him stowed away in the hold with enough to eat and drink for a couple of days or more. Any time he could do it without notice he's been hiding food there, and so he'll have plenty to eat. The water casks are there and so is the rum. I'm hoping he goes easy on that."

"And how will he manage to sleep? It's a good thing it's late summer. But even in summer the ship's hold can be damp and cold."

"Oh, he'll dress warmly and snug himself away somehow. Sailors can sleep on a pile of coal if need be. He'll crawl in between kegs and casks, hide himself effectively, and sleep like a stone."

"I do hope the stone will awaken when needed," she chortled. "It'd be really bad to have him wake up to a roaring inferno or water up to his waist. He must be ready to pounce like a tiger on the man who comes to scuttle the ship. Otherwise we could face disaster."

"I'm convinced he'll do his job well. The part of the operation that could be difficult to carry off is the drowning. He found a box of door hinges in the hold and smuggled them to my cabin. I don't know of anything other than a box of rifles that would make a louder splash and sink rapidly. The rifles were too heavy and too bulky to get on deck and heave overboard unnoticed by the man at the wheel.

"But wouldn't he see you heave the hinges overboard? And how will you have him believe the bo'sun and not some other seaman went overboard? It's not an easy thing you're planning to do."

"Somehow," I answered, "I must do it when he's not looking in my direction. Also I must get him to believe the bo'sun's aft before he hears the splash. That could be a real problem."

"May I offer a suggestion?" Emma asked.

"By all means, and I hope it's a good one."

"The man at the helm can be deceived. The night will be dark and deception is easy in the dark. When the watch changes and the carpenter goes below, it will be you on deck again and a new man at the wheel. The new man ought to see the bo'sun as he makes his way to the helm. You and the bo'sun can be talking near the wheel. The man will hear his voice but not make out his face. Then the two of you walk away."

I listened carefully to every word she spoke. One could say she was my teacher at that moment and I her pupil. She was outlining a plan of action that had not occurred to me, and it seemed feasible. Her father sat sleeping in the chair, and she was looking at him as she spoke. Anyone only a few feet away would think she was talking to him.

"As the two of you stand there in shadow, another person quickly appears and stands beside you. The bo'sun slips away instantly and hides himself in the hold. The box of door hinges is hidden in one of the lifeboats. You and the person pretending to be the bo'sun will go to the boat and make a show of examining its trappings in the interest of safety. Unseen by the helmsman, you take the box of hinges to the rail, and the pretender slips away in the darkness. When he's gone you hurl the box overboard and cry out."

"I see nothing wrong with the plot you describe, not with a single detail," I said, unable to conceal my admiration for her sharpness of mind. "However, I see one little problem that might be a big one. Who is going to replace the bo'sun? Charnook is dead and I can't depend on the steward to take on a role so daring."

"And what about me?" Emma quietly asked. "Can't I do it?"

"You could, of course, but there's still a problem. You don't look like the bo'sun in any way whatever. Maybe as tall but not as wide, and your hair is a bit longer than Burdick's. He's balding, you know."

"If you will find some of his clothes for me, I'll put them on and see to it that I'm wider. Also the hair will go under a cap and the face will be concealed by the darkness of the night."

"I see it all vividly, and I'm thinking I should be calling you Emma the Brave, or Woman Thinking, or both. A sou'wester will allow for several layers of clothing. It can also cover your hair, but a cap might be better. I'm sure the bo'sun can supply some old trousers you can wear. However, if the night isn't dark we have to postpone everything."

"I understand. We move with the first dark night," she said with a half smile, her blue eyes shining. "I'm so glad I'm able to help."

"All joking aside, you are truly brave," I replied, unable to hide my admiration. "And so very efficient! Why, you're fit to command a ship."

"Well, thank you, Captain Doyle!" she trilled in undertone. "It's a compliment I gladly accept, a bona fide sailor's compliment!"

Then looking at her father asleep in a chair in the sunshine, she turned serious. She hoped the uncertain future would bring a workable solution to our problem, and she wanted her father home again and healthy. Gently she woke him from his slumber and assisted him in walking to their cabin. I was left alone on the poop to squirm under the weight of what we were planning. With utmost anxiety I waited for the hours to go slowly by and for the night to come.

I thrilled to the thought of carrying out the scheme successfully, but wallowed in anguish and foreboding as I found myself thinking of failure. Quine on discovering the plot would show no mercy. I would die and the angry crew would violate Emma Waterhouse one by one and kill her father. There could be no margin for failure.

CHAPTER SEVENTEEN

"Man Overboard! Come About!"

Quine came on deck as my afternoon watch was ending. I saw the bo'sun walking toward us and decided to talk with him, if I could, without incurring the carpenter's suspicion. I said to him in the hearing of Quine that I would get my chart, spread it out on the cuddy table, and have him take a look at it. I was reasonably certain my calculations were correct but felt a double check wouldn't hurt. I placed the chart on the table under the skylight for Quine to see it all if he so desired. While pretending to work on the calculations involving navigation, we were able to complete the details of the bosun's carefully devised plan.

Burdick admired the boldness of Emma's idea, saying he would just as soon trust her to be his doppelgänger as any man he knew. He chuckled and grinned widely when I said she would have to wear his clothes. He told me he would make up a bundle of his Sunday best for her if I could get it to her cabin without being noticed. It would include a heavy sweater for bulk and fill up the sou'wester to his size with no problem.

"She can shorten sleeves or trouser legs or whatever happens to be too long," he said, "and you better tell her to walk like a man if she can. You can always spot a woman on stage that's supposed to be a man 'cause of the way they walk. They sort of glide, you know."

"That shouldn't be a problem. She can imitate your walk, but the night has to be very dark. What weapon do you plan on using?"

"I got me an iron bar the size o' my leg," he answered. "And I know how to use it. Don't wanna drop it by accident on my foot or toe."

When I glanced upward and saw the grim face of the carpenter staring down at us through the skylight, I murmured that our conversation was being monitored. Whether the plan would become more than mere conversation depended on the night being dark. If by a fluke of weather the ship would be in half darkness come nightfall, we would have to wait. Certain the bo'sun understood we wouldn't be able to act if the crescent moon were shining brightly, I went back to my cabin with the chart. I was about to put it away when I noticed one of the lockers was slightly open. I bent to inspect it and found the contents not in order. It was the same locker in which I had found the bag of coins, but when I thrust my hand inside to find them, I quickly realized they were gone. Only Quine could have taken the coins, for the cabin was off limits to all the crew. I had already discovered he was a liar and a murderer, and now it was clear to me he was also a thief. Well, it didn't matter.

If things worked out as we were planning, the silver dollars would be more weight to drag him down should he fall overboard when deserting the ship. Being near dinner time, I ordered the steward to take three plates of food to the cabin occupied by Gilbert Waterhouse and daughter. I knew the carpenter would be coming off duty, and I didn't want to eat at the cuddy table with him. The cook, of course, went about preparing the food, and Simpson delivered it. I went to the Waterhouse cabin a little before 1800 and had a pleasant meal with them. Although Cookie was coarse in many ways, he lived up to his boasting of being an expert cook. The food was quite nourishing and tasty. Before leaving I informed Emma I was on my way to the hold.

I went quiet as a mouse down the ladder that took me to steerage.

It was fifteen feet abaft the mizzen mast which placed it some distance from the wheel, and so I had no worry of being seen. In the bowels of the ship were two kerosene lanterns fully fueled and ready for use. I had to light one of them to dispel the darkness but managed to conceal all but a small circle of light with my coat. The hold was dark, dank, and dreary even near the end of summer. Along the starboard side of the ship were several hundred boxes of door hinges. Each box made of sturdy cardboard measured 23 by 23 inches, small enough to be portable but heavy enough to simulate a human body splashing into the sea. I looked for something that might serve even better but found nothing. Anything in wood might float. An iron bar would be heavy enough but would enter the water with too little a splash. So without too much difficulty I managed to get the box to my cabin and to the quarterboat under my coat just as daylight was fading.

The Dutchman, who had been steering, was surrendering the wheel to another crewman. The two of them were chatting and paying no attention to me, especially when they began to share a plug of tobacco. When the Dutchman began cutting off a piece for his friend, I hid the box of hinges in the boat and walked. The bo'sun on his way to the cuddy saw what I was doing but appeared not to notice. In few words, looking straight ahead, he said I would find clothes the lady could wear in a bundle just inside my cabin door. Because the carpenter had become suspicious of our being together so much, he walked on ahead of me and went below as if alone. I lingered on deck to check the weather. The night promised to be dark. The sky was thick with clouds and if they held, no moon would appear. The wind from the southeast had freshened, and the *Windhover* was beating against it at eight to nine knots.

I stood at the rail and looked at the shadows of night gathering on a leaden sea. A dozen storm petrels whirled and glided in our wake, and the sight left me with feelings of dread. From the time I was a little boy growing up on the Maryland shore I had heard the sea legends involving Mother Carey and her chickens. She was presented to me as a supernatural figure in charge of a threatening sea, and she rode across the angry waves like a witch on a broom. The storm petrels, thought by sailors to be the souls of dead seamen, swirled around her and did her bidding.

To shoot one of the birds would bring disaster to the shooter and the ship on which he stood. Now as night was approaching I was looking at Mother Carey's chickens dipping and flying astern of our ship. I watched them skimming the surface of the waves until I could see them no more. I am not a superstitious person, and yet I felt a cold chill as I remembered the woman's chickens were said to bring bad luck. However, since Mother Carey herself wasn't on the scene, I quickly reached the conclusion the birds were not out to do harm. I had more important stuff to think about. Reality demanded my attention, not fantasy.

It looked as though Mother Carey's chickens were bringing good luck instead of bad because the night was coming on dark. Even though my deck watch was coming to an end, as the breeze grew stronger I ordered the men to furl the main top-gallant sail and put a reef in two topsails. The adjustment didn't seem to affect either the speed of the ship or the degree by which she was heeling. I called for no other sail trim because the vessel seemed to be sailing fast. At eight o'clock the carpenter came on deck, and I went to awaken the bo'sun. Then as he made ready to go on watch I carried the bundle of clothes to the Waterhouse cabin. I gave Emma the clothes and also my sou'wester to wear on top of several layers. That way her slender body would look more like the broad form of the man she would be emulating.

"How will I receive your signal?" she asked.

"I will strike three sharp blows with my heel on that part of the deck that makes the roof of your cabin."

"I won't have any trouble hearing the sound even though it might wake up my father. If it does, he'll go back to sleep and I can leave him as soon as I'm in the bo'sun's clothes."

"You won't have to rush. We have plenty of time. Burdick will relieve Quine at midnight. Then I'll join him when the carpenter has gone below. Here, take my pocket watch to know the time."

"Do we have the advantage of a dark night?"

"I'm happy to say it's very dark. Dense clouds and no moon. The ship is scudding along under half sail in a brisk wind and steady. As far as I can tell, things couldn't be better."

"Let's hope all remains that way. Nothing must go wrong."

"The bo'sun is sound asleep and snoring in his cabin. At the appointed time he'll be in the hold with a crowbar. The carpenter will find it harder to scuttle this ship than he ever imagined."

Back in my cabin I lay down for what I thought would be rest and not sleep but slept as soundly as the bo'sun until eleven. The ship now seemed more on even keel, and that meant the breeze had diminished or shifted aft. I put my face against the glass of the porthole to size up the night and found it pitch black. I lay in my bunk thinking over our plot and lit my pipe to prod my thinking and keep me awake.

The one weak point I could find was the matter of the hold. Burdick would have to kill or knock unconscious the man who came to scuttle the ship without making a sound. He would have to do it as fast as possible and by surprise. How would he move without notice from his hiding place and when? Would he wait for the man to come to the piano crates with lamp oil and matches, or perhaps with an auger to bore holes in the hull? Would he silence the man as soon as he entered or wait for the right moment? Well, the bo'sun would surely manage. He was well acquainted with the hold and the placement of its cargo.

When I thought about how the man intent on scuttling the ship would react on seeing a dark figure flashing forward to attack him, I couldn't resist a quiet laugh or chuckle. Superstitious to begin with, he would think a vengeful devil or malignant ghost had suddenly arisen from nowhere to strike him down. Yet the bo'sun with that bar as big as his leg wouldn't give him much time to be terrified. One quick blow and the man's troubles would instantly be over. As eight bells were being sounded topside I heard Quine's heavy footsteps on the companion-way ladder. I wanted him to look in on me to see me sleeping, but instead he roused the bo'sun who went immediately on deck. I expected the carpenter, tired from his watch, would turn in with no hesitation, but instead he went to the pantry and brought back to the cuddy a bottle of rum and a tumbler and drank a full glass. Then drying his lips on his sleeve, he replaced the bottle and glass and went to his cabin.

I had waited with my door slightly ajar for Quine to retire, and when he did I quietly went on deck. Acting as skipper, I could be there at any time day or night and cause no suspicion, particularly since we were supposed to be approaching land. So if he should decide to come up before sleeping, he would see me there watching the weather and taking note of the ship's course. The night wasn't as dark as it seemed when looking through my porthole, but dark enough. From only a few feet away it was difficult to see the man at the wheel, and the masts of the ship dissolved in darkness. The bo'sun stood near the mizzenmast.

"Are you ready?" I asked, careful to speak in a whisper.

"I am."

"Gonna make friends with the rats?" I lamely joked.

"No time for friends," came the laconic reply. "Got a job to do."

"That lamp in the cuddy is throwing too much light on deck. I'll go talk with the helmsman if you'll take a tarp from the starboard quarterboat and throw it over the skylight. Who's the fellow steering?"

"The Dutchman."

Burdick concealed the light while I spoke with the Dutchman. Everyone called him that. I never learned his formal name. He was the man who had knocked off my shackles, and we chatted a few minutes with no animosity whatever. In the meantime the bo'sun found the tarp and covered the skylight. The ship's decks from stem to stern were shrouded in the darkness of a night without a moon.

"Now," said I to the bo'sun. "Walk with me a few turns on the poop so the helmsman will see us together. Then stand in front of the binnacle to block his view of the deck."

As he went aft I walked to that part of the deck over Emma's cabin. With the heel of my boot I struck three smart blows while slapping my chest as though warming myself. Then I walked to the break of the poop and waited. In a minute or two a figure came on deck, mounted the poop ladder, and stood by my side. Emma had done herself up elegantly in Burdick's clothes and my sou'wester, and except for the face half concealed she looked like a man. When the bo'sun saw her with me, he slipped quietly away in the darkness en route to the hold.

"Now," I said in a very low voice, "our scheme begins. Keep your fingers crossed and hope for the best. We must walk to let the helmsman see us. You will be to windward and I to leeward to take advantage of the ship's heeling. It will make you look taller."

We walked slowly to the quarterboat where I had hidden the box of door hinges. I placed it on the windward rail and asked her to hold it while I went aft to speak to the man at the wheel. He was carefully reading the compass, intent on keeping an accurate course, and he didn't appear to notice us or anything on deck. He raised his face from the binnacle just as I approached.

"She seems to be sailing herself almost," I said to him. "Heeling a bit but no effort to keep her on course?"

"None whatever. She's a sweet little ship. Sails better than any I been on. One tiny yank o' twist on this here wheel and she's jumpin'."

"Good, good. I'm gonna walk forward and check the fore rigging. We may need more sail on the foremast if this breeze holds steady."

I walked forward and drawing near Emma at the rail I paused for only a moment to tell her to place the box on the deck, move away low to her cabin, get out of the bo'sun's clothes, roll them in a bundle, and hide them. She heard every word and in seconds was gliding away like a shadow. Except for the rush and whistle of the wind, all was quiet forward and the main deck deserted. I lifted the box of hinges to the rail, took a deep breath, and looked all around to see nothing but darkness. Then I heaved the box overboard. It hit the water with a thumping, slapping splash as all along I had hoped it would. Even before it could sink I roared out at the top of my lungs, "Man overboard! The bo'sun overboard! Come about!" Then I ran aft as fast as I could, ripped off a life buoy, and flung it with a mighty heave far astern.

The Dutchman brought the ship into the wind. The sails banged against yards and rigging loud enough to wake the dead. The ship beat against the waves like a mighty drum before falling into irons. I added to the noise with excited cries.

"Steady there! Ahoy! All hands on deck! All hands! For God's sake, lend a hand somebody! The bo'sun's gone overboard! Bo'sun overboard! Get a boat in the water! We don't have a minute to lose!"

CHAPTER EIGHTEEN

"The Bo'sun's Drowned Dead"

As the ship lay stalled with gentle waves stroking her weather side, I bawled as loud as a trumpet call. My urgent cries brought sailors rushing along the main deck. The canvas beating on yards and rigging, the clatter of boots and bare feet, and the shouts from me and the crew made a fine uproar. The seas and wind had moderated, and so when the ship lay in irons I didn't worry about losing or ripping sail. But slowly, despite the helmsman's efforts, she was turning broadside to the waves for a new tack. As she rolled from side to side, moving about on deck became difficult even for the most seasoned sailors. The carpenter had been hired for his skills as a carpenter and was not a seaman in the true sense of the word. Yet he was one of the first to reach me.

"What in hell is goin' on?" he bellowed. "Whut's the matter?"

"The bo'sun fell overboard!" I shouted above the rattle of the canvas. "We brought the ship around to pick him up but can't see a damn thing in the dark. Shouldn't we launch a boat?"

"Hell, no! What good would that do? We could be dismasted sloggin' like this! And you know that better'n I do. The bo'sun's done drowned by now. Give the crew orders to get the ship underway!"

When I hesitated, he bawled to his mates. "Look at the way she wallows! Do you want the masts to go? Do you want the first vessel that comes this way to put you in shackles? You want every single one of ya to hang 'cause the bo'sun fell overboard?"

Grabbing me roughly by the arm, he said to me in a voice so hoarse I could barely hear him, "Give the crew orders, man! Sing out to the men, goddamn it! The bo'sun is drowned dead and that's that. We can't save him! But we gotta save this ship 'fore she loses her masts!"

With a show of great reluctance I went over to the poop-rail and delivered the necessary orders. For half an hour the crew worked hard and well. The ship fell off, picked up the wind, and surged along but not on course. In time we eased her into position and she galloped in a rising breeze. The carpenter worked as hard as any man, bawling all the time that if the *Windhover* should lose her masts all hands would be hanged. His cries animated the crew to work skillfully and fast. It took less than an hour, for it was now 0100, to drown the bo'sun, put the ship in irons, and move her out again. Quine came from the main deck to the poop, breathing hard from heavy work, to ask for details. He wanted to know exactly how the bo'sun could have fallen overboard.

My first response was to say I didn't know. How could anyone know? The night was very dark and he was alone. When he kept pressing for details, I gave him the full story. I told him I had come on deck to be there until midnight. It was my usual watch and I concerned myself with how fast the ship was moving and whether she was still on course. I looked at the compass, chatted a few minutes with the helmsman, and left him to walk forward to the bowsprit.

"And then what happened?" Quine asked impatiently.

"At the rail on the weather side of the ship I stopped to say a few words about the weather to the bo'sun. He seemed all right but was looking downward at the ocean and had nothing really to say. I went on forward and was inspecting rigging and sails near the bowsprit when I heard a splash, a loud splash that alerted me. It was then I realized the bo'sun, a capable man, was nowhere to be seen. Crazed with excitement and dread I ran the full length of the ship, ripped a life buoy from its brackets, and threw it as far as I could astern. Then, as you know, I sang out at the top of my lungs Man Overboard!"

"Well, it ain't a sailor's worst accident," Quine muttered. "More than once I seen a man or even two poor devils fall from the masthead of the main mast. Not a pretty sight, I tell ya. They splatter all over dependin' on the way they're dressed and how they hit the deck."

"I think we could have saved that man, Mr. Quine. Certainly we should have tried. But even though I'm called the skipper, I know very well that you're the boss. So I couldn't argue."

"And you did right by that," the carpenter crowed. "Never argue with the boss 'cause most of the time the boss is right. So it ain't no use sayin' we could have saved him when I say we couldn't. It ain't easy, and you know it as well as I do, to bring a ship around in breezy conditions to pick up anything from the ocean. Even if we did, who could see a head in the dark? Oh, we got flares but they light up the sky, not the sea."

Without saying more he turned on his heel and walked briskly aft to speak at length to the man at the wheel. After a few minutes I sauntered over to find the Dutchman explaining how he heard but didn't see the bo'sun fall overboard. He was corroborating my story in every detail. It could have been a different story had he not seen the bo'sun and me standing together shortly before I gave the alarm. Any story to cause the slightest suspicion would have meant a thorough search of the ship and my scheme exposed. But the stratagem we had so carefully planned was working well. I knew Emma would be pleased to hear it.

The next day the seas fell calm and the wind boxed the compass, shifting from the southeast to the northwest to put the ship on a broad reach. We had a steady, pleasant breeze under blue skies, and no one on board save the cook and his helper seemed to be working. The carpenter had made it clear to him that he was to keep the galley clean at all times and prepare simple but tasty meals from the ship's stores. His helper was a Chinese boy we called Chin Fang. I never knew whether that was his real name.

I know Cookie often called him a lazy oaf even though the boy seemed to have tremendous energy and was always working. I asked him once how he managed to be on board a merchant vessel on her way to Europe. He merely looked at me as if not understanding, then shook his head. Finally he said he goes where Cookie goes, but of course Cookie was not his father nor a blood relative whatever. He was the owner of the boy, or so the rumor went among the crew, but that I had no way of ascertaining whether true or not.

Near noon as I was about to use Charnook's coveted sextant to take a noon sight, I saw at some distance from us the outline of a large ship. Through the glass I could see that she was under full sail and on a course almost parallel to our own. As I looked at her I got to thinking how I might come into some sort of communication with her that could lead to a good result. Since we were not exactly on a parallel course, the big ship was coming steadily closer to us and flaunting a wonderful tower of canvas. I thought I might signal her when she was closer but quickly canceled that thought as too dangerous. I knew I could be punished severely the moment any man saw me near the signal halyards. I thought if by good fortune the two vessels came within earshot I might hail her vocally, but if they failed to hear my shouting or refused to acknowledged it, where would I be? Quine and his men wouldn't fail to hear me, and instantly they would kill me. So in silence I watched the splendid ship come closer, sailing faster by at least five knots.

Otto Jones and another man came along the main deck, and Jones came up to me with a look of some concern when the other man went into the cuddy. I remembered he had gone with me to the wreck and had shown himself a brave seaman, but now it seemed so long ago.

"The men are worried, Mr. Doyle," he said. "They say we're coming too close to that ship, and they don't like it. We gonna have to come into the wind and sit for a while or come about."

I was about to reply that to do either would attract attention, but then I decided to say it to the crew. "Jones wants me to bring the ship about," I called out loudly, "but if I do the skipper on that vessel will know something is wrong. You don't suddenly come about in a good beam wind, and you don't swing into it even close hauled."

"Take us away from that ship any way you can," someone cried. "That's all we want! Just get us the hell away from them."

The shouting brought the carpenter running to the poop with nothing on but his shirt and drawers.

"Whut in hell?" he cried out fiercely. "Whut in hell is goin' on? Answer me, Doyle! Are you tryin' to put us alongside?"

Before I could reply he spit orders to Haythorne at the wheel. "To port, goddamn it! To port! Run across her wake under her stern!"

"Don't," I calmly said, eager to show good intentions. "If you do that, it will attract attention and cause suspicion."

Then seeing the huge merchant ship pulling rapidly ahead, I cried to our helmsman, "Steady! Take her one point off course to leeward."

The carpenter scowled at me and made a threatening gesture but said nothing. Most of the crew mounted the poop to stare at the ship and then to stare at me. I well understood their meaning. I had brought the *Windhover* a bit too close to another vessel that could set into motion a series of events to see them hanged. But when the vessel moved fast away from us, their hostility soon disappeared. They let me know, however, that if I valued my life I was not to play tricks on them.

I was not surprised when the vessel hoisted her colors as she moved away. The Union Jack soared gracefully at the end of a gaff near the stern, and people were looking at us from the taffrail.

"We must answer that," I said to the carpenter. "Bend on the ensign and run it up. It's a courtesy we can't ignore."

I suppose Quine saw no harm in our displaying the flag we sailed under, and so in his leisurely raw-boned way he had one of the hands run up the stars and stripes. When she saw that we had answered her, the British ship hauled her ensign down and slowly moved out of sight.

"You did all right," Quine said grudgingly. "Better'n comin' about I reckon. And the men liked your way of doin' it too."

"All of our sails are full and working and it's steady as she goes. We're now back on course with no worries," I said quietly.

Quine went below to put on the clothes he had worn every day since the voyage began. The time was 1600, or four o'clock in the afternoon, and time to relieve me. He shambled to the poop looking tired and complaining of not enough sleep.

"I'm sick o' the sight of ya, Mr. Doyle. You look exhausted too but you stand there all stiff and proper like a soldier on guard. I'm sick o' the poop and this voyage and the goddamn ship and the mess we made. First part o' passage me and my fellas was starved for food. Now with no real skipper to keep things in order I'm starved for sleep. How much longer is it gonna take us to lay off that Spanish coast? I gotta know!"

"If the weather holds and we get a good breeze, I think I can safely say we can be there in just a few more days. I've done my best to take us where you want to go, but I'm real sad we lost the bo'sun."

"Well, are ya now?" he responded with a shade of sarcasm.

"He was a good man, a good sailor, maybe the best of the lot."

"Well, that don't matter at all now, does it? We just have to take it as one of them things and get over it. You whine too much, Mr. Doyle."

"What really bothers me is not stopping to try to save him. He deserved at least an attempt on our part even if it meant putting the ship in danger. If we couldn't have found him, we could have said at least we tried. Just that could have made us feel better about losing him."

"Well, you already said what you just said, Doyle. I'm thinkin' you better try to get a job on land. Maybe you're too soft for a sailor's life. I said to try was too much a risk, and when I says No I mean No."

"But the crew thinks I'm a heartless bastard for not launching a boat to search for the poor devil," I said pretending anger.

"Some of the hands didn't like him and some did. I'm one o' the few that did. I would of tried but feared the masts crashin' down."

"I'm forced to agree that groping about in the dark for a drowning man would have been a dangerous maneuver."

"I'm glad you see what I been gettin' at, Doyle. I had the ship and all us on her to consider. We couldn't run the risk of losin' every livin' soul on this ship just to save one man. Now let's have no more talk of Rinehart Burdick. He's down there with Davy Jones now."

"No doubt about that," I replied. "I'm dead tired and ready to turn in for forty winks. You know the course, Mr. Quine. You might have a hand climb up and set the fore-topmast stun'sail. Could help a little with our speed. I'll be on duty again in a few hours."

With a civil nod I left Mr. Quine on what seemed almost friendly terms. He was convinced the bo'sun was dead. Our subterfuge seemed to be working better than ever we expected. I wanted to tell Emma all about it but heard no sound in her cabin and so passed on to my berth to get some much-needed sleep and rest before going on duty again.

CHAPTER NINETEEN
A Slaughter Of Hens And Pigs

Things went all right on my watch and I finally got around to seeing Emma Waterhouse at breakfast time. As usual the steward brought the breakfast she and her father would eat to their door and tapped on it. Taking the tray she saw me at the cuddy table and came into the room. She was dressed in the sleeping gown she had made of the serge I had given her when she was new on board. I marveled at what she had done with it. In the makeshift gown she looked tall and slender and very pretty. Her shining blonde hair flowed softly to her shoulders, and I found it hard to remove my eyes from her. Then as I was about to say how nice she looked I heard her speaking.

"Please excuse my appearance, Kevin, but I just had to talk to you. Did it go all right? Oh, I've been so anxious to know!"

Her blue eyes were flashing as she asked that question, and I could tell she was eager to get an answer. She sat down across the table from me, and I sipped my coffee before replying.

"It went as we planned it, even better than expected."

"The bo'sun is down in the hold," she asked, "and no one knows?"

"Only you and me. He's there with food to sustain him, and every person on this ship, save you and me, believes he fell overboard."

"Oh, that is so good to hear!" she exclaimed, smiling faintly.

"We couldn't have done it without you, Emma. You played your role very well and bravely too. Burdick admires you much and so do I."

"Don't look up as I say this," she whispered, "but the carpenter is peering through the skylight. I will leave you alone, but can you tell me when the ship will reach the place where they intend to leave us?"

"I can't tell you exactly because we depend on wind and weather, but I'm thinking about two days from now, maybe three."

Because Emma knew Quine was watching, she merely looked at me calmly, rose from the table, and went to her cabin. My thoughts centered on her and her father as I finished my breakfast. It was a dire situation confronting them through no fault of their own. Their lives and mine, and that of the bo'sun, hung by a thread. Whether we were to live or die depended on courageous action at the last moment. But the real problem we had to face was not knowing exactly when and how the crew would leave the ship. Would they scuttle her and remain on board until she began to list? Or would all of them leave while one man went to the hold to set fire to the piano crates or perhaps to bore holes? It worried me that I could not supply an answer to those questions.

On deck to stand watch I found myself alone except for the man at the wheel. All the hands were eating breakfast, and the carpenter left the moment I appeared. The breeze had become a splendid sailing wind, and our sleek little ship skipped along across moderate seas like a very expensive yacht in a race. I cast my eye upon the horizon and turned around 360 degrees to scan it entirely. I saw not a thing but sea and sky. For a moment all seemed right with the world, a sailor adoring his ship and taking pleasure in her performance. Then ugly reality barged in as I saw the carpenter walk along the main deck and enter the fo'c's'le. After breakfast

I expected Quine would immediately crawl into bed. He didn't. Instead for half an hour or more he was with the crew.

Then of a sudden he tumbled out of the fo'c's'le with Sylvain, the cook, and a couple of other hands. They went directly to the chickens on the port side of the longboat, and I began to hear screeching hens raising a ruckus. I walked across the poop to see what was going on and found all four men wringing the necks of the fat hens. I thought it might be some sort of cruel game they were playing, but they were not laughing, not even smiling. Grimly they killed nearly twenty hens and placed them in a heap near the coop. Then with the job finished each man gathered an armful of hens and carried them into the galley. I could draw only one conclusion from what I saw. The carpenter had decided on a culinary reward for the men before they would be leaving the ship.

As I wondered whether the poultry would be cooked up and served as a one-time feast or added to daily rations, a gang of men came on deck and went to the enclosure where the pigs were kept. Two men sprang into the pen brandishing knives and went for the pigs. The noise the squealing pigs made was hideous. It bothered me that Emma and her father couldn't help but hear it and be disturbed by it, but there was nothing I could do. The pigs screamed like human babies being tortured but only for ten minutes or so. It seemed apparent the men had killed pigs before and knew their work, for the screaming and shrieking of porkers having their throats cut lasted only a few minutes.

Most of the crew had gathered around to witness the sport and were now looking at six or seven slaughtered animals gushing blood all over the deck. When the pig-stickers climbed out of the pen stepping on dead pigs to boost themselves over the fence, the cook jumped into the enclosure. His hands, face, arms, shirt, and britches were soon bloody. Emitting a loud, high-pitched laugh and dancing a little jig, he threw the carcasses into the crowd of onlookers. They screamed when the bloody pigs hit them but also roared with laughter. Two weeks earlier a sow had given birth to four piglets, and these became live footballs in the hands of the riotous crew. They tossed the little pigs from one man to the other and cried out in boisterous laughter when a good catch was made. Within minutes the piglets were dead, and hoarse with mirth the rowdy men looked as bloody as the pigs. The entire ship was in an uproar, raucous and vulgar. Only the sun was silent.

I watched it all from my station, even laughed at some of their shenanigans, and felt a queasy sensation in the pit of my stomach when fiercely they began to fight one another. A big muscular sailor rushed at a smaller man with a knife upraised but was struck down like a bowling pin by a dead pig hurled against him. In another encounter a big, beefy fist pounded a bloody face to blacken both eyes. The din the group made was an ugly medley of groaning, growling, laughing, yelling, and cursing. The melee came to an end with half the men reeling half stunned like drunkards and all of them panting for breath. To a person they surged into the fo'c's'le to clean themselves, leaving Sylvain and the cook to carry the pigs into the galley. I was not to find out until much later whether they gutted the pigs and prepared the meat for eating, or simply threw the dead animals on the tiled floor to rot.

As I viewed the revelry, if one may call it that, I began to understand it was a prelude to leaving the ship in a few days. If Quine and his men were to make their way to a strange beach from a distance of fifty miles off shore, they would need ample food supplies from the ship's provisions. In their minds, though every man hungered for roast pork, that justified killing the livestock. After cleaning themselves of the blood and gore, they made no effort to clean the decks but went to their bunks for rest and sleep. For the remainder of the afternoon the steaming decks were clear of all hands and stinking under the sun. I saw only one man topside, Haythorne at the wheel. As the blood dried I could see a bluish vapor rising from it and could smell the stench even from the poop. As skipper it was within my power to issue harsh orders, and yet I knew I wasn't the skipper. The entire crew had become the henchmen of the carpenter and obeyed his orders. Only when sailing the ship did they listen to me, obeying me only when the spirit moved them.

The next day as the sun was rising several men began to wash away the blood. Two of them got inside the longboat and scrubbed the sides and chine with lye soap and a wire sponge. They rinsed their work with buckets of sea water, turned the boat on its side to drain, and left it to dry. The decks too were rinsed after scrubbing and when dry looked fairly clean. Later the carpenter came aft with the Dutchman, and I heard him speaking gruffly to the steward. Within a few minutes the Dutchman came along rolling a cask of cuddy bread. Behind him was Simpson carrying two huge bottles of rum. These provisions they placed near the foremast and went to the ship's stores for more. When it seemed they had gathered enough, they covered all the items with a tarpaulin for the time when they would go into the longboat.

Obvious preparations for leaving the ship brought home to me with something of a shock the reality of my situation. The departure of the crew was no longer an operation planned for an uncertain future but a real action unfolding step by step in front of my eyes. If only two men, myself and the bo'sun, had to plan a reaction to what was happening, it would have been easier. But I had in my custody a courageous young woman, her sickly and perhaps dying father, and the unpredictable steward, a straw man at best. Though Emma had helped greatly in our scheme to survive with the ship intact, the two deficient men could prove a burden. Even so, I managed a show of composure and a high degree of interest in all the activity on board.

It wasn't long before the carpenter came on the poop and nodded to me with a half frown on his leathery face. He didn't pause even to say a word but went directly to the starboard quarterboat and appeared to be inspecting it. Then he crossed over to the portside boat and looked it over. Afterwards with a grin wide enough to show his bad teeth and with a little prancing motion in yellow trousers, he came to me.

"I need your help figurin' out somethin'," he said. "How many hands would you say can fit into the longboat? Comfortable like."

I looked over to where the boat was stowed on deck and measured the vessel with my eye before answering.

"That boat was designed for fifteen to eighteen men escaping a disaster at sea. In a pinch it could hold twenty or more."

"Oh, like sardines in a can!" Quine blurted. "That ain't no good. If we gotta go fifty miles in open ocean, we gotta have some room!"

"So you've decided to use that boat? Seems a good choice."

"We gonna put off in the longboat and one o' them here."

"You probably don't want my opinion, but I'll offer it to you anyway. I think all aboard should go in the longboat. The boat has a wide beam and will carry all of us with no problem. Not only that but she's fitted with a sail. Also if we should be picked up before landing, we can say both quarterboats were lost in the wreck."

"We mean to put off in one of them quarterboats and also the longboat," Quine muttered after some hesitation. "We can use the quarterboat to store our water and vittles. Then if we get to a barren spot on shore we got food and drink to last two or three days."

"I see the reasoning behind that and have no objection. The two boats can easily carry the whole crew and all necessary supplies."

He walked away nodding and began to talk to Sylvain as they went forward. In a few minutes they returned to the poop with a pry bar and hammer. To my dismay and disgust the big fellow got inside the portside quarterboat and began to tear it apart. He ripped away half the planking and threw it overboard. The carpenter stood close to me watching Sylvain at work. Evidently

166

he wanted me to ask why the man was destroying the boat, but feeling a surge of anger in my throat I kept my mouth shut. They wanted no lifeboat on board that my companions and I might use when the ship began to sink. Deliberately they were seeing to it that four people, or three if they planned to kill the steward, would be forced to go down with the ship and drown.

Even before Sylvain's job was done several men came aft and began to provision the remaining quarterboat. Into it they put the best food supplies the ship had to offer: bags of sweet biscuits, meat preserved in cans, kegs of water and rum, slabs of salt pork wrapped in cloth, and bags of coffee and tobacco. I was amazed when a man came with a little kerosene stove for the boat, but no lantern of any kind. On top of the food supplies they put heavy blankets to protect them from the sun and from shifting. Also the blankets could be used for warmth in the cold of night. At the time all this was going on, others were busy with the longboat preparing her for gaff-rigged sailing but also including oars.

The morning passed rapidly with the entire crew busily working but doing little to sail the ship. I could see and hear a festive atmosphere on board, a loose freedom with all the men laughing and joking and insulting one another in rough horseplay. The carpenter bustled about supervising the work, chomping on a cud of tobacco and squirting the juice wherever he went. He was clearly excited but not once did he speak to me. As far as he was concerned I was not even on the ship. Shortly before noon when I made ready to measure the sun's altitude, the men near the longboat suspended work to watch me. Ordinary sailors are mystified by the sextant and have high respect for it.

When I sang out eight bells and went below to calculate my noon- sight observation using the *Nautical Almanac*, Quine followed me and stood looking on. His behavior convinced me he couldn't trust my navigational mumbo-jumbo and had to be present to set it right even though he knew nothing of what I was doing.

"Now, Mr. Doyle," he asked petulantly, "where are we now?"

I picked up my pencil and pointed to a mark on the chart. He leaned over to get a closer look. "That is our position at this moment," I said. "It'll change as the ship moves along but that's it right now."

"But it looks awfully close to land," he exclaimed. "This squiggly line here is the Spain-Portugee shore, right?" He was tracing the shore line with a dirty thumb, leaving a greasy trail behind it.

"Yes, Spain just to the south of Portugal. Might be better for us to land in Portugal south of Lisbon and make our way to the city, but a landing in Spain would be a lot closer."

"Then let it be Spain. You say it's gonna take two more days to get there? Looks like we're close enough already."

"Don't be deceived by the chart, Mr. Quine. A sheet of paper doesn't have room for a lot of miles. Look at the scale. When we're fifty miles offshore, the ship will be approximately here." And I made a tiny mark with my pencil very close to the squiggly line.

"Hell, I could swim that distance!" he said with a laugh. "But you'll tell us when it's time to lower the boats, I'm sure."

"I will indeed, but can you tell me more about your plans? I need to know more if I'm to do my part effectively."

He looked at me askance as if sensing a plot on my part but sat down and scratched the back of his head, tilting his cap forward.

"I thought you already knew our plans, Mr. Doyle."

"I need to understand them more clearly."

"Well, I thought they was very clear. All the hands say so."

"Why did you rip planks off the quarterboat this morning?"

"I didn't. Hector Sylvain did that. You saw it. The idear is not to have a boat driftin' about with the *Windhover's* name inside o' her."

"But if the boat is on davits, how can it drift?"

"How should I know? You the one that knows these things. You the fancy officer with fancy trainin'. Anything more?"

"Yes, do you mean to leave the ship with her canvas standing?"

"We gonna leave her just like she is when hove to," he said with a show of impatience. "No man's gonna work a ship he's leavin'."

"A ship may sight her sitting in irons and wonder why she's not moving. They could find her abandoned, put a crew on board, and sail her to the nearest port as salvage. Then would come a Court of Inquiry involving a lengthy investigation. Abandoned vessels bring investigation."

I thought this might get him to admit the *Windhover* was to be scuttled and sunk, but he was too cunning even to hint at such a thing.

CHAPTER TWENTY

"We Gonna Leave This Tub"

A s we talked Quine was telling me more of his plans than I ever expected. But I suppose he wanted me to believe that every person on board was included in those plans even though I already knew he would take only the mutinous crew with him. It all began with killing the livestock, gorging themselves at a riotous party, and later carefully placing supplies in both the longboat and the quarterboat for departure.

"I can't wait to get off this tub," he was saying. "Any poor wretch that finds her can keep her. Any more questions, Mr. Doyle? All this chit-chat is takin' up too much o' my time."

"Well, I do have one more question, Mr. Quine. Do we take extra clothing with us or just what we can wear?"

"Won't be room for extra clothin'. Dress warm and put any valuables you might have in yer pockets. Also you gotta remember we gonna be shipwreck survivors, poor sailors as the newspapers will say, come away from a vessel sinkin' under our feet. So we'll have no time to gather extra clothes, jest barely time for a bit o' food and water. We gotta say the stubborn skipper went down with his ship, and the first mate jumped for a boat and missed it and got drowned."

"And the second mate?"

"Oh, him and the skipper were like two peas in a pod, and he went down with the ship too jest to be with the skipper."

"Then where does that leave me? I'm officially the second mate of the *Windhover* even though you and the crew named me skipper. Are you saying it's best not to admit I'm second mate when questioned?"

He stared at me with a look that suggested he wasn't understanding a word I was saying. Then a wide, malevolent grin turned into a burst of forced laughter and a slap on the back. He brought his ugly face close to mine and stared at me as if meeting me for the first time.

"Oh, hell!" he cried. "I done forgot all about you and yer rank! Been thinkin' all along you was jest a ordinary sailor. No, you can't be second mate when you get ashore. You gotta be somethin' else."

"What then do you suggest?"

"Why you can be a passenger or maybe the ship's doctor. Yer hands not rough enough to be a sailor, no calluses on yer fingers or thumbs from hempen rope. I'll tell ya what you gotta say as we move along. Have to tell the others too. We gotta tell jest one story and keep it straight and don't go changin' it. We gotta stick together 'fore we go our separate ways. That girl and her daddy might be a problem."

"Don't you worry about them. They will go as passengers, as indeed they are, and so will I. The three of us will say nothing to anybody unless questioned, and then all three of us are passengers."

"That could work, but you gotta understand we can't have no girl and a sickly old man slowin' us down. Anyway, you do yer part to get us there and we'll do the rest. It can't be long now, Mr. Doyle, coz the crew is gettin' restless for ground under their feet."

Already standing in an awkward and self-conscious position, Quine swung around with a gesture resembling a grotesque salute and quickly left my cabin. Whether he knew it or not, and I think maybe he did know it, our conversation had revealed more than he wanted me to know. It was all the more reason for me and my friend the bo'sun to act at the right moment. If we didn't, our lives wouldn't be worth a plug nickel.

As soon as the miserable leader of the mutineers left I made up my mind to bring the terrible time of waiting to an end as soon as possible. We were now in the afternoon of an August Wednesday. I would wait no longer than the afternoon of Friday. Regardless of the weather, calm or storm, I would tell the carpenter we had arrived at that spot on the chart, the coordinates indicating some fifty miles off the Spanish coast. I no longer cared how far our ship would be from shore. Several time-consuming delays and severe storms that threw us back hundreds of miles and the indecisiveness of the mutineers after taking over the ship had doubled the time Redstone had in mind for a crossing. So everyone on board was eager to be on land again. It was the not the location of the ship, however, that concerned me. It was the final struggle fast approaching, and the lack of firearms was foremost in my thoughts.

I had the revolver in my possession, the six-shooter filled with bullets, and was glad I had found it before some member of the crew. But I would have felt less worry if the bo'sun or even the steward also had a pistol. When no one was looking I went to Turpin's old cabin, thinking I might find a weapon there. However, when I opened the lockers I could see at a glance that someone else, surely Mr. Quine who now occupied the cabin, had rifled through the contents searching possibly for the same thing. I hoped Turpin had not owned a pistol, for if he did it would now be in the grubby hands of the carpenter. I made it a point not to sit down with him at dinner, and he didn't object.

The steward told me the men were having a bodacious feast in the fo'c's'le. A dozen chickens strangled in the morning were baked for the crew's dinner. The cook also prepared in a thick sauce an abundance of pork from the slaughtered pigs with plenty of rum to wash it down. When the men were not gulping down the food they were singing loudly off key, laughing, and shouting. It seemed obvious to me they were enjoying themselves as perhaps never before in their impoverished lives, and the celebration was coming shortly before they would be leaving the ship. Believing that every man would eat, sing, and make merry until he was too drunk even to walk, I went to Emma's cabin to explain the ugly sounds she had been hearing most of the day.

She opened her door immediately, hustled me inside, and invited me to sit. Her father stood with his back to the door, leaning against the wall, and looking through the porthole. Even though he heard me talking to his daughter, he didn't acknowledge my presence. Emma took him by his thin shoulders and stiffly turned him around as one would turn a mannequin. Only then did he speak, his eyelids fluttering as he looked upward into my face. He spoke just above a hoarse whisper.

"Ah, my dear sir! You have come to visit us! How kind of you. I do wish I could offer you a snifter of sunny brandy, but as you can see our accommodations here are rather spartan."

"Thank you for your gracious welcome, Mr. Waterhouse. I know you lack comfort here, but you'll be pleased to know that very soon now you and your daughter will see things getting better."

"I do hope so, dear sir! My poor Emmie and I have suffered greatly today because of ugly noises somewhere out there. So much bumping and scraping and screaming and screeching! Oh, my! Didn't bother Emmie at all but got on my nerves I must say."

"I must apologize for that, sir. The crew has been a bit rambunctious today, and there was little I could do about it."

"But you are the captain of this ship, my dear sir! Why did you not tell them to stop? The crew on any ship of mine would never ignore a direct order from the captain. On my ships the captain's rule is law!"

I was trying to come up with an answer when Emma took the old man's hand and gently led him to a chair in the small cabin. She turned away from him as his head fell to his chest in instant slumber and shook her head. I could see in her beautiful eyes a deep sadness that prevented me from commenting on her father's condition. In just a few days a visible and rapid degeneration had conquered the old man, leaving his loving daughter mournful and helpless. I didn't know how to answer his last remarks and could only wait for Emma to speak.

"Most of every day my dear papa stands there looking through that porthole, looking at the horizon, entranced by the sight of nothing but water and sky, driven deranged by the sameness of it all. Oh, I do wish we could be off this ship. It's becoming an agony for me."

"I'm in sympathy with all you say, dear Emma. If I had it within my power to alleviate your suffering instantly, I'm sure you know I would gladly do so. It pains me to see you suffer, but I'm here to tell you that all this will be coming to an end soon."

Gilbert Waterhouse was suddenly awake and wanted to lie down. When he stretched out a trembling hand for assistance, I quickly stood up to help him. Again he looked into my face with a strange expression on his own. His watery eyes were blinking and his thin old mouth quivered as though trying to speak. He withdrew from me with an air of offended pride and stood as tall as he could, inhaling deeply. His daughter helped him into his bunk where he lay as one dead.

"You mustn't be angry with him," she whispered, drawing closer to me. "He's unpredictable and doesn't mean half of what he says or does. I really believe I shall lose him soon."

"Oh, no, your father will live and prosper again as soon as we get him on dry land. Ashore he'll recover rapidly. It's the confinement that's getting to him, this stuffy little cabin, the constant tossing of

174

the ship, the absence of comfort. Summon courage, Emma. I know you have it."

"You are the one with courage," she answered with a fleeting smile. "You have it in such abundance you give a good part of it to me. For that I'm thankful. And of course I must thank you again for saving our lives."

I looked into her brave, soft, intensely blue eyes and found them swimming in tears. Even so, I found there a look of resolve. My heart skipped a beat as I held her close and peered into her winsome face. I remained silent for a moment to gather my wits.

"You will not want to go on deck today," I said, feeling a constriction in my throat. "Please remain below until I call for you."

"Why must I stay here? Is there danger on deck?"

"Nothing you need to fear, just some ugly behavior going on. The men believe they are nearing the time when they will leave the ship, and so all day from early morning they've been a bit boisterous."

"Yes, we heard. What were they doing up there knocking about so? Every now and then we heard a loud thump like someone falling down, and a lot of cursing and yelling. And once I heard *babies* crying!"

"Not babies, pigs. They killed the chickens and all the pigs, and even now they're having a little party with rum flowing like water. They're thinking only of themselves, but it's best for you to keep out of sight."

"I will do as you say."

"Good! Good! They're getting drunk and we don't want an incident. Now let me tell you what's in the works. Friday afternoon begins the big adventure. At that time I will tell Quine the ship is approaching fifty miles off Cadiz, Spain. I will back up my claim with these coordinates here on the chart: 36º31'37"N and 6º17'19"W. A line drawn from that mark to Cadiz will be further proof."

"Yes, I understand. I know how to read coordinates: thirty-six degrees, thirty-one minutes, thirty-seven seconds North; six degrees, seventeen minutes, nineteen seconds West. And then what?"

"If the night is calm, and I'm hoping it will be, I will order the ship hove to. The maneuver, as you must know from having sailed on your father's ships, will render the ship stationary in the water. And quite still if the weather is calm. Two boats will be slung over the side. The longboat, Quine tells me, will hold the crew and the other will carry supplies. The longboat will have a sail and will tow the quarterboat."

"That demented carpenter and his minions figured all this out?"

"They did indeed," I chuckled, "even counting the pieces of beef jerky and shots of rum for every man. It's certain the boats will go over the side, but then I begin to doubt what happens next. Will the crew remain on board until their man comes back from the hold? Or will they wait for him in the boats? If they wait for him alongside or decide to push off without him, the ship will belong to us. The bos'un and I both believe they'll sacrifice the man they send below, but of course we can't be certain. If they wait on board we have a problem."

"How so?"

"Circumstance will push the bos'un to become an actor. After he overcomes the man they send, he will have to pretend he's that man. If they call to him he will have to answer in a muffled, counterfeit voice."

"What do you think he'll say?"

"He will say his job is nearly finished but taking more time than expected. He will tell Quine to get his men on the boats in orderly fashion to prevent dropping in a panic to the boats as the ship sinks."

"But where does that leave the supposed scuttleler?"

"Yes, I forgot! He will tell them when his job is done he will jump overboard and swim to a waiting boat. Chances are they'll lose patience and shove off. That's how they'll thank the man who scuttles the ship."

"It's a clever scheme we have," said Emma softly. "I just hope it works. The bo'sun's life depends on it, and ours too I suppose."

"He will do what he has to do, I'm sure of that," said I, not willing to admit I feared they might recognize the bo'sun's distinctive voice. "It's likely they'll take to the boats and wait for the scuttler for a few minutes and shove off in a hurry if they find he's taking too long."

"And if they leave the ship, what then?"

"Then I will be calling on you to help me."

"What will I be able to do? Please tell me now if you can."

"I will, but there's a third way of overcoming that odious carpenter and getting this ship under our control."

"Really? I'm eager to hear it."

"The carpenter has only three or four cronies among the crew that he can trust. It's my belief that he and his lackeys will try to rid themselves of the others to cut the chance of being identified and arrested. Leaving the scuttled ship with the man in the hold means one less person to worry about. Four or five others could be stabbed and thrown into the sea for the sharks. I thought I might sound out the crew to find out who is really with Quine. Surely some of them don't like the idea of being in an open boat fifty miles from an unknown shore."

"I do believe Quine is capable of acting the way you describe. He places no value on human life. I do, but if we have to kill him to save our own lives, I will help you any way I can. However, any attempt to question the crew would leave you more vulnerable to

Quine than ever. Even if some of the crew agreed to come over to our side, you couldn't trust them. The carpenter would get wind of the scheme, and then what?"

"Yes, I had to put that one out of mind as too dangerous. I'm hoping the stratagem we finally hit upon will work. In the end it may not, but you and I both know we can't just stand by and do nothing."

"We won't, my dear Kevin. We won't go down without a fight. I hope what we're up against will not put us on Quine's level, but if it means fighting fire with fire, so be it."

"That carpenter," I added, "lost his calling when he became a carpenter. He was born to become a murderer. He'll take a human life without hesitation any time it's necessary. We must keep that in mind."

"Indeed we will. A very old passage in the Bible says it best: 'Never trust your enemy. Watch yourself and be on your guard against him.'"

Her blue eyes were flashing assertively. I admired her spunk profoundly. I could not have found an ally braver or stronger than she. The bo'sun hidden in the hold and subsisting on the roughest of food was ready to act and so was Emma. I hesitate to say it for all the world to hear it, but I loved her dearly. I fought against becoming too fond of her, for she belonged to a world of wealth and luxury far from my own, but I lost the battle and now admit it.

"Must you leave so soon?" she whispered, glancing at her father who was snoring in his bunk with a very audible snuffle and wheeze. "On this small ship we see so very little of you. Nothing would please me more than to have you near me more often."

"I must go. If Quine goes looking for me, I prefer that he find me in my cabin and not in yours. You must know I don't leave you willingly."

She smiled and took my hand as I opened her door. Moving closer to me, she murmured, "I know. I know. I will not see you go willingly."

I wanted to take her in my arms and kiss her tenderly but resisted the urge. It was not the time to allow heart to control head. When she turned to look again at her sleeping father, I left and closed the door. In my cabin my thoughts centered on her even when I knew they should be elsewhere. It was suppertime but I didn't feel hungry. At the cuddy table I ate only a biscuit with pork and drank my ration of rum. I was glad to go on watch shortly afterwards. Quine joined me on the poop.

He asked me how the coast would appear from the ship when she was hove to. I told him it was doubtful we would see the coast even on a very clear day, but we would fetch it with no problem if we sailed the longboat easterly. He wanted to know if the ship had an extra compass beyond the one in the binnacle. I replied any skipper worth his salt would have a backup compass, or more than one, and he could certainly have one I had seen in the captain's cabin. He seemed relieved to hear that, and I assured him that even without a compass *we* — I was careful to emphasize *we* — would have no trouble reaching the shore.

"We will not be sailing to an island," I said, "but to the mainland. If we were going to an island we could miss it depending on weather conditions, but not the mainland. And it will be the Spanish coast. Portugal lies much farther northward. Is the longboat ready?"

"Aye, she's ready all right and provisioned for a month."

"That could be a mistake, Mr. Quine. If a ship came to our rescue, and let's hope it won't happen, but if a ship picked us up they'd question how we managed to leave a sinking ship with so many supplies."

"We can say our ship went down real slow like. Now don't try to get me to dump even one little thing 'cause I won't."

"You're the leader of the operation. We have to rely on what you decide. I was just trying to help. But I do have a question. When the longboat is brought alongside, will all of us jump into her?"

"Well, why would she be alongside if everybody didn't get in?" he grumped. "Of course we all get in but there ain't gonna be no jumpin'. I don't want no pesky injuries. We'll have a ladder and maybe block and tackle to let old Mr. Waterhouse down easy and his darter too."

"Another question, will anybody be left on the ship? Will the ship be totally abandoned, or will someone you don't like be left on her?"

"Will anybody be left? What are you sayin', Mr. Doyle? What in hell put that in yer dumb Irish head?"

"I'm thinking some men want to be rid of the steward for calling bad pork good and for siding with Captain Redstone. More than once Simpson has told me the cook and some of the others hate his guts."

"I don't have no love for the steward neither, but it never entered my noggin to leave him behind. If I leave anybody, it'll be that cocky brown cook. But I'm not the kind o' skipper to leave anybody aboard a sinkin' ship. Well, it ain't gonna be sinkin' far as I know, just abandoned."

It was a slip of the tongue I pretended not to hear. I told him I had read about a crew wishing to leave their vessel. They had only two boats that would hold only part of the crew. So twelve men out of eighteen conspired to lower the boats and leave the others behind. But they had to do it with great caution because the men left behind would become desperate, jump into the boats, and fight for their lives. Anybody knows a man fearing death has the strength of two or more, and so the odds would be equal. He listened with great interest and wanted to know how the problem was solved. I told him the solution was easy. Twelve men jumped into the boats and shoved off real fast. The remaining six jumped into the water to catch them, swam as fast as they could, but the boats moved faster. Exhausted, the six sank and drowned.

"Ah, now I see!" Quine cackled with glee. "Them chaps as wanted to get away got away in a hurry. Didn't hang around none, rowed hard. And when the six jumped in the water they rowed even harder. Hah!"

Looking aloft and finding something wrong, he pretended not to hear my reply. In haste he called for two men to get into the ratlines and secure a sail that had broken away from its clew. He walked forward to the bow of the ship while I remained on the poop. When finally I left my watch and went below, the night was calm and the moon had placed a shining, silvery path upon the water. The men had stuffed their bellies with roast pork and fowl with plenty of rum, and some appeared sick. One or two fights broke out as several got drunk, but by the time I retired all was quiet. It had been a day of dramatic and memorable activity. I was glad to get under my blanket for a few hours sleep.

Chapter Twenty-One

"Get Them Boats Over The Side!"

As I lay in my bunk I thought of the bo'sun in the hold. I wondered about his comfort crammed in with the cargo and what he was thinking when he heard the shindy going on above his head. I asked myself whether the man had a timepiece. He had been there for some time now, and he could be losing track of time. What if he fell asleep and didn't hear the man who came to scuttle the ship? What if the man bearing a candle or lantern to penetrate the darkness found him and kicked him in the head before he could awaken? Ah, terrible thoughts! I had to put them out of my head. But knowing he was there in the dark and the cold with only the rats for company was not a good thought either.

By the time I began to sleep I could tell the wind was blowing freshly and would probably hold all night. On watch the next day I had up and working well all the sail the ship could handle. The *Windhover* skittered across the sea like a great bird, and I felt a spot of joy watching her perform. The joy came in spite of knowing she was moving toward a dreaded destination. Later the wind fell light and shifted to the northwest. That placed us on a broad reach with slower speed. It didn't matter because neither the carpenter nor crew seemed to care about our speed. They believed we would reach our destination the next day even if the vessel began to move at only five knots. On the chart they had seen an X close to shore, and that had convinced them.

When the afternoon came with bright skies turning blue-yellow, the men got the longboat ready to swing over the side. Tackle was made ready to lift the boat from her chocks. Another set of block and tackle would lower her to the water. These preparations made it clear to me they were eager to depart. It would be the climax of a long party lasting two days and supplying them with all the food and drink their bellies could hold. The carpenter told me in a tone of disgust that several of the men had eaten too much and had made a mess of their berths in the fo'c's'le. Yellow puke, he said, was all over and he made the steward clean it up. All day the men ate prodigiously but went easy on the rum.

Toward evening we sighted three ships. One was moving in a northerly direction and the other two sou'easterly. Their presence convinced Quine that we were nearing the coast. Then a seabird skimmed across the waves and that convinced him even more.

"I can't believe it!" he said with some excitement. "But we gonna be there soon! I was thinkin' it wouldn't never come. Them two ships look to be headin' for Gibraltar, other for Lisbon. Me and my men can't wait to get them boats over the side."

I assured him we would be there on the morrow, barring some unforeseen obstacle. That evening I spoke briefly with Emma, asking about her father. Sadly she reported he was no better, seemed to be steadily losing his grip on reality. I tried to comfort her in a few words by saying it was perhaps the way he had chosen to handle distress. She said nothing but I could tell by the look on her sad, expressive face that it was something more. Again I cautioned her not to show herself on deck. A night of boisterous and bawdy celebration had already begun.

The men were sky-larking on deck and in the fo'c's'le, slowly getting drunk, and making a lot of noise. Joshua Haythorne, who often spent time at the wheel, had found a concertina and was passionately squeezing it to make a sound that imitated music at times. Several sailors were dancing, or trying to dance, to the erratic, squawk-box music. All were laughing and hooting and having a good time. Their fun would have been innocent enough had they been ordinary sailors on a disciplined ship instead of unrestrained mutineers at liberty to act as they pleased. So the party went on and on until one by one the men dropped from exhaustion or excess or both. Shortly after 0200 all was silent.

Once speaking with Emma she had told me she knew how to steer a ship. At the time I didn't think much about it but now began to see how that ability might help us when we began to act. I had to be certain I had heard her correctly, and so I asked her bluntly during our brief conversation whether she could steer. Her answer was a curt yes. I waited a moment for her to say more, but she didn't. I really needed to know how much experience she had, and so ventured another question.

"You say yes because you'll do whatever you can if I ask you to steer the ship, or is it more than that? It's important for me to know."

"I say yes because I really understand how to steer, how to read the compass, how to keep the vessel on course with all sails working."

"Where did you learn all that?"

"I learned on a voyage to the Cape of Good Hope. I watched the man at the wheel like a hawk and began to memorize every move he made according to the movement of the ship. I asked the captain if he would let me steer on a good day. The vessel belonged to my father, and so he couldn't readily refuse. We treated the lessons as a joke. He would give me orders, and I would steer accordingly."

"If I gave you an order to put the helm to starboard, you would pull the spokes in which direction?"

"To the left," she answered with no hesitation. "In nautical language, to port." She spoke the additional remark jauntily.

"If I called out 'hard over' what would you do?"

"With the wind to starboard, I would turn the wheel all the way to the left, thus hard over. I know the terms, I can steer."

I believed her and I told her that if we were lucky enough to gain control of the ship after the crew departed, her role as helmswoman would be of utmost importance. When she asked me why, I said with her at the wheel three men could work the ship instead of only two. She smiled at that, touched my arm to show gratitude, and drew herself up in a mockingly arrogant pose to show how important she was feeling. I was beginning to love that woman, but I liked her very much too. Even facing a situation that could be deadly, her sense of humor held firm. She was smart, brave, competent, resolute, warm, and funny.

Friday came with most of the men sleeping off the noisy festivities of Thursday night. The day was sunny and a breeze came from the south with just enough strength to keep our sails working. Shipboard discipline had disappeared and regular watches abandoned. Now that the voyage was nearing its end, Quine was markedly distrustful of me and was nervously pacing the deck when he should have been sleeping. He looked at the compass, stared at the water to guess the ship's speed, stood with me on the poop at times, and at other times went to the fo'c's'le to be with the crew. Often I saw him talking with men I deemed his inner circle, the ones he trusted most. He said nothing of Gilbert and Emma Waterhouse. It was as if he had forgotten their existence.

I couldn't help but notice, as the day wore on, that he didn't want to be in my company. Any time I appeared forward of the poop he went aft, and when I approached the poop he had business elsewhere. I took that as proof he had no intention of taking us with him but nonetheless remained calm and methodical in my duties. The weather by noon was hotter than any day of the entire voyage. The sun beating down on the deck melted the tar between the wooden seams. It stuck to my boots as I made my rounds, and

I could smell its pungent odor. Even the paint work of the ship seemed to fry in the sun and gave off a stink. But the greenish water looked cool, and the sky was intensely blue.

The crew was quiet as they sailed the ship. In the rigging I heard no singing of sea chanties and very little chatter. At intervals a man would climb to the top of the main mast and scan the horizon while those on deck watched anxiously for a sign. The carpenter was constantly gazing around the horizon, looking for a tiny black dot that might be a ship, and twice in half an hour he checked the compass. We were under plain sail, and the ship appeared to be making five knots even though I logged it as seven. When I came with my sextant to take sights, most of the men gathered around with curious looks. I could tell they were eager to learn whether our journey would soon end. To please them I worked out my calculation in their presence. Then unfolding the chart I put my finger on the spot we were supposed to have reached.

"Put a mark there with yer pencil," said Eddie Calvert. "Then all us can have a good look. You say it's fifty miles from the coast?"

"Give or take a mile or two either way," I answered. "And if the wind holds we'll soon be closing in on the mark and ready to heave to."

"When we stop she'll look to be sailing if a vessel sights her," said the carpenter, "but she'll be in irons and makin' no headway."

I went below to my cabin and seeing the steward in the pantry, I asked him to bring me a couple of biscuits and some sherry. I wasn't hungry but had something to say to him. If Quine saw him come to my cabin with a tray in his hand, he would suspect nothing. Simpson put the tray down and was about to leave when I asked a question of him that made the poor man turn more pale than usual.

"Do you want to go on living?" I said to him, looking him straight in the eye. "I'm assuming you do. So listen to me carefully. Near sunset the crew is planning to leave the ship in two boats. They will scuttle the ship first. Exactly how I don't know, either by drilling holes in the hull or setting a fire to make her sink. They will not be taking us with them."

"Oh my God! Oh my God!" he muttered, wringing his hands. "Are we gonna be left on board to go down with the ship?"

"That is their intention. But the bo'sun is in the hold ready to kill or knock unconscious the man who goes to scuttle the ship."

"But how can that be? Everybody knows the bo'sun fell overboard a few days ago. I heard it from the cook, and people are talking."

"It's good they are because it means they really believe he went to Davy Jones's locker. He didn't. He's in the hold and ready to act, and it's time for us to do the same. If we want to save our lives, we have to make sure no man gets on board again after dropping to the boats. If any man tries we must hit hard. If we are defeated we are dead. If we manage to defeat them, we own the ship and go on living."

"You can count on me to do my best, sir, but you'll have to tell me what to do. I never was in a fight in all my life, sir. I'm afraid."

"You'll have to cram your fears into a bottle and cork it, Simpson. If you show cowardice, if you run and refuse to fight, if you do not do as I tell you, then you must remember this one thing — I'll put a bullet in your brain. I'll kill you for betraying us, for not helping."

"You have a pistol, sir? A pistol with bullets? What can I use?"

"The first belaying pin you can get your hands on. The ship has plenty. Now go about your work as usual but say nothing. If you reveal anything I've said to you here, you're a dead man."

He went away pale as a ghost with thin shoulders trembling. The man had no courage whatever, but good eating had made him strong again. I couldn't be sure what he would do when the time came, and yet I know the meek can be formidable antagonists. Fear can render a weak person desperate, and the frenzy created by fear can be daunting. Fighting for his life, the steward might surprise me. I returned to the poop sooner than usual because I wanted to keep a close eye on what the crew was doing. I found the breeze diminishing.

The hot blue sky was promising calm. In the distance the green water looked glassy. Lying close to the mild breeze, we made no progress at all. Calm would certainly make lowering the boats and putting off easier, but it also meant the longboat would not be able to move under sail. Also I wouldn't be able to swing the yards around to get the *Windhover* underway as soon as the men were off her. Then it occurred to me that the promise of calm could mean a radical change in the weather, the well-known calm before a storm. That thought unnerved me, for if we were in for a storm the men would have to postpone their plans for the time being and stay on the ship. And the bo'sun could die of privation.

At the appointed hour the crew went to dinner in the fo'c's'le, and Quine apparently joined them. I glanced through the skylight and saw Emma Waterhouse looking up at me. I leaned forward and spoke to her just loud enough to be heard.

"Keep a stiff upper lip," I said, mimicking a British accent to keep my heavy message light. "Whatever is going to happen will happen soon. Be ready to act when I give the signal."

"I'm ready," she answered, her face showing she got the humor of my phony accent. "I shall be ready, my lord, at a moment's notice!"

"Remain in your cabin. Don't let any of the men see you. If Quine or the cook should happen to see you, they might try to force you to go along with them in the boats. Be vigilant, take care."

"I will stay out of sight. The steward will give me a little brandy for Papa. He isn't well, Kevin. He's very weak and rambles in his talk."

She went into the pantry, was given a tumbler of brandy, and returned to her cabin to lock the door. The steward came under the skylight to tell me he would fight for his life not because he valued himself all that much, but because his wife and five children needed him.

"Just remember three things," I said to him. "One, move quickly; two, strike as hard as you can; and three, stay away from the booze. Don't drink to bolster your nerve, man. It won't work. If I find you drunk, I'll let the crew drown you."

He nodded without saying a word and went back to his pantry. The men were spending far more time at table than usual and were quieter than usual. That caused me to wonder whether some had not already gone to the hold to scuttle the ship. Maybe they would bore holes after all, half a dozen with an auger. It would take a long time for the ship to fill with enough water to take her down, and they could be off as soon as she began to show signs of settling and listing. If the wind were to come up strong, however, they might have to stay on the ship and would not want her less than seaworthy.

A seaman came aft — I think he was Ben Webster — to relieve the man at the wheel. Finding the ship sitting like a duck in a mill pond, he locked the wheel in position, pulled out a pipe, sat down on the taffrail, and began to smoke. I didn't bother to go over to converse with him, and shortly afterwards Quine came along the main deck to the poop.

"Looks like a dead calm," he said in a monotone, "and hotter than hell. It's getting into late summer, so why is it so goddamn hot?"

"Beats me," I answered. "Weather unpredictable. Not even the best of us knows what the next day will bring. We just have to guess. Are you planning to leave the ship standing as she is, or take in sail?

"I dunno. I'm impatient with details, y' know. You have something in mind?" He was looking aloft, deliberately feigning indifference.

"I would shorten sail, snug her down."

"Why?" he demanded.

"Should another ship find her, it would look like we had to abandon her in the middle of a storm."

"Something can be said for that," Quine replied.

"Then I should tell the men to shorten sail?"

"Sure. Why not?" he said with an odd grin I tried to ignore.

I wanted to snug down as much sail as I could while I had men to do it. So I called out, "All hands! Shorten sail!"

Instead of springing aloft to obey the order, the men near the fo'c's'le roared with laughter. One glance at Quine snickering and grinning let me know how foolish the order sounded. What was it to any of them whether the ship sank with sails full or furled? They laughed and laughed, shaking their heads in high amusement. They knew the *Windhover* was doomed to sink; the joke was on me.

CHAPTER TWENTY-TWO

Suddenly He Sprang Upon Me

W hile I could have gone below to get away from the derision, I sat on my haunches in the shade and smoked my pipe as calmly as I could. The sun was unrelenting in a cloudless sky. The sea was empty and glassy. Our perky ship sat patiently as if waiting for something to happen. Carefully I looked at her sails, her slender masts, her scrubbed decks, and her gleaming brasswork. I concluded the crime against her the gang intended to commit was beyond belief. How could anyone in his right mind sink so beautiful a vessel, and with people aboard to go down with her? Could they not have pity on a young woman with her life ahead of her? Or upon an old man already close to death? And how could they murder another sailor, one of their own, who had done them no harm? How could any sailor loving ships sink the *Windhover*?

Near 1800 the carpenter ordered his men to get the longboat ready for launching. As he was calling out to them I saw cat's paws on the water, and the sky to the southwest was turning a slightly different shade. It meant to a sailor's eye that a breeze, possibly a strong one, was coming up to reach us soon. The men busily obeying Quine's order didn't appear to notice. Before their job was done a gentle wind had touched the ship and taken her aback. The carpenter seeing this quickly ordered the vessel hove to with her bow to the southwest. Then he went to the wheel, lashed it, and went forward to supervise the work of getting the boats off the deck and down to the water.

I took up my station on the starboard side of the poop and remained there to see as much as I could of what the crew was doing. Carefully I looked at each person and found them all there, including the cook and even his helper. That let me know they had sent no person into the hold. So I had to watch closely to determine when someone was missing. Since they knew they had little or no twilight to rely upon, the men worked hard at getting the longboat from her chocks and over the bulwarks. It took them only half an hour to attach the yardarm tackles and lower the boat gently to the water. Two men made her fast alongside.

"Now get the quarterboat over the side!" I heard a man yell.

I think it was the Dutchman's baritone voice, and I wondered why the carpenter wasn't giving the orders. The operation was repeated with the smaller boat. Tightly packed with provisions, three men lowered it to the water. Then of a sudden my vigilant eyes told me the carpenter was missing. I looked for him, even peering into the boats alongside and through the skylight of the cuddy. He was nowhere to be found.

I had to admit beyond a doubt that he had left the deck to scuttle the ship. All along he himself had been planning to do the job. Not once had I thought he would be the man to set fire to the ship or bore the holes. And the bo'sun was there to kill him! Oh my God! If Burdick killed Quine, nothing good would come of it. He was the leader of the mutinous gang, and if he didn't return in the allotted time they would go in search of him. Surely they wouldn't quit the ship without him.

Discovering the carpenter was not among the men ready to drop into the boats, was perhaps engaged in a deadly struggle with the bo'sun below, hit me like a rabbit punch to the back of my head. My vision blurred and I felt dizzy. My lips were parched and my mouth dry as a desert. My throat burned when I tried to swallow. Beads of sweat stood on my face, and I bit my lip in supreme anxiety.

It was all I could do to resist finding a place to slump into apathetic torpor. With effort I summoned my strength to stand and wait. For what I didn't know.

Even though their leader wasn't there to supervise them, the men went about provisioning and launching the boats efficiently. It was a festive scene with them laughing and passing jokes, whistling, and humming a tune. All of them seemed excited and happy that at long last they would be leaving the scene where they had endured misery and where murderous events had taken place. I got the impression they were viewing their departure almost as a holiday to celebrate.

The sun was sinking faster than they wanted, and so they worked to prepare the boats as fast as they could. I doubt that any of them noticed a shadowy disturbance on the horizon. But I did, and I hoped it was a good stiff breeze that would hit us in time for me to get the ship out of irons and moving again as soon as they departed. Yet that couldn't be done without the bo'sun's help, and I kept wondering what had happened. Was Quine lying dead somewhere in the hold with a split skull? Or had the bo'sun — I shuddered at the thought — become the victim?

The minutes went by at a snail's pace. Five, ten, twenty came and went. The sound of men laughing and joking, sky-larking as sailors say, grew dim in my ears. The sun now sat like a red-hot cauldron on the water, turning it blood red and purple in places. Though we still lay in a sizzling calm, a wandering breeze was beginning to rustle the sails. Some of the men were now going over the side, leaving three or four on deck near the gangway. They glanced at me as they went laughing over the bulwarks but said nothing. I stood alone only a few feet from them.

Then of a sudden the carpenter came from the galley, striding with long steps, and went quickly to the launch site. I had thought I would never see him again, and the sight of the man, robust but favoring his left leg, startled me more than I'm willing to admit.

"Hop into the boats, mates! Look alive! Move it!" he cried. And quickly the men on deck obeyed.

One after another they dropped like stones into the longboat, the carpenter going last. The boat's painter was tied to a chainplate, and quickly they cast it off. Within a few minutes the longboat with the quarterboat in tow had moved away several hundred yards from the *Windhover's* hull. The men in the boats sat staring at the ship as if waiting for something to happen. Then as the orange sun was drowned by the purple sea, darkness came on fast to obscure them.

I stood as one made of salt, too amazed at what I was seeing even to move. When I saw the carpenter on deck again, I concluded immediately that he had killed the bo'sun. Yet his behavior contradicted that supposition. If indeed he had killed Burdick, would he have left the ship without killing me too? What, then, was the meaning of it all? Had the bo'sun *died* during his stay in the hold? Though the thought upset me terribly, it had to be true. Burdick lay dead and hidden when Quine entered the hold, and the carpenter had performed his task of scuttling the ship without hindrance. So while I stood there with awful thoughts running through my skull, a fire was raging or water was pouring into the hold. The sea without hesitation would be taking our vessel.

In near panic I flung myself off the poop and began to shout at the top of my lungs down the forescuttle.

"Below there! Hey! Hey! Below there! Can anyone hear me?"

I got no answer.

"Below there! Bo'sun! Burdick! Burdick, can you hear me?"

From somewhere in the bowels of the ship I heard a thumping sound like a wooden mallet against wood.

"Anyone there?" I shouted for the third time. "Hey!"

I paused to listen and heard nothing. Then as I was about to shout again, I heard movement in the hold and a face all black and greasy appeared under the forescuttle. I had to take a second look to identify that black face in darkness, but to my great relief it was the bo'sun's.

"Did them sons o' bar hags finally leave?" he calmly asked.

"Oh, my God, man! What happened to you? What happened down there?" Though he was deadly calm, I was numb with excitement.

"Nothin' much. I been pluggin' them leaks or holes or whatever you wanna call 'em. Got two done already and gotta go lookin' for the third. Don't believe there's more than three. Talk later."

And with that he moved back into the gloom. I now began to understand what might have happened there in the dark and dank hold but would have to wait to find out for sure. I heard the bo'sun hammering away at the last of the leaks and waited impatiently. I was thinking the mutineers might have forgotten something important and would return to the ship to get it. They could easily climb up the lines that had lowered the boats and be on deck in minutes.

Then as I was about to cry out to the bo'sun for help in removing the launch lines, he suddenly appeared in the hatchway.

"Did you get the job done?" I asked.

"Aye, aye, sir! She's tight as a coconut!"

"Good, good! Now get up here real fast and help me get the ship underway. We have a breeze that'll help us. Them savages are somewhere close by waiting to see the ship settle, convinced she'll sink."

I ran to the bulwarks to pull the launching lines up but found them too heavy for one man. Then as I struggled Burdick began to pull and we got them up and on deck. I paused for a minute or two to look at the boats and the men in them, but all I could see in the gathering darkness was the mast of the longboat and some attempt to get a sail up. The two boats lay side by side, and the men appeared to be eating and drinking and chatting among themselves as they waited.

"We have to move it, Mr. Doyle," the bo'sun said in a tone of urgency. "Time's very important. How many hands we got?"

"Three. You, me, and the steward. And we have Miss Waterhouse to steer our ship when needed."

"Our ship! That warms me heart!" the bo'sun cried. "Let's make haste to get her away from them apes in the boats and keep her our'n!"

I called the steward and Emma in one breath, directing one to the poop and the other to the wheel. Both showed themselves on deck almost instantly, and both were happy to hear all the men we had feared for too many weeks were off the ship.

"Put the wheel to starboard," I called over the breeze to her.

Quickly she cast off the lashing and expertly ran the wheel over to stop exactly where needed. The *Windhover*, sensitive to the helm in any position, responded as though alive and slowly began to move. The topsail, top-gallant, and royal yards came round with the main yard, swinging to fill the sails, and the ship moved faster.

Bracing myself as I stood to windward to scan the water where the lifeboats had been, I caught a glimpse of men in the quarterboat rowing hard to reach us. I could hear the grinding of the oars in the oarlocks, the sloshing of the water, and the cries of men in the longboat urging the quarterboat men to overtake us. The carpenter had seen three men on our ship, and that convinced him a trick was afoot to baffle their scheme. He knew Gilbert Waterhouse was too sick to leave his cabin, and so a third man, whoever he was, meant a mighty effort was in motion to save the ship and get her sailing.

On the longboat they got the mast up in record time and bent on the sail. If they could catch the wind just right, they could reach the *Windhover* at about the same time as the quarterboat and grab a chainplate to climb aboard.

"If they board this ship, they do it over my dead body!" cried the bo'sun. "We must work like a dozen men to be sure it don't happen."

"Steward!" I shouted. "Whip out a belaying pin and stand by to use it on the first head that comes within reach. Emma, steady as she goes! We don't want the wind too far aft!"

We positioned ourselves near the main and lesser shrouds, knowing the enemy would climb aboard from the chainplates. Each of us had a heavy belaying pin ready to swing with force against the first head we saw. As we waited I drew out my pistol and made ready to shoot Quine. I could hear him cursing us furiously and knew he was nearby. Then it occurred to me that none of them had a firearm. So instead of shooting the man and having his followers scurry away to tell anyone who would listen that their leader was killed in cold blood, I decided to wait until we could take them all one by one.

The quarterboat came alongside, bumping hard against the hull. A man quickly grabbed one of the ship's chainplates, passed the painter around it, and made the boat fast. Then several men with knives in their mouths like the pirates of old came clambering up the hull. So close they were I could identify their faces. I looked for the carpenter but didn't see him. Then suddenly he sprang across the bulwark and to the deck exactly where I stood. With a knife that must have come from the ship's galley and cursing fiercely, he lunged at my throat. For a moment he was so close I could feel his spittle on my face and smell his foul breath. As he threw me to the deck, I had no time to use the belaying pin or the pistol in my waistband. Then as Quine drew back to plunge the knife into my neck or chest, I heard a loud whack like wood on wood. My assailant staggered up, spun around, and fell overboard.

He screamed a cry of agony as loud as any I've ever heard, and hitting the water with a hefty splash sank rapidly. Eighty-five silver dollars hidden in a pocket might have dragged him down. Then as the steward moved away to use his weapon on another man, the huge figure of Sylvain caught my eye. He held a shroud tight in his big hands and was ready to spring upon me. I swung the belaying pin and missed his head. He laughed and cried, "c'mon little man, show me somethin'!" I swung again, striking his shoulder and right arm. He let go the shroud, muttered a jumble of curse words, reeled backwards, and toppled into the sea. I heard a loud groan as he fell and a heavy splash when he hit the water. I couldn't tell whether he tried to swim or sank.

The bo'sun had swung his deadly belaying pin at Otis Bearclaw just as the man's enormous head appeared above the bulwarks. With one blow the head exploded like a melon, and a gush of blood stung the face of the bo'sun. Bearclaw fell dead or dying to lie in the boat alongside. The steward to my surprise was fighting like a madman. With a knife I didn't even know he had, he stabbed the Dutchman deep in the belly. Dazed but not dead, the man hung over the bulwarks with head and arms hanging downward toward the water. With a loud groan and writhing hideously with the knife still in his guts, he dropped to the water, hit the side of the quarterboat, and silently slipped under the surface of the sea.

Of the five who had climbed the hull, only Cookie remained alive. He was agile as a squirrel, quick and cunning. In seconds he was behind the bo'sun ready to stab him in the neck. I fired my pistol to stop him but missed. The bo'sun swung around and struck him with the belaying pin. It made a sound like the one that saved me, and the knife went flying. The steward, seeing his old enemy sprawled on the bulwarks, grabbed him by the feet and yanked him to the deck. The fall appeared to have broken his back, for he lay there groaning and motionless. The steward stood over him ready to kill him, ready at last to taste revenge.

"Don't do it, Simpson!" I shouted. "Don't kill him! We may have use for him later. The man's a scoundrel but knows how to cook."

We tied him to the rail and left him there looking at us aghast as if we were strangers he had never seen before. The breeze was up enough to fill the sails and give them power, and the *Windhover* responded admirably with Emma at the helm. The quarterboat, now vacant except for Bearclaw's body, wobbled and splashed alongside as the ship moved into her traces and began to heel. Astern I stared into the gloom hoping to see the longboat. When I could see nothing but darkness, I fetched the night-glass and gazed through it. With its aid I was able to catch a dim outline of a small sail some distance from us. Those in the longboat were no longer a threat to our safety and that of the ship.

"Bo'sun!" I shouted. "Come here, please. Our helmswoman wishes to check on her father, and I want to go with her. Tell the steward to break open some brandy and adorn the cuddy table with it. As soon as we know Gilbert Waterhouse is all right, we celebrate."

"Beggin' yer pardon, sir, but it's best we postpone any celebratin' till we know we have full control of this here ship. There's work to be done on deck. I say shorten sail while the wind's light."

"If the steward will take the wheel," I said, "you and I can do it."

"Let's put Cookie on his feet," replied the bo'sun, "and see if he's willin' to help. Hey, Simpson! Can you steer?"

"No, sir," the man responded. "I can't. I don't know how."

"Damn it!" Burdick exclaimed. "I'd rather be a miserable landlubber than a no-good steward that can't do nothin'!"

"I must differ with you there, my friend!" I cried. "That man saved my life! He fought like a tiger and took out two of the four."

"Oh, then I stands corrected," said the bo'sun hoarsely. "He's as good a man as any of us, and I won't bad mouth him no more."

"Take hold of these spokes and look at the card, Mr. Simpson," I urged. "Do you see how the compass card points southeast? If the letters swing to the left of the lubber line, turn the wheel to the left until S.E. comes to the mark again. If S.E. goes to the right, shove the spokes to the right. That's all there is to it. Do you understand?"

"I think so, sir. I'll give it a try."

"Just keep your eye on the card. Don't let them letters get away from you. If you do, you'll have men climbing on board again."

I left him clinging to the wheel and staring at the compass, his eyes full of wonder and bulging. With the bo'sun I went along the main deck to where we had left the cook. Though he lay like a sack of grain against the rail, his wits had returned and he was cursing a blue streak.

"Go ahead and kill me you sons o' bitches! Kill me, goddamn it, and get it over with! But before you do maybe you can loosen this here rope so I can breathe again. It's too goddamn tight!"

He was a feisty little hoodlum even in defeat, and he was having his say. For a moment I rather admired his grit. He was certain we had come to kill him but wasn't begging for mercy. All he wanted was a little comfort before we shot him between his little black eyes.

"How in hell you get the idear in that l'il brown skull o' yours we come to kill ya?" cried the bo'sun in a voice hoarse with thunder. "Don't wiggle yer jaw whinin' about breath, ya little no-good bastard. You ain't gonna have none in five minutes!"

"Then do it, goddamn it, and be damned! What made you come over to Doyle's side anyway? We thought you was with us! Well, I remember Quine sayin' he didn't trust ya much, but I thought you was all right. Now you gonna kill me. So do it!"

"Tossin' you overboard is too good fer the likes o' you!" retorted the bo'sun. What you need is a good whuppin'! Just wish I had a good bullwhip to flog ya. Then arterwards I would . . . ah, I won't say it."

"We'll spare your life, Cookie," I said with more calm, "if you agree to help us run the ship and do some cooking on the side. But understand we'll keep an eye on you. If you get out of line even by an inch, you die."

"Well, Mr. Doyle," he answered in a softer tone, "I didn't belong to that bunch 'cause a cook ain't a sailor. And that bastard carpenter beat fiery hell outta me, and when I complained the crew beat me. So to hell with all of 'em. I can be with you the same as I was with them. You won't get no trouble outta me. I spent all my angers against Redstone and Turpin and that sneaky steward and later that bastard Quine."

"Do you think he can be trusted, Mr. Doyle?" asked Burdick, playing something of a role. "He's got a blood-thirsty look on that ugly copper face o' his, and them little beady eyes are full o' murder."

"Loosen the goddamn rope and let me breathe, and I'll be as good a friend to you, bo'sun, as you ever had. You gonna eat good too!"

"He was Quine's chief mate, Mr. Doyle. We can't trust him. Let's heave him. Or maybe leave him here a few hours 'fore we decide."

"Let's give him a try, Mr. Burdick," I said at last. "If we ever have cause to suspect he's not with us, then overboard he goes."

"You can trust me, Mr. Doyle, I swear! I'll cook for ya and do what I can to work the ship. I'd rather be here than in the longboat. Them guys ain't never gonna make it to any kind o' shore."

We hoisted Cookie to his feet and sent him off to the galley. Burdick hadn't eaten a decent meal in days and was half starved. Cookie would prepare us a fine meal. To the bo'sun I said we needed to get the quarterboat on deck because Quine had made its duplicate useless. With some effort we managed to heave Bearclaw into the sea and drop the heavy boat into its davits. We managed also to save its food and water, items too precious to lose though some were soiled with blood.

CHAPTER TWENTY-THREE

Low Glass and Lightning

*A*ll this time the steward was steering the boat and doing a good job of it. My papa often told me that when a man takes on a job he can't refuse, he finds a way to do it. That was Simpson. I went over and spoke briefly with him. In the light of the binnacle I complimented his newly acquired skill and thanked him for bravely saving my life. He responded with a broad smile and a nod of the head. I couldn't recall having seen him smile at any time since our long voyage began. The hour was very late, but I told him all on board our ship intended to eat a sumptuous supper prepared by Cookie. Afterwards he would be relieved to eat also and rest. He was amazed to hear he would be working again with Cookie but seemed free of fear. I believed the man had become a man.

I went to the Waterhouse cabin to inform them we would be eating a belated supper in one hour. Immediately Emma opened the door and said to me in that soft and feminine voice of hers that her father had asked for food earlier but was now sleeping. I apologized, saying the events of the evening had required a necessary postponement of supper, but now with the steward at the wheel we could eat a fine repast in peace. She asked incredulously how in the world could we enjoy "a fine repast" with no cook on board. That's when I told her about Cookie and assured her he would be working for us and with us.

The cook found an abundance of meat in the galley and gave us big chunks of well-prepared roast pork along with good wine. At the cuddy table three tired and hungry people ate well, and then we called the steward to table after Emma volunteered to relieve him at the wheel. I urged him to eat all his belly could hold, and he did. Then as the bo'sun relieved Emma at the wheel I called in Cookie and invited him to eat. It was a gesture he had not expected at all, and I could tell he was pleased to be accepted as an equal. I was thinking if we treated the feisty little man kindly, we would get no trouble from him. I'm happy to report that we didn't. He proved to be a valuable member of our small crew and worked as hard to save the ship as any of us.

After supper I mentioned to the bo'sun that because the glass was standing at the low mark, we should try to get in all the sail we could before a blow came. With Emma again at the wheel, the two of us worked as hard and as fast as we could to clew up the three royals. Then later we doused the mizzen-royal and the main-royal and went on to reef the top-gallant sails, jibs, and staysails. Afterwards, if we had any strength at all left, we would have to furl and snug the mainsail. I knew the steward would be no good attempting to work aloft, and so I asked him to help Cookie clean the galley and get things back to normal there.

He hesitated, saying Cookie hated him and would try to kill him. Then he drew in his breath, righted his shoulders, mumbled something like "no matter," and did as he was told. Because our situation required it, they worked together in that tiny space without conflict and quickly learned to get along with each other. The slaughtered pigs had left a terrible mess, and they had to decide whether to dump all the meat or keep what didn't seem spoiled. I learned later they threw two dead pigs and three fowls overboard and cleaned the entire galley with lye.

As we worked aloft Burdick and I had a chance to talk. I asked him to tell me exactly what went on in the hold. With no pause in the work we had to do he gave me a full explanation.

"Well, as you know, I went down there with an iron bar intendin' to split the skull o' the first sun o' gun that come near me. But then I got to thinkin' it might not be a good idear to do that 'cause the gang might take it into their head to wait for him. Then if he didn't show, they might go lookin' for him and find him dead and kill me dead. So I decided to keep out of sight and plug up any holes he bored after he left."

"But how did you know they would bore holes in the hull after they floated the idea of setting fire to the piano crates?"

"I told myself they abandoned the fire idear as too dangerous. The ship could go up like tinder, and some other vessel might see the fire. So a man would come with an auger and bore half a dozen holes and leave. Well, he came and bored only three and soon as he left, I plugged all three to make this little ship tight as a fiddle."

"But how? What did you use to fill the holes, and will it stay there or eventually wash out? Where did you find it? And the hammer for pounding. Where did you get a hammer?"

"I had my knife with me and a box o' matches and lit a small piece of packin' material for a flare and found a broomstick. So all I had to do was break the stick, whittle the ends, and pound away."

"And what did you use to pound away? Ah, don't tell me. The bar!"

"The end o' that bar made as good a hammer as you'd ever want. I see the carpenter workin' away at borin' a hole. Then the water comes rushin' in, and he goes and bores another hole and the water rushes in. Then he bores a third hole and tosses his candle aside and scampers outta there when the water's rushin' through all three holes."

"And then you went to work in the dark?"

"No darkness at all, plenty o' light! The crazy coot tossed away his candle scurryin' outta there like a jack rabbit. I picked it up still burnin' and plugged two of them holes about as quick as it took him to get on deck. Then as you know I went for the third."

I roared with laughter and we shook hands warmly. Even now years later I think about the bo'sun and our conversation aloft in the dead of night among the sails. The immense height, for example, and the swinging of the masts back and forth and us on the top. And looking down at the ship in black water with traces of phosphorescence. I can remember the black sky merging and mingling with the black water. Then glancing at the horizon, we could see a faint play of lightning that told us a change in the weather was coming.

From the towering height of the fore-royal masthead I could see the lightning growing more vivid on the horizon. It was coming not in horizontal flashes as earlier, but as jagged blue bolts racing downward to the sea against the dark sky. The wind was increasing slightly but remained a breeze to push the ship forward with almost no sound except for the bow wave. The stars were high in the sky and pale, unlike some nights at sea when they appear so close you feel you can reach up and touch them. When we eventually reached the deck to sprawl against the rail and rest, I was far more scant of breath than the bo'sun. But I was glad we had managed to shorten sail. Now if a gale came, as the glass appeared to promise, we would be ready for it.

All the time we were handing sails aloft Emma was at the wheel expertly steering the ship to maintain a steady speed in light air. Though not fully recovered from the heavy work we had just completed, I went to her and expressed my thanks for all the help she was giving us. She listened to every word, but when I resorted to a tiny bit of flattery to show my appreciation, she stopped me in my tracks.

"I want you to forget all about my gender, Skipper, and view me as an able-bodied member of your crew. I don't wish to be treated as different from the other hands. You can't afford to make a small crew smaller, and so I hope you realize you can't do without me"

Her keen intelligence was at work again, and all I could do was stammer how right she was. The bo'sun stood by smiling from ear to ear as if to say, "She really laid one on ya there, fella!" He liked her too.

"Look at the lightning over there!" she was saying. "We'll get some wind pretty soon. And I'm sailor enough to know our masts would come tumbling down in high winds with all that sail we had up. You and Mr. Burdick have saved the ship. I stood here doing nothing while you two worked as hard as a dozen men and probably more efficiently."

"I will not disagree with you, my lady," I said to her as gallantly as I could. "I know the ship needs watching, and you have the eyes for it. So stay longer if you wish. I'll go to your cabin and check on your father."

I went below and opened the cabin door just wide enough to see the old gentleman sleeping. His daughter had already lit the lamp, and it shed a faint light in the room. Closing the door gently so as not to wake him, I went into the pantry for a bottle of sherry and some biscuits.

"Your father is sleeping soundly," I said, "and so you need have no worry concerning him. I know you must be tired. So I've found a little treat for you, some wine and biscuits."

She thanked me, and I went forward to help the bo'sun stow more sail. I crawled out on the long bowsprit, the ship splitting the black water below me, and gave the man a hand to stow the jibs. Then we climbed the ratlines to the fore-topsail yard and worked away at reefing the big sail. In the dead of night, two men somehow did the work of a dozen. I was proud of what we had accomplished. We had reefed two of the three topsails, stowed the three jibs, the three royals, two top-gallant sails, and the staysails. And we had done it all in heavy darkness which made our work much harder than in daylight. Exhausted, we made our way aft and squatted near the wheel. Emma had been steering for some time now and was proving herself well qualified for the task. It seemed to me as I looked at her that she and the ship had formed a special bond. A beautiful girl and a beautiful ship, what more to say?

"Go below now, both of you," she insisted, "and get some sleep. I'll keep watch and call you if something out of the ordinary happens."

"Did you hear that, bo'sun? This young woman wants us to turn in. She tells me she'll keep watch and call us if a gale smacks the ship."

"I called her a wonder a while back," said the bo'sun, "and I'll say it again right to her face I will. That girl's a wonder, Mr. Doyle, a downright wonder! Well, she ain't a girl no more. That I gotta say. She's a full-grown woman to my eye and a proper sailor in all respects."

"I'll say amen to that!" exclaimed the steward, approaching with the cook. "A proper sailor she is without a doubt, and the best!"

"And you, Cookie!" said the bo'sun standing up while I continued to sit. "You, Cookie! Now tell me to my face you was plannin' to let this here woman sink with the ship the carpenter tried to scuttle."

"No, no!" urged the cook, carefully watching the bo'sun for any movement in his direction. "I never thought o' the lady even once, I swear. I forgot she was even on board, Mr. Bo'sun. I just went along with Quine like all them others, but I'm glad to be here now."

"Mr. Doyle!" came a feminine voice interrupting the cook. "A question. Will all four of you go lie down and sleep while I watch? I'm fully capable of sailing this ship in mild conditions."

"Of that I have no doubt, Miss Waterhouse. But not yet. We have more work to do. We'll go in a little while but you need rest too."

"That lightning's growin' powerful," said the bo'sun from astern as he tried to light his pipe. "It's slow as a dog with worms and a lame leg but comin' straight for us, I warrant."

Our heading was south by southeast and a gentle breeze was off the starboard beam. I was thinking the lightning might be the remains of a passing thunderstorm and so no worry. Yet the mercury was at the bottom of the glass and seemed to have no ambition to move upward. The air was very warm but less oppressive than in daylight. I checked my watch to find the time was 0300, and I knew it wouldn't be long before dawn would be breaking. Emma went below to check on her father, and all of us waited for daylight, hoping for sunny skies and fair weather.

"Now that the girl's gone," said the bo'sun, puffing on his pipe, "maybe it's time to talk about what's a-layin' ahead."

"Of course we can talk, bo'sun, but Emma Waterhouse can be present at any discussion we have. I view her now as a member of the crew as efficient, capable, and strong as any of us. Not only that, but you know as well as I that Miss Waterhouse is sharp of mind and may help with any plans we try to bring to fruition. And of course she'll be on hand to steer when we need her."

"I understand, sir. No doubt about it. She's a strong-minded lass. I was just sayin' maybe it's time you and me had a good long talk, but there's the steward squattin' on his hams eager to listen, and so I guess it won't be just you and me after all. I don't mind the girl, you understand. But won't the men folk make the big decisions?"

"I've been thinking while we were working and will tell you what I have in mind. When we brought the ship into irons yesterday, I was careful to note that our true position lay some ninety miles due west of Cadiz. If we stay on an easterly course and veer a little to the north, we should have no trouble making that port in one or two days. With only a few hands on board we may not be able to dock, but there ought to be room in the harbor to drop anchor. Then at our leisure we can use the quarterboat we wisely rescued to go ashore."

"I need some time to mull it over," the bo'sun replied, slightly frowning as he spoke. "I'm a-thinkin' it might be better to go on to where the ship's expected, and that's Gibraltar. In Catalan Bay there's plenty o' room to anchor, and there we can pick up extra hands to take us on to Italy. The owners' agents are a'waitin' our cargo, and if we deliver after all the trouble we been through we get a big bonus."

"I can see yer point," exclaimed the steward with some excitement. "It's a good idea. But how do we explain needing a new crew?"

"We don't have to explain nothin'. Plenty o' seasoned sailors hang around them bars there just waitin' for a berth. We can select a dozen one by one and make no bones about it. Just shove off when we got a crew with no talkin' to any nosey authorities."

"It sounds like a good idea," I replied, "but I'm not so sure we can do it. A ship in our time doesn't escape an inquiry when arriving in a port without a crew. Gibraltar could be the end of the voyage for us. What's more, we could be burdened by legal complexities for months. We could be required to stay there until an investigation is completely over."

"And wouldn't we have the same problem in Cadiz?" interposed Emma, who had rejoined the group unnoticed. "Might even be worse in Cadiz. The Spanish navy is quartered there, and they look with a jaundiced eye upon any single ship arriving in trouble. The authorities there are tough and thorough in these matters. Gibraltar is British but looser in its laws, more free wheeling. I know from experience."

"I can believe it," said the bo'sun. "Gibraltar ain't my idea o' the best place on earth and it's not as pretty as Cadiz, but a bloke that speaks English can do business there better than in Spain. We might round up a crew there without causin' a lot o' ruckus."

"All right then," I said with some reluctance. "Let's try to make it to Gibraltar. When we left Bermuda the Rock was to be our first landfall. On a clear day we expected to see it from as far as the human eye can reach. No missing Gibraltar like so many ports tucked behind the shoreline. The Rock of Gibraltar towers a thousand feet above any ship moving past it. Our little ship on leaving Bermuda was slated to go past it to the Mediterranean and on down the coast of Italy as far as Naples."

"Let's do it!" cried the steward. "Sooner or later it's gonna come out we suffered a mutiny, but if we deliver our cargo in spite of the goldarn mutiny it stands to reason we gonna get a handsome bonus and also our names in the papers. I never had my name in the paper. My wife would be so proud of me and also my little ones."

"FAs the daughter of a ship owner, I know the owners of this ship would want us to deliver her cargo. Those pianos in the hold are worth thousands. The cargo could be as valuable as the ship."

"The long night is finally coming to an end," I said. "While the rest of you sleep, I'll try to get a noon sight and fix our position. Then I'll plot a course for Gibraltar to the southeast and hope for the best."

"The steward is right," said Burdick sucking on his pipe. "And so is Miss Waterhouse. We would be earning some kind o' fame and maybe a bit o' money from the owners if it should get about that we brought this here ship through a bloody mutiny and to her destination with cargo intact. I never saw my name in print neither. I'm a-thinkin' I'd like it."

"What is yer full name, Mr. Bo'sun?" the steward inquired.

"Well, and you better not laugh neither, they named me Rinehart Algernon Burdick. Don't ask me why. When I was a young'un they called me Riney and sometimes Algie, then later Burdick, and on Sunday Mr. Burdick. Then when I goes to sea they call me as now, the bo'sun."

"Well, bless my soul! I know a Burdick that lives in South Boston. Old man now but I recall he went to sea in his younger days."

"Do yer now? Well, now you know two. And did he? Good for him! As I was sayin', Mr. Doyle, it ain't a bad idea to complete this voyage and deliver the cargo as if nothin' happened. We might benefit from it."

"We might indeed, bo'sun, but now let's think about what has to be done here and now in the present. Most important, we need rest. I'll steer the ship and call you if I need you. Emma will see that Cookie provides a substantial breakfast for anyone who wants it."

My stalwart crew — a weather-beaten sailor, an uncertain steward, a wizened brown cook, and one amazing girl — left me alone at the helm. I was glad the air was light and less hot than the day before. Though very tired from hard work and no sleep, I was able to keep the *Windhover* on course with little effort. Strong winds promised by the low glass and the lightning on the horizon didn't materialize, and that sometimes happens. The weather continued hot and mild with enough wind to keep us moving steadily. When noon came slowly — in my solitude time seemed to creep along — I lashed the wheel and went below to get my sextant for a sighting. The sun was peeking through cumulus clouds, and I had no trouble measuring its altitude. The figures in the *Nautical Almanac* seemed much too tiny for my weary eyes, seemed in fact to dance from one sterile column to the next. But in time I got a fix on our position and set the course our ship would sail for several days.

CHAPTER TWENTY-FOUR

"Stand By! Here Comes The Wind!"

In late afternoon the bo'sun came on deck all clean looking in a striped shirt and yellow trousers. He stood for a moment to inhale the salt air deeply, stretch himself after sleeping, and adjust his suspenders. At a glance I could tell the rest and bath had done him good, and I hoped Emma was recovering her strength and well-being. Earlier when I had the steward deliver lunch to her and her father, he reported she opened the door just wide enough to take the tray and thanked him almost in a whisper. That led me to believe her father was asleep, but on second thought I began to wonder how the old gentleman could sleep so much. As we worked through the night he was sleeping, and now he seemed to be sleeping all day. When the bo'sun relieved me of duty, I decided to knock on the Waterhouse door and inquire about her father. I waited a few minutes before Emma opened the door. She looked drawn and pale, not at all rested as I had expected.

"Oh, Kevin!" she cried, throwing herself into my arms and burying her face against my neck and shoulder. She was sobbing.

"What's the matter, dear Emma?" I asked, attempting to comfort her. "Did your father take a turn for the worse?"

"My father . . . my dear father is dead!" she moaned without removing her face from my shoulder. "He's dead, Kevin, dead! All the time we thought he was sleeping he was lying there in his bunk

212

dead. I tried to wake him. I slapped his cheeks and tried to wake him. I couldn't."

It was sad news to hear but didn't come as a great surprise. His health had been declining day after day in that tiny little cabin. Had he been able to walk the decks for exercise in fresh air, he might have lived. But circumstances, a mutinous crew in command, didn't allow it. His mental capacity had been shaken by the wreck from which he was rescued. Confinement took a toll on his physical well-being. It caused him to spend most of his time in his bunk mumbling strings of nonsense and nostalgia. In his final days, Emily reported, he spoke of turning his business over to her but only if his partner, Claude Dukenfield, approved. She had tried to convince her father that he would be in control of the business for many years, but he must have had a premonition of sorts, must have known that he was dying.

The *Windhover*, our beautiful little ship so graceful and so full of life in every movement she made, had become — and it saddens me to say it — a ship of death. Gilbert Waterhouse lay dead in his bunk. His loving daughter, inconsolable in her grief, sat nearby sobbing as though every fiber of a gentle heart had been ripped and torn. Dumbfounded, I could only look on the scene and be reminded of all the others who had died on this one ill-fated voyage. The first to go was Captain Oliver Redstone, a handsome, healthy, and capable seaman with too little patience. The second was Andrew Turpin, his chief mate, also an able seaman but an angry man without sweetness and light. Enrique Santos, rescued from the wreck of the *Diana Huntress*, was mad when he came aboard. Young and handsome, he died too soon in a burst of agony. All three were unceremoniously flung over the bulwarks into the sea. Soon afterwards our navigator, Peter Charnook, died of natural causes. With dignity we committed his body to the elements. Then came the bloody battle with the mutineers who tried to storm the ship. In the attempt, four of the five died. Eight men had met death on what I cannot bring myself to call a ship of death, and now we had another.

It was my duty to break the sad news to my small crew. All three wanted to place the body in a shroud made from a canvas hammock and dispose of it as soon as possible. As with all sailors, they were superstitious and fearful of a dead body on board, fearing not the body but the bad luck it could bring. At the cuddy table, discussing the matter, they reminded me that a storm was bearing down on us. That made it even more imperative to rid ourselves of the body. Yet we had to think of Emma Waterhouse and be respectful of her wishes. She wanted a dignified ceremony for her beloved father but insisted it need not be long and time consuming. She wanted me as skipper of the ship to speak a few words. Then she would follow with the eulogy. The bo'sun, the cook, and the steward would be silent witnesses. Should the wind come up, the bo'sun might leave to take the ship's wheel.

The ceremony was held in the shelter of the cuddy rather than on deck. With my help Emma had placed the body in a clean sheet, and the two of us made the canvas tight around the sheet. I said a few words in praise of the old gentleman and then his daughter spoke from the heart to describe him, his work, and the good he gave to the world. She was tearful as she spoke but eloquent, and she didn't lose her composure for an instant. Once more she exhibited a strength of mind and spirit not to be found in most human beings. She seemed in fact more angelic than human as she delivered a simple though moving eulogy. My heart went out to her in that hour of her deepest pain. I loved her; I can't say more. We lifted the body gently, carried it to the deck, and slipped it over the side. Burdick left us to go quickly to the wheel. Emma retreated to her cabin, saying she wished to be alone and would sleep if she could.

I stood alone looking at the sky. A bank of clouds, low-lying on the horizon in the early morning, had now risen to cover most of the gray sky rapidly becoming darker. In the distance a blue dagger of lightning stabbed the heavy clouds and went flashing to the sea. Yet I could hear no thunder. Then as I continued to study the dome above me big drops of rain splashed on my face, and I knew it was the beginning of a downpour. I dashed below to don my oilskins, and coming on deck again I saw the bo'sun was already wearing his storm gear. I have never seen it rain so hard. Sheets of heavy rain blocked our vision entirely. At the helm looking forward we could see only half the ship. The bow and bowsprit lay somewhere beyond the bo'sun's keen sight, and though the rain poured as if from barrels there was no wind behind it.

"Where is the steward?" the bo'sun muttered. "As one o' the crew Simpson should get his slow-movin' carcass up here on deck. We're in for a storm, Mr. Doyle, and all hands gotta do their part."

"And that includes the cook," I said in reply. "Both men have duty as cook and steward but also as crew. I'll go roust them."

I found the steward wedged in a corner in his pantry. It was a habit of his when the ship began to rock. He was dry and comfy but blinked like a frightened animal as I demanded he get into oilskins and get on deck. In the galley I found the cook sort of guarding his stove from the wet or warming himself in the cold the rain had brought. He had opened a new keg of sweet biscuits and was gnawing greedily on one when I appeared. He too I ordered to get topside and be ready to perform as a seafaring man when the approaching storm hit us. The ship was tossing and pitching in a mighty swell. Moving about on deck was difficult and dangerous. Then as the rain fell harder and harder it flattened the seas, leaving us with not enough wind to move with any force.

At the helm the bo'sun talked wisely of the weather. "That slow-movin' storm," he said, "ain't driven by the wind but creates wind o' its own. That kind o' storm wanders across the sea just lookin' for a ship to pester. When it finds a vessel worth wreckin', then watch out. It'll bust down on ya in a dead calm like dynamite. You wanna snug yer ship to the last reef and keep her stern toward it."

The cook and the steward sat on their hams in a little knot and pretended to listen. Their heads were between their legs shielded from the rain. They said not a word, but to show they were listening they glanced at the bo'sun from time to time with quizzical looks. I listened too, for the old seaman had wisdom to share. He wasn't speaking nonsense. Nature in a fury would soon support all he had said.

"When the tempest hits," I asked, "should we run with it? Or do you think we should bring the ship around and keep her pointed into it?" The rain was making such a noise I had to shout these questions.

"It's the mother o' gales that's a-comin'," he replied. "I can smell it! But we're snug enough to lay close to it, I warrant!"

"We'll bring our ship close if you say it's best, but I'm almost convinced we'll have to run before the storm later."

"If we run for it, it's gonna throw us back a hundred miles or more when we thought the shore was coming up."

"We may have to reckon with that," I said. "In the meantime while the wind is light and to get out of the rain, I suggest we lash the wheel, find shelter below, get something to eat, and rest."

The steward and the cook were gone as soon as the last word was out of my mouth. Laughing sardonically, the bo'sun called them scared rabbits and leisurely lashed the wheel. Our ship would take care of herself until the wind came to blow away the rain and require us to give her direction. Then we would have to struggle to keep her upright in the storm and save her from damage or even sinking. She was small as merchant ships go, but she was seaworthy. With a full crew to work her there would have been no worry. We didn't have so much as what seafaring men call a skeleton crew.

"Before I do any restin'," said the bo'sun, "I guess I better go down and check on my plugs. I don't want one o' them poppin' loose in the storm. We gonna be plenty busy on deck when the blow comes, and I want our vessel to be plenty seaworthy. I'll take a hammer with me."

"Hot coffee will be waiting for you when you return," said I. "Cookie will boil up some good strong coffee for all of us."

As I went to my cabin I hoped Emma was sleeping soundly and would gradually come to terms with losing her father. I knew it would take time but knew also she wouldn't surrender to loss and grief. She was stable and strong and would put her pain aside to help us run the ship. Of that I had little doubt. Already with her fine ability to keep the ship on a steady course, she had proven her worth. As I thought of her I saw her once more at the wheel, her dress hitched up to allow freedom of movement, wearing my straw hat. I smiled as I remembered her yellow hair struggling to escape the hat, a curl or two falling across her finely chiseled Grecian face. I saw a serene but weary face, her beautiful lips pale and quivering with fatigue. Then at last, as I lay in my bunk to rest, those stunning blue eyes flashed into memory. Reflecting purity of soul and fire within, they were extraordinary. They also mirrored the excruciating pain of an ordeal that seemed unending.

On the poop again after catching forty winks of unintended sleep, I saw the sun peeping from behind a vast bank of clouds that seemed to be sitting like a land mass on the horizon. I can't explain it, but the sudden appearance of sunlight in a sky of iron gladdened my heart. Perhaps it meant no storm to wrestle with at all. Perhaps the clouds would disperse and give us the gift of blue and sunny skies. The bo'sun, who could read the weather better than any barometer, had said the storm was slow moving and unique. So I dismissed the thoughts of a fine day as wishful thinking and prepared myself for the inevitable. Looking at the horizon from the weather side of the ship, I could see a black object riding on the ocean swell that came and went in light air.

Cookie was on his way to the steward's pantry with an armful of food and wanted to know what appeared to be so interesting. I pointed out what I had seen and he saw it too. With the naked eye neither one of us could make it out, but raising my telescope to it I saw detail that surprised me. It was an open boat with a short mast and a sail half hoisted.

"It's the longboat!" I cried. "The longboat with men in it."

"Oh my God!" the cook bawled. "With this storm a-comin' they gonna be doomed for sure! That boat won't stand the storm! That boat was never made to stand up to a bodacious storm!"

"They know it's coming," I said, "and they've lowered their sail to be ready for it. Thing is they need that sail for stability."

The bo'sun suddenly appeared on the quarterdeck calling out, "She's all right below! Snug as a bug in a rug. No fear of a leak!"

"Come here!" I yelled. "And see for yourself. The longboat's wallowing in a trough out there. Not making any headway, just riding the swells and waiting for the wind."

"Yep, it's the longboat all right. No doubt about it," nodding his head as he looked through the glass. "They're headin' this way. If they catch a bit o' wind they could be alongside. Might have to fight 'em again."

"Well," I answered, "I'm not at all sure about that. They don't like the weather, bo'sun, and they may want to save their lives rather than take ours. Looks to me like they're done with fighting."

"I agree, sir," the steward exclaimed. "Now that Quine is gone, all their spit and vinegar is gone too. I betcha they'd be glad to come aboard and work the ship if you'd lay by for 'em."

The bo'sun looked askance at the steward and snorted. He said nothing and neither did I. Though we needed hands desperately, and even though the ringleader of the mutiny was dead, I couldn't trust them. I was thinking that when the storm passed and they found themselves in favorable weather, they would murder us as they had murdered Redstone and Turpin. The steward who believed they were now harmless would also die. And the fate of Emma Waterhouse in their hands was too ugly even to imagine. No, that bunch of cutthroats had not ceased to be dangerous. They would kill us all hoping to escape justice, hoping to avoid being arrested and tried as mutineers and murderers.

The lightning was now becoming almost constant, and we could hear a rumble of thunder in the distance. It meant the storm we couldn't avoid would be hitting us hard, and soon. I have often thought how vulnerable ships at sea often are; no ship, not even the fastest steamer, can outrun a storm. So the crew must wait and prepare and hope for the best. I've heard that on some vessels the entire crew is called upon to kneel in prayer, beseeching whatever gods may be to go easy on them. Yet I believe every sailor knows it isn't God kicking up a tempest at sea, but nature without heart and without mind. Mariners on the wide ocean know it is ruled by laws as old as the universe. And they know too that while nature may govern the sea, it pardons no mistakes.

When the cook came aft with a big pot of coffee, Simpson went to his pantry to get the food Cookie had taken there. He set it on the skylight, our outdoor table, and we ate with ravenous appetites. Because many uncooked pounds of pork had gone bad, as well as some of the chickens, we had a breakfast of preserved meat warmed by the cook, biscuit, butter, coffee, and lime juice the steward had stowed to ward off scurvy, but no eggs. I finished first and ordered Simpson to prepare a good breakfast for Emma and have it ready for her the moment she left her cabin. I was yawning as I took the wheel. My eyes were red and sore from lack of sleep and my entire body ached, but the thunder was loud enough to keep me awake. The sky was growing darker by the minute. A dead calm had fallen upon us and the *Windhover* lay motionless in glassy water with not a ripple or cat's paw. Then came the rain, torrential rain, pouring upon us like a waterfall.

"In this rain I lost sight of the longboat," said the bo'sun. "You see it, sir? It's out there and close to us but can't see it."

"It's hidden somewhere in these sheets of rain. Could be close to us and not see it. Grab hold the wheel while I run and get my 'scope."

I was back at the helm in a few minutes, and Burdick ran for his protective clothing. He bumped into the steward who wanted to stay below but was told to get in rain gear, get on deck, close the skylights, and batten all hatches. The cook was in his galley complaining the rain had put out his fire. He too was ordered to show himself on deck. In a violent storm all hands would be needed. Only Emma Waterhouse would have the privilege of staying below in the shelter of her cabin. Yet soon after the storm began she was there in a sou'wester too big for her to do all she could as a seasoned sailor.

The rain came so heavy and so hard we had to shout at the top of our lungs to be heard and still not be understood. I can't explain which I dreaded most to see and hear, the rain or the thunder and lightning. Buckets of water fell from the sky, not mere raindrops but buckets. We had sailed into a cataract and there seemed no way of getting out. The rain was so dense we couldn't see the sky or the sea or even each other. We were finding it hard to breathe because, as far as I could tell, the wet had robbed the air of oxygen. Then of a sudden, boom! crack! crack! The rain had given way to hail, balls of ice almost the size of eggs. I lashed the wheel securely, and we ran for cover.

With no wind to give the downpour a slant, the hail and water fell in a perpendicular line of ninety degrees. The lightning flashing through it made it look like a shining, transparent curtain in a theater. For half an hour or more we stood transfixed in the midst of a wild and natural concert, an overwhelming display of nature's sound and power. I for one felt like a bug ready to be stepped on by the boot of a heavy man. And then it passed. As suddenly as it came it went, leaving us soaked to the skin and shivering in a dead calm.

Our little ship was drenched too but standing proud with decks cleaner than ever I've seen them.

The skies brightened with light, and I felt on my wet cheeks a subtle breeze. To leeward the rain and hail went roaring like a creature in a child's nightmare. I squeezed the water from my eyes to watch the spectacle gallop across the water. Then turning, I saw the wind upon the sea rushing toward us, a mighty wind chasing the rain. "Stand by!" I bawled to my crew. "Here comes the wind!"

"And here comes the longboat on top of it!" yelled the cook.

I glanced to windward, and sure enough the longboat was flying toward us with prodigious speed. The gale struck the *Windhover* like a hammer to a nail, and over she heeled to lay her portside gunwale close to the water. With just a little more sail aloft she might have gone farther to turn turtle and end everything. The longboat with only half a sail was bearing down on us to come alongside. In a flurry like a chicken with its head cut off, it swept past our stern as the ship righted herself. I held my breath as the boat came about, certain it would capsize when coming broadside to wind and waves. But somehow the seven men and a boy managed to keep her upright. Again they whirled past us, flying in full disarray like a great wounded bird. One poor wretch in ragged trousers and no shirt grasped the rickety mast and stood on the gunwale, beseeching us for help we were helpless to give.

"Oh my God! Oh my lovin' God!" screamed the cook who stood near me, "I might of been in that god-forsaken boat! Oh my God!"

CHAPTER TWENTY-FIVE

"We Makin' Landfall? Good!"

G enerally I pride myself on being able to read the weather even though I know without a doubt the bo'sun has a better eye. I thought on this occasion we were in for the blow of our lives, a survival storm as some call it, but it didn't happen. Even though it blew hard enough to turn the rain horizontal, it was not the worst storm of my life. Because we had prepared for the worst, our little ship managed to hold her own quite well. We lost some headway with leeway drift in high winds but didn't lose the many miles we would have lost had we been required to run with the wind. I got her on course again with three close-reefed topsails, and about an hour later we put on more sail but cautiously. I wasn't sure the terrific thunderstorm was not a precursor of something worse to come, another even stronger blow that could wreck the ship.

Since we were not able to surmise when a vessel might heave into sight, I had the bo'sun bend on our ensign and run it up. A train of flag signals would have caught the eye far better, but that I decided against when the wind continued to blow hard. With my 'scope I carefully swept both windward and leeward horizons for any sign of a ship but found nothing. So with the bo'sun at the wheel, the cook in his galley after getting the fire going again, the steward in his pantry ready to serve the mid-day meal, Emma Waterhouse resting or sleeping in her cabin, and I in mine looking over precious marine charts, the *Windhover* skimmed across moderate water sou'easterly toward Gibraltar.

Earlier I had discovered quite by accident that Cookie before becoming a cook had been an ordinary sailor. The little scoundrel had deliberately kept this vital information from me because he knew I would have him go aloft to perform dangerous work, and he preferred the safety and shelter of his galley. As he spoke to me about his past, he said he had given up long ago his identity as a sailor and for that reason had made no effort to hand sail or take the wheel.

"You were a sailor? Did I not hear you say you were once a sailor?

"I was, but a long time ago. So long I don't remember nuthin'."

"You know the old saying, Cookie: 'Once a sailor, always a sailor.' As of this moment you've become a full-fledged member of our crew. Your first job is to cook, but you will also work the ship with us, and that means duty aloft when necessary."

I wanted to flog him for his lack of honesty. But for a slip of the tongue I wouldn't have known he was an experienced sailor. Even so, I was glad to hear it because it meant three men instead of two would now be on call to trim sail. When Emma and Simpson were not available to steer, Cookie would do it. Also when necessary, whether he liked it or not, he would work with the bo'sun and me aloft. I would soon discover he was a competent helmsman though certainly not the best I've known. Aloft he was quick and nimble.

With Cookie at the helm the rest of us gathered around the cuddy table to eat the food he had prepared. Emma came into the cuddy all prim and neat after abundant rest and after bathing in the tub we provided her. She looked so much better than when she left the wheel near exhaustion with the horror of her father's death fresh upon her. It seemed to me she had recovered fully, and that gladdened my heart. She was friendly and gracious and ate with a good appetite. Moreover, she wanted the latest news concerning the ship, her condition after the storm, and her current position. While the steward had little to say, the three of us engaged in amicable and productive conversation.

"We oughta be sightin' a vessel soon," the bo'sun observed "since we ain't far from the shippin' lanes. The steamers come this way from the Medi'ranean on their way to points west and so do the mail packets."

"Should be no lack of sailing ships," I replied. "As we get closer to the strait we'll see them, but we're still pretty far out."

"Let's suppose we encounter a vessel," Emma said. "What do you mean to do? What procedure are we expected to follow?"

"I'm thinking we'll try to come within hailing distance and ask for some men to help us work our ship into the strait to drop anchor in Catalan Bay just beyond the town of Gibraltar."

"But what if their ship is going in the opposite direction?" she asked. "What if they happen to be short-handed too?"

"Then we're out of luck. They won't oblige us."

"I'm sure you know few ships go to sea these days without being short-handed. We could sight fifty vessels and get no help."

"I'm fer takin' our vessel into the bay ourselves," said the bo'sun. "We finally got to know that little scoundrel the cook is a sailor. He's maybe a mite rusty but counts anyway as a extra hand. Simpson is no good with sail but can steer, and we know this young lady can do all sorts of good things. So I'm for callin' up some self-reliance and doin' the job with no help from others. We might have to do some tackin' when we get in the strait, but it's wide enough for our size and won't be no problem under short sail."

"You make a good argument there," I replied. "Let's say we get help from another ship and dock in Gibraltar. That means a long and tedious British inquiry that could take weeks or even months to complete. Means, too, we don't get the cargo to its destination."

"That's what I'm sayin', sir. This ship set out to deliver them pianos in the hold and all them rifles and bird cages and door hinges and other stuff. A Court of Inquiry would confiscate ship and cargo. We might get the ship back eventually but not likely the cargo."

"I'm in agreement with the bo'sun," Emma asserted. "We wouldn't want to try docking, just drop anchor and be on our way in a day or two. Like I said before, the authorities don't have to know anything more than a ship is passing through the straits."

"But what's gonna happen," the steward asked, "when we get on down the coast of Italy to our destination and have to dock?"

"Oh, there's plenty of room to anchor in the gulf off Naples," Emma replied. "Then we can go ashore, find where the *Windhover* is scheduled to dock, round up a temporary crew, and dock for unloading."

"Let that be our plan," I said as the final word. "Haul down the ensign, steward, and stow it. No help needed, at least for now."

"Aye, aye, sir!" he responded in sailor fashion. "I'm on it."

Just as the steward was rising from the table to leave us, the bo'sun announced he would relieve the cook for an hour or so at the wheel and then go below to sleep. He had gone without sleep for more hours than I can count and needed rest desperately. Emma assured him that she was fully capable of taking the helm for several hours, should we encounter no more heavy weather, and she insisted that all the men on board rest until nightfall while she stood watch. The bo'sun was inclined to argue with her, saying he had plenty of energy left, but in the end she had her way. All four men slept during her watch, and when we came on deck she reported good sailing without incident. Once more that remarkable woman had proven to strong men that she too was strong.

The wind picked up during the night but went down again near morning. That required more work aloft to add sail but not too much. My one worry as we moved along on course was to have too much sail when another gale might hit us. Our ship was heavily laden and riding low in the water. One sail too many in a blow could mean the loss of the vessel and disaster for all on board. So even though our speed was never more than seven or eight knots when it could have been more, we lived and worked with satisfaction. Several days went by, one much the same as the next, until finally the cook with sharp eagle eyes sighted something in the distance that didn't look like a cloud. I was below at the time but could hear a loud, high-pitched shriek.

"Mr. Doyle! It's land I see! At last we makin' landfall? Good!"

I ran topside to investigate and sure enough a peak of hard rock could be seen above a cover of cloud.

"I believe you're right, Cookie! It's the Rock of Gibraltar unless your eyes and mine deceive us. Fetch my glass, I'll take the wheel."

Like a nimble squirrel he scurried to my cabin, found my telescope and also my one pair of binoculars. Through the former I could see a little round circle of blue-gray accented by a darker form. Through the binoculars the field of vision was wider, and that confirmed the sighting. The bo'sun and the steward heard our excited cries and came to the poop for a good look. Both did a grotesque little jig, dancing for joy and roaring with laughter. Though we were making landfall in the nautical sense, we were still some thirty miles away in uncertain seas.

"Go break the good news to Miss Waterhouse," I said to the steward. "No, on second thought I'll do it myself. Mind the wheel, Cookie."

She opened her door as soon as I knocked. "What's all the excitement on deck? Someone having a party?" she asked facetiously.

"Landfall!" I said excitedly, drawing her close to me. "Landfall!"

"Then you must know we enter another phase of our voyage," she replied, smiling. "Another adventure you might call it. The Mediterranean is another sea, of course, but not the same as the Atlantic."

"Yes, yes, you are right. The first sight of land after any voyage is exciting, but behind this landfall is another thousand miles in different water. I've heard the currents at the entrance to the Strait of Gibraltar can be strong at times, and we have to look out for that. We should have no trouble entering, depending on the weather, but the strait is only eight or nine miles wide as we go into the Mediterranean, and that we may have to worry about later."

"We will take it as it comes," she answered. "Now will you relax and have a cup of tea with me? Someone placed some rather good tea on board this ship, and the steward was good enough to bring me some."

I was about to tell the lady that American sailors, particularly sailors on cargo vessels, don't usually drink hot tea. And I couldn't explain how tea got on board our vessel, but how could I resist her entreaty? So we sat at the cuddy table and drank tea from porcelain cups. I couldn't remember ever having tasted hot tea, but it was good. In a way it was better than coffee or the cold tea I frequently drank when younger. Our conversation, as we enjoyed the tea, dwelt mainly on what to do with our lives when our ordeal ended. Emma wanted me to help her run her father's business. She would take control of it for a year or two while I learned the ropes, and then I would take over to run the entire operation with Dukenfield as a silent partner. All that implied she wanted me as husband for the rest of her life. She loved me more than I can say.

The gist of that conversation troubled me for days. I loved that beautiful woman dearly and now that she was professing her love for me, I should have felt the deepest joy of my life. But how could we marry? What lay between us was an enormous gulf as wide as the Gulf of Mexico. Her background was one of wealth and luxury, mine of semi-poverty and struggle. Oh, I had become a junior officer on a merchant ship, and I had saved her life. But for all that, I was a common sailor and self taught while she was the product of a fine university. I knew the world better than she perhaps, but she had book learning and culture. More than that, on shore again she would be wielding influence and power in a world beyond mine. Yet I didn't feel inferior to her, only troubled. Try as I might, I couldn't reconcile the reality of her existence with mine.

As the Rock hove more clearly into view it wasn't necessary to work out coordinates for its location, and yet I did anyway. I reasoned that any hour a heavy mist or fog could descend upon us and block our view of the grand sight even as we got in closer and closer. It is fog that every sailor dreads when approaching a shore. In the daytime it renders a lighthouse useless, and even if the light has a horn or bell seamen find it difficult to zero in on the harbor entrance. You might say just follow the sound and move in toward it, but in a heavy fog sounds have a way of bouncing around to deceive the ear. Many a ship attempting to follow the horn have been lost on shoals for that reason. So carefully I took my noon sight and figured our position as 36º8'N by 5º21'W and found it was close to the recorded coordinates for Gibraltar. We planned to come in from the south and enter the strait mid-channel from the west. I felt we were fortunate to be arriving in a spell of good weather. It meant less work and more safety for our short-handed crew.

To pass the time, I decided to jot down in my journal, perhaps to jog my memory at a later date, some observations concerning those on board. People become very close when thrown together in a life or death situation requiring them to endure uncertainty for long periods of time. That describes our group as a whole, but now it's time to view each one as an individual. I will begin with Burdick the bo'sun. His full name, as he gave it to the steward, is Rinehart Algernon Burdick, and I record it here for posterity. I have no idea how he got that name and don't have the courage to ask him. I know only that while he has no formal education he is smart, brave, courageous, level-headed, strong, and wise. Where he gets his strength in his early fifties I don't know, and yet it's there with the power of three men or more when he needs it. Without him the rest of us would be lost.

Emma Elizabeth Waterhouse is the full name of the lady on board. Of all the women I've had the privilege of knowing, she is without doubt the very best. I found her facing death in a perilous situation. She and her poor father were certainly as close to dying as any living person has ever been, and yet in deep despair she was calm and eager to help me help her. But it was not her own well-being she cared most about, rather that of her father. She wanted him in the lifeboat first even if it meant she herself could be swept away into the sea. She came aboard the *Windhover* exhausted and sick. Through sheer strength of will she overcame it all to become a valuable member of my tiny crew. But before that could happen she had to endure the danger of living in close quarters among mutinous men who might have raped or killed her. And quietly she used her good mind to help me overcome those men. Then when it seemed all would be well, her father died.

The steward is the next on my list. We almost never call him by his name, rather by the office he serves, but the ship's papers show his name as Daniel Simpson. He is known simply as the steward who serves the meals on this ship and oversees the pantry. Now he does whatever he can as a sailor, and I can never thank him enough for saving my life when we were forced to kill or be killed. Before the untimely death of Oliver Redstone, the steward was something of a lap-dog and despised by all aboard except the captain. I must admit I had no love for the man either. I saw him as something of a coward hiding in a corner to avoid conflict. But to his credit when the chips were down and we needed him most, he found a special courage we never suspected, and he fought as well as any of us. He tells me he has a wife and five children living in poor housing on coarse food in Baltimore. His one aim is to return to them with money to make their lives better.

Cookie takes the third place on the list. If he has a formal name I've never heard it. His position among us is unique to say the least. He was one of the mutineers, even one of their leaders, but agreed to be loyal to us if we would spare his life. Because the four of us needed another man desperately to work the ship, we took him on with a warning that he would die if he got out of line even one inch. He told us he would just as soon be with us as be with them, and he would cook for us. Later I found out in his early years at sea he had been a common sailor able to steer, work aloft, and do other chores. So in two identities, though even now we don't fully trust him, he became a valuable member of the survival crew. He's a crafty little man with a thin body and a big head. He favors one or both legs when walking but moves about as quick and nimble as any squirrel. He is steering the ship even as I write this. Soon he will fire up the galley stove and cook us a good meal. He calls himself the best cook on the seven seas and prefers keeping to himself.

Though I must go on duty in a few minutes, I believe I must take the time to jot down a few words about Peter Charnook, our deceased navigator. I remember Charnook as a sickly man from the moment I met him. He was a good navigator, precise and accurate and dependable until he fell ill. On many merchant ships the captain or first mate do the navigating, but for reasons I have never quite understood the owners of the *Windhover* hired in the person of Charnook a professional navigator. He was seen by the crew as an odd duck, not one of them and not an officer, but respected for his knowledge of celestial navigation, a mystery to them. When the crew rebelled and took over the ship and killed the captain and first mate, they didn't harm Charnook. However, in time he died at sea and was given a proper burial even though Captain Redstone and First Mate Turpin were flung like garbage into the water.

Gilbert Waterhouse, Emma's father and a gentleman if I've ever met one, deserves mention as the last person described in this journal. He owned the ship that was wrecked by a powerful storm and was close to dying when we found him and brought him aboard the *Windhover*. I can't say that I have ever met a any man more proper than Mr. Waterhouse. He was suave, smooth, refined, educated, and a shrewd man of business and the world. But gradually the horror of the wreck affected his mind. He lost his memory and became old before his time and died on board our vessel in the tiny cabin he shared with his daughter. With unspeakable grace she delivered his eulogy, and in a dignified ceremony we committed his emaciated body to the insensate sea. He was a very wealthy man, and now his wealth will go to his daughter. To my dismay, she wants me to share her life and her wealth as her devoted husband. I must end this now and go on deck. The ship needs me.

CHAPTER TWENTY-SIX

"A Man In A Ship Is A Man In Jail"

The next day near the end of August we found ourselves in excellent weather. The sun broke from the eastern horizon bright and clear and not as hot as when the mutineers were on board. Our ship came alive with all five of us happily enjoying good times and looking forward to being at anchor. We had a lively breeze from the south-southwest off our starboard quarter. The vessel was moving smoothly in mild conditions, so smooth in fact we hardly knew she was moving at all. Then looking up we saw billowing white sails with full bellies, and that told us the wind was fresh even though we couldn't hear it. But we heard the bow wave and saw our wake behind us and seabirds dipping across it. We heard the rigging sort of whining and marveled at how blue were sea and sky. Our ship was sailing well, and we expected to enter the Strait of Gibraltar and reach our anchorage before sundown.

At breakfast both the cook and the steward, the only occupants of the fo'c's'le, complained bitterly of the smelly, poorly ventilated, creaky wooden world where they sleep. Underway the fo'c's'le located close to the bow receives the full brunt of the sea in any weather. A sailor lying in his bunk or hammock there can often read the speed of the ship by the vigor of the bow wave. Some mariners love its sound and find it soothing, but these two complained the noise kept them awake. The ship moans at night, they muttered, and the stuffy fo'c's'le has the smell of rank clothing and sea dogs

232

who never bathed. With a smile more stern than flippant the bo'sun explained our ship has seen her lover go to sea never to return, and it's out of loneliness she moans. Even though the old sea legend and the way he told it brought a laugh from me, the complainants received it with frozen faces. I solved the problem by declaring each man could have a cabin of his own. Until we could enlist a new crew the fo'c's'le would remain empty and well-aired.

As we were approaching the entrance to the strait in late afternoon, a beautiful steamer emerged and made rapid progress westerly. The sun low in the sky shined upon her at just the right angle to enhance her beauty. Emma and I stood on the poop to admire the ship, and possibly the young woman was thinking how wonderful to be on it and headed for the States, perhaps even to Baltimore. The steamer passed to the south of us not more than a mile away and sounded her horn in salute. It was fascinating to watch her move powerfully through the water, gaining speed in the open ocean. But surely both of us felt unspeakable dread to see help so close at hand and yet so far away. A man in a fancy uniform was standing on the ship's bridge watching us. Other people safe and secure were probably watching our little ship too and agreeing that she was a living symbol of the past.

We entered the strait under short sail. Up and working were the fore and main topsails, the spanker, and two jibs. Immediately a strong and fast current rushing from the sea to the ocean spun our vessel half way around. I was steering at the time, and to my surprise I found I was not able to control the helm alone. With four hands on the spokes we finally got back on course and moved sedately eastward. The wind was off our starboard quarter. If it shifted just a little, it might fall directly behind us to cause the yards to swing aback in limited space. As skipper of the ship I felt it was my duty to be at the wheel and take her safely to the anchorage. I thought we would never get there. The distance was farther than expected, and we were moving slower than expected. But as the sun sank lower and lower, almost touching the water behind us, we came into a little patch of water called Catalan Bay. With dispatch we let go the anchor, the bo'sun doing most of the work.

Cookie and the steward stood beside the windlass to pay out the cable for a scope of 8 to 1, the lead line showing the depth of the water. With the anchor rode securely cleated, our ship slowly began to point her nose into the sou'westerly breeze that had remained constant. Though two other vessels were anchored in the bay, we hardly had time even to glance at them. Before darkness came we had to snug all sail, and we had only three men to do it. The cook was ready to prepare the evening meal, but that would have to wait. With some reluctance he worked with the bo'sun and me aloft to furl and snug topsails, spanker, and two jibs at the bowsprit, sails that had brought us from the Atlantic. We finished our work in record time to discover on descending that Emma and the steward had prepared a tasty supper for tired men. All five of us sat around the cuddy table to eat, chat, and rest. When a silvery moon was rising in the east, we went to our separate cabins to lose ourselves in deep and luxurious slumber. Selfless Emma volunteered to arise in the night to check on the ship's position.

Out of habit I awakened early and went on deck to look at our surroundings. A steady rain was pelting the decks and I was glad the hatches and skylights were closed. I looked across the water at the little fishing village sharing the same name as the bay. It was located on the eastern side of the Rock away from English Gibraltar. To the west and slightly to the south, the Rock stood out forcefully even in the rain. The Rock of Gibraltar is surely one of the most impressive sights Europe has to offer. The village of Catalan Bay is picturesque and peaceful but nothing to write home about. On its broad sandy beach were many colorful fishing boats. Later I learned it's an official refuge for fishermen. An edict declared near the beginning of the century that only fisherman could live in Catalan Bay, and that goes on even today in 1871. To get out of the rain I quickly returned to my cabin. I could hear no sound whatever on the ship. Very tired mariners were sleeping undisturbed.

The cook had boiled up some coffee for anyone who wanted to begin the day with it. Also we found in the pantry some biscuits and preserved beef. I poured myself a cup of thick black brew and went back to my cabin. While sipping the coffee I decided to look through the lockers to see if I had missed anything when I had searched them rapidly and found a pistol. This time under seafaring items, mainly clothing, I found a curious little notebook maybe half an inch thick with red covers. It was a vivid account of a young man's first ocean voyage. Though I had no proof, the narrative appeared to be the work of Captain Redstone. Often to pass the time in good weather seafaring men jot down their thoughts and feelings to send to loved ones back home or keep as a memento. I saw no indication of authorship and nothing revealing a specific year. His ship departed New York harbor on October 27, year unknown.

When I compared the handwriting to entries in the ship's log, I could tell the logbook entries were hastily written and sloppy compared to the careful cursive of the notebook. Yet both were clearly in the same hand. Redstone mentioned a problem common to sea captains the world over, and I will quote him: "The captain wanted to leave with the noontide, but as we prepared to cast off he discovered three of his most dependable crewmen were missing. They were experienced men who had shipped with him on other voyages, and their failure to show for this one made him testy with disappointment. At the last moment he had to take on a couple of rough characters, sailors or would-be sailors, who happened to be on the wharf to watch the vessel depart. The crew including me called them 'wharf rats' and kept a close eye on them."

I thumbed through several pages of the notebook, reading passages here and there, and began to see Redstone not as a tyrannical ship's captain, but as a likable young sailor slowly acquiring his sea legs. Here is the way he described the ship's cook: "I'm a new hand but I carry my share of the load and I'm learning as I work. I help the laughing cook from time to time as a galley boy. No one seems to know his full name, but we call him Dan. He's a big fellow and sweats in the heat of the galley and smells like a dead goose, but I have to admire him. Every day he cooks for a dozen people in a tiny cubbyhole where pots and pans are always swinging. I don't envy him his job but he likes it, and he's more than just the cook. In his own way he's a homespun philosopher and a medicine man. He cured me of my bout with seasickness when the seas were rough and the ship rolling." I was seeing a side of Redstone hard to believe. The arrogant and domineering captain of the *Windhover* had once served as a galley boy! On any ship the cook, though important to all the crew, is at the bottom of the social scale. His helper is usually a nobody without rank of any kind.

Though I found that relic of Captain Redstone's past intensely interesting, I decided to put it back where I found it and make no mention of it to anyone. It was, after all, a very personal piece of writing that might prove valuable some day in a maritime museum. Until it became public, or so it seemed to me, I had no right to read it. I didn't like Captain Redstone when he was alive. The stresses of leadership had made him a different man from the days of his youth. Yet I felt I owed him the honor of preserving what he had written as a sea-going novice. So believing another man might find it later, I put his notebook back into the drawer.

One brief passage in Redstone's journal rang and sang in my head, and for reasons I don't understand it sank into memory not to be forgotten. It was a quote from Samuel Johnson, the old dictionary maker of the eighteenth century. Young Redstone had copied the quote carefully. *"No man will be a sailor who has contrivance enough to get himself into a jail,"* Johnson had written. *"Being in a ship is being in a jail but with the chance of being drowned. A man in jail has more room, better food, and better company."* Redstone, it seems, never forgot Johnson's pungent remark and neither did I. The old sage had become a social critic.

Two or three times I read what Dr. Johnson had written in the eighteenth century of life at sea. Though he wanted the remark to be taken as humorous, it was heavy with truth. Even on government ships a sailor's life was hard and ugly. On a pirate ship it was brutal. When the notebook was back in the drawer, I listened for life on our vessel. All I could hear was the rain. It was coming down steadily as an all-day thing, and every person aboard had decided to remain below in silence and repose. I thought I might knock on Emma's door and ask if she wanted company, but decided against it. She needed to be alone now that she had a future, and so did I. My bunk seemed to beckon me with open arms. I kicked off my boots, crawled into it, and went back to sleep.

I dreamed of being on a picnic in a green meadow flecked with daisies. My companion was a woman as beautiful as Emma. We were sitting in the shade, and she was holding in her slender hands something good to eat and offering it to me. As I reached out to accept it, suddenly and violently I was jerked back into the hardknock world. The steward was roughly shaking me awake. Half asleep I thought a mutineer was on board and assaulting me. I lashed out with a clenched fist, striking him hard in the chest and causing him to roar with pain. His anguished cry brought me to my senses at once.

"Sir! Sir!" he was crying. "We have visitors! We think it best you talk to them. Three men in a boat making inquiries."

I rolled out of my bunk, jerked on my boots and hooded sou'wester, and went topside. The day was gray and still and the rain continued to fall. On the weather side of the ship was a small rowboat. Three men in rough clothing becoming very wet sat looking at me. One called out in a language I didn't understand. Another spoke in broken English.

"We come here 'cause you need someting from shore. We bring you anyting you like — fresh water, good food, anyting you write down. Prices here very high, but us don't charge much for helpin'."

"We anchored here at sundown yesterday," I replied, careful not

to tell them more than they already knew. "We haven't checked our inventory as yet, but I doubt we need anything."

"Whar yo boat come from?" the man asked. "And whar you goin'?"

Though it sounded like an official question, I was in no mood to answer directly. But not wanting to anger the men I replied, "We came from nearby and will go into the Mediterranean."

"And you don need no supplies? Den you will have to pay us for de trouble coming out here. You fly American flag, fee twenty dollar."

It was a shakedown. The man was making me angry, but I replied as calmly as I could. "We have no money on board. We get paid only when we reach our destination. I'm sorry to disappoint you."

Before anyone of them could make reply I turned on my heel and walked away without looking back. The bo'sun later told me they sat there at least ten minutes looking fiercely at the ship and grumbling before pulling for shore. Unseen he had been watching them.

"Them fellas are poor fishermen just tryin' to make a quick buck. They probably won't trouble us, but we gotta keep a lookout anyhow."

"Right you are, bo'sun. From now until we leave, each of us stands a nightly watch. We have to keep an eye open days too."

Noon came and we gathered around the cuddy table to eat and make decisions. The first question on everyone's mind was how many nights should we remain at anchor? Moving out too soon could make for difficulties later in the voyage. Remaining too long could attract attention, perhaps from the authorities on shore, and that we wanted to avoid. So we agreed after some discussion that two nights fell within the margin of safety and would allow us time to rest. We also agreed it would be folly to launch the quarterboat and row ashore in a pelting rain unless we needed essential supplies.

I asked the steward about our food and water. He replied we had several kegs of good drinking water and enough food for two weeks or more. Then looking downward and speaking softly, he said it would be a good idea for me to check the hold for edible provisions. Later I went with him to do as he requested and discovered to my happy surprise the backup provisions the mutinous crew believed were there. Proudly he told me a good steward always orders backup supplies for the officers, though not necessarily the crew, for an ocean passage. In the hold alone we had enough water and food for several weeks and several kegs of rum. We had no need to go ashore.

All day long it rained. Although we had a hankering to set foot on land after being on the water all of June and July and most of August, we were glad to have an excuse to remain aboard. Launching the quarterboat in the rain or retrieving it afterwards wouldn't have been easy, and there was also the risk of being questioned by the British authorities. So we stayed out of the rain as much as we could on this first day at anchor. On the second day we planned to move out, going through the most narrow part of the strait before entering the Mediterranean Sea, passing between Corsica and Sardinia, and making our way down the coast of Italy. One look at the chart revealed scattered islands and shoal water near the islands that would have to be navigated with care.

In my cabin with Emma sipping coffee and looking on, I began to plot the new course our ship would take. I thought of Peter Charnook. More than ever I could have used his skill and knowledge. He could have taken us safely to Naples. Although Emma was present to strengthen my resolve, I wasn't sure I could do that. When we dropped anchor, most of us felt our voyage would soon be over. Now I discovered our destination lay more than a thousand miles across a treacherous sea I knew very little about. Though battered by storms, our ship was seaworthy and capable, but was the tiny crew up to the challenge? I had my doubts but knew I had to overcome them. If we could catch a steady breeze under blue skies, perhaps we could sail all the way to Naples. However, any sailor will tell you ideal conditions are seldom a reality at sea. Even so, encouraged by Emma's gentle manner and smiling face, I plotted with high hopes the first leg of the new journey.

CHAPTER TWENTY-SEVEN

"The Ship's Leaking Badly!"

When the steward relieved the cook forty minutes after midnight and reported to me afterwards, he said nothing of consequence had occurred on either watch. I had told him he was to keep an eye out for any small boat that might approach the vessel and sound the alarm if he saw anything suspicious. I got the impression he slept during most his watch but was relieved to hear he saw nothing when awake. He had shown up late, claiming he overslept, and was told to keep a stiff watch until dawn. Later the bos'un told me with mounting anger that vandals had left a long slash of black paint on the white hull of the ship. On whose watch it happened I had no way of knowing. We found no other damage.

During the night the wind moderated, the rain stopped, and the barometer began to rise. When morning came our ship was riding perkily at anchor. I went on deck at dawn and found Simpson huddled against a lee wall well out of the weather sleeping soundly. I kicked the soles of his boots to wake him, and he jumped to his feet as though I had hit him with a bullwhip. It's good I had no such instrument, for in my anger with the man I might have used it. With numerous apologies he shuffled below to help the cook with breakfast. I remained alone near the bow, looking eastward and thinking of what lay ahead. After breakfast and after a meeting to discuss this new phase of our adventure, we would be moving into those blue waters that blended so completely with the sky that even a practiced eye saw no demarcation.

At the cuddy table all five of us sat for breakfast. The cook had prepared a meal that would stick to our ribs all day long, and the steward was there to serve it. Later the two of them joined us, hoping not to be singled out and reproached for indecorous conduct on watch. Vandals from ashore had defaced the hull of the ship during the watch of one of them. While I had no power to punish the guilty party, even were he identified, I knew the matter could not be ignored. The bo'sun was more adamant than I, asserting the ship could have suffered serious damage because two men were too lazy to keep watch. Then after a few well-chosen words in which he insisted it must not happen again, he let the matter drop. As he spoke I realized that shipboard discipline is a complex abstraction when normalcy has fallen by the wayside. Among the five of us there could be no hierarchy of command even with me as supposed skipper. It was every man for himself, every man depending on the good will of another, every man driven to do his best. However, half of the men of our tiny crew had not done their best.

Before hauling anchor I looked at the chart again. Our new course would be due east off the southern tip of Spain, and then nor'eastly with the Balearic Islands to the north of us. At Palma de Mallorca with its well-protected bay we could drop anchor for one or two nights. Then weather permitting, we would move onward to the big islands of Corsica and Sardinia and sail between them to reach the Tyrrhenian Sea. From there our course would be sou'easterly to the Bay of Naples. If we could make this last leg of the voyage without mishap, I expected no trouble with water depth. However, the shoal water surrounding islands worried me, particularly that off Corsica to the north and Sardinia to the south. We would have to be careful at all times when passing between the two islands to stay in mid channel.

Emma wanted a bath before we set out, and so I ordered the cook to bring her some hot water for her tub while the rest of us hauled anchor and prepared to leave. I looked at the black slash of paint defacing the white starboard hull and realized it wasn't paint at all. It appeared to be a mixture of coal dust and mud that would quickly wear off when we got underway. Apparently the vandals were too poor to afford good paint to express their anger and went to the earth for help. Though it was a small matter, I was somehow relieved because I wanted to deliver the ship to her owners with as little damage as possible. The day promised good weather, and we found ourselves moving slowly away into the rising sun, into an ancient sea once thought to be the center of the world.

Emma finished her bath and came on deck to greet the morning. She looked fresh and rested and sort of funny in the seaman's clothes she had fashioned for herself. All signs of despair had departed from her fetching face and were now replaced by hope. Though she had suffered dreadfully during several terrible weeks, somehow she had found the strength to endure. My admiration was as deep as the ocean beneath us, and she knew full well that I loved her more than life itself. She didn't know we would have to go our separate ways when finally we left the ship, and I didn't have the courage to tell her. As I have said earlier, she wanted me to be the skipper of one of her father's ships. I told her I had papers to qualify only as a first mate. She responded with a musical laugh, saying I could easily pass the examination to secure the skipper's certificate. Then quickly I would assume command of a fine ship, and we would travel the seas together. After turmoil and tumult, suffering that had driven a strong sailor mad, she was dreaming broad and big.

I stood at the wheel with hope for a good and positive ending to all our troubles too. I looked aloft and found the bo'sun and the cook already adding sail. I called to them to go easy on shaking out the reefs, for if the weather should change we wouldn't want more sail than we could handle. They bellowed back to me in good-natured banter. Even the steward, inclined to be weepy at times, seemed to have new life in him. When I had to go below to check the chart, he quickly assumed his position at the wheel and managed to keep the *Windhover* on course. We sailed at six knots with a nor'westerly breeze off our quarter. After weathering a storm with mountainous seas, we were fine again.

My overriding ambition, though unexpressed at the time, was to take the ship all the way to Naples. There I would contact her owners, surely worried about their overdue vessel, and ask for instructions. I would tell them the heavily laden ship had endured a great deal of stress and strain but had arrived at her destination with cargo intact. A considerable number of hand-crafted pianos and hundreds of finely made Remington rifles, along with other items, would be unloaded at their discretion. All that would surely place me in their favor, and I could expect a berth at good pay on a larger ship. I allowed my thoughts to run on until I saw myself commanding a vessel with a large crew. That image brought a stream of thoughts concerning Emma Waterhouse. She wanted exactly what I wanted. It was unreal.

Just as I began to study the chart with care, the steward came below breathing hard and speaking excitedly.

"Slow down!" I said to him. "What seems to be the trouble?"

"The bo'sun sent me to tell you the ship is leaking badly! He measured the water in the hold and came up with twelve inches! Oh my God, sir! Is the ship gonna sink just when we finally seemed out of trouble?"

I clambered on deck as fast as I could. The bo'sun was standing near the fo'c's'le with the iron measuring rod in hand.

"Bad news, sir." He said in that laconic way of his. "Twelve inches o' water. And the rod don't lie when it's used properly."

"Twelve inches!" I cried. "The pumps suck all but four inches, right? And we pumped two hours ago before weighing anchor. That means in two hours we've taken on eight inches."

"Yes, sir. And that's too much to my way o' thinkin'."

"We must get the pumps operating again, and soon. Get Cookie and Simpson. I'll be along to help too. We're pretty much on even keel right now, and so the sounding should be accurate."

I hoped there was some mistake but really couldn't doubt the ship was leaking. I asked the bo'sun if he had checked his plugs. He said they were tight as a drum. He thought a hempen seam hidden by cargo might have pulled loose. If so, even though we had a good supply of oakum, we couldn't reach the seam to repair it. Hearing this brought on a fit of despair. My dream of saving the ship was shattered. All I could hope for was to launch the quarterboat close to an island and abandon ship. The misery Emma had suffered swept in upon me like a flood to drown. Each deadly blow demanded notice. First was the shipwreck, and then the murderous mutiny, and then the storm that seemed to last forever, and then the death of her father. Then when all seemed bright and sunny comes the dark fear of the ship sinking beneath us.

Within minutes I heard the clanking of the pumps on the main deck, the bo'sun singing out to encourage the other two and doing the work of two. Hearing the commotion, Emma appeared to ask if all was well. At my urging she took the wheel as I ran to help with the pumps. With the four of us working on the heavy levers, we got most of the water out in good time but paid for our effort with exhaustion. The bo'sun sounded the well again to find just under four inches.

"In another couple hours," he said, "we gotta pump again. So beggin' Mr. Doyle's pardon if I seem to speak fer him, let's get some rest now."

The steward was already sprawled on his back, the cook was bundled up in a little knot against the rail, and I squatted out of breath on my hams. The bo'sun walked aft to the wheel and asked Emma politely if he might take it from her. Politely she refused, urging him to rest. Reluctantly he went below for grog, and I joined him there. As I looked into his weathered face, lined with all his years at sea, I'm sure he must have noticed a flicker of admiration in my demeanor. Rinehart Burdick had the courage of ten strong men, the nautical know-how of ten, the strength of ten, and he was more than fifty years old. In all my life I have never met a finer, more capable man than Burdick.

Our latest problem was the leak, and on that I centered my thoughts. If the ship made no more water than eight inches in two hours, the pumps could certainly keep her afloat for any number of days. With Emma at the helm, four of us could shoulder the load. But if the hidden breach of the hull got larger, it could mean more water coming in than going out and pumping beyond our strength. Also, if the pumps failed as they've been known to do, we would have to abandon ship. However, the bo'sun assured me a repair might be possible. Pumps are not all that complicated, he said, and the ship's hold is likely to have spare parts for any that might fail. I asked if he knew how to repair a pump. He looked at me over his grog, blinked twice, and nodded.

When noon came I went on deck to fix our position. The ship was sailing well in water so blue it dazzled the eye. Emma was still at the helm, smiling broadly and breathing deeply. Steering the *Windhover* in good weather was a joy for any helmsman. For Emma it was more than a feeling of joy; it was something transcendent that I could read in her face. I riveted my glance upon her but said nothing. In my cabin with *Almanac* and chronometer I got a complete reading and entered our position in the ship's log. It was a comfort to know the Balearic Islands to the north of us were not too far away. With navigational instruments safely tucked away, I went back on deck and to the wheel. The cook and the bo'sun were on the main deck preparing to sound the bilge again. I knew when they began pumping I would have to be present. But for now I wanted to be in the company of a remarkable young woman.

"You have too much energy," I joked. "You must give some of it to the rest of us. You've been here all morning!"

"I like doing this," she responded quietly. "And I like working with you and the others, pulling my own weight. If you must know, I will never be a doll in crinoline. I absolutely will not be a doll in starchy petticoats either now or later when all this is over."

"You want to be a sailor in a mess jacket too big for you? Well, that's fine with me for now. But the time will come, my lady, when you will dress again in resplendent gowns that accent your beauty. You will drink no longer stale grog from a pewter cup but sparkling fine wine from delicate, long-stemmed glasses. Also, and soon I hope, your tiny cabin will become a mansion surrounded by acres of green lawn."

"You have a lovely imagination, Mr. Doyle, but now that we have a few minutes to chat I wish to bring you down from whatever cloud you seem to be riding on to plain and cold reality."

"And what do you have in mind, Miss Waterhouse?"

"I've been thinking for some time now about what lies ahead when we finally make land. What will we do, Kevin? What will happen to us?"

"There will be an inquiry, of course, and we'll have to answer questions. Well, more than that. I will have to relive all the terrible events of this voyage, give the Board of Inquiry full details. They will not have it any other way. I doubt that any punishment will come of my revelations, but I expect no rewards either."

"But there will be rewards for you, Kevin, rewards aplenty. I will see to it that you will command one of my finest ships and without delay."

"As recompense for saving your life? For thrusting you into a miserable mutiny? For having you endure day after day, week after week, the misery of storm-tossed seas?"

She withdrew her eyes from the compass card and with both hands clutching the top of the wheel looked at me sadly but sternly. "I never thought you would speak to me like that, Kevin, I really didn't."

"I want no recompense for anything I've done."

"I haven't offered you any!" she retorted with muted anger. "Why must you be so blind? Why must you be so dumb when I know you're one of the most intelligent men I ever met? I simply want you to be happy doing what you like most. I love you, Kevin. I know I shouldn't say it first and yet I will. We are not living in polite society at the moment. Our lives are moving very fast and we must rise to the challenge."

I covered my confusion by taking one of her delicate hands and smothering it in my own two hands. I think I spoke my love for her, and yet to this day I can't remember. I was looking into her deep blue eyes searching for three simple words when the bo'sun came strolling from the main deck with good news about the pumps.

"Pumps sucking!" he roared. "Sucking! Only four inches at most!"

"Good for you and your mates!" I shouted. "Down below now for grog all around and no stinting. Give them all they want, steward. Then it's off to rest for all of you. I'll have you up again shortly to sound the bilge, but now for an hour or so get some rest. The ship is practically sailing herself and so no work for you except the pumps."

"I'll get me grog," said the cook and come back to steer. Then the lady can get some rest. She's been at it all mornin'."

"No, Cookie. It's nice of you to offer but go get some rest. I'll take the helm after I persuade the lady to leave."

With some hesitation she went to the cuddy for a bite to eat and then to her cabin. On the ladder she turned and said, "You didn't really say it, my brave young man, but I do know it. Call if you need me."

Not quite understanding what she had said, I remained alone at the wheel. The breeze was steady and seabirds whirled in the blue sky. The bow wave was singing an old familiar song, and it warmed my heart to hear it. The weather was good, so good I hoped it would last forever. But any sailor will tell you the good weather never lasts for long and certainly not forever. On board we had a leak to worry about even in the best of weather, and beyond that we had unfamiliar seas with islands and shoal water and the unknown.

CHAPTER TWENTY-EIGHT

We Anchor Off An Island

As I sailed the *Windhover* in breezy solitude, the leak became dominant in my thoughts. What could we do about it? Would we be able to control it, or would it begin to control us? We needed only to get to it but how? Only two parts of the ship's hold were accessible to a man seeking a leak — forward near the forepeak and aft near the lazarette. Between these two points lay tons of cargo to be lifted only by heavy machinery. If the leak were located there, we had no chance of getting to it. No human hand could push aside even one piano carefully strapped in place. However, if the leak ran only a foot in two hours, we had control. In time without enough rest or sleep we could lose our ability to operate the pumps, but if we could anchor after sailing a day or two we might find a much slower leak and thus get more rest. So in spite of what seemed to all of us a malicious wallop by fate, I didn't lose hope.

The wind had shifted to the south, and so we sailed on and on in a nor'easterly direction with the wind off our starboard quarter. Each man took his turn at the helm and so did Emma. Every two hours we manned the pumps after finding the usual foot of water. Each time we brought the water down to only four inches, but soon discovered it was taking less than two hours to make eight inches. That worried us, for if we had to pump the hold every hour, the task would soon go beyond our strength. Also with all that wear and tear the pumps could fail. So I decided to drop anchor in the lee of the first island we could reach, but that too posed a problem. Night was coming on. It wouldn't be wise to pull in close to a shore in darkness. We would have to go through the night and look for an island when morning came.

My hope lay with the largest of Spain's Balearic Isles, Majorca. It offered sheltered water in both the south and the north. The chart told me the anchorage at Palma de Mallorca was preferable, but if the wind happened to be blowing hard from the south, we might have to anchor in the little bay to the north. Regardless of wind direction, we would find calm and peace in one or the other. While knowing that lifted my spirits enormously, sailing all night in unknown waters did not. Yet it had to be done and we would do it. When I was a little boy I learned that as a basic fact of life. "When you have to do it," my papa would say, "you do it. When it has to be done, son, you do it." He practiced what he preached, working at several jobs he didn't like for many years.

As night came slowly with stars close in the sky, the bo'sun had the watch from eight till twelve. Then Cookie agreed to take it until dawn. At that time I would be on deck again to figure our bearing. The one thing that broke the routine was the absolute necessity of sounding the well and pumping the bilge every two hours. It meant not many hours of sleep for anybody. Emma did no pumping but had to be on hand to steer. Even so, we pumped only three times during the night hours and managed to keep the ship on course but never at full speed. When dawn broke and I stood alone at the wheel, I could see in the blue distance the vague outline of land above the sea. Sailing one night and most of two days, we had managed to clock three hundred miles. If the good weather continued to hold, we expected to be there in a few hours.

The dim outline slowly became a land mass and the land gradually transformed into an island. Coming closer it grew larger, and through the glass I could see the beach and activity on shore. The chart told me the island was Spanish and named either Mallorca or Majorca. A town or city called Palma de Mallorca fronted the wide harbor. A street, probably the main street of the town, ran parallel to the beach. Several ships were anchored there, preparing perhaps to cross the Atlantic. We could anchor as one of many and not be noticed by the Spanish authorities on shore. Or we could deliberately ask for their help and give up the ship. It would mean the end of the voyage and possibly the loss of all cargo as well. I asked the bo'sun what he would do. Without hesitation he said we should steer clear of government people, hang on to the *Windhover* in spite of the leak, and make every effort to take her to Naples.

Under short sail and sounding with the lead line, we moved gingerly into the anchorage. We let go the heavy anchor in six fathoms of clear water. Our ship fell back in place and rode gently in moderate calm even though outside a northerly breeze was blowing hard. Looking around, we could see if the stiff breeze shifted to the south we might have to move out. In that direction the bay was wide open with no protection. The number of ships already at anchor convinced us that few expected a radical change in the weather. Cookie and the bo'sun climbed the ratlines, furled three top-gallant sails and two royals, and tied them tightly. The staysails they reefed to be ready when needed. Then for an hour or two in the warm sunshine all on board relaxed. Shortly before supper it was necessary to man the pumps again. We were pleased to see the leak had not increased. At bedtime the bo'sun sounded the well with the measuring rod and found only seven inches. As we had thought, the motion of the vessel under sail made for a faster leak.

It was good to be at anchor again. We could look for the leak and also make decisions involving the next leg of the voyage. When morning came all five of us had an affable, leisurely breakfast at the cuddy table. Emma in her morning clothes was the center of attention. From the material I had given her when she first came aboard, she had fashioned an attractive dress that revealed her figure more seductively by far than any of her mariner clothes. I liked looking at her, like the way she moved her slender body, liked the sound of her voice. She never flaunted her beauty and though very intelligent, she never paraded that quality either. She spoke softly in a thoughtful way that made us all take notice.

"I hope we may be able to stay here longer than one night," she was saying. "I'd like to go ashore but understand it wouldn't be in our best interest to do so. We must attract as little attention as possible."

"I'm with you there all the way, Missy" said the bo'sun. "If the Spanish authorities get wind that somethin' ain't quite right on our vessel, we'd be forced on the spot to give up all plans for Naples."

"And we all agreed to take this here tub all the way to Napoli," said the cook. "I can't wait to get there. Good climate, good food, even music in the streets. But that ain't the main reason I wanna be there. We gonna cash in big when we pull into port there. I jest know it!"

"I wouldn't be too sure about that," I cautioned. "It'll be entirely up to the owners to give us a bonus, or accuse us of foul play and give us nothing but trouble. I can't say much for ship owners too cheap to buy edible provisions for a long ocean voyage. Even so, Cookie, I can't believe rational and grateful men wouldn't reward us somehow."

"Oh, they gonna do right by us, just you wait," chimed in the steward who'd been silent all this time. "We gonna be on easy street, fellas, and I'm gonna get home again with money in my pockets."

"It isn't money I want," said Emma earnestly. "I want to see all of you safe in good health on terra firma. And I want to see good things happening to you in your future. Too many bad things have happened in the present. I'm thinking you'll have to rebuild your lives, and I'll help with whatever money is necessary."

"Ah, Missy," said the bo'sun, rising from the table. "You are a good and generous woman, but I could never accept yer offer. I been makin' my own way all my life and won't be stoppin' any time soon. But I do wanna thank ya much anyway."

"And I wanna thank ya too, Miss," said the steward. "I got a family in Baltimore needing all the help they can get, and so much obliged."

"It's time to man the pumps," I said before Emma could answer. "I'm hoping we'll find less water at anchor. Maybe the job won't take very long, and then we have to go looking for the leak."

All day long the leak was foremost in my mind. We had less water to pump, but somewhere the sea was entering the vessel. Any sailor will tell you even a tiny leak is a major concern. Mariners on the whole love the sea but take great pains to keep the water at bay. When it begins to penetrate a vessel it becomes a seafarer's relentless enemy and causes alarm. As every sailor knows, men weren't made to be water creatures. Any man at sea is out of his element. With those thoughts in mind, I went with the bo'sun to the hold and looked in every nook and cranny. We found nothing. We had to conclude the leak was hidden behind cargo and beyond our reach.

The day went by very fast. During the afternoon we sat on deck and watched the activity in the harbor. We pumped on schedule but found less water than when moving, and so pumped every three hours. That allowed us to get plenty of rest before moving eastward the next day. I looked at my chart and plotted our course as carefully as I could. It would be a long one, more than 300 nautical miles, and we would take the ship between Corsica and Sardinia before stopping again. When night came I took the first watch until midnight. I asked the steward to relieve me at that time, but the man claimed he had bursitis of the knee and found it painful to move about. Simpson was constantly trying to escape hardship and work. So I couldn't be certain he had anything at all wrong with him. Even so, I asked the cook to spell me at midnight. It would be a real burden for him if he had to cook shortly after going off duty, and yet the bo'sun had more than earned a good rest. I couldn't bring myself to ask Emma to stand watch in darkness even at anchor.

Even though the *Windhover* rode gently in sheltered water, the wind continued to blow briskly. Overhead was a fine, quiet sky filled with stars, a glorious night promising another good day. Cookie relieved me at midnight, and after pumping I tumbled into my bunk with my clothes on and fell asleep in five minutes. I'm sure all of us wanted to stay at anchor longer but knew we had to move onward. "We can rest," the bo'sun had said, "when the voyage is done." And of course if we could make it all the way to Naples, we could unload her cargo and save the ship. I can't explain it, but after a while that one goal became almost an obsession not just with me but with Emma and the bo'sun. Everyone knew the cook and the steward had no love for the ship, but if they were to save themselves they had to go along with us.

Near 0300 after sleeping like the dead I was awakened by the clanging of the pumps. With nothing but my boots to put on, I managed to get on deck in record time. The bo'sun had sounded the well and come up with less than a foot of water. The leak couldn't be considered very serious with only that amount coming into the ship every two hours or so. When the pumps sucked, I said we wouldn't be pumping again until we were ready to leave. Then I urged the men, including Cookie on watch, to get back to their cabins and sleep until 0600. All three had no reason whatever to resist the order and quickly went below. Alone on deck I made a couple of rounds, walking from stem to stern, and found nothing amiss. A large ship to the west of us had moved out, and the crew of a smaller one to the south appeared to be making ready to leave. As the black of the eastern sky slowly turned gray, I could hear sea dogs singing out as they worked in the rigging. I went below for more sleep.

We pumped again shortly after 0600 and found the leak no better and no worse than earlier. We gathered in the cuddy for breakfast, and not long after that we hauled anchor. Under short sail we moved in a southerly direction to round the point near Ses Salines. The wind had remained in the north, and in the lee of the island seas appeared almost calm. But away from the island we encountered three-foot waves in a breeze much stronger than earlier. Our course was nor'easterly and so the wind was off our portside bow, a comfortable sailing position. Our little ship seemed to gallop along, like an old horse heading for the barn the bo'sun said. Since our destination, the strait between Corsica and Sardinia, was more than 300 miles away, we would have to sail all day and all night to get there. Then late on the second day, if all went well, we would move through the strait into the Tyrrhenian Sea for the last leg of our voyage. It would be less than 250 nautical miles.

Near noon we spotted a sail that seemed to be coming directly toward us. Because we were in a shipping lane used heavily by ships crossing the Mediterranean, it came as no surprise. Yet at sea, as I have mentioned elsewhere, one never ignores the approach of another vessel, or even a sail in the distance. It breaks the monotony and arouses curiosity and appeals to the human need to know others are like you, crazy enough to be on the open sea. I got my telescope and could see a big ship under full sail except for reefed skysails at the top of her masts.

The steward clambered into the mizzen rigging for a better look, and Emma stood at the rail. The bo'sun exhibited no excitement whatever. In half an hour the ship in a churning sea was close to us. Even with the naked eye we could see people on deck looking at us, women and children, and for a few minutes I thought the big ship would heave to and speak us. Then suddenly she altered her course, hoisted the Italian flag when she saw our colors, and moved rapidly away. People at her stern waved white handkerchiefs. Sighting another vessel so close to us made for jumbled emotions, but not a word of feeling was spoken later.

As night came on the mercury went down and the wind came

up. Because we needed to keep the leak under control, we stood watches at the wheel for three hours instead of four. We shook out a little more sail to take advantage of the wind, and the *Windhover* moved at nine knots. The night passed without incident even though thick clouds moved in low to obscure the stars. When morning came I could tell we were in for a storm with gale-force winds that could last a day or more. All the sunny hope of reaching Italy in good weather was suddenly dashed.

Grimly we prepared our ship for the inevitable, taking in as much sail as we could and still keep moving. The disturbance came slowly across the water from the southeast, the sky above and behind it sort of green in color. I wanted to be at the helm when it hit. The bo'sun stood by to help me should the force of the wheel become too much for one man. The others I sent below to be on call when needed. For almost an hour we waited. I wanted to believe the storm might veer westward and miss us. I could remember that happening more than once when sailing the Atlantic. Storm clouds would bear down on us, hover over the ship threatening havoc for what seemed a very long time, and then quickly and suddenly swing away. Burdick, more seasoned than I, stared at the thing approaching us and shook his head.

"She's gonna hit us, that's fer sure," he said, "and I hope we have the guts and the muscle to handle what she's gonna give us."

I gripped the wheel, looked aloft, looked at the wide expanse of water on our starboard side, looked at the compass, and riveted my gaze on the ship's bow. It was all I could do just to stand and wait. The bo'sun went for woolen sweaters and hooded oilskins, found them, and returned in minutes. Quickly we snuggled into the storm gear and waited. For what and for how long we could only guess.

Chapter Twenty-Nine

Shrieking Winds And Torn Canvas

During that first day at anchor, fearing the ship could spring more leaks, we made the quarterboat ready for launch. The mutineers had done a good job stocking supplies. It had four kegs of water and many cans of preserved meat, fruit, vegetables, and sea biscuits. Also we found fishing tackle and tools and matches in a water-proof container. It had no mast and sail because their intention was to tow the quarterboat behind the longboat equipped with sails. In about two hours the versatile bo'sun jury-rigged the sturdy little vessel for sailing. He found a spare top-gallant stun'sail boom to step as a mast, and I added a compass and chart. Emma suggested placing oil and lanterns in the boat, extra clothing, and blankets. I included the ship's log and papers and my personal papers. Then we worked together for a speedy launch if necessary. So it was a comfort to know we had a chance to survive should the *Windhover* suffer another breach or be wrecked in the approaching storm.

In warm sweaters and hooded storm gear we stood at the wheel, the bo'sun and I, and gaped in astonishment at what appeared to be an avalanche of green water hurtling toward us. A strong sea was quickly rising, and the wind suddenly became so strong one had to lean against it merely to move. Though not very tidy, our sails were snug enough aloft. The bunt of the mainsail wasn't tight enough, but the other sails lay secure upon their yards. The gale might batter them but not beat them.

As the wind and rain came on hard, I went below for my skull cap. I was in my cabin not more than five minutes, but in that brief time the storm increased enormously in force. The moment my head reached the top of the companion-way ladder as I attempted to go on deck, I thought the wind would blow it off my shoulders. Its fury and force convinced me it was stronger than any wind I had ever experienced. To reach the bo'sun at the wheel, I had to crawl on my hands and knees. Walking would have swept me overboard. I grabbed the spokes to stand and clung to them, looking aloft in dismay.

The mainsail had blown loose and was raging in a thousand rags upon its yard. The foresail was split in half and flapping like thunder. The mizzen topsail had lost its sheet and was striking other sails with the noise of rifle shots. Though under great pressure our masts stood strong even though the beating of the mizzen topsail made the mizzen-mast shiver. We put the helm on center and raced before the furious storm. The last gale was but a summer breeze compared to this one. Though bewildered by the screaming winds, the thunder of torn canvas, and the cold spray ripped from the sea and hurtling through the air, the two of us remained grimly calm. Glancing at my companion, I could see he was biting his lip. It was the first sign of anxiety I had ever seen on the bo'sun's leathery face. It was there because he reckoned our ship might not survive this most terrible of storms.

"We ain't gonna be able to run fer long," he bellowed. "She'll be pooped as soon as the high seas come, and that ain't good. We gonna have to heave to while we can."

"Let's do it now!" I bawled.

Burdick tried to bring her about, but even with his strength he couldn't control the wheel alone. The awful force of the sea against the rudder made it hard to hold the wheel steady even for the two of us. I called as loud as I could for the steward. After a long pause he emerged like a rabbit from a hole, but no sooner did the wind hit him than he tumbled down the ladder. I hauled him up by the collar and drove him to the wheel. With three pairs of hands on the spokes we managed to heave to with the ship's nose slightly off the wind. Immediately the helm became lighter, and we found it easy to hold the wheel.

However, the violence of the wind was more than I could bear. It stung my face like needles, roared like a freight train in my ears, rolled me to my hands and knees, and required me to hang on to whatever I could grasp, or be swept overboard. The ship lay steady as the compass goes but rolled and wallowed as though half full of water because of her heavy cargo. Tremendous seas crashed over the decks. I half expected to hear the cook cry out that unrelenting water had smashed his stove. If we lost the stove it would mean no hot meals, only food barely edible. Yet my foremost worry was losing a mast to the violent wind. We had stripped the ship of sail, all but a close-reefed main-topsail, but already the jibs on the bowsprit were ripping loose and causing a terrible clatter. Risking his life, the bo'sun later cut them away to fly like kites.

Hanging onto the wheel I looked aloft to inspect the main-topsail. The survival of the ship depended on that one sail. If it blew away, the only sail remaining would be the fore-topmast staysail, and that sail would not be enough to keep the ship in irons. She would turn away from the wind and begin to run with the rampaging sea. It would soon overtake her, dump tons of water on the decks fore and aft, and cause her to pitch stern over bow and sink. Strong men of a full crew could get the storm trysail working if the topsail blew away. Three exhausted men, the steward not able to work aloft, could never do it. Alone at the wheel with heavy seas thundering, with the most violent gale I had ever seen howling and roaring like a wild beast, I grew despondent. I began to believe the wondrous forces of nature were bent on crushing our ship to take our lives. The power and immensity of the storm would absorb us like a raindrop in the sea. I had to resist that kind of thinking.

I held my post at the wheel while the others rested below. Should Cookie or the bo'sun fall ill, or even the steward, then we would be in real trouble. The same would hold should any mast give way. While the mainmast seemed stable enough, the biting wind and slashing seas were causing the mizzenmast and foremast to wobble. Dreading what might follow, I called for the steward to rouse the bo'sun and cook and send them on deck. They looked at the foremast and shook their heads, saying there was no way to wedge it to stop the quivering. The shrouds on the weather side were as tight as banjo strings and couldn't be rendered tighter. On the lee side they hung loose. Then suddenly a monstrous wave smashed against the ship, throwing the bow up and the poop down. The entire sea, or so it seemed, crashed across the decks and soaked us. The stern of the *Windhover* sank into a hollow, and the bow rose high in the air to fall with a sickening thump on hard water. That brought the foremast crashing down, half of it in the water.

I gave the wheel to the steward and rushed to help the cook and bo'sun cut away shrouds and halyards. It was hard work that left us panting and exhausted, but in time we managed to saw the spar in half and push it off the ship. Unfortunately as he struggled to perform a task beyond his strength, the cook's foot got tangled in the rigging and he went into the sea with the mast. I threw a lifesaver to him, but within minutes he was gone. Before I could fully understand what had happened, I had to reckon with a new trouble. The steward came staggering forward, his face bluish-gray and his eyes protruding. He had left the wheel to spin out of control, and he was shrieking nonsense. He jumped on the rail and was about to throw himself into the sea. I caught him by his ankles and dragged him down from the rail with force enough to knock him unconscious. He lay huddled as if dead on the wet deck.

"Maybe it's good that happened!" cried the bo'sun over the noise. "Let him lay there for a while, I'll tie him to the rail. He'll come around with his brain intact, I warrant. Wouldn't be the first time I've seen it."

261

"Let's get him below," I said. "Not good to leave him there. The exposure could kill him. Emma will hang on to the spokes."

The steward was not a heavy man, and though our strength was ebbing fast we got him into his cabin and into his bunk. Just as we were about to leave he rolled over on his side and appeared to be sleeping. When I went to check on him an hour later, he was sitting bolt upright and looking downward at his hand. With his forefinger he traced the lines in the palm. He looked up when I spoke to him and smiled wanly. Even though he had regained consciousness with no apparent damage, he was not entirely sensible as the bo'sun had predicted.

As night came the raging tempest subsided in force and eventually passed on to the north. It left us battered and shattered and shipping water but still afloat. The *Windhover* had sprung another leak and water was rushing into the hold. We no longer had the strength to man the pumps, and we knew as soon as daylight came we would have to abandon ship. The wind and waves would be down by then, and we could launch the quarterboat as planned. I lashed the wheel to let the strained and leaking vessel drift through the night. We gathered at the cuddy table to eat our last supper before leaving. It was not a good meal. Everything we ate had a bitter, metallic taste. Though hungry, the steward wouldn't eat a thing. He sat rocking back and forth at the end of the table looking at his hands and smiling wistfully.

"No, you have my word," we heard him say. "I won't eat the cuddy food, not one biscuit, not a morsel, nothing."

In his delirium he was speaking to the mutineers. I thought about that wife of his in Baltimore and the five children and their struggle to make ends meet. It wouldn't be a good thing for him to return to them all broken in mind and spirit. His presence would be another burden on the poor family. I said as much to Emma who disagreed.

"Perhaps returning to his family will be the cure he needs. In the bosom of his family, loving his wife and children, maybe he'll forget the horror. I'll see to it that he and his family get the best of care. An endowment or trust will relieve them of worry."

Shortly afterwards we went to our separate cabins. Before closing her door Emma threw her shapely arms around my neck, hugged me tight, kissed my cheek, and then my lips. Surprised but transported by strong feelings, I returned her kisses with fervor.

Then I whispered over and over, "I love you, I love you!"

"I belong to you," she whispered in return, kissing my neck. "You snatched me from certain death and gave me hope."

"Do you give me the life I saved because you think you owe me?"

"I give you my life — I give you me — because I love you."

Putting her finger on my lips to ask for no response from me, she stepped away as I was about to embrace her and closed her door. I went to my cabin forgetting the ship was sinking, forgetting that on the morrow we'd be on the open sea in an open boat. An old sage once said love conquers all, and he seemed to be speaking directly to me.

In my bunk I could hear the Mediterranean Sea beating against the wooden hull as our ship drifted. I could tell she was listing to starboard as more and more water came into the hold. Half asleep I thought of the fine pianos there that no human finger would ever touch. I dreamed of Emma resplendent in evening dress drawing celestial music from a gleaming grand piano. Awake momentarily, I remembered I had never asked whether she could play, had merely assumed it. Her wealth and station required it, and then I was sleeping again.

Early in the morning before the breaking of dawn I was jarred out of bed by a hard and mysterious jolt. The bo'sun too had felt the jolt and had raised the alarm by piping all hands on deck. I jumped into my trousers and ran to the poop in my bare feet. He was hanging well over the rail attempting to inspect the side of the ship.

263

"What's the matter?" I cried excitedly. "More trouble?"

"More trouble, yessir!" he replied. "Appears she hit a reef or rocks and knocked a hole in her bottom. Reckon we gotta leave her."

Emma was now on the wet deck and showing concern. The steward, though not entirely with us mentally, stood on the companionway ladder looking bewildered. Having slept in his clothes, he was fully dressed in duck trousers, a heavy sweater, and a cap but wore no boots. I would have to find time to get his boots on and help him safely to his seat in the quarterboat. The bo'sun in his seaman's clothing and cap was already in the hold. Again he was proving his worth.

"Go back to your cabin and prepare to leave the ship," I said to Emma. "Looks like we'll have to abandon ship sooner than expected. As soon as the bo'sun's back on deck we'll launch the quarterboat."

"I'll be there to help," she replied simply and firmly.

Streaks of cloud were appearing in the east. A light breeze was coming from the south. On the poop I spoke with the bo'sun. With a lantern he had gone into the hold and found more than two feet of water.

"Up to my knees," he said. "Coming in fast. Big gash in the hull just aft of the bow. I give it maybe twelve feet to sink her. Got time to leave her, but we gotta move now and fast."

I was thankful we had prepared the lifeboat earlier for lowering. It wasn't a difficult task with block and tackle to put her over the side, and in semi-darkness we got the gangway ladder over the side. The bo'sun got in the boat first to help Emma descend the ladder and see her safely seated. The steward shied away and was about to run away when I grabbed him by the waist and pushed him forward. He was ready to resist when the bo'sun cried out that his wife was waiting. Hearing that, the addled man scrambled down the ladder and into the boat.

We pulled away a few hundred feet. By then the gray of early morning surrounded us, and we sat in calm water to watch the *Windhover* sink. She was listing as the water poured in on one side, and we believed it wouldn't be long before the deep took her. Broken now and shorn of use, she had braved and conquered terrible seas while giving us shelter. Though hating the terrible violence that had taken place on her, I loved that little ship with her well-defined lines and perky performance. She was a thing of beauty and deserved to live. In a tiny open boat miles from any shore we wasted precious time to watch her die.

Chapter Thirty

"No Livin' Soul Will See Her Again"

Since we had begun the day before first light with no breakfast, I opened a tin of ham and prepared a meal. The bo'sun and steward ate heartily, chewing the salty ham and smacking their lips, but Emma took only a biscuit and some water. I couldn't persuade her to take more. Her tired blue eyes were fastened on the horizon. As the sun climbed higher, she stared at a cloud bank in the distance.

"Isn't that land?" she asked. "I believe it's Sardinia or maybe Corsica. Before the trouble began we were sailing fast in that direction. It could be we are much closer to land than you think."

"You are looking at clouds, dear Emma. I wish I could say we're close to land, but my reckoning yesterday didn't show it. Even so, these waters are traveled heavily. A ship could spot us before day's end. I guess we should be trying to move toward shore, but it seems only fitting to wait and watch until our ship goes under."

"We have no wind for the sail," Emma replied, "and the boat is awfully heavy loaded with all these supplies and four people. So to sit and wait for a breeze seems right for me."

"Me too," assented the bo'sun. "And to say goodbye. An old sailor don't leave his ship willingly, and she ain't leavin' us willingly."

Two hours passed and the *Windhover* floated low in the water.

Any minute I thought her decks would be swamped and she would sink, but her cargo though heavy had lots of wood and she was a fighter. I was speaking encouragement to Emma when the bo'sun cried, "Look! There she goes!" I gazed toward the ship and found her hull had vanished. I could see only the spars, the two masts, slanting at a forty-five degree angle as her stern went down. They sank lower and lower, slowly at first and then very fast. In the blink of an eye they were gone. All that remained of our little ship was gone. Awestruck, we stared in silence.

"It's over!" said the bo'sun, hoarsely breaking the silence. "No livin' soul will ever see the *Windhover* agin!"

She sank in calm water under blue skies and a bright sun. When we pulled away in the quaterboat, we thought it would take only minutes for her to go down, not more than two hours. A breeze was stirring and we tried to get our jury-rigged sail working, but we barely moved. I tried to get a noon sight, but the boat was too unstable for an accurate reading. I brought out my compass to set an easterly course. When the calm persisted we tried to row but soon discovered that rowing was work as hard as pumping. The afternoon came and went with amazing rapidity. Daylight quickly yielded to darkness under a canopy of stars. We got our lanterns working after finishing a spare supper. The brightest I hoisted to the masthead. We hoped a vessel sailing to America might see us and rescue us before the night was over.

It didn't happen. For most of the night we drifted in that boat. The steward lay face down in the bottom, so still and so unmoving I thought he might have died. But on occasion he assured me he was alive by groaning or grunting and shifting position. The bo'sun found a place to rest near the bow and was soon fast asleep. Emma and I sat in the stern section of the small boat talking quietly. As our conversation was coming to an end, I said I would move the steward and make a bed for her with blankets in the bottom of the boat.

"It will please me to see you sleeping," I murmured. "The night is balmy, the seas are calm, and you have no cause to be afraid of anything. I want you to get plenty of rest while this good weather lasts."

"I don't wish to disturb Simpson," she whispered. "He needs the rest more than I. If you don't mind, I'll sleep sitting here beside you."

Her proposal I couldn't resist. I passed my arm around her, drew her closer to me, felt the warmth of her breath on my neck, and saw her close those blue eyes in preparation for sleep. In minutes she slept like a little child, limp and relaxed against me, her face angelic in the light of the masthead lantern. For two long hours I sat without moving so as not to waken her. Then curious to know how far into the night we had gone, I drew out my watch to look at the time. As I tried to return it to my pocket, Emma raised her head and spoke softly.

"It's so eerie!" she exclaimed. "Floating and drifting in a little boat in the middle of a wide, wide sea. The night calm under twinkling stars, and the silence so very heavy. What is to come of us?"

"The time is after midnight," I answered. "We have a few hours before dawn and when the light finally comes, a ship will see us and take us on board. A big, beautiful ship with comfortable cabins and caring people and beds of goose down. It will happen, my love, trust me."

"I do trust you, my Kevin, and when you say we'll soon be rescued I believe you implicitly. We didn't go through all that struggle and turmoil to die on a sea of glass. Now you must rest, my worn-out friend."

She couldn't have found a better way to describe my condition. Like an old shoe in tatters I was absolutely worn out. I was drained emotionally, intellectually, and physically by the heavy strain put upon me from the time I showed Captain Redstone the rotten biscuit. At that moment I incurred his wrath and became his enemy, and the stress of untoward events soon became very difficult to bear. He threw me into irons, and he threatened to bring me before a court of law charged with mutiny. But all that was tame compared to what happened later. Stress and strain became a daily burden until that interval of peace at anchor. But even then I had to worry about saving a leaking ship and the lives aboard her. I was surely worn out, no better way to describe it, and yet I had Emma. She had come to me like a priest, like a visitant from another world, to exorcize my demons.

The steward was no longer lying full length in the bottom of the boat, but sitting up with his arms around his knees and his head slumped between them. Under a heavy blanket Emma and I managed to sleep maybe two hours while the bo'sun stood watch. I was beginning to lapse into a fitful dream when he suddenly cried, "Mr. Doyle! Listen!" Jarred awake, I scrambled from under the blanket.

"What's the matter, bo'sun? You hear something?"

"Listen! Just listen!"

"I cocked my ear to listen but heard nothing more in the still air than the wash of calm water against the boat.

"You don't hear it, Mr. Doyle? You don't hear it?"

Emma was now awake and he was asking her the same question. "Miss Waterhouse! You hear nothin'? Don't you hear it?"

A minute or two passed in silence before Emma answered. "I think I hear a kind of rhythmic groaning or growling."

"It's a kind of throbbing!" I exclaimed. "I hear it now! It's an engine of some kind, a steamer! I hear it but how far away is it? This calm water carries sound so well the ship could be miles away."

"It's getting louder!" cried the bo'sun whose ears at more than fifty were keener than mine. "Swing yer lamp there on an oar, Mr.

Doyle! And I'll dip the masthead lantern up and down. If we keep movin' the light, as they get closer they gonna see it!"

"I see something now!" cried the muddled steward, standing from his sitting position. "It's a monstrous shadow and gettin' closer!"

"That ain't no lie!" exclaimed the bo'sun. "I see it too! Just hope they see this lantern goin' up and down the mast."

Then of a sudden we saw a red light on the sea. It meant someone on board a vessel had spotted us and was probing the water. I waved my lamp furiously, but there was no need to wave longer. The dancing red light drew nearer, the throbbing of the engines grew louder, and the propeller beat a tattoo under water. The "monstrous shadow," as the steward had called it, loomed larger and became a shape. A man's voice barely audible from a distance called out, "What light is that?"

My voice was too weak to answer, but the bo'sun roared back, "Ahoy there! Shipwrecked seamen adrift in an open boat!"

The shadow moved in closer and suddenly became a long, black hull with a tall funnel spouting smoke. A huge vessel moved closer and closer until she stopped, her engines turned off and silent.

"Who are you?" came a strong voice. "Is that a raft or a boat?"

"Shipwrecked sailors!" shouted the bo'sun. "Seamen adrift in a quarterboat! Three men and a girl!"

"Can you come alongside?"

"Aye, aye, sir! We can and we will!"

I grabbed an oar and we began to row toward the steamer. That's when I realized how terribly weak I was. I trembled so smartly that even in the half light that gathers before dawn the bo'sun noticed and took both oars. The man pulled with the strength of three men, but deceived by her size we found the vessel was farther off than we had reckoned. Twenty minutes passed before we bumped her hull. A line fell from the towering deck and the bo'sun caught it, singing out "All fast!"

"Are you strong enough to climb the ladder?" came a voice from the deck of the steamer. "If not, we'll give assistance."

"We can use some help," I answered. "Please send down a couple of men to help the lady aboard. Also we have an addled man here who needs help. Two of us remaining can manage."

They lowered a ladder and within minutes two men scampered down to the quarterboat. They were young as I remember and strong. They spoke with a Bostonian accent and were courteous.

"Take the lady first," I said, holding on to the mast as I spoke. "And there's a man here not in full command of his wits. Take him next."

"Are you all right, sir?" asked a young man who looked to be only eighteen or nineteen. "You don't look so good. The lady's on her way. We can take you next if you oblige us."

I mumbled something in reply. I think I said, "No, take him."

Of a sudden I felt myself becoming dizzy and terribly sick. I sat down in a stupor. The men lifted Emma easily to the ladder, and she climbed it to the deck. The dawn was breaking now and I could see all that was going on. It was a sight I had long dreamed of — Emma rescued by compassionate people and gently put down in a safe place. Her long dark night of painful but patient endurance was over. Her intense suffering had ended with a characteristic show of strength. Before I could say thank you to the young men, they were lifting the steward from the bottom of the boat. He muttered incoherent strings of half sentences as they carried him up the ladder. Then suddenly a heavy and nauseating darkness closed all around me. I could feel a moment of sheer helplessnes, like falling from a cliff, just before the bo'sun sprang forward. He caught me just as my senses left me.

CHAPTER THIRTY-ONE

I Lay In A Feverish Delirium

With amazing strength, as Emma told me later, the bo'sun slung me over his shoulder and began to climb the ladder. A crewman quickly descended to help him place my lifeless form on deck. A group of men gathered around me, and one knelt to examine my pulse. I was still breathing, my pulse seemed strong enough, and so perhaps I had merely fainted. Perhaps the excitement of being rescued after several weeks of struggle, turmoil, and torment had become just a little more than I could handle. Release had come with a torrent of blood rushing to my head, causing me to lose consciousness just when I needed to be most alive. Emma and the bo'sun were certain if I could have rest in a comfortable bed for just a few hours, I would be well again.

They put me on a stretcher, took me to a cabin near the sick bay, and placed me in a clean and comfortable bed. Emma insisted on sitting beside me until I woke up. It could take a long time, the doctor had said. "I don't care how long," was her reply. "I will stay with him for as long as it takes." After many hours when she was seen exhausted and weeping, she was persuaded to retire and rest. An orderly on the ship, one of the doctor's assistants, took her place. He was told to keep an eye on me through the rest of the day and into the night. If I had not awakened by dawn, he was to call the doctor. It was a well-meaning diagnosis delivered by a competent physician, though a bit too optimistic.

I lay in a feverish delirium for several days. Lucid and talkative at times, I told my story to everyone who came to look after me. I explained in detail how and why the mutiny had taken place, emphasizing its causes and effects and the immense pressure it put me under. I spoke of coming across a sinking ship and going to investigate the wreck against the wishes of my commander, who later placed me in irons. I mentioned becoming embroiled in deadly conflict with the mutineers, and surviving outrageous storms. I divulged how we ran down and capsized a fishing boat and went on in the mist without stopping. I praised the bo'sun as the one man who brought positive results to a deadly ordeal. To this day I don't know whether I told my story in chronological order or any kind of order. The ship's physician, as well as the captain, later informed me they were made acquainted with all the particulars of the *Windhover* voyage from the time we left Bermuda until the moment my Emma was taken safely on board the *Valkyrie*. Anything beyond that was a blank. *Valkyrie* was the name of the big ship.

When at length I became sensible enough to sit up propped against pillows, I found myself in a comfortable, well-appointed cabin obviously equipped for well-paying passengers. The bunk was almost as wide as a bed, had a good mattress, and was scrupulously clean. I didn't have the remotest idea as to where I was, and my memory was no help at all. But viewing the ceiling and a porthole with a sailor's eye, I knew it had to be a ship. I had never been on a steamer, and the sound of the engines throbbing and thumping puzzled me. Because the vessel was so huge and heavy, I felt no sensation of movement whatever. All my adult life I had worked only on sailing vessels highly responsive to wind, weather, and water. This behemoth of a ship solid, warm, and eminently safe was beyond my experience.

I lay back and closed my eyes and began to wrestle with a gigantic puzzle. It had a thousand random pieces to fit together to form a picture I had never seen. I tried to remember what had happened to place me in my present position but got no answer.

My muddled brain was off balance and refusing to work. It was able to receive only what my senses delivered to it in the present. I could recall bits and pieces of the past but in no organized fashion to reveal what had happened. Then the door opened and a man of considerable girth walked inside. He wore a white jacket and a smile on a broad, good-natured face.

"Well," he said, "it's good to see your eyes open, dear man. Proves you're still alive. Staring about you, I see, and wondering no doubt. Good thing, curiosity in a sick man. Shows the blood's flowing. I'm Flynn, ship's surgeon. You've been in my care several days now."

He was taking my pulse as he talked, "Hungry I bet."

"Yes, sir, hungry and thirsty."

"Well, how do you feel overall? Any aches, any pain? Weakness? Raise your arms and try your muscles. Straight out and hold."

"I can do that," I said, raising my arms and holding them straight before me but noticing a slight trembling.

"You feel a bit of strain doing that. Easy to see it. Not ready for a boxing match, I wager."

As I dropped my arms I found myself breathing deeply, winded by no more exercise than that, and he was asking more questions.

"What about memory? How's your memory? Got it all back? For several days now you've been sort of wandering, bouncing from one continent to another."

"Give me a clue, a couple of hints, please, and I'll see."

He looked at me kindly and with interest but said no more. Nodding his shaggy gray head, he seemed to be working on some sort of equation, a solution to a problem that perhaps concerned me.

"I'll send you in something to eat and drink," he said. "The person who brings it will be able to help you more with that memory than I ever could. But don't get excited. Talk calmly and not too much."

Ten to twelve minutes went by and the door opened again. A tall young woman came in holding a small tray. On it was a glass of water and a bowl of beef stew with golden crackers on the side. She set the tray down on a table just inside the door, sprinted to my bed, and pressed her wet cheek to mine. In a moment I realized she was crying, and I hugged her as tight as I could. Her beautiful blonde hair covered my face, and its fragrance was that of rose petals in springtime.

"My darling!" I murmured. "My Emma! Is it really you? I'm not in heaven and I can't be dreaming. So it has to be my darling Emma."

Her blue eyes flooding with tears, she kissed my face time and again before saying a word. That silvery voice of hers — "It is I, my Kevin!" — was the panacea to cure all. Slowly like a chrysalis, like a caterpillar becoming a butterfly, my memory returned in full glory. I wanted to speak a thousand terms of endearment, but all I could do was look into her beautiful face. On it was a mixed expression of joy and concern.

"I was so worried, my love. I thought I might never speak to you again. You lay in a coma for so long. I sat beside you. After a while they wouldn't let me. I looked in later and you seemed to be dying. Oh, but I mustn't give way to feeling. Here, take your food. Eat and drink."

She brought the tray to my bed and held the glass of water to my lips. I was so thirsty I wanted to drink it all in one gulp, but quickly she drew it back after a few sips, saying I must drink slowly. She wanted to feed me, but I insisted on taking the stew myself. It struck me as very salty at first and then became delicious. I ate it all with two crackers and began to feel stronger almost immediately.

"How long have we been on this vessel?" I asked.

"Almost a week," she answered. "This is the sixth day. You fell unconscious the moment I was placed on the deck of this ship. The bo'sun caught you and carried you half way up the ladder himself. Several men crowded around me. A woman wanted to lead me away. I wouldn't move a step until I saw you on board. And the bo'sun, that wonderful man, bending over you and sobbing. He thought you were dead."

"Where is Rinehart Burdick at this moment? I must see him and thank him for all he's done. A finer man I never met."

"He's alive and well, as chipper as ever. He's been entertaining the crew of this ship with his stories, and they love him. The doctor will let him see you in time, but for the present no excitement."

"And the doctor? I think he said his name was Sullivan."

"No, that's the name of the ship's captain, Patrick Sullivan. You'll meet him after you become stronger. The doctor is Harper Flynn. I'm told he has excellent credentials, studied at Johns Hopkins and has a good reputation in the medical community."

"The steward, my old nemesis and good friend. I'm having a hard time remembering him, but he saved my life. He got aboard all right I suppose. Where is he now? Someone caring for him?"

"The poor man seems improved physically but appears dazed and disoriented. He occupies a bed in the sick bay. I visited him a couple of days ago. He recognized me but made no effort to talk to me."

"It pains me to hear that, but his reason like my memory could return. I hope so. And you dear Emma. Through it all you remained steady, calm, courageous. With all my heart I admired you as you insisted on climbing that ladder all by yourself. Then suddenly something swirling like a dark and menacing waterspout spun me around and knocked me down. I woke up with no memory of anything."

"I wanted to be the first person to greet you when you woke up. I wanted to be holding your hand and ready to kiss you. But they insisted I preserve my strength. Said I needed rest."

She turned her face to the light, and I could see that in spite of her mental and physical suffering she was beautiful. Her blue eyes were bright, her delicate skin smooth and clear, and her shapely lips as red as a new rose in springtime. Moreover, she was well dressed in a gown of dark blue silk. I didn't notice it was too big for her until she rose to leave. A generous British passenger had given her the dress shortly after she came on board.

"Must you leave so soon?" I asked. "You came here only five seconds ago, and you are leaving me already?"

"The doctor made it clear to me that I was to see you for only ten minutes. Already fifteen have gone by."

"Stay longer please. I can't let you go now. You're giving me back all the energy I've lost. I can't understand why I swooned. A sailor worth his salt should be able to handle shipwreck."

"You claim weakness when really you were very strong. Try to remember what you were forced to endure. No rest, no sleep for days."

She kissed me, patted my cheek tenderly, and with a smile of affection left the cabin. It vexed me to lose her even for a short time. Conversation with her couldn't possibly hurt me. The doctor was surely mistaken. I had no idea what time of day it was but hoped she would be returning soon. I found the strength to leave the bunk long enough to use the chamber pot. Then quickly I fell back in bed and slept. How long I don't know but probably for hours. I awoke not with tremors and bewilderment as before but feeling refreshed.

Three persons were standing near me. One of them was Emma in different clothing, this time a sky-blue dress that fit her better. Another was Dr. Flynn, rotund and smiling with a stethoscope around his neck. The third was a thin, straight, angular man perhaps as old as the bo'sun. He wore blue trousers and a white coat with gold braid on the shoulders. I learned he was the captain of the *Valkyrie,* a steamer of many tons berthed in Boston. I thanked him earnestly for his kindness and compassion, for the extraordinary humanity he had shown us.

"Ah, but the pleasure is mine," he replied. "You couldn't have lasted long in that open boat when the wind kicked up. But we were able to save all the occupants: two brave men, a confused man, and a very delightful young woman who loves you very much. All of you, Mr. Doyle, are getting the best of care."

I thanked the affable captain again for all he had done. I said I was grateful for his kind words concerning me, but the man who merited his attention most was the bo'sun. It was he who made our rescue possible. If not for him we would have gone down with our ship. He saw to it that we were safe in the quarterboat to watch the *Windhover* sink.

"I've met the man and I've heard him talk, and I want to tell you right now that unless you have other plans for him, I will take him at good pay and gladly. In these times I know the value of such men."

The captain turned and motioned to a seaman at the door who ushered in my old companion. I wanted to stand on my own two feet to meet and greet him, but could do little more than hold out my hand. The honest fellow clutched it with such warm cordiality that it later ached, but I didn't mind one bit. All the trouble we had endured together had made us fast friends for the rest of our lives.

"Mr. Doyle!" he exclaimed in that gruff but mellow voice of his. "I'm real happy to see you all improved! There was a time when I thought you wasn't gonna make it, and I blubbered like an old woman to think o' you dyin' after all the trouble you got us through and jest when you was on the brink o' marryin' this here brave, high-spirited woman."

As he poured out his feelings to me he was also addressing the others in the room, particularly Emma. It was a deeply emotional scene for her, and when I looked into her pretty face I saw a big tear stream from the corner of one eye. Another might have wept, but she quickly gained control of herself and made light of the situation.

"I know, bo'sun! You would give your right arm to see my Kevin whole and happy, and so would I. When we "set down on the bench o' matrimony," as you put it, I must absolutely have you there to hold the ring. I do thank you for your kind words."

I thanked him too, and heartily. I could have praised him more warmly than he had praised me, but picking up on the tone established by Emma and observing the clothes he was wearing I joked with him. The crew had given him articles of clothing that made him look more like a jester than a sailor. Yet I said he looked more handsome in harlequin clothing than ever I had seen him. Roaring with laughter, he tweaked his forehead in salute, and left the room. Emma left with him to bring me something nourishing from the galley.

I asked Captain Sullivan what he could tell me about the steward. He answered that the man appeared to be in good health physically but wandered the decks with a vacant face seldom speaking to anyone.

"He's clearly unhinged," said the captain. "He won't taste any food other than what is served to the crew. I offered him dishes from my own table, but he wouldn't touch them. Shunned everything and eyed me with fear and suspicion. I don't know what to make of it. Perhaps you can explain his behavior if you're not too weary."

"The mutineers threatened to hang him if he touched the food reserved for officers. I managed later to get him to eat what we ate, but in his present condition he lives in the past and remembers how the crew promised to kill him. That's why he appears terrified and will eat only the food prepared for the crew members of this ship."

"Perhaps in time a good doctor will find a way to help him. It's remarkable what's being done with mental disorders these days."

Changing the subject, I asked the captain about his ship, her destination, and how long it would take to get there. He said their home port was Boston, but their destination on this voyage would be New York. They were sailing from Genoa with a cargo of Italian wine. "Not your usual bottles," he laughed, "but wooden barrels, 1,300 of them." And in addition to the cargo the ship carried more than a hundred passengers.

"We've just left the Port of Gibraltar to cross the Atlantic," he continued. "We expect to put you and your friends ashore near the end of September. By then your summer of trial and tribulation will be long over. Sunny days for you now, my friend, and the wind behind your back. I understand you sailed initially out of Baltimore. I'm sorry to say it, but you'll have to travel there by train from New York."

"If you can get us to New York, sir, you'll have our undying thanks and more. Emma has told me that you and your staff will be handsomely rewarded for all you've done for us. We can certainly find our way home from New York with fond memories of your ship."

"And when do you plan to marry, if I may ask? New York would be a fine city in which to tie the knot. It has every amenity one can imagine and would be a fine place to spend your honeymoon."

"I'm not at all sure about any of that," I laughed. "That's Emma's department. Until now we haven't had much leisure to plan a marriage or a future or anything resembling either."

"She has told me her father owned ships that now belong to her," said Dr. Flynn lightly as if joking. "So when you marry there will certainly be no financial worries. I daresay you were lucky to rescue an heiress, and a pretty one at that. I know men in my circle who've been looking to marry a substantial woman for years."

"Her wealth is no concern of mine, Doctor," I replied quite seriously. "I love her very much, have loved her now for what seems a very long time, and would marry her in an instant just as I found her. You must know from all the babbling you were privy to as I lay confused that I found her shivering and sick with just the clothes on her back."

I was about to say more when Emma entered with a bowl of beef, bean, and broccoli soup to end the conversation.

Chapter Thirty-Two

"You Speak As My Sailor Boy!"

Thanks to Emma's devotion and loving care, I was able to leave my sickroom three days after regaining consciousness. During that time any number of passengers inquired about my condition, and Emma informed me with that little musical laugh of hers that people were curious about what had happened on the *Windhover* and wanted the full story. From her and the bo'sun they had gotten just enough to tease their curiosity, and now they would hear what the skipper had to say. It was not an endeavor I cherished, not by any means. At heart I'm a rather shy person and don't enjoy being the center of attention.

Yet remembering the teachings of my father, I made up my mind to do what I had to do. In time I delivered a little speech to most of the ship's guests assembled in the ballroom. I gave them the full story of our ghastly voyage but limited my remarks to fifty minutes. Afterwards as well-meaning people shook my hand and said good things about me, I tried to be gracious in my response but felt discomfort. Emma was quick to notice and came to my rescue, assuring everyone that I very much appreciated their concern and good wishes. The second mate generously offered to share his wardrobe with me, but I politely declined. While I was confined to bed the ship's laundry washed and pressed all my clothing, even my underwear. As soon as I could walk about again I wore my own simple sailor's clothes.

As noon was approaching on the third day, I rose and dressed myself after a spare lunch in bed and sat waiting for Emma. She came a few minutes late, and I folded her in my arms and hugged her tightly.

"Oh, I can tell you're much stronger, my Kevin!" she scolded. "That hug almost squeezed the life out of me!"

I was too happy and too excited to think of a clever retort and settled for a kiss on her broad and smooth forehead. Laughing, she grasped my head and drew my face down to her lips and kissed me deep and long on the mouth. While the chatterers of the day were saying a young woman so feminine and so virginal as Emma should in no way display passion for the opposite sex (if she valued her honor), I knew beyond a doubt that the woman I loved paid little attention to what pundits were broadcasting. My lively lady was a free spirit and her own person. She was strong, capable, outspoken, supremely intelligent, and independent. In other words, it was she who commanded her emotional life as a young woman, not the dictates of a middle-class dowager or the mutterings of some dry-as-dust parson. At that moment, accepting her kisses, I loved her more than any words can say. I love her now even more, and the years since we met have passed altogether too fast.

On leaving the cabin we found ourselves in a spacious, luxurious saloon. Handsomely furnished and decorated, it stood in stark contrast to the plain and small public room of the *Windhover*. Stewards in spiffy uniforms were preparing a table for lunch. What appeared to be fresh flowers nestled in gilded vases on the table. Instead of a wooden deck or sole in sailor language, I felt to my amazement a rich and deep carpet underfoot. Against the wall I saw a fine-looking piano and original paintings by well-known artists adorning the wall. Even though skylights brought in sunshine, an abundance of lamps lit up the room, making it as bright as the day outside. For a moment I could hardly believe this sumptuous drawing room befitting the mansion of any great man was actually the interior of a ship on its way across the Atlantic. On a comfortable sofa two women sat knitting. They smiled and nodded as we passed through the room and went on deck.

The ship was immense, so large I thought even a village could have gone to sea in her with no overcrowding. Men, women, and children were walking up and down as though promenading in a street. Others sat in deck chairs taking the sun. Some children were playing ball in a netted court, and several men and women were engrossed in a game of shuffleboard. We stopped for a moment to watch the heavy disks glide down a narrow lane over the smooth deck to the scoring area. How strange it was to see people playing on a ship's deck instead of working. We strolled the full length of the ship and found her most impressive. She was steaming over moderate seas under blue skies at fifteen knots, or better than seventeen miles an hour. I marveled at that. The top speed of the *Windhover*, considered fast, was nine or ten knots. I could feel the breeze on my face but had no sensation of motion.

Smartly dressed in a pristine uniform designating rank and position, Captain Sullivan came from the bridge to chat with us. Kindly he shook my hand and offered sincere congratulations on my recovery. His first mate also approached, and some passengers crowded around us to offer good wishes. When the luncheon bell rang they went below, and the chief officer went off to perform his duties. To my satisfaction we had a good portion of the deck to ourselves.

"You said more than once, Emma, that our lives would be spared. You never gave up believing that, and now the dream has come true."

"I predicted, too, that my dear father would get through that awful ordeal, but of course he didn't. That saddens me no end, my Kevin. It saddens me even now. So my dream of somehow overcoming a terrible ordeal that threatened our lives seems indeed to have become a reality, but not without cost and not without pain."

"The loss of your father saddens me too, and I'm sure you know that. In recovery I was feeling it wasn't quite right for me to go on living when so many others had died. It seemed a violation of natural law for me to triumph over forces so incredibly strong."

"We must not overlook the fact that you are alive and well. You can philosophize all you want, but all that matters to me now is that you are here with me and alive and becoming strong again."

"The ship will dock in New York. That's some distance from your home, but you can take a train and be in Baltimore overnight. I'll go on to Culpeper to visit my family. I sincerely hope you'll meet them when the time is right."

"I look forward to it, my love, and I will bring them presents. You must tell me what material thing they would like most to have."

"They are plain, hard-working people and too proud to accept expensive gifts. Simply to know you are mine will make them happy."

"If they need anything at all, I want you to tell me. My father had banking interests in New York, and so money is waiting for us there. Isn't it strange to be a passenger on this luxurious ship and not have a dime to pay for anything? But I'm keeping a record. I intend to pay Captain Sullivan very well for his kindness."

As she spoke of money and wealth my sense of poverty reasserted itself, and I felt I had to make my position clear to her. My station in life was not the same as hers and might never be the same. Though she had called me her "sailor boy," she was an heiress far beyond my reach. I knew she loved me but felt it wouldn't be right for her to marry one so poor as I, a man not of her class and without a formal education.

"Emma," I said to her seriously, "I'm very poor. All I owned went down with the *Windhover*. I cannot and will not marry you as I am. When we're off this ship and in the States again, I'll look for a berth on another ship, work hard to advance in my occupation, and save all the money I make. In time I'll be ready to . . ."

"No, no! I won't listen to that!" she interrupted. "I cannot listen! You are going to tell me you'll work hard, become the captain of a ship, save a little money, and when many years have passed come asking for my hand in marriage. Ah, Kevin! Your foolish pride disturbs me! Will you sacrifice your life and happiness simply because the rules of our society say you can't marry a woman with more money than you?"

"But Emma, try to understand."

"I do understand. Like thousands of women in these cruel times, I'm expected to wait for you in spite of my wealth. Wait for you until I'm an old maid! Would you love me less knowing I'm poor? Did you save my life suspecting I was rich? You fell in love with me because I am me, Emma Waterhouse, a young woman. I loved you and do now because you are Kevin Doyle, a brave and clever young man."

"I know, but but . . .," I mumbled. She was leaving me speechless.

"Would you abandon me because you are too proud to make us both happy? Oh, don't speak of being poor. I will sign over to you all that I own. You alone will be Dukenfield's partner in a thriving business. I will stay home and be the mother of your children and not say a word about the business." She was crying, but softly.

"Emma, dearest," I said earnestly as I tried to console her. "I will put away what you call my foolish pride. Never, never, would I ever be able to leave you. But please understand I cannot accept any part of your inheritance. I must work for my living. I will get a job and together you and I will accept whatever the future holds."

"Now you speak as my sailor boy!" It was all she said.

After that conversation we spoke only of how soon we could marry. In time we arrived without incident in New York and made our way to Baltimore. In that city Emma got in touch with Claude

Dukenfield to inform him of his partner's death. Together they worked out the details of how it would affect the business. I insisted Emma become Dukenfield's senior partner, for that is what her father would have wanted. After some hesitation she agreed, but only if I accepted a responsible position as an officer in the company.

As winter was coming we traveled to Culpeper to visit my parents. They found her refreshing, charming. My papa told me later he thought I would never find such a woman. At sea for months as a time, sailors never meet any kind of woman. Ashore for a week or two, they meet only the women of the waterfront. But I was to marry a woman of quality, and he couldn't believe it. Although we wanted them to be honored guests at our wedding, they had to refuse because Mama was arthritic and found travel very uncomfortable. A year later when her condition was much improved, thanks to Emma, we persuaded them to go to Europe on a steamer similar to the *Valkyrie*.

At the beginning of the new year we married. Cookie might have come if not for an unfortunate accident, but the steward in good health attended the wedding with his wife and older son. Emma had seen to it that when addled he got the best of care. She bought a house for him and his family and found him a good job that didn't tax his abilities. Rinehart Burdick, exemplary bo'sun and warm friend, was our best man. Out of stubborn pride he wouldn't accept more from Emma or me than a select collection of new clothes. However, when spring came he went back to sea on a ship owned by Waterhouse and Dukenfield. He proved himself a seaman and within two years became the chief mate on a fine vessel called the *Symphonie*.

Though at times even now I'm inclined to accept command of one of the ships belonging to Waterhouse, Doyle, and Dukenfield, as president and chief officer of the company I know I shall never return to the sea. Dear Emma laughs and says I'm too old to resume the seafaring life. She is pleased to have me live out the rest of my life on shore, and I feel content with it too. However, one of these days our little son Bert may develop a love of the sea and follow in the footsteps of his father.

So now my ghastly tale is told. The heart within me, ceasing to burn, hears tinkling bells promising peace.